"A refreshingly original twist on the vampire story. Fast-paced and fun."

—*Kelley Armstrong, New York Times bestselling author*

LYNDA HILBURN

Medallion Press, Inc.
Printed in USA

5 OUT OF 5 QUILLS

"THE VAMPIRE SHRINK by Lynda Hilburn is a can't put down, spine-tingling, laugh out loud book that will keep you glued till you turn the final page. Even then I found myself wanting more and praying that there would be a continuation. Devereux is pure delight for the senses, a vampire to delight any woman. Alan is a complex soul that deserves to be explored more thoroughly. And Kismet Knight is the very meat of the story. I love her expressions, her sarcasm and wit, and the inner workings of her mind that are shared with us. I can't wait for more of Kismet! So if you only pick up one vampire book this year, make sure that it is THE VAMPIRE SHRINK by Lynda Hilburn. You won't be disappointed!"

—*Gotta Write Network*

"A very well written horror fantasy! Keeps the reader's eyes glued to the pages up to the very end. Scary yet sensual! The characters seem to leap from the pages. As the plot flows along, the horror deepens. Great intrigue! A marvelous unique writing style causes the suspense to build as the mystery unfolds . . ."

—*Wanda Maynard, Simegen.com*

"Lynda Hilburn creates a fascinating world—wicked and sexy!"
—*Kerrelyn Sparks, USA Today Bestselling Author of*
BE STILL MY VAMPIRE HEART

"A great blend of humor, horror, and quirky mystery. Fans of Laurell K. Hamilton will love Lynda Hilburn."
—*Jennifer Armintrout, author of BLOOD TIES, BOOK ONE:*
THE TURNING and BLOOD TIES, BOOK TWO: POSSESSION

"In THE VAMPIRE SHRINK, Lynda Hilburn takes readers on a well-crafted roller coaster ride where the line between reason and madness blurs and the worlds of science and fantasy collide."
—*Jeanne C. Stein, bestselling author of THE BECOMING*

"Fans of paranormal romance will welcome Lynda Hilburn's steamy new series about a psychologist who finds herself treating an unlikely clientele, who have a lot of serious issues. Hilburn is the latest Denver author to show us a dark, dangerous, and sexy layer under the city's wholesome surface."
—*Marta Acosta, author of MIDNIGHT BRUNCH and*
HAPPY HOUR AT CASA DRACULA

The Vampire Shrink

LYNDA HILBURN

DEDICATION:

To my son Daniel, the light of my life.

Published 2007 by Medallion Press, Inc.

The MEDALLION PRESS LOGO
is a registered tradmark of Medallion Press, Inc.

Typeset in Baskerville
Printed in the United States of America
10-digit ISBN: 1-9338362-3-7
13-digit ISBN: 978-1933836-23-2

10 9 8 7 6 5 4 3 2 1
First Edition

ACKNOWLEDGEMENTS:

Many thanks to the wonderful people at Medallion Press, who believe in me and my book, my agents Joshua Bilmes and Steve Mancino, and my supportive, talented critique partners — Rita Sable, Anna McLain, Jeanine Berry and Patricia Crossley — who keep me motivated and sane.

Chapter 1

My involvement with vampires began innocently enough. Long before the blood hit the fan, so to speak.

Like most psychologists, I'd been trained to view the world through a diagnostic lens, hearing my clients' stories through my metaphorical ears, searching out the deeper meanings. Thankfully, my tendency to reduce each person to a prevailing neurosis was tempered by my irreverent, dark sense of humor, which kept me from taking myself and the world too seriously.

While I never was as bad as some of my colleagues about believing only in what I could prove—if you couldn't quantify it, it wasn't there—I had seen enough bizarre stuff in my private psychotherapy practice over the years to make me more skeptical than I was comfortable admitting.

My private practice had its share of UFO abductees, demonic possessions, satanic cult survivors, religious cultists, attached entities—all the newest selections on the menu of emotional and mental pain. Plus, all the "regular" therapy issues.

So, when I opened the door separating my reception area from my office that fateful Friday to welcome my new client, I was only momentarily surprised. Waiting for me was a young woman wearing a long, black dress covered by a dark purple velvet cape. Rings adorned all ten fingers, and a long snake bracelet, with sparkling ruby eyes, wound its way up her arm from wrist to elbow. She had waist-length, light brown hair with multi-colored streaks, and she wore white theatrical makeup, dark red lipstick, and remarkably lifelike, high-quality, removable fangs.

My mind began to pick out the various category boxes I could put her into. Hmmm, Goth? Vampire wannabe? Acting-out teenager?

"Please come in and have a seat." I gave my warmest therapy smile and waved my hand in the general direction of the couch and chairs in the center of my office. "I'm Dr. Knight. Please call me Kismet."

That's quite an outfit. Spectacular, really. This sweet, young thing has a flair for the dramatic. What's that delicious fragrance? Sandalwood?

She walked in silently, handed me the packet of paperwork she'd filled out in the waiting room, and sat down in the chair farthest from where I was standing. Scanning the information, I noticed she'd listed her name as Midnight.

"Midnight? That's a lovely name. Is there a last name?"

"No. I have no need of anything from my human past," she said, with exaggerated seriousness.

Okay. Let's not assume the obvious. I chose a chair across from her and picked up my note pad and pen. "Tell me how I can help you."

"I'm only here because my family made me come. They can't accept my choices and they're hoping you'll talk me out of wanting to be a vampire. They want you to fix me." Her voice separated each angry word like little staccato notes.

She gave me the once-over I'd come to recognize from my younger clients: the smirking scan that evaluated my tailored, light blue suit and sensible, black heels and found them hopelessly conventional. Then, inevitably, her eyes moved to my hair, which was very long, curly, and often had a mind of its own. The dissonance between my conservative suit and unintentional rock-star hair disrupted the inner picture she was constructing of me. I always enjoy the flash of confusion that washes over their faces at that point. My inner trickster is never far away.

She hiked her dress up until the hem rested on her knees and crossed her legs dramatically. "You're not what I expected."

I smiled. "What did you expect?"

"Someone old, with her hair in a bun and no makeup. You're not that much older than me. And you're pretty. You remind me of that singer my mother listens to all the time. Sarah Brightman. The one with the long, dark hair and blue eyes."

"Thank you. I enjoy her, too. Are you comfortable with someone who isn't old and who doesn't have her hair in a bun?"

She frowned. "I guess so."

I could see that her need to connect was struggling with her automatic protective defenses, and the jury was out about which one would continue the session.

"Well, tell me about your desire to be a vampire. How long have you wanted to be one?"

She tilted her head, pursed her lips and sat silently for a few seconds. Quick flashes of emotion danced across her face as fear, disappointment, and resentment gave way to hope.

"Ever since I met Devereux—or Dev, as we call him—about a year ago," she said, dreamily.

Ah, connection won. Maybe she'll let me in.

"Why would meeting Dev make you want to be a vampire?"

"Well, *duh*, because he is one." She rolled her chocolate-brown eyes, and made that "tsk" sound with her tongue against her teeth.

I kept the warm smile on my face, and ignored the teenage angst. "Can you tell me about Dev?"

She hesitated, staring down at the floor, using the tip of her tongue to play with the fake fangs. "I don't think I'm supposed to talk about him. He wouldn't want me to. He says it's better if no one believes vampires really exist."

Oh, I see. Her sharp little fangs fit perfectly over her own canines, with an almost-invisible band holding them—similar to braces. How clever.

"Do you believe that vampires really exist?" I tried not to sound as if there was only one right answer to the question.

"Oh, yes. You wouldn't believe what I've seen. Denver has tons of vampires," she enthused.

"Really? Midnight, I want you to know that anything we talk about in here is completely confidential. You can feel free to tell me anything you want and it will go no further. I'd really like to hear about all these vampires."

Vampires. Well, that certainly is a change of pace from aliens and demon possessions.

She raised an eyebrow. "How do I know you won't tell my parents?"

"Unless you're going to hurt yourself or someone else, I will never tell anyone anything that we discuss," I explained, giving her my ethically required disclaimer.

She paused a moment, studying me. "Well, I guess it's okay then, since you can't tell anybody."

She uncrossed her legs and shifted forward in the chair. "So, what do you want to know?"

"Why don't you just start at the beginning?"

She nodded. "I met the vampires right after I graduated from high school last year. My friends all went down to that cool club that used to be a huge, old church in the funky section of downtown—it's called The Crypt. We've got the best fake IDs so we just slide right in. But it's weird. Even though we've got the perfect IDs and they let us in, they never let us buy alcohol. If we go up to the bar, the bartender just laughs at us. Pisses me off. What's up with that?"

I scribbled notes on my pad. It was a delicate dance to get the words on paper without letting my clients feel abandoned by my split attention. I always wound up with a cramp in my hand after each session from all the fast writing.

Interesting that the club wouldn't sell drinks to her. Maybe they'd gotten in trouble for serving minors before?

She worried her bottom lip with the tip of one of her fangs, as if it gave her time to think before speaking again.

"Anyway, there are several levels to the club and one of them, down in the basement—we call it the dungeon— is private. There were curtains over the doorway, but my friend, Emerald and I, we waited 'til the guy who guarded the door left for a minute, and then we sneaked down and peeked in through the crack and saw all these amazing people," she reported, with an expression of awe on her face from the memory.

"Amazing people?"

"Yeah, two different kinds, really. A whole bunch of kids around my age, maybe a few years older, all dressed up sorta Goth, but not really, wearing white paint on their faces and red on their lips. Then there were the other ones. So beautiful. They were wearing regular stuff like leather, and didn't have the white makeup on, but they were totally awesome. They were a little older, maybe in their 20s or 30s, and they all had gorgeous, long hair . . ."

She stared off for a moment, her mouth hanging loosely open, having gotten lost in the vision.

"So, they were totally awesome?"

Nodding her head gently, she said, "Totally."

"And then what happened?"

"We were just standing there, scoping out the room, and a hand came through the curtains, opened them, and the hottest guy I've ever seen asked if we wanted to come in. Emerald didn't want to go in—she's afraid of everything—but I really wanted to check out all those people, so I said yes. The hot guy reached out, took my hand and actually kissed the back of it and said his name was Devereux. I thought I was going to pass out just from looking at him. There was something about his eyes." She paused and glanced over at me, trying to gauge my reaction before she shared any more details.

I felt the muscles in my neck and back tighten, which happened sometimes when I worked too hard at holding in all the opinions that wanted to tumble out of my mouth. Often, having to remain silent was the hardest part of my job.

She met a strange man in a bar. A man dressed in leather, who invited her into a private room. What's wrong with this picture?

I smiled. "And then?"

"Then he sorta led me inside and Emerald followed us. There must have been fifty people in that room and they were all incredible. Dev walked us over to a table, and he was so polite. He pulled out the chairs for us, like in the old movies, and asked if we wanted anything to drink. We both ordered beers—we had to try—but he brought us Cokes, and we just sat there, staring at him. He wasn't drinking anything and I asked why not, and he said he'd already had his fill for the night, and he just kept smiling and giving us those psychedelic eyes. I didn't know what he meant back then, but I do now."

"What do you mean?"

"Are you sure you won't tell this to anyone? I don't want to piss Dev off," she said, reading my face for signs of deception.

"I promise," I assured her.

She nodded. I'd evidently passed the test.

"Well, he drinks blood, ya know? That's what vampires do. So, when he said he was full, he meant he had already 'eaten' for the night," she explained, her voice light and casual, as if we were talking about the weather.

Yuck. He drinks blood. Can you say mental illness?

"Do you drink blood?"

That, obviously, was a loaded question, because Midnight started scraping her lower lip against her upper teeth. She twisted the edge of her cape nervously in her hands and stared down into her lap.

"Midnight? Are you all right?"

Squirming in the chair, she said, "Yeah. It just feels creepy to be talking about this."

"Do you mean because of what your family would think?"

She hesitated. "No, because of what Dev would do if he found out," she said, softly. "We're not allowed to drink blood."

Thank heavens for that.

"We'll come back to the blood in a minute. What's your relationship with Dev?" I was becoming more and more suspicious of this seemingly charismatic character.

Catching the drift of my concern, Midnight shook her head. "He's just a friend. All the girls are after him, but he said we're too young and that he's into older women. We all hit on him but he never goes out with any of us. He's in charge—the boss, I guess."

The vampire Bruce Springsteen? "The boss of what?"

"The vampires. And the apprentices."

"The apprentices?" I had a sudden vision of several vampire wannabes sitting around a conference table in New York with Donald Trump. A vampire Donald Trump. I fought to keep the amusement from creeping onto my face. My sense of humor is such a challenge.

"That's what we call ourselves."

"Let's go back to the drinking blood part. You seemed to have a strong reaction when I asked you about that. Why?"

She lowered her eyes and started chewing her bottom lip again. "Dev lets us hang around with him and the other vampires, but he won't let anyone take blood from us and he won't let us drink blood, either. He said that only real vampires can use blood the way it was meant to be used. Since we're officially still human, we could get diseases that vampires can't get. He has lots of rules about what we can and can't do if we want to be with them."

Okay, so maybe the guy isn't totally whacked if he keeps them from the blood thing.

"So, what is it you don't want him to know?"

Long pause.

I waited silently and watched waves of conflicting emotions flow across her face as she decided what, if anything, she was going to tell me.

"There's this one guy, Eric, who wants to be a vampire real bad. Dev told him that he wasn't ready, that he needed to go out and learn about life before becoming the undead, but Eric doesn't listen. He set up all these rituals at his apartment, where the apprentices drink each other's blood. He gave us all these neat little necklaces with tiny knives on them, so we can make little cuts in each other's necks and drink," she said, her voice breathy. "It would be really bad if Dev found out because he'd be totally angry, and I don't want to do anything to make Dev mad at me."

My eyebrows crawled up toward my hairline.

The apprentices drink each other's blood?

Holy shit.

I hoped she was simply acting out and all this blood stuff was imaginary. I needed to find a non-threatening way to convince her the entire vampire thing was a fantasy.

"Are you afraid of Dev?"

"No. Not the way you mean."

"But, despite Dev's disapproval you go to the rituals at Eric's apartment?"

She scooted forward excitedly in her chair. "Well, yeah. It's so much fun. I never would have thought that drinking blood could be so sexual—so romantic," she gushed.

I tried very hard to keep the neutral expression on my face.

"Sexual? Romantic? What happens at these rituals?"

AIDS! Not to mention viruses, bacteria, and things I can't even comprehend. What about infections from the cuts? Red alert, Kismet.

"Well, first we order a pizza or something and drink some wine—maybe get high—just the same as any other night. Then we pick a partner, and after we take turns drinking a little blood—not much, just a couple of teaspoons—we have sex. It's the most amazing feeling. I let Eric cut my boob last week and suck on it. It was so hot."

Is this what she thinks intimacy is? Where did all this come from?

"Are you having safe sex?"

She nodded vigorously. "Don't worry about that. I've got a purse full of rubbers!"

I tried to visualize a rubber big enough to fit over Eric's entire body. I didn't want to come off as sermonizing or lecturing because she wouldn't come back, but I had to find a way to get across to her how dangerous this was.

"Midnight, what about diseases you can get through blood transmission? What about AIDS? Drinking blood is very dangerous."

"Vampires can't get diseases."

"Eric and the other apprentices are just regular guys, aren't they? Human?"

She stared into her lap, silent.

"Will you consider holding off on any more cutting and drinking blood activities until we explore the consequences more thoroughly?"

She stayed silent for so long that I feared she might leap up and flee the office, but she finally gave a loud sigh. "I guess."

I let out the breath I'd been unconsciously holding.

Whew. Talk about a pregnant pause. Even if she's just humoring me, it's a start.

"Thank you, Midnight. I appreciate your open mind and your willingness to trust in our work together.

"So, outside of the rituals at Eric's apartment, the apprentices mostly just get all dressed up and hang around with Dev and his vampire friends at the club downtown?"

She nodded.

"Tell me more about Dev."

She got that faraway look in her eyes again and lifted out of the subdued mood she'd retreated into.

"He really rocks. So hot. He's over six feet tall. I am so into tall guys. Gorgeous, long blond hair, aqua—not blue, not green, but aqua—eyes, and a killer bod. He's always wearing some kind of tight, dark leather." She sighed and drifted off again for a moment.

Hmmm. That does sound interesting.

Chuckling, I said, "I get the picture. But what's his story? Why is he hanging out at a bar in downtown Denver? What does he do? Who is he?"

"He doesn't talk much about that. He told me once that he's been a vampire for eight hundred years and that he really loves Colorado because the mountains remind him of some place in Europe he lived before he died. But he seems to have a ton of money. He has this amazing loft down the street from the bar, which, by the way, he owns, and the loft is so cool. Sometimes he lets us come over and blast some tunes, and he always keeps lots of food around, even though he doesn't eat any of it."

Why does this supposedly gorgeous, wealthy man hang around with teenagers? He has lots of rules for them. Does he see himself as a father figure? Or is he a clever predator?

I glanced over at the clock. "Well, Midnight. Our time is up for today. I'd like to meet with you a couple of times a week for a while so I can get a good sense of how I can help you. Would you be willing to do that?"

"I guess so. You seem cool, and it's a relief to finally be able to talk to somebody about all of it. Usually I have to be careful what I tell anyone—even Emerald."

We scheduled our next appointment and I walked her out into the waiting area, wondering how she'd look without all the makeup. I shook my head and thought about what a miracle it was that any of us survived our teenage years.

Since Midnight was my last client of the day, I sat down at my desk, kicked off my shoes, and created a case file for her. I hadn't been able to decide on a specific diagnosis yet, but I selected some possible options and then added a sheet of informal notes to her case file:

Female, nineteen years old. Referred by family. After some half-hearted resistance, she readily shared her experiences. In fact, she seemed overly eager to unburden herself. Almost too willing to share all the out-rageous details. I need to explore how seriously she takes this fantasy world she's created. She's articulate and intelligent, but naive. She has an outgoing personality and a trusting nature that is both sweet and problematic. Is this a bid for attention or a cry for help? She is partici-pating in some very dangerous activities, and is reluctant to acknowledge what she's doing because this peer group is probably her main support. Explore disconnection from family. Set boundaries and create a contract for healthier behavior.

Geez. Life isn't weird enough. We need to go out and

drink blood. Why didn't I think of that?

But I had to admit, the topic had already captured my interest. I was, after all, subject to the same rules as any other psychologist: publish or perish. I was due to write another book and the pressure was on. And, if truth be told, my life had become boring. I had accomplished all the goals I'd set for myself and settled into a listless rhythm. After the excitement of always graduating earlier than expected from every academic program I'd ever attended, adapting to the monotony of private practice was less than thrilling. It would be good to have a challenge.

I turned on my office computer and searched for everything I could think of about the subject: vampires, vampirism, blood, blood drinking, cults, mind control, immortal beings, etc. I was inundated with fiction stories about vampires, historical research on blood-drinkers, case studies involving the self-proclaimed undead, and websites for wannabes. Talk about an education.

I printed out examples of the most informative sources and spent a good three hours at my desk, reading through psychological reference books, seeking a trail of crumbs. By the time I came up for air and checked the clock, it had become full dark. I usually tried to avoid walking out of my office by myself at night. Too many lost souls wandering the streets.

"Shit, shit, shit," I said out loud as I gathered the papers and tucked them into my briefcase. I put my shoes back on, found my purse and my car keys, locked up my office and headed out to the elevator.

Normally at that time of night there wasn't much traffic in the building and the elevator came right away. I rode down, holding my keys with the car alarm clicker in my hand, and strode out the front door of my six-story office building. Luckily, I had parked conspicuously beneath one of the street lights in the parking lot across the street. My champagne-colored BMW was the only car left, so I figured I would be safe.

Just as I walked out of the building, I caught a blurred movement out of the corner of my eye, felt the hairs on my arms raise and noticed a shadow to my right. A male figure stepped away from where he'd been leaning against the wall. He stood there, gazing at me, smiling. Almost close enough for me to touch. We locked eyes for a long moment. The light shining out of the front of my building was bright enough for me to notice that he was scrumptious. Long, blond hair, dazzling eyes, and tight leather pants.

Hey, wait a minute. Stop ogling the good looks of the guy who's about to jump on you and RUN!

And I did.

For someone who sat on her butt all day talking to people, I could still move pretty fast when I wanted to. I was blessed with one of those long, lean, runner's bodies, an inheritance from my father's side of the family, and my body fat percentage was on the low end. But due to my mother's genetic contribution, I was too "well endowed" to actually enjoy running on a regular basis.

The fight-or-flight instinct is an awesome thing.

I sprinted over to my car, clicked the lock, yanked the door open, jumped in, and secured the door. My heart was pounding out a heavy metal drum solo in my chest as I turned the key in the ignition.

Once I was safely barricaded in my car, and the reasoning

portion of my brain sauntered back to the party, it occurred to me that I hadn't heard any footsteps following me as I ran. Scanning the area in all directions, I could find no threat of any kind. The handsome mugger or rapist had vanished. Or maybe it had been some regular guy, enthralled by my grace and beauty, and I'd scared him off when I'd bolted. *Yeah, right, Kismet.*

My heartbeat began to slow down to some semblance of normal. I'd have to say that was the most exciting thing that'd happened in weeks, which said a lot about the pathetic state of my social life.

I sat there until the adrenaline rush subsided and then shifted into drive. *I need a new office.* I drove out of the parking lot and steered the car along one of the many one-way streets that confound the traffic in downtown Denver.

I caught a red light a few streets over, which gave me a moment to check out the nightlife in this popular part of town. Taking up an entire city block was the club Midnight had told me about; the old church that had supposedly been converted into a play temple for the Children of Darkness. It really was a beautiful building. All that incredible stained glass. Funny that I'd never noticed it before. Just as the light turned green and I put my foot on the gas, I saw a tall man with long, blond hair standing on the entrance steps. He smiled and waved at me when I passed.

I drove home to my new townhouse, punched in my security code and locked myself into my own, personal sanctuary.

I lit an aromatherapy candle, poured myself a glass of white wine, sat down in my favorite chair—one of those puffy, huge chairs with an equally large ottoman—and stretched out, letting my thoughts wander back to the blond man.

That was just too weird. My mind must be playing tricks on me. It couldn't possibly have been the same guy, could it? Well, wait a minute. That club was only a couple of blocks from my office, and if he had been the one who saw me run to my car, then it made sense that he could have recognized the car again when I passed him. It was merely a coincidence he was at that particular club, which I only noticed because I'd heard about it today.

Just a coincidence.

But, then again. The guy in front of my office building re-sembled the blond, gorgeous, blood-drinking—maybe mentally ill—guy Midnight had talked about. Could I be so desperate for male company that I conjured up the image from her words? I have an active imagination, but this was ridiculous.

I carried my glass of wine over to my desk, opened my briefcase and spilled out all of the vampire material I'd printed. I turned on my computer, clicked on the TV and prepared to spend the next couple of hours researching pos-sible topics for a new book.

"Allow me to introduce myself. I am Count Dracula," blared from the speakers.

Startled, I looked up at the TV then smiled. There he was, the sexiest vampire ever. Frank Langella as Dracula, circa early 1980s. He had the best lips—pouty, full and defi-nitely come-hither, and eyes that wouldn't be denied. One of my college roommates had been a real vampire fan, and she had an extensive collection of bloodsucker movies.

I sat back and enjoyed watching Frank's lips for a while, finishing my glass of wine. As the end of the movie approached, I clicked off the TV, because I didn't want to watch those sweet lips get fried by the sun in the film's finale.

I had a sudden memory of the last time I'd watched this movie in college, sitting with my roommates and listening to them scream at the end—rooting for the vampire to break free and fly away. Afterward they all talked about what fun it would be to invite some dark, window-tapping stranger into their beds.

Hmmm. Vampires as erotic fantasy material. Listening to my roommates that long-ago night, the budding psychologist in me had been intrigued, but I considered vampires to be horror movie and comic book fare. I was not the kind of person who believed in the supernatural or the mystical. I'd found that most things turned out to have rather bland explanations.

Of course, since then I'd taken the required class in Jungian Psychology in graduate school and I knew all about his theory of synchronicities—the interconnection between inner and outer realities based on the idea of a collective unconscious. Jung said that there are no coincidences and the universe functions through an unknowable intelligence. I could even agree with that on an abstract level. And yes, it did seem odd I was experiencing things that appeared to be related on the surface. But contemplating the cosmic possibilities of metaphysics was a helluva lot different from believing in vampires.

But, still. This had been one strange day.

Chapter 2

$\mathcal{I}$ spent most of the weekend immersed in my vampire research. It turns out there were thousands of vampire pretenders in the world. Reading through some of the web sites gave me a better understanding of the scope of the illusion. Most of the wannabes were very sad—young people searching for meaning, connection, and love in a world where they hadn't found any. Some were simply drawn to the excitement, danger, and forbidden fruit. Then there were others—the wounded souls who had crossed the line between acting out and psychosis.

By Sunday afternoon I had formulated a plan of action, and I was excited. It had been a long time since I'd felt passionate about my work. I was going to become the Vampire Psychologist. Well, Vampire-Wannabe Psychologist, anyway. I would run ads in all the local newspapers, offering both individual and group psychotherapy for vampires.

Yes, I thought, mentally rubbing my hands together, this had bestseller written all over it.

I had found a brand new dysfunction-of-the-week, which mixed in just enough mental illness with some scary occult sensationalism to be a bona fide hit. Maybe I'd even get to go on Oprah!

While I daydreamed about my impending stardom, my stomach growled in angry protest. When was the last time I'd eaten? I tended to forget mundane details such as food and, as a consequence, strolled into the kitchen foraging for something edible. As usual, the refrigerator was cluttered with old take-out boxes—the contents of which were no longer recognizable—bottled water, and something that was probably cheese. My kitchen was a potent reminder that I was exceptionally organized and efficient in my professional life but completely oblivious to the other aspects.

Shopping was torture for me. Not only did I have the impatience of my "Type A" personality to deal with, but being around all those people—their energy I guess, for lack of a better word—seemed to wipe me out. According to my family, I'd always been "too sensitive" and receptive to the moods of the people around me. Well, I guess that's why I became a psychologist, but my sensitivity certainly complicated the rest of my life.

Deciding to call out for Chinese, I picked up the phone and heard the beeping sound that told me I had messages. The phone hadn't rung, had it? I checked the ringer volume and remembered that I'd turned the phone off. Damn. How many days ago? Since all my client calls went to my business number, I sometimes forgot all about my home phone. Luckily, my answering service had my cell phone number in case they needed to reach me for a client emergency.

I poured myself a cup of coffee then punched in the retrieval number to access my calls.

The first message made me smile. It was from Vaughan, the very cute chiropractor I'd met when we'd both volunteered to answer phones at the local PBS fundraiser a couple of months ago. I think he'd called me once before, but I couldn't remember if I'd returned the call or simply thought about returning it. He really was adorable with his light green eyes, curly chestnut hair, and that delicious dimple. It probably wouldn't hurt to call him back. I was such a coward about dating.

Hearing the next voice made me catch my breath. Dr. Thomas Radcliffe. The man I'd been willing to change my life for. The man I thought was the answer to my prayers. The man who told me I didn't excite him and who dumped me for an airy-fairy astrologer who wore crystals and smelled of patchouli oil. After all this time, thinking about him still made me want to cry. It had been two painful years, and I had only recently started to feel good again. Two long years of going over everything I'd said or done, trying to understand what it was about me that hadn't been quite good enough. Shades of my childhood.

He said he'd be in Denver for training and he wanted to get together for lunch, to "catch up and touch base." He always talked that way. I wondered if his vocabulary had expanded to include all the astrological information he surely must be privy to. But, no matter. I had no intention of meeting him for lunch or anything else. The welcome mat had definitely been pulled out from under Tom Radcliffe. He might still have the keys to my libido, but the rest of me wouldn't go along for the ride anymore. I erased his message and called the Chinese restaurant.

Midnight came in for her second appointment on Monday.

She was still wearing the white makeup and the fake fangs, but instead of being shrouded in a long cape, she was dressed like that campy TV vamp, Elvira, Mistress of the Dark, in a very low-cut, cleavage-enhancing, tight, black dress. She glided into the room and bonelessly melted into the chair. She seemed to be in a very good mood.

I picked up my pad and pen and sat down. "It's nice to see you again, Midnight. I can't help but notice that you're smiling a lot today. What's got you in such fine spirits?"

"I met someone." Her smile spread wider.

Now we're talking. I settled back in my chair. *Maybe a nice college guy or Peace Corp volunteer?*

"Well, he must really be something to light you up this way. Tell me about him."

She selected a lock of her long hair and began nervously twirling it around her finger. "He's one of the new vampires who started coming to the club. His name is Bryce and he is so hot. I'd seen him around for a couple of weeks, but it wasn't until this past weekend that he came over and talked to me. We spent the whole night together last night and it was like a dream. It was the first time I'd ever had sex with a real vampire."

Vampires, again! I struggled to keep the dismay from my face. To give myself a moment to regroup, I jotted down a couple of notes on the pad. *Well.* I gave a mental sigh. *I guess it was too much to hope that the fantasy would start to fade already. I wonder if they'd take away my license if I locked her in a closet until she passed through this phase?*

I met her eyes. "You had sex with a stranger?"

Her body language altered ever so slightly, just enough for me to notice that my question had pushed a button.

"That makes it sound bad or dirty. It wasn't dirty. It was beautiful. We just got swept away." She almost sang the last two words. Still smiling, she carefully smoothed out the wrinkles on her dress and flipped one side of her hair back away from her face, avoiding eye contact.

I wish someone would throw away the book that we women keep handing down to each other. The one with all the ridiculous reasons why we lose our minds in the presence of some man.

"How old is Bryce?"

She examined the blood-colored fingernails on her right hand. "I'm not sure. I don't think he's as old as Devereux— around 200, maybe—but he looks about 30."

He's 200 years old? Well, I did ask.

"Don't you think Bryce might be a bit too old for you? What are you hoping will happen between the two of you?"

"I think he's the one I've been waiting for."

Waiting for? You're only 19. I need some magic words, here.

I started to respond, but just then she turned her head and stared out the window, deep in thought. I waited, and after a while she brought her gaze back to me, all the joy wiped from her face. "Bryce says he'll bring me over if I want."

"Bring you over?"

"Make me a vampire."

Okay. She said she wants to be a vampire, and this guy is offering to help her out, but it doesn't appear that she thinks it's a good thing. She's definitely sending out mixed signals. What's really going on here?

I noted she'd raised her chin at the end of her last statement, exposing the attitude of defiance that had also crept into her voice, so I decided to push the envelope a bit.

"I thought Dev wouldn't let you do that. Have you talked to him about this?"

Come on, Dev. Be a father figure instead of a predator. It sounds like Bryce wants that job.

"No." Her fists tightened in her lap. "He hates Bryce. He already asked me to stay away from him, but why should I? Why shouldn't I have a relationship with Bryce? Who is Dev to make those decisions for me? He isn't my father."

Ah. Bingo.

"Did he tell you why he wanted you to stay away from Bryce?"

The anger that had started out as a slow leak now flooded the room.

"He said Bryce was one of the bad guys, that he used people and he didn't care about anyone but himself. Then I had to sit there while he went on and on about how vampires are no different from humans—there are good ones and bad ones—and how I'm not 'mature' enough to know the difference. Who does he think he is? He doesn't care that I finally found someone who wants me."

She burst into tears.

And the wall comes tumbling down . . .

I moved the tissue box closer to her and said softly, "It sounds like Dev hurt your feelings . . ."

She blew her nose, and nodded.

"Why is Dev so important to you?"

"He's the first person who ever paid any attention to me,"

she sobbed. "I hoped he'd change his mind about me being too young for him. I really love him, and he treats me like a kid."

"That must be very frustrating."

"Yeah," she sighed. "But I know he cares about me. Just not the way I want him to."

"Is it possible that having a big brother type of love might be special in its own way? After all, having someone who watches out for you is worth a lot."

"I never thought of it that way." She frowned and paused to think about it. "Maybe I should talk to him?"

I nodded and relaxed my tight shoulders. "I think that would be an excellent idea."

Maybe this Dev guy isn't so tweaked, after all.

We sat quietly for a couple of minutes.

"Midnight, are you seriously considering becoming a vampire?"

Becoming a vampire had started to sound like a euphemism to me, and I was getting the same vibe I got when a client hinted about suicide, without actually talking about it.

"I don't know. Last night Bryce and I took a little blood from each other. It was the first time that a real vampire had bitten me and he did it while we were having sex, which felt great, but I think I must have passed out for a while because I couldn't remember what happened after that. He told me he had chosen me because I was ready. I don't want to let him down."

Let him down?

Bryce was setting off all my inner alarms. I wished I could see the skin hidden by all that hair so I could tell if she had any cuts or bite marks.

Did he drug her? He's obviously playing into the vampire fantasy. Is he a manipulative slimeball or something even worse?

"I thought we made an agreement that you'd hold off on any blood drinking activities until we talked about it? What if Bryce has some kind of illness? Is he worth dying for?"

She scowled. "I think you're making it a bigger thing than it is. I know I told you I'd wait, but we got so caught up in the moment. Bryce said that if I really loved him, I'd want to share everything with him. I know how that sounds, but at the time it made perfect sense. He just looked at me and I knew it was the right thing to do. Besides, Bryce said if I do decide to become a vampire, any disease that I might have would go away."

Shit. We've crossed the line now. I'm legally required to report harm to self or other and, even though Midnight isn't a minor, she's at risk. If I get the authorities involved in this, Midnight will never trust me again. But if I don't . . .

I leaned forward in my chair, locking eyes with her. "Would you be willing to give this some time? Will you promise me—I mean *really* promise me—that you won't make any decisions about becoming a vampire or drinking blood without talking to me first? It's a very big deal."

I let the honest concern I felt show in my face, and I watched the suspicion in her eyes soften into possibility as she sensed my sincerity. I really didn't want to bring in the police unless I absolutely had to, and I needed time to deepen our connection.

She heaved an exaggerated sigh. "Well, I guess I could do that."

I persuaded her to put off the decision for a couple of weeks and we spent the rest of the session exploring some of her background. "Tell me about your father," and she did. The hour flew by.

As she stood to leave she said, "I told some of the other kids about you and a few of them might want to come and talk. Would that be okay?"

"Sure. That would be great." I picked up some business cards from my desk and handed them to her. "Just ask them to call to schedule an appointment."

I walked her into the reception area and she stopped with her hand on the doorknob and turned toward me again. "Oh, yeah. I forgot to tell you. I told Dev I was coming to see you that first time—that my parents were making me see a shrink—and he was very interested in that. Well, anyway, he was waiting for me after our appointment, and he asked me lots of questions about you and what we talked about. He asked me how you look. I told him everything. He said he might drop in to meet you sometime, and that I should tell you."

"If he'd care to make an appointment, I'd be happy to see him."

"It would have to be at night." She smiled.

I nodded. "That's perfectly fine. I often see clients in the evenings." I didn't add that it was one of my least favorite things to do. But if I was going to specialize in vampire wannabes, I'd have to get used to the nocturnal schedule.

She left and I went back into my office.

I met with a few more clients that afternoon and early evening and was just kicking off my shoes when I heard the door to the reception area open. I quickly scanned my appointment book to make sure I hadn't forgotten anyone. Finding I hadn't, I put my shoes back on, and opened my office door.

Sitting in one of the chairs in the waiting room was the very same gorgeous, blond-haired, leather-clad man I'd seen outside my building.

My stomach lurched and I think I made a gasping sound.

He stood when I opened the door and it was fluid motion. As if he had simply willed himself to stand. His body was all lean muscle radiating some kind of primal power. He moved elegantly over to me, gave a slight bow of his head, and offered a glorious smile.

Dressed all in black, his snug leather pants, form-fitting silk T-shirt and long leather duster gave the impression of high fashion rather than Harley Davidsons.

I froze in the doorway with my mouth hanging open, speechless, staring into the most amazing pair of turquoise eyes I'd ever seen.

He picked up my hand gently and kissed the back, his lips soft and silky. "I am Devereux. Is this a good time for an appointment?"

Chapter 3

There were so many emotions slamming against each other inside me I didn't know which one to act on first.

Fear decided to step to the front of the line, and my mind began weighing options in case the man physically attacked me. He didn't seem menacing at the moment, but he was much bigger than me—much stronger—and I hadn't spent as much time in the gym as I probably should have. Hell, I hadn't spent any. And, obviously, he had.

My heart raced and still I hadn't formed a coherent sentence or done anything beyond stare at him like a deer in his headlights.

What was happening to me? My eyelids felt as though they were wearing cement overshoes, my jaw sagged open, the air was suddenly thick, and there was a sumo wrestler on my chest. The normal background white noise acquired a sharp edge and turned into a persistent buzz, vibrating in my ears. I felt as if I was in some kind of trance.

He took a step back from me and released my hand. "I am very sorry. I have frightened you. That was never my intention. Sometimes I forget how intense we can be. You must be a keenly sensitive individual. I will endeavor to control myself. Please accept my sincere apologies."

You will endeavor to control yourself? I'm the one having the meltdown.

He shifted his gaze down for a moment, and when he met my eyes again, the tension drained from my body, and I could breathe. It felt as though a switch had been thrown, and I was once again in charge of my body functions. I could still hear the hum in my ears, but it had diminished in volume. I ran my tongue over my very-dry lips.

"You did startle me. I wasn't expecting anyone this evening."

Both times I'd seen this man, he'd caused my anxiety levels to blast through the roof. I wanted to scream at him that it was absolutely *not* acceptable he'd come unannounced to my office, and that his habit of lurking around me was going to earn him a trip to the police station. He seemed altogether too sure of himself. I wanted him to know he couldn't just stroll in and expect me to drop everything and attend to him. No matter how gorgeous he was.

But I swallowed the irritation, opted for whatever remnants of professional demeanor I could summon, and said instead, "Well, Mr. Devereux, why are you here?"

He cocked his head and flashed that god-like smile again. "Just Devereux. As I mentioned a moment ago, I had hoped this would be a good time for our appointment. I trust Midnight told you I wished to meet with you?"

His voice was unusually pleasant—the timbre of it flowed through me like a favorite song, as if I listened to him with my entire body. He had a lilting European accent, almost old-fashioned sounding—like he'd stepped out of another century. Strange, how a voice could be so enticing.

I closed my eyes and sniffed the air. What was that wonderful aroma? It seemed to hover around him like an olfactory aura. Maybe he used a special kind of soap or shampoo. Something spicy and masculine and unusual.

He brushed a finger lightly along my arm. "Dr. Knight?"

My eyes flew open and I realized I'd been standing there, blatantly reveling in his scent, making sniffing noises. *How embarrassing. What the hell is wrong with me?*

Come on, Kismet. Talking has always been your strong suite. Just one word at a time. Concentrate.

I cleared my throat. "Yes, she did mention that you might call to set up an appointment. Would you care to schedule one for later this week?" I inhaled a deep breath and tried to remain professional.

I was so nervous my solar plexus contracted, my hands were sweating and my knee was twitching. I'd always had a fear of small spaces, and something about this situation gave me that same, closed-in, panic feeling. He had done nothing obvious to make me afraid, but my entire body felt as if it was waiting for some other shoe to drop. Something about him radiated danger. Almost primal.

"Would it be terribly inconvenient for us to meet now, since I am here?"

That voice. Maybe he was a hypnotist and he knew how to use it to put people under. So soothing. I could stand here and listen to it all night.

I felt myself sliding down that slippery slope again and rallied. I needed to get this guy out of my office before I made a complete fool of myself.

If I'd known I was going to have a mental breakdown today, I'd have penciled it into my book.

"Well, I was just leaving. It would be much better if we could schedule another time . . ."

He reclaimed the step he'd given up, and stated, as if the outcome was already a foregone conclusion, "I would appreciate very much the opportunity to speak with you about Midnight. I am concerned about her."

Through the cotton candy that had taken up residence in my brain, the voice in my head was screaming NO! but my mouth said, "I guess I could give you a few minutes. Please come inside."

Please come inside? Hey, wait a minute. That isn't what I meant to say. Where'd that come from?

I backed away from the door, drawing it open so he could enter, leaving it that way so he wouldn't be encouraged to make himself too comfortable.

I was about to invite him to sit down when I noticed he'd already seated himself in the chair I usually sat in. I realized he had no way of knowing that was "my" chair, but it still annoyed me.

"Would you mind filling out a little paperwork for me?" Out of habit, I handed him a packet of papers on a clipboard.

He took it. "My pleasure."

I sat down across from him and studied him while he wrote. His hands were very artistic-looking, with recently manicured nails, trimmed close. He had very pale skin, with a lovely, translucent sheen to it, which gave him an ageless quality. It wasn't often that I encountered someone with skin lighter than mine.

His eyes were extraordinary. Midnight was right. They

were aqua and beautifully shaped with long, dark eyelashes. I was surprised that his eyebrows and eyelashes were dark because his hair was so light, but the combination was very appealing.

His thick, lovely hair flowed down over his shoulders to mid-chest. It appeared soft and silky and very touchable. And his mouth. Studying his soft, full, generous lips caused a visceral reaction in me. I could imagine the feel of them against mine.

Okay. Take a breath, Kismet. You're in your office. This is a professional situation. Stop thinking about what you want to do to those lips and pay attention.

As I raised my gaze up from his mouth to his eyes, I found him watching me with an amused expression, apparently finished with the paperwork. Embarrassment warmed my face as I reached out to take the clipboard from him. For some reason, I couldn't take my eyes off him long enough to even glance at the forms he'd filled out.

I struggled to regain control of myself. "What is it that concerns you about Midnight?"

"Before we speak of that, would you mind if I ask you a question?"

"Well, you can ask. I can't promise I'll answer."

"Do you believe in vampires?"

"What?" Surprise radiated up my spine, and I stiffened in my chair. The buzzing in my ears got louder and I was suddenly very thirsty.

He toyed with a beautiful antique medallion on a chain around his neck. "Do you believe what Midnight has been telling you?"

Okay. Maybe he has a suggestion about how to help Midnight move beyond her vampire fantasy.

To steady myself, I walked over to the small refrigerator in the corner of the room and selected two bottles of water. I set one of them down in front of Devereux, opened the other for myself, took my seat and drank deeply.

Breathe. Just breathe. This can't be hot flashes. I'm too young.

"I can't discuss anything that Midnight may or may not have talked to me about. It's all confidential. But in general, I can tell you that I've never seen any evidence to support the existence of vampires or any other supernatural beings."

He smiled. "Ah, you are a scientist. Do you wish to see evidence?"

I was getting that claustrophobic feeling again. Maybe this handsome man really was a nut case and I'd allowed myself to be distracted by his obvious assets instead of following my professional instincts. I switched into the noticeably calm voice I used to soothe disturbed clients. "Is it important to you that I believe in vampires?"

He threw back his head and laughed with pure delight. "I have never been called insane in such a lovely way ever before. I can assure you that it is of no importance whatsoever if you believe in vampires or not, but I think the information could prove useful to you. What if I told you that everything Midnight has shared with you is absolutely true?"

Oh, geez.

"Since we can't talk about anything Midnight might have told me, I can only suggest that you tell me directly what you want me to know."

"I am a vampire."

Of course you are. "Tell me about being a vampire."

He laughed again. "As you wish. Until I can convince you of the truth of my words, I will be the good therapy client and follow the rules."

He seemed to find me very amusing. *Hmmm. Inappropriate humor. That's a symptom in several diagnoses.*

I wonder what he's basing his role on. I've never seen a movie vampire who went around telling people he was a vampire. Wasn't that the point? To avoid the stake in the heart thing? Maybe I could just rattle his delusion a little bit.

"Why do you want me to know you're a vampire? Isn't that supposed to be a secret?"

"I want you to know about me because I have a feeling about you. I believe you have an important role to play in my life."

An important role in his life?

This was definitely getting out of hand. Maybe I should rework my idea about counseling vampire wannabes. These folks were much more delusional than I thought, and it wasn't going to be as simple as I first imagined. I'd assumed all my pretend vampires would be similar to my alien abductees: creative, needy, acting out and harmless. I hadn't considered the possibility that this sub-culture would be populated by psychotics. That would require a totally different treatment plan.

No problem. This is good. I need to know what I'm dealing with.

I glanced over at the clock, thinking of ways I could gracefully end this session.

"Shall I show you one of my vampire abilities?" he asked, his voice deep.

My solar plexus tightened. "I don't know. What kind of ability is it?"

"Simple telepathy. Allow me to tell you what you have been thinking."

He repeated back all my thoughts about things getting out of hand, reconsidering how I'd work with vampire wannabes, that he was being delusional and my wanting to end the session. Word for word.

My body rode a rollercoaster of emotion.

I immediately felt embarrassed that he'd known what I really thought about him, which was then made even worse by the humiliating possibility he'd been aware of my earlier appreciation of his physical attributes, but then I got angry. The buzzing in my ears had morphed into a headache and I was rapidly approaching some inner line in the sand. I hadn't given him permission to stroll through my mind or to inconvenience me with his unexpected presence or his sideshow antics. Since I had no intention of taking him on as a client, I felt justified in letting myself have a reaction.

I held onto the arms of the chair so tightly that my fingers were even whiter than normal.

"That's quite a clever parlor trick. Are you a mind reader? A psychic?" There was more heat in my voice than I'd intended.

Something is very wrong here. I've never had this reaction to any client, ever. I've never gotten angry at a client before. I've never been so attracted to a client before. This is unnatural.

"You are angry. Once again, I apologize for upsetting you. It is my nature to be able to read the thoughts and sense the emotions of others. It has always been that way for me, even before I was born into darkness. I cannot be other than I am. All vampires are telepathic, but not all are as skilled as I am—it is one of my gifts. I can teach you to shield your thoughts if you wish."

"Can't you just stay out of my mind?" I demanded, much louder than I'd meant to. I couldn't honestly say I believed he'd read my mind, because that just wasn't possible, but I had to admit I couldn't explain how he knew what I was thinking. Not being able to explain it made me nervous.

He smiled, and gave another bow of his head.

"With most humans, there is little pull to their thoughts. Their minds are filled with ordinary, unimportant details and I can easily turn my attention elsewhere. But your mind is very powerful and you have your own abilities that you have not acknowledged yet. That is a very strong attraction for me. But I will do my best to stay out of your mind."

"Thank you," I said, standing up. *What abilities?* "We need to stop now."

He stood and smiled at me. "Yes, of course. I am grateful for your indulgence. Midnight holds you in high regard and I am pleased that she will be spending time with you. She has most likely told you that she is involved with another vampire she met at my club. This . . . individual . . . is dangerous, and I wish to discourage their relationship. She is most upset with me, but I must be firm on this. I hope that as you learn more about him, you will agree with me. Perhaps she will listen to both of us."

He has such interesting speech patterns. I feel as if I've fallen into a time warp. Or into an episode of Dark Shadows.

There were many questions I wanted to ask him since he'd started talking about Midnight, but I didn't want to encourage him, or breach her privacy, so I kept my face pleasantly blank and said nothing.

"May I have your permission to come and visit you again?"

Ah, the vampire wannabe is tapping at my window, wanting in.

"Is there something you wish to talk to a therapist about? Because I believe I've made it clear that I can't talk about Midnight with you, so it might be best if I refer you to another therapist."

"There are many things I wish to talk about, but only with you. Would you come to my club sometime, as my guest?" he said, his voice smooth velvet again. "It would give you an opportunity to see the world Midnight lives in."

What was it about that voice? Why did it cause me to have very un-therapist-like thoughts? I gathered my professional aura around me like a protective cloak. "I don't think that would be appropriate, but I appreciate the kind offer. If you decide you want to speak with a therapist, I'd be pleased to refer you."

I guided him into the waiting area and he turned to me, lifted my hand and kissed it, his mouth lingering just a bit longer than necessary. His aqua gaze locked onto mine.

"Please allow me to give you a parting gift."

Before I could answer, he placed his index finger gently on the skin between my eyes and made a circular motion. I jumped as if he'd burned me. The touch had felt like a mini lightning bolt.

I gasped. "What did you do to me?"

"I provided a layer of protection over your third eye—your sixth chakra—so you will no longer be overwhelmed by what I am. Your symptoms are already subsiding."

My symptoms?

"Until next time." He turned and left my office as quietly as he came in.

I rubbed my forehead, half expecting to find a gaping wound, and was pleasantly surprised to find nothing out of the ordinary. In fact, I felt almost clear-headed again. I suspected I was right about him being a hypnotist, because he certainly understood the power of suggestion. But, regardless of why the fuzziness, buzzing, and pain had gone away, I was relieved it had.

I closed and locked both the doors, noticing that my legs were shaking and my knees were dangerously close to bailing on me. I shuffled over to the couch, flopped down and stretched out along the length of it, kicking my shoes into the air as I surrendered into the soft cushions. I could still feel his kiss on my hand and I was very aware that my hormones were jumping up and down on my arousal trampoline.

That was, without a doubt, the weirdest experience I'd ever had.

After lying there for a few minutes, trying to figure out what had just happened, I sat up and reached for the information sheet he'd filled out, noticing that he hadn't answered many of the questions. He listed the club downtown as his address and phone number, and under date of birth he wrote August 8, 1172 and October 31, 1201.

Oh, I get it. In keeping with his story, he'd given me both a human birth date and a vampire birth date. Very clever. According to this, he was 29 years old when he was "brought over." So, something must have happened to him when he was 29 that caused him to retreat into this masquerade. Since he didn't appear to be much older than that, it couldn't have been very long ago.

I suddenly felt very sad. What a shame it was that this obviously intelligent and unquestionably gorgeous man was caught up in this bizarre pretense. Or, even sadder, that he was mentally ill enough to actually believe he was a vampire. But there was still that business about him guessing what I'd been thinking. I remembered reading an article about mental illness and enhanced psychic abilities. I'd have to do some more research on that.

But why had I let him get to me? I was thoroughly ashamed of myself for behaving so unprofessionally—so irrationally. I've never had that kind of reaction to a client. I owed Devereux an apology. First, I'd let myself be attracted to a potential client and then I'd lost my temper. Both those things were completely unacceptable and very unlike me. It was undoubtedly time for me to make an appointment with my own therapist again, who would lecture me on the necessity of having a balanced social and professional life. I mean, how unnatural was it for a 30-year-old woman to be a celibate hermit?

If my bad experience with Tom had caused me to be so uncomfortable around men that I was incapable of dealing professionally with a sexually desirable client, then I'd better take some steps toward correcting the problem, or find another line of work.

I decided I'd call the cute chiropractor when I got home. I'd have to get back on the horse sometime.

Chapter 4

The next couple of days were uneventful. I called Vaughan the chiropractor and we arranged to meet for dinner the following weekend. He seemed so pleasantly surprised and delighted to hear from me that I was actually excited about our date. Maybe I'd even force myself to go to the mall and buy something new to wear.

The ads I'd placed in the newspapers announcing psychotherapy for vampires had started to draw responses and I'd begun the screening process for setting up appointments and forming groups. I was beginning to understand that screening was going to be very important. After my experience with Devereux, separating the mildly delusional from the profoundly confused was imperative. As expected, the ads attracted calls not only from vampire wannabes but also from people interested in other forms of the paranormal. Unfortunately, it also included those who defined their lives by hating anything they didn't understand.

One such caller was Brother Luther. He left messages on my voice mail, reminding me that I was going to burn in hell for consorting with demons and the minions of Satan. I wasn't sure if Brother Luther was affiliated with any organized group or if he was the sole member of his congregation, but he was very enthusiastic and dramatic in his opinions. He spoke with a southern accent and reminded me of the fire and brimstone preachers I'd seen as a child while visiting relatives in the Smoky Mountains. I usually didn't take those kinds of calls seriously, and I assumed he was a harmless windbag.

I was still troubled by the way I'd behaved with Devereux, and I knew I should call him and apologize, but for some reason I couldn't make myself pick up the phone. Even thinking about him caused me to have that same strange, overwhelming reaction. I was afraid of him yet very attracted to him, and those conflicting emotions seemed to create some terrifying third thing inside my psyche. So, I did nothing except brood.

When Midnight came in for her next appointment she wasn't wearing her vampire costume and she wasn't alone. I almost didn't recognize her until she spoke to me. Dressed in jeans, Renaissance Faire T-shirt and athletic shoes, with her long hair pulled into a ponytail, she was the fresh-scrubbed girl next door. It turned out that underneath all the makeup was a beautiful young woman. Sitting quietly next to Midnight in the waiting room was a thin, frail-looking female, with dark circles under her green eyes and tangled, black hair.

"Dr. Knight, this is Emerald. I brought her with me because I didn't know what else to do. Something's wrong with her." Midnight put her arm around her friend's shoulders and propelled her into my office.

They sat down on the couch together. Emerald gave me a vacant stare. I had seen that reaction before in clients who'd been traumatized. It was as if the body was still functioning, but the personality had gone into a dark closet and closed the door.

I stood next to them. "What happened to her?"

Midnight turned frightened eyes to me. "When I came home this morning at dawn, I found her sitting out on the front stairs, staring off into space. Just like a zombie. She hasn't said a word since."

"Emerald?" I moved over to squat down in front of her, glad my pantsuit was made of a flexible material. I held up my index finger in her line of sight and shifted it from side to side, watching to see if her eyes followed the motion. There was no reaction from her at all. I reached over and touched her hand. It was icy cold.

"Midnight, is Emerald usually this pale? How long has she been sick?"

"I guess I didn't really know she was sick. She's been complaining about being tired and sleeping a lot, but I've been so into Bryce that I didn't pay attention. I guess I've been a crummy friend." Tears glistened in Midnight's eyes.

Well, maybe it's good for Midnight to focus on her friend for a while. Get her mind off the vampire thing. Even though she's feeling sad, I'm glad to see her expressing her emotions.

Still kneeling in front of her, I touched Emerald's cheek with the back of my hand. "I'm not a medical doctor, but I think we need to take Emerald to the emergency room. It just isn't normal for a person to have such a low body temperature." And, now that I was close to her, I could see some bruising on her neck and chest. I gently angled Emerald's head to the side so I could investigate and noticed several sets of small puncture marks running down her neck. I pulled back the collar of the jacket she was wearing and found that the wounds went all the way down to the top of her breast. There was a little dried blood on her skin and clothing.

I was just about to say it appeared Emerald had been attacked by some kind of animal, when Midnight said, "Those are vampire bites."

I was tempted to say something to challenge the claim, but the helpless expression on Midnight's face stopped me. She was truly worried about her friend.

By this time, all I was thinking about was getting Emerald to the hospital. I was in no mood to play "let's pretend," but I also didn't want to damage the fragile trust that had been built between Midnight and myself. Creating a therapeutic bond was a crucial turning point in therapy, and I didn't want to burst the bubble.

I stood. "Let's get her to the hospital. We can take my car." I knew that Midnight usually walked or rode the bus to her appointments, so I assumed I was the designated driver. Besides, I wasn't going to let them out of my sight until I knew they were in good hands.

Midnight rose and held Emerald upright while I gathered my purse and car keys. I opened the door, supported Emerald's other side, and the three of us shifted sideways to get through the narrow space.

"Hey, Ronald," said Midnight, talking to a sweet-faced young man sitting in the waiting room.

"Oh, Ronald. I'm afraid we're going to have to reschedule

our appointment. We have a bit of an emergency here," I explained, stating the obvious.

Ronald was one of the "apprentices" Midnight had referred to me and this would have been our first session. I'd wondered if he'd show up in costume, and he hadn't. His squeaky-clean-looking auburn hair flowed down over his shoulders, and his round, copper-colored eyes were warm and friendly. In fact, the only indication of his alternate lifestyle was his "Theatre of Blood" T-shirt and a pentagram earring hanging from one ear lobe.

He stood. "Can I help?" he asked, with concern in his voice. "Emerald is a friend of mine. My van is parked right in front of the building."

Without waiting for me to answer, he stepped out into the hallway, trotted down to the far end and called the elevator.

Nice guy, I thought.

Under other circumstances, I might have hesitated before accepting his help. After all, I'd only spoken to him on the phone before today and didn't really know much about him. But since my inner radar wasn't sending me any warning signals, I decided to take a chance and trust him. Besides, if it came down to needing to carry Emerald, I wasn't going to turn down another set of muscles.

I had imagined that Ronald's van would be something you'd find on a Grateful Dead album cover, but it was surprisingly nice—and very clean. He opened up the sliding door on the side and Midnight and I climbed in, holding Emerald, who seemed to be fading fast. Her head drooped as if all the muscles and bones had been removed from her neck, causing her chin to bounce against her chest. She made tiny whimpering sounds that seemed to come from deep inside, and every few seconds her eyelids fluttered as if she were in REM sleep.

The hospital was only a few blocks away, but we managed to catch every red light and construction detour on the trip.

Ronald's eyes peered at us in the rearview mirror. "Who do you think did that to her, Midnight?"

"How would I know?" Midnight snarled, her voice loaded with hostility.

I raised my eyebrows at her, and she answered, "Ronald doesn't like Bryce and his friends, either."

My eyes shifted back and forth between them. "Is somebody implying that Bryce had something to do with this attack on Emerald?" The discussion already had me thinking about the call I'd make to the police. As a licensed therapist, I had a legal requirement to report harm.

"Nobody knows who hurt Emerald. Ronald's just being a jerk," Midnight fumed. "He's mad because Bryce chose me instead of him."

"I'm not the one being a jerk," Ronald snapped.

Apparently, there are more dramas in the vampire wannabe game than I know about.

We finally arrived at the emergency room entrance and Ronald pulled the van into the "no parking" zone, came around to let us out and took my spot holding Emerald, who had slipped into unconsciousness during the ride over. "Dr. Knight, you go on ahead and deal with the red tape."

Appearing as official as I could manage, I hurried to the admissions desk and enlisted the aid of a nurse. A gurney was wheeled over for Emerald and she was taken away.

Since Midnight was the only one of us who had any information about Emerald, she filled out the hospital paperwork while Ronald went back outside to move his van before it was towed.

After she answered the nurse's questions, Midnight and I sat in the hard, orange chairs in the huge, white, noisy waiting area. The emergency room was filled with people in various states of crisis, and more trauma victims arrived every moment. There was that ever-present hospital smell: a combination of antiseptics, body fluids, and fear. I couldn't even imagine how it would be to work in a chaotic environment such as this, where the adrenaline was constantly pumping. It was almost as if I could see the tension in the air.

It was times like these when my "sensitivity" really became a problem. Sensory overload. Strong emotions and physical discomforts bombarded me from all sides, and I began using all the mental tricks I'd learned to help me distract myself from the unwanted sensations. I closed my eyes tight and imagined myself surrounded by a fortress of thick, high walls. That visualization usually did the trick, but this time it barely soothed the chaos. I still felt anxious.

I'd always been aware of peoples' feelings and emotions, but it was usually through clairsentience. Just my normal idiosyncrasy. I simply somehow knew what was going on inside their psyches. It came in very handy in therapy sessions, where I could do a little skillful intuiting—skip ahead a few pages.

I didn't know why exactly, but I had the notion that my discomfort had something to do with the weird experience with Devereux the other night. Maybe the suggestion he'd given me about my *third eye*—as if there was any such thing—

had caused me to revisit yet another unwanted ability. I had the fleeting thought that it would be helpful to speak with Devereux about this new development—that maybe he'd have some advice. But then the part of me that was already dangling outside her comfort zone slammed the door on that idea. She wasn't fooled. She knew I only wanted to see him again. In fact, I couldn't stop thinking about him.

Somebody help me. I'm possessed by a vampire wannabe.

I jumped off that train of thought, grabbed onto a piece of consensus reality and turned to Midnight. "Would you care to fill me in on what you and Ronald were talking about?"

She slumped down in her chair and crossed her arms on her chest. "I'm sorry I got mad. I'm really stressed out. I'm just so tired of everyone telling me that Bryce isn't good for me or that he's going to hurt me. They don't know him like I do. He would never hurt Emerald. He knows she's my friend. Besides, I think more than one vampire did that to her."

Back to the vampire fantasy. I made a mental note to ask her more about that later.

She relaxed her arms, sat up abruptly and turned toward me. "Then there was the thing with Dev. About you. He told me he came to see you, and he went on and on about how pretty you are, and how your eyes are so blue that they reminded him of the daytime sky he hasn't seen in over eight hundred years, and your dark hair this and your long legs that. Blah, blah, blah. I was so pissed that I went and spent the night with Bryce just because I needed someone to want me like Dev wants you."

I opened my mouth to speak, but then closed it because I didn't know what to say. It was normal for clients to transfer their feelings about their parents or some other significant childhood person onto me, but I'd never found myself in the middle of a love triangle before. But, this wasn't the time or place to discuss those issues. Apparently, Devereux was clueless about the depth of Midnight's feelings for him. Or maybe he was simply a heartless bastard who didn't care. But in the midst of my annoyance at him for his insensitivity, there was a part of me that'd been pleased to hear Devereux thought I was pretty.

I was saved from having to figure out anything to say about it by the approach of a handsome, official-looking man dressed in brightly colored scrubs with a stethoscope around his neck, who I assumed was a doctor. He had shoulder-length, golden hair and dark brown eyes framed by wire-rim glasses, which gave him a professorial, academic look. One of my personal favorites. By this time Ronald had returned and the doctor addressed the three of us.

"Are you the ones who brought in the young woman with the neck wounds?"

We nodded.

"Are you family?"

We shook our heads.

Midnight explained that she'd left a message for Emerald's parents, telling them their daughter was in the hospital, but she wasn't expecting them to show up, because they'd given up on Emerald a long time ago.

"Doctor . . .?" I said, searching for a nametag.

He scooped me up with his soulful dark eyes. "Dr. Mitchell. Lee. And you are?"

Available.

"Dr. Knight. Kismet. I'm a psychologist. Can you tell us anything about what's wrong with Emerald? Can we see her?"

"We've stabilized her, but she's lost a lot of blood and she's receiving a transfusion now. This is an unusual case; the patient should be covered with blood to account for the excessive blood loss, but she isn't. And, it appears that she has older puncture wounds on her neck and chest in addition to those we're treating today. We're running tests on the wounds to see what kind of animal caused them. Do you have any information about where she was when the attack occurred? Did you see anything?"

I glanced over at Midnight, sliding the questions into her lap. She shook her head. "I thought Emerald was staying home last night and I didn't get back 'til early this morning, so I don't know what happened. I'm so sorry that I wasn't there for her," she whimpered, as tears ran down her cheeks.

I put my arm around her shoulders. "Dr. Mitchell, when will you get the results of the tests back? I'd like to know as soon as possible."

"Is the patient a client of yours?"

I started to say no, but then I remembered the lost, empty eyes of the vulnerable young woman we'd brought in, and I decided to lie. I wasn't sure how far professional courtesy was going to get me, and I wasn't willing to be another person who abandoned Emerald.

"Yes. We just started working together."

"I should know something by tomorrow morning. I could call you when the results come in, if you want." He smiled and tilted his head to the side.

Was this guy flirting with me? I must have crossed into

some twilight zone, because this kind of stuff just didn't happen to me. First the vampire wannabe gave me Jello knees, and now the handsome doctor was smiling at me in a most inviting manner. I'd bet the combination of the smile and the head-tilt thing always worked for him. I could definitely verify its effectiveness.

"I would appreciate that." Slightly flustered, I finally managed to pull out one of my business cards and handed it to him. "Just leave a message any time and I'll call you right back."

If one of my almost-clients hadn't been lying in the hospital, missing several pints of blood, I might have been tempted to pull my own smile and head-tilt out of the garage and take it for a test spin. But under the circumstances, I just put my professional face back on and behaved myself.

"The patient isn't going to be able to have any visitors today, so it would be best if you returned in the morning," he explained, stepping back into his official persona. "Don't worry. We'll take good care of her." He winked at me, smiled, and walked away.

Well. That's it. I've definitely entered a parallel universe.

Ronald went to fetch the van and Midnight retreated in search of a restroom. I sat back down in one of the uncomfortable chairs, closed my eyes and circled my head around, stretching out the tight muscles in my neck. After a few seconds, I sensed someone behind me and turned to investigate.

Wow. I've died and gone to hunk heaven.

A tall, absurdly attractive man was inching toward me, madly scribbling into a notebook, totally oblivious to the fact that I was staring at him. He must have sensed he'd reached my chair because he started talking, eyes still on his writing.

"Dr. Knight? I'm Special Agent Stevens," he said, finally making eye contact. "I didn't mean to sneak up on you. Seems I really can't walk and do anything else at the same time. I couldn't help but overhear the conversation you had with the doctor. The victim of the attack is your client?"

"Special Agent Stevens? You don't look like a special agent." I noticed he was wearing jeans and a white T-shirt. "Who do you work for?" *Who knew the hospital was where they kept all the great looking men?*

"Sorry. I'd just gotten home and changed clothes when I picked up the call that there'd been another attack." He pulled out his identification from his back pocket and handed it to me.

Federal Bureau of Investigation, Special Agent Alan Stevens. I shifted my eyes from the photo to his face and back again. The picture didn't do him justice. It didn't even begin to convey the intelligence and depth in his sapphire eyes or the golden highlights in his dark hair. *Well, now.*

I handed the ID back to him. "Why would the FBI be interested in an animal attack in Denver?"

He paused and studied me as if he was trying to figure out if I was serious or not. "This wasn't an animal attack. I've been tracking these cases all over the country. The local police are involved, too. So, is Emerald Addison your client?"

"You know I can't confirm or deny that." *Shit.* He'd obviously heard me confirm it to the doctor.

"That pesky confidentiality thing, eh?" He smirked, making excellent eye contact.

I got distracted by his face for a moment. *He has wonderful eyes. Depending on how he moves his head, sometimes they're blue and sometimes purple. Like the ocean at twilight. Snap out of it, Kismet!*

"Uh, what cases have you been tracking? What does Emerald's situation have to do with those?" It was definitely time to change the topic.

He smiled. "Oh, so you won't answer my questions, yet I'm supposed to answer yours? I don't think so. But I'd like your contact information, just in case I think of some questions you *can* answer. Could I have one of those business cards you gave to the doctor?"

I wonder how it would feel to run my fingers through all that gorgeous hair.

Making sure that thought was not written on my face, I gave him one of my cards, and he fished in his wallet for one of his. "Here's my card. If you think of anything that might help me find whoever did this to your client, you can call me. Day or night."

I nodded, feeling like a hormonal 13-year-old. "Thanks, I will."

We locked eyes for a few seconds and then he shifted his gaze back down to the notebook, began writing furiously again, and shuffled back a few feet toward the nurses' station. Midnight, who had been standing off to the side, listening to the exchange, joined me and reported that Ronald and the van were out front. We were just going out the door when Special Agent Stevens suddenly reappeared and grabbed my arm.

"Oh, by the way, doc. Watch out for the vampires."

Chapter 5

By the time we left the hospital, the mountain skyline shimmered in the midst of a breathtaking color and light show. Brilliant shades of red, orange, blue, and purple swirled around and through each other, muting into pinks, peaches, and lavenders as shafts of sunlight streamed through openings in the kaleidoscope of colors. And off to the east, faint points of light floating in an indigo void sparkled as the sun retreated behind the towering peaks in the west. Nothing's as magical as a Rocky Mountain sunset.

We were all exhausted and the ride back to my office was a silent one. It appeared my companions had buried the hatchet, because Ronald offered to take Midnight home, and she accepted. Before they left I rescheduled Ronald's appointment and thanked him for being such a big help. He seemed ill at ease with my expression of appreciation, but gave me a tentative smile. I looked forward to finding out if I could help alleviate the sadness I saw behind his warm tawny eyes.

I wrestled with myself about whether I should go up to my office and work for a while or head home to a glass of wine and a hot bath. Guilt won the match and I rode the elevator upstairs, daydreaming about sinking into an aromatic, bubble-filled tub.

I was gratified to find several voice mail messages from prospective clients, and I sat at my desk for the next hour returning calls and answering emails.

I had just decided to pack it in for the evening, when my office door opened and two of the whitest men I'd ever seen walked in. I don't mean just pale, like the British actors on the BBC. Chalk white. Unlike the makeup that Midnight used to adorn herself, the tone of their complexions hadn't come from a tube. Suffice it to say they weren't sun worshippers.

One of the men was tall, dark-haired, and handsome and the other, short, odd-looking, and muscle-bound.

Startled, I asked, "Can I help you?"

How did they get in? I'm positive I locked those doors.

No response.

They ambled into the office and circled around, prowling through the couches and chairs in the middle of the room, their eyes fixed on me.

The smaller of the two came and sat on the corner of my desk and leered at me. He smiled a closed-mouth smile and reached out a tattooed hand to touch my hair. He was wearing a sleeveless T-shirt that showed exaggerated biceps and triceps rippling across his upper arms. His hair was that artificial color of burgundy that was so popular with the Goths, and it flowed down his upper body like stringy octopus arms. His eyes were so light blue they were almost white. He reminded me of a demented, miniature muscle man. A nightmare come to life.

These guys made my stomach hurt. It wasn't only that they'd invaded my privacy, or that they appeared dangerous, or even that they could assault me at any moment. It was something else. Some basic, preverbal fear that caused the hairs on my arms to stand up and the warning system in my head to fire a red alert. I kept having the odd, less-than-comforting intuition that death was in the room, and my usually manageable radar was picking up so much fearful information that it plunged into overload and threatened to shut down.

I glanced over at the phone on the far corner of my desk and began sliding my hand in that direction.

The tall man stepped around behind me and put his hands underneath my jaw, pulling my head back. He bent down, brought his mouth next to my ear and whispered, in a very sensuous voice, "I've heard so much about you, I thought it was time we were formally introduced." He grabbed the hand moving toward the phone.

"Who are you? What do you want?" I tried not to sound as worried as I felt.

His hand trailed across the hair at the back of my head as he moved to sit directly in front of me on my desk, which caused his legs to be jammed into the space under the desk with mine.

I instinctively reacted, making an unsuccessful attempt to push away. He bent in close, his hands straddling my chair, effectively blocking any move on my part. I was glad I'd worn a pantsuit instead of a skirt, because I wanted as many layers between us as possible.

He lowered his mouth to within an inch of mine, and I twisted my head to the side, shifting away from his hot, un-pleasantly sweet breath. He grabbed my chin between his thumb and first finger, holding tightly enough that I knew there'd be bruises, and forced my face back level with his. "I'm Bryce. I believe you've heard of me."

"Stop it! Let go of me . . ."

He swallowed my words with his mouth, clamping his lips on mine with enough pressure to cause my teeth to break the skin on the inside of my lip. Then he sucked my lower lip into his mouth, holding it with his teeth until I made an involuntary yelp of pain. Only then did he pull back, giving an evil grin, and gazed at me with his dark green eyes, which seemed suddenly magnetic. I tried to look away, but I couldn't. I literally couldn't. It was as if his eyes were pulling me. I managed to briefly squeeze my eyelids shut, and he dug his fingers into my chin again, jerking my head roughly. He roared, "Open your eyes."

My eyelids flew up and his eyes were directly in front of mine, the green darker than before, almost black. I fell into them and felt the edges of my vision blur—a strange haze settling over everything—as part of my mind drifted off on a cloud.

I felt as if my arms and legs were encased in armor, that even thinking about moving would require way too much effort, and that it really wouldn't matter, because they were too heavy to lift anyway.

Bryce cocked his head to the side and watched me, smiling. "See? You're feeling much more relaxed now. Aren't you sorry you put up such a fuss?"

"What do you want?" I mumbled.

I made what I thought was another valiant effort to raise myself out of the chair. Since nothing happened, I could only assume the message hadn't made it from my brain to my body. My muscles were pudding and my mouth was dry as the Sahara. Maybe I'd had a stroke and was spending my last moments on Earth in the company of a psychopath.

He laughed. "I enjoy when you struggle. It excites me. I'm not sure you really want to know what I want. Let's just keep it a surprise, shall we?"

Bryce selected a piece of his long hair and brushed it against my cheek. "You really are quite lovely. All that long, dark hair and sexy eyes. I can see why Devereux is attracted to you. I'm here because I overheard him talking about you to my little servant, Midnight. I think he's quite smitten, if you want my opinion. Nothing would make me happier than to keep Devereux from having something he wants or, even better, to take it away from him after he has it."

"No one has me," I asserted, despite the fact that I didn't have any idea what he was talking about, and the part of my mind that had floated away was still missing-in-action. False bravado was one of my favorite defenses.

All this time the smaller man had been laughing and slapping his leg with one hand. I slanted a glance at him and he showed me his top row of teeth, exposing a very real-looking set of fangs. He definitely had the best pair of fakes I'd seen so far. I wasn't sure what kind of reaction he thought I'd have to his cosmetic dentistry, but I obviously didn't give him whatever he wanted because he lurched at me and growled, "I could rip your throat out with these."

Abnormally fast, Bryce reached over, grabbed the small man by the throat, and threw him onto the floor. He snarled, "Leave her alone, Raleigh. I told you. She's mine."

Raleigh glared at Bryce, making noises that sounded more animal than human. He got up off the floor, stumbled to the nearest couch and stretched out, lacing his fingers behind his head.

She's mine? What does that mean? Am I his to harm, or . . . ? I wish I could find the "on" switch for my brain.

I hadn't worked with any physically dangerous or psychotic clients since my residency at the psychiatric ward during graduate school, and I tried to remember the skills I'd learned for dealing with them. Since I'd seen Bryce throw the small man around like a cardboard cutout, I knew I had no chance of doing anything that required physical strength, and I thought my only hope would be to use my tools as a therapist. Maybe I could reason with him. Or maybe I should just keep my mouth shut. I definitely needed to keep a clear head and that had become a problem.

Bryce turned his attention back to me and searched for something in my expression. He leaned in, ran his tongue over my lips and then kissed me again. I twisted my face away and yelled, "No!" He angrily shoved my chair back from the desk, stood up and lifted me, holding me like a child in his arms.

I ineffectually pushed against his chest and kicked my legs, trying to get him to put me down, and for one sick moment I was reminded of a scene from that old science fiction movie, *The Day The Earth Stood Still*, where the robot picked up the woman and she couldn't get away. Bryce felt that cold and alien to me.

I still had little control of my limbs and I was forced to acknowledge that this situation wasn't likely to end up any way I'd choose.

"Let me go! What are you doing?" I screamed, as he walked me over to a couch back against the far wall. The motions I was making with my arms and legs were pitifully useless. I hate feeling helpless. I thought about all the opportunities I'd had to take self-defense classes and how I'd always come up with some excuse to avoid them. I didn't know if learning to take down a guy wearing a big, foam helmet would have helped me fight off these two vampire wannabes, but it would have been better than nothing.

"Let's have a therapy session." He sat down on the couch, holding me tight in his lap. I kept pushing against him, getting more and more pissed about whatever he'd done to cause this bizarre paralysis, but his arms were steel bands. The sweet, coppery smell that rode his breath seemed stronger now.

"What do you want? Why did you come here?" I demanded, trying to sound more confident than I felt.

"Maybe I need someone to talk to," he said in a fake whining voice. He opened the top button of my blouse, and ran his finger across the section of exposed skin. "Maybe I'm just a lonely vampire searching for my soul mate. What do you think?" He threw back his head and laughed, enjoying some private joke, and then he recovered himself. "I hear you don't believe in vampires. I thought I'd change your mind. Watch."

He lifted his top lip so I could see the upper row of teeth and, as I watched, his canines got longer and longer until they protruded a good quarter- to a half-inch below his other teeth. Then they contracted back up into their normal place and extended again, as if he could will them to move in and out of his gums. He grinned at me. "How do you explain that?"

I didn't say anything. I stared at his mouth, trying to figure out how the trick fangs worked.

He smiled, his eyes sparkling. "Go ahead. Touch them."

Touch them? I wasn't going to stick my fingers in some psychopath's mouth. He'd probably bite me. I didn't want to think about where those teeth had been.

"No."

"Oh, but I insist." He grabbed my hand and forced it up toward his mouth, laying the tip of my index finger on one of his fangs. It contracted while I touched it, and I was able to snatch my hand away. Maybe my instincts could over-ride whatever he'd done to me.

He laughed. "I'm old enough to have total control of my fangs, but if you get me aroused or angry enough they seem to have a mind of their own. And, right now I'm feeling very aroused."

He grabbed my hand again and shoved it down into his lap, which was filled with a large erection. "Let me show you what else has a mind of its own."

In one quick motion he had me lying flat on the couch with him on top of me, roughly pressing his lips against mine. I pushed at him again, my muscles finally deciding to re-join the party, but he grabbed my wrists, holding them over my head in a vice-like grip as he forced his tongue into my mouth. After a few seconds I felt him kissing his way down to my neck and there was a flash of pain when he bit me.

I screamed and kicked and pushed against him in a futile effort to dislodge an immovable object. I tried to raise my knee to administer the only effective self-defense strategy

I knew, but he weighed on me like a slab of cement and I thought that maybe I wouldn't have to worry about him raping me, because he'd probably crush or smother me first.

He was making loud sucking sounds at the wound on my neck and I started to feel lightheaded. Suddenly, the pain stopped and I opened my eyes—which I hadn't realized I'd closed—and he wasn't on top of me anymore. I could hear male voices yelling and the sound of furniture being pushed around.

I sat up, feeling like the morning after, and saw Devereux and Bryce struggling with each other, dancers in a strange ballet. Raleigh was nowhere in sight.

Watching the two of them was surprisingly entrancing, and I couldn't shift my eyes away. It was as if they were in slow motion. I was fascinated by Devereux's light blond hair contrasted by Bryce's dark, silky veil. I hallucinated that their hair was flowing out around their heads as if they were submerged under water and, while some part of me knew that couldn't really be happening, I was lost in the spectacle.

I was jarred out of my trance by the harsh sound of Devereux's angry words.

"If you touch her again, I will kill you," he bellowed in an unnaturally amplified voice. "She is under my protection now. Ignore that at your peril." He released Bryce, who laughed and then vanished.

I stared at the empty place where Bryce had been and tried to get the neurons in my brain to fire in some helpful way. I quickly blinked my eyes a few times to clear the fog. Perfect. I'd finally lost my mind.

Devereux straightened his clothing, smoothed his hair

back away from his face and walked over to me. He sat
down, opened his arms and I sagged against him, forgetting
for a moment that I had my suspicions about his mental state,
and allowed myself to be held. I could hear his heart beating
and felt his warm breath on the side of my face.

We just sat like that, with him holding me, collapsed and
shaking against him, for several minutes. "I am very sorry
that I did not get here sooner. I never thought Bryce would
risk my anger by coming here. I will pay much closer attention in the future."

"Thank you," I mumbled, but I didn't know what I was
thanking him for. Had he appointed himself my bodyguard?
Was he saying that he was the reason I'd been attacked?

He stroked my hair and I surrendered into the calming
rhythm of his hand. I didn't know how to make sense out
of anything that had happened. I prided myself on my logical mind, and none of the puzzle pieces fit. My body was in
shock, and the wound on my neck throbbed. I couldn't really
have seen someone disappear before my eyes. That was impossible. It was probably a delusion triggered by the attack.
But it had seemed so real.

I was grateful to find that all my clothes were still but-
toned, snapped, and zipped. Thankfully, Bryce hadn't been
able to follow through on his intention to penetrate more
than my neck.

I'd listened to many rape and assault victims talk about
their horrible experiences, but I'd never truly understood how
it felt to be at the mercy of someone who meant you harm. I
sat there drowning in an unfamiliar mish-mash of feelings,
second-guessing myself about what I could have done to talk

him out of hurting me. Or, at the very least, what I could have done to shake myself loose from the effects of whatever drug he must have slipped me.

Maybe it was some new version of the date-rape drug that could be passed along by body fluids. That would explain why he focused on my mouth so much. He wanted to make sure I got the whole dose. Yeah, that must have been it. Right. Even I didn't believe that.

I knew better than to blame myself for any part of what had happened. I was well aware how damaging it was to blame the victim for her own victimization. But I couldn't sort out the avalanche of emotions.

I *should* have been able to do something. What was all my training for if I couldn't handle one maniac?

But, damn it to hell. I couldn't move my arms and legs! What the hell kind of weirdness was that? Are all vampire wannabes closet hypnotists?

How dare those assholes waltz in here and make me feel unsafe in my own office? Unsafe in my own life?

I'd never thought of myself as someone who'd ever need to be rescued. I didn't like the feeling.

Devereux gently turned my head and inspected the bite on my neck.

Something about what he found made him frown. "You have lost some blood. You will probably feel dizzy for a while. May I?"

He moved in closer for what I thought was a better view, and I felt his tongue brushing against the bleeding holes in my neck. Outraged, I pulled away and yelled, "What the hell are you doing?" I immediately felt woozy from the sudden movement. But I'd be damned if anybody else was going to snack on me tonight.

"I am stopping the bleeding. One thing about the vampire legends that is true is that we have a coagulant in our saliva which helps wounds heal faster. And, of course, blood is a wonderful delicacy and I would never pass up the opportunity to partake. It is my nature."

Something about the words, "It is my nature," roused me from my stupor. Suddenly, it all came back to me. I was in my office and Devereux was one of the lost souls pretending to be vampires. And I'd been attacked by a lunatic.

"I am not pretending to be anything. I apologize for invading your mind, but I do not think we have the luxury of continuing this interesting dance we have been doing. Bryce is indeed a lunatic, and you need to fortify yourself with facts. I do believe that facts are important to you, are they not?"

I struggled up from the couch, my face hot with anger, and I was just about to vent some of it on Devereux when he stood and picked me up in his arms, all in one invisible movement.

Now, I'm not a small person. In my 2-inch heels I easily reach 5'10", and no one has ever complained about how I filled out my swimsuit. But for the second time in one night, I'd been scooped up like a sack of potatoes and made to feel like a helpless infant. I can't even remember the last time anyone had the nerve to touch me without my permission and it seemed it was the name of the game with these people.

I pushed against him and, just as it had been with Bryce, it was impossible. His arms were unyielding. Closing my eyes tight to hold back the waterworks I felt gathering there, I tried very hard not to cry, but I was so exhausted I didn't know how much longer I could keep everything inside. Part of me just wanted to curl up in his arms and sleep.

"You must listen now." Devereux moved gracefully around the room, apparently trying to soothe me. "There is much I need to tell you."

I shook my head. "Please put me down. I'm sure you mean well, but this has been a terrible night and I just want to go home. I appreciate you pulling Bryce off of me, and you've been very kind, but I've had enough." The tears I'd been trying to hold back slid down my face, and I made a pathetic sniffing sound.

He studied me briefly, lifted my chin up toward him and kissed my lips gently. He pulled back, gazed at me with soft turquoise eyes for a few seconds more, and bent down and kissed me again, lightly at first, then deeper. His lips were warm and silky and, without even thinking about it, I put my arms around his neck and kissed him back. He let my feet find the floor and wrapped his arms around me, never altering the intensity of the kiss. He brushed his tongue along my lip and I opened my mouth for him. Whatever else he might have been, he was one awesome kisser.

Somebody hose me down, I'm going to spontaneously combust.

We reluctantly pulled our lips apart, and he enveloped me into a warm hug. I could feel both of our hearts beating out different rhythms and it occurred to me that my sensing Devereux's heartbeat was proof he wasn't a vampire. Everyone knew the dead had no heartbeat.

The ridiculousness of that thought made me want to laugh out loud—or scream. I didn't know which was more upsetting: my giving validity to the possibility of the existence of vampires or kissing a beautiful nut case. I was in deep shit any way you sliced it.

He stepped back from me and brushed a stray lock of hair from my face. "I think you have had enough excitement for one night. Please allow me to drive you home. I promise I will be a perfect gentleman."

I was going to argue that I could drive myself, but it just wasn't true. I could either take Devereux up on his offer or call a cab, and, since I needed my car the next morning, the choice was clear.

Well, there you have it. If Devereux was really a vampire he wouldn't know how to drive, right? Don't they all sprout bat wings and fly?

Devereux chuckled softly. I was going to ask him what was so funny, but my body's lack of cooperation suddenly captured my attention.

I had intended to walk over to my desk and gather my things to leave, but even that small attempt to move under my own power seemed to be too much for my legs, and my knees buckled. Devereux caught me and lifted me into his arms again. I'm not saying it wasn't pleasant, but I felt like a limp rag doll, and I didn't understand what had happened to cause me to be so lethargic. "What's wrong with me? Why am I so weak? What did Bryce do to me?"

"He bespelled you and then he drank your blood. Bryce is a master of enchantment. We all have the ability to use our eyes to entrance mortals, but Bryce takes special pleasure in manipulating and controlling. He is very powerful and, to use your psychology terms, he altered your brain waves. That is why you feel so confused. He had intended to drain you to near death, and he would have had I not arrived when I did."

"Do you mean he used his fake fangs to make holes in my neck and actually sucked my blood out and swallowed it?" My mind refused to accept what Devereux was telling me.

He raised one of his perfectly arched eyebrows and stared down at me for a few seconds. "Humans have the most remarkable ability to not see what they do not wish to see. The stronger the mind, the harder it is to accept what is hiding in the shadows. I would rather we had the time to introduce you slowly to the ideas you resist, but that is not possible now. This is not something that will go away like a bad dream."

I started to ask more questions, but he shook his head. "No, that is enough for tonight."

He walked me over to my desk, bent down so I could pick up my briefcase and my purse and we left to find my car.

I must have fallen asleep on the ride to my house because the next thing I knew, we were there and he was lifting me out of the passenger side of my car.

He carried me up to my front door and I asked, "How did you know where to go? I didn't give you directions to my house."

"I performed my little parlor trick. I can do the same with your alarm code if you wish, or you may simply punch in the numbers."

I gazed up at his beauteous face, decided I didn't have the energy to argue, entered the code, and unlocked my door. We stepped into my living room and I blurted, "Hey, I thought vampires could only come in if they were invited."

The moment I said it, I couldn't believe it had come out of my mouth. I must have some kind of head injury or something because I'd never make light of someone's delusion if I was in my right mind.

"I'm sorry. That was very thoughtless of me."

He laughed. "I am pleased you are getting into the spirit of things. But, that particular bit of vampire lore is false. We can come and go as we desire. Where is your bedroom?"

I tensed. "My bedroom? Why do you want to know where my bedroom is?"

He stared down at me, the warmth in his eyes replaced by something remote and cold. "Yes, it is wise for you to be afraid of all of us. No matter how much some of us might wish to pretend, we are not human and we do not live by human rules. But, for tonight allow me to put your mind at ease. As delightful as it would be to take you to your bedroom and make love to you, I am only offering to carry you to the comfort of your bed. I would be lying, however, if I said I do not hope for an invitation in the future."

He carried me upstairs to my bedroom, held me easily with one arm while he pulled back the bedclothes, and laid me down. He removed my shoes, covered me with the blankets and gazed into my eyes. The last thing I remember was that wonderful voice saying, "Sleep."

Chapter 6

I'm falling. Can't breathe. My entire body is contracted in terror as I plummet down into what I'm certain will be beyond my ability to withstand. The void. Darkness so complete that there's no comprehension of it. Falling and falling, with no sense of speed or location, just the continuous, ever-building dread. I feel enclosed, as if I'm spiraling down some long tube, dense with stifling, hot, thick air. And then, without notice, pulled out into an empty, cold nothing. My very essence fragmenting in all directions. Death. The descent seems to last a long time, as a distant voice shrieks horrible-sounding words I can't understand, echoing in oblivion. The voice crawls over me and through me, penetrating my skin, like hundreds of carnivorous insects, and I scream in the darkness, flailing my arms and legs. Is there something even worse than death? Then the shock of crashing down into warm liquid. Blood. Sticky, thick, coppery-scented and old—very old. The intensity of the harsh landing keeps me afloat for only seconds before I discover there's nothing underneath me—no foundation. Nothing to hold me. No one. I go under, still screaming, gasping, and swallowing blood. Drowning in the blood and the overwhelming hopelessness. Terror larger than I can hold. And someone is laughing.

"No!" I screamed. A shrill ringing startled me and my eyes flew open. I bolted up, heart beating fast and hard. Shaking, I leaned back against the headboard and noticed all the blankets and pillows from my bed were on the floor. Fragments of the dream swam back into my awareness and the feeling of terror intensified. I knew I was safe in my bed, but the memory of spiraling down into that darkness pressed against my chest, and I struggled to slow my breathing. Rivers of sweat snaked down my face and pooled between my breasts, and I distantly observed that I was still wearing the clothes I'd worn yesterday.

The annoying sound continued to intrude, louder now. A headache, which had started as a dull throb over my left eye, infiltrated my entire brain and beat a strong cadence of its own, rivaling what I finally understood was the telephone ringing. I took some deep breaths, pushed the wet hair back from my face and cleared my throat. Rolling over toward the night stand, I picked up the phone.

"Yes?" I croaked.

"Dr. Knight? This is Special Agent Stevens. We met at the hospital yesterday. I'm sorry, did I wake you?"

"Who?" My brain stubbornly refused to connect the dots, and the inside of my upper lip had become hermetically sealed to my teeth.

"The FBI guy from the emergency room. Special Agent Stevens."

I ran my tongue over my teeth in a vain attempt at hydration, and wound up making dry, smacking noises with my lips. "Special Agent Stevens? Uh, yes. Okay, I remember. I recognize your voice."

Idiot. You let the phone ring a thousand times—of course you woke me. And you'll never know how grateful I am that you did.

Groggy, I squinted over at the clock to see if it really was as ungodly an hour as I imagined it to be, and it was.

I sucked in another deep breath, held onto the solid reality of the phone, and forced myself to calm down. I cleared my throat again. "Why are you calling me at 5 a.m., Special Agent Stevens? And how did you get my home phone number? It's unlisted."

"I work for the FBI, enough said?"

"So, why are you calling?"

"I want to find out if you've heard from your client, Emerald Addison, the one you brought to the hospital?"

"What do you mean? She's still in intensive care, isn't she?

"Well, that answers my question. No. She isn't still in intensive care. Sometime between 1 a.m. and 4 a.m. she went missing."

"What are you talking about?" I barked, the pain in my head slam-dancing in heavy shoes. I pressed the palm of my hand against my forehead as if that would keep my skull from exploding. "The last time I saw Emerald, she was in no condition to do anything. There's just no way she could have gotten up and walked out of the hospital. What are you doing about it?"

His voice held the verbal equivalent of a smirk. "It sounds like we're a little cranky when we don't get our beauty sleep, doc. Even though you're being testy, I'll answer your question anyway. This case is being treated as an abduction or a missing person. Each one of those categories has its own protocol, and the local cops are in charge. Since your client was attacked in the same manner as the other cases I'm investigating, I'm being included in the information loop. So far we have zip. I'm hoping you can tell me something that'll give us a lead."

Okay. He gets points for pulling me out of that nightmare, but cute cop or not, there's no way I'm sharing client information. Even if I knew anything.

I took a deep breath, pushed "play" on the "I'm a Professional" tape in my mental repertoire, and began speaking in my therapist voice. "As I mentioned yesterday, I'm not at liberty to tell you anything about anyone. But if there is something general I can help you with, as a psychologist, I'd be willing to do that."

"Great. I'll be right there. Put on some coffee, okay?"

"What?"

The pushy bastard. I didn't expect him to take me up on it.

"Wait a minute! I need to take a shower and get dressed. You can't come over now!"

"How much time do you need?"

There was that cocky tone again. The tone that said he assumed I'd be spending hours primping in front of the mirror.

"Give me half an hour."

"Half an hour. Will do."

"Hey, hold on. Don't you want me to give you directions to my house?"

He chuckled. "FBI, remember? We've got all those handy little records. See you in thirty."

I hung up the phone and rolled out of my warm bed, still on automatic pilot. I stumbled around the bed, managed to remove all the damp sheets, threw them into the laundry hamper, and headed to the shower. It took ten minutes of standing like a statue under the hot spray before the sensation of something crawling on my skin receded and I felt somewhat normal again.

I stood, my arms braced against the tile walls enclosing the bathtub, willing the hot water to wash away the fearful residue from the nightmare. The sound of the hideous laughter still echoed through my inner world, reverberating like a ghostly memory.

I picked up a bar of soap and reveled in the sensation of it gliding over my skin and began to feel renewed—to come back to myself. I slid the bar over one side of my neck, kneading gently, and when I lathered the other side, I was startled by a sharp jolt of pain. Instinctively, I dropped the soap, which hit the bottom of the tub with a loud thud as I explored the tender skin with my fingers.

"Shit!" I stepped away from the water and gingerly slid my finger over the painful area, mentally shaking off another layer of drowsiness.

Touching the wound on my neck brought the horrible events of the previous evening back to me in living color. Some demented maniac had broken into my office and punctured my neck with his teeth.

His teeth! What movie was it where the guy put on his grandmother's sharp dentures and chewed on his victims? And how the hell did they get into my office? What a miserable night. First the psychopaths then the dream. Oh, yes. And let's not forget cocky FBI agents, although I guess this didn't qualify as "night" anymore.

That nightmare was off the charts. I couldn't remember

ever having such a vivid, terrifying dream before. All that blood and existential emptiness. Maybe those assholes coming to my office last night frightened me even more than I realized. The dream was probably a reaction to their threats and my feelings of mortality. The standard death dream, maybe. Or an indication that my brain was turning into scrambled eggs. Well, whatever it was, I'd have to sort it out later.

I hadn't even begun to think about whether or not I should report the attack to the police. There was the confidentiality issue to consider. Bryce was connected to Midnight, and I couldn't involve her, but if I pressed charges, she'd probably be dragged in.

But I was definitely moving my office to a building with security—cameras, doormen, the whole deal. No more uninvited visitors.

I finished my shower, stepped out and wrapped myself in a thick, extra large towel. Enjoying the warm feeling, I went over to the mirror, wiped away a patch of fog, and checked out the wound on my neck.

"Damn! What the hell?"

I stared at the carnage. There were two blatant, swollen holes surrounded by a sea of red with purple and yellow blotches. It looked as if I'd been ravaged by some kind of wild dog or something.

I opened the medicine cabinet, rummaged around for my antiseptic salve, and read the label to see if it said anything about being an effective defense against human germs. I remembered reading something about the germs in a human's mouth being worse than anything else. I hoped that wasn't true.

Anti-bacterial? Well, I guess that's better than nothing. I wonder if there's an anti-vampire-wannabe medicine? An analgesic to ward off those pesky undead cooties? I probably should get a tetanus shot, at the very least. Yeah. Here I am, thinking about this as if it's just another day at the office. Maniacs "R" Us.

I dotted some of the medicine on the wound and held an inner debate about the merits of covering it versus letting it breathe. Breathing won. For now.

Touching the bite mark reminded me of Devereux's tongue sliding over my neck, and I had a pleasant body rush. Then I remembered the feel of his lips and noticed my nipples were hard and the area between my thighs grew warm and wet. I took a quick ride down Possibility Lane as I imagined how it would be to feel his hand there.

The human mind really is resilient. What am I thinking about while patching up the leftovers of my very own psychotic Bela Lugosi's munch-fest on my neck? Sex. Sex with Devereux. I definitely didn't get enough sleep.

Still tingling from the mental afterglow, I toweled my hair, sprayed it with a super anti-tangle concoction and flipped my head over so that my hair hung down in a thick curtain in front of me. I picked through it with my wide-tooth comb, snarling as I struggled with the clumps of hair that refused to play nice.

I stopped, mid-pick, when a simple realization washed over me. It finally penetrated my sleep-clogged brain that I could have told Agent Stevens I was unavailable and would see him at my office later. I could have continued snoozing in my warm bed. I definitely knew better than to make any decisions before I've had my caffeine fix. Apparently, the events of the previous night plus the demonic nightmare caused me to have an even more intense case of fuzz brain. The annoyance of my obvious act of stupidity caused me to fling my head back up with such momentum that the weight of my hair almost gave me a whiplash.

"Ouch! Dammit!"

I strode into my bedroom and flung open the door to my walk-in closet, knocking a picture off the wall.

Okay. Temper tantrum accomplished. Next?

I climbed into my favorite baggy jeans and a University of Colorado T-shirt and headed down to the kitchen, fantasizing about that first cup of nirvana.

After I started the Mr. Coffee, I checked my office voice mail to see if Emerald had left a message. She hadn't.

I was pouring my first cup of coffee when Agent Stevens knocked on my door. I didn't usually get up that early, but every time I did, I was reminded of how much I love watching the sun come up. There's that wonderful feeling of a new beginning, of endless possibilities. And this morning, in particular, I appreciated the beauty, light, and warmth of the dawn.

I let him in, stood for a moment in the open doorway, watching the light reclaim the sky and enjoying the early fall breeze, and I jumped when he spoke.

"Hey, Earth to Dr. Knight? Where do you keep your coffee mugs?"

I glared at my visitor, who was making himself quite at

home. He wandered around the kitchen, opened every cupboard and drawer and then parked himself in front of my open refrigerator. "Holy cow. There's nothing in here but take-out food. Don't you know how to cook? There isn't even any milk for my coffee."

Is this guy for real?

Waking me up before the crack of dawn was bad enough, but inviting himself over and having an opinion about the state of my refrigerator was over the top. My head was pounding and I simply had no patience for dealing with this arrogant cop. If it hadn't been for my concern about Emerald, I'd have kicked his tight little butt right out the door.

But the longer I studied him, the more the wind leaked out of my anger sails. He looked exhausted—as if he hadn't been to bed yet. He was either wearing the same clothes I'd seen him in at the hospital, or he had a collection of jeans and rumpled white T-shirts. His eyelids drooped slightly, the purple-blue of his eyes seemed less vibrant and his hair was a monument to what happens when you use your fingers as a comb.

Come on, Kismet. Don't go getting all warm and gooey now because the guy's worn out. This is a professional consultation. No caretaking allowed.

"Sit down, Special Agent Stevens." He eased his long frame into one of my kitchen chairs. I poured us each a mug of coffee, carried them over to the table, and joined him.

"You can call me Alan, doc."

I pulled another clump of my hair over my shoulder, making sure it still covered the ghastly souvenir on my neck. "Well, Alan, how can I help you?"

"Why are you counseling vampires? Don't you know how dangerous that is?"

And to think that for the past thirty years I doubt if I heard the word "vampire" more than ten times, and now everyone I talk to seems obsessed with it.

I shook my head. "Dangerous? What's dangerous about helping people free themselves from a destructive delusion?"

He paused. "That's the second time you've said something that leads me to believe you don't know what kind of tiger you've got by the tail. Are you seriously telling me you think vampires are delusions? You really don't see the big picture?"

Oh, please. I'm not awake enough for this. I can't believe an FBI guy is talking about vampires.

"Can I see your identification again, Agent Stevens?"

He pulled his picture ID out of his pocket and handed it to me, smiling. "You think there's something fishy about an FBI agent talking about vampires?"

I inspected the ID. It appeared authentic, but I really had no way of knowing.

"You read my mind, Agent Stevens."

"No, I read your face, Dr. Knight."

I handed his ID back to him. "Don't FBI agents usually work in pairs? Where's your partner, Agent Stevens?"

He grinned. "I'm temporarily between partners. I seem to be an acquired taste. My partners keep asking for transfers. If you're nervous about whether I'm who I say I am, you can call the local police. They know all about me and what I'm doing here. So, will you answer my question now? Why are you working with vampires?"

My neck was throbbing and my patience was gone. The

good feeling I'd gotten from the hot shower was retreating at the speed of light.

"Special Agent Stevens, I didn't get up this early to discuss fairy tales or cartoon characters, and unless there is some aspect of psychology that I can help you with, I think we're finished."

"Wow. You really don't know. I figured when I saw your ad in the paper that you knew what you were dealing with, but you're flying blind. You're messing with things you don't understand and somebody needs to enlighten you. It might as well be me."

"I don't think that's necessary." I sighed and stood.

He grabbed my wrist. "Wait. Please. Hear me out. I think you'll be intrigued by what I have to say."

Please? I stared into his watery, bloodshot eyes and saw what appeared to be sincerity. Or maybe it was simply exhaustion. Something about the determined set of his jaw and his easy smile convinced me to sit back down at the table. "I'm listening."

He let go of me. "First, let me give you a little background, to show you that I didn't start out as a believer, either. You and I actually have a lot in common, because I have a Ph.D. in Psychology, too."

My eyebrows winged up, and my mouth formed into an "O."

He saw the surprise on my face. "Yeah, Doctor Stevens at your service. But I never intended to be a therapist. My interests lie with the criminal mind. So when I was recruited by the FBI's Behavioral Psych unit—think *Silence of the Lambs*—I jumped at the chance to become a profiler. I specialize in cases that have paranormal elements. Yep, I can see by the gleam in your eyes that you're drawing comparisons between my work and a certain television program. It's true. Some clever coworker or another is always putting *X-Files* posters on my door, and my official nickname is Mulder."

So, Special Agent Stevens isn't your normal FBI agent. Interesting.

I had to laugh. I'd enjoyed that program and Agent Mulder's dry, sarcastic sense of humor. Of course, I fancied myself to be more like Scully.

I sipped my coffee. "I'm impressed. So, what's a profiler like yourself doing in my kitchen wanting to enlighten me about vampires?" I had to admit that thinking of him as a colleague rather than only a cop was making him even more attractive to me. I was a sucker for a clever mind wrapped in a handsome package.

He relaxed back in the chair and stretched like a cat. The white T-shirt material molded to his chest muscles and accented the outlines of his nipples. Very distracting.

He saw me notice and smiled.

"About a year ago, I started tracking a pattern. Dead bodies showing up with holes in their necks, drained of blood. At first I did just what you're doing: I wrote it off to some creative form of mental illness. I assumed I was searching for one predator who moved around a lot, or maybe a copy-cat murderer who was picking up on the vampire theme. And, as I suspect you've done, I did research on everything involving blood drinking."

He downed the last of his coffee, carried his mug over to the pot, poured himself a refill and returned to the table.

Why, yes, thank you. I'd love some more coffee.

He drummed his fingers on the side of his mug. "I showed up at the murder scenes, checking for similarities, and the cases just kept getting weirder. Some of the bodies had multiple bites that the lab results showed came from different sets of sharp teeth. No human or animal DNA in the wounds. But there were never any signs of struggle—no needle marks for drugs. It was as if the victims simply lay there and let themselves be drained. Almost like some form of hypnosis or brainwashing."

He stopped talking, scanned the kitchen and pointed to a bag of cookies on the counter.

"You mind? I haven't had any breakfast yet."

Without waiting for my response, he got up, fetched the bag of cookies, and returned to his seat.

"Help yourself." I wondered if he was always this comfortable with strangers or if he was simply oblivious.

No, I'm sure. Oblivious.

"Then something happened to turn me into a believer," he continued. "I was in Los Angeles, following through on some leads about the latest murders, and I was attacked by a vampire."

He saw me tighten my lips and raise my eyebrows, and he said, "Let me finish. I know this pushes all your 'this guy needs therapy' buttons, but hang in there with me." He opened the cookie bag, selected one and took a bite.

He scooted to the edge of his chair and excitedly pointed his finger up in the air and brought it down in a quick dive toward the floor. "I saw this thing fly down—I kid you not—from the roof of a 12-story building. He landed in front of me as if he'd just stepped off someone's front porch. Not a hair ruffled. He came at me, with his teeth bared and these long, sharp canines, picked me up by my neck, like I weighed nothing, and threw me down on the ground. He was on me so fast I didn't have time to be afraid. I started shouting questions at him—asking him to tell me about himself. For some astounding reason, he stepped back and started answering. At the risk of being boringly unoriginal, it really was an interview with a vampire."

It sounds as if poor Special Agent Stevens is missing a few of his marbles.

I bit the inside of my mouth to keep myself from smiling. "What did this vampire tell you?"

Alan raised an eyebrow, tilted his head, and mentally dissected the expression on my face to determine whether I was being serious or sarcastic. He must have decided my question was on the level.

"That's a very long conversation for another day, but what's important is that my education was vastly expanded. He gave me a graduate course in the strange and impossible. I think I must have connected with him at exactly the right time, because he was willing to spill all the vampire secrets. Actually, I think he was suicidal. Maybe I should refer him to you for therapy?"

He ate another cookie.

I shot him a frosty look. "Okay. Let me get this straight. You're honestly trying to get me to believe that there are such things as vampires—preternatural, blood drinking ghouls— living among us. That they aren't only myths or psychotic humans?"

He leaned over and stared into my eyes. "That's exactly

what I'm telling you. And I'm prepared to put my money where my mouth is. I can show you. I think the vampires have Emerald Addison. There's a coven in one of the clubs downtown—a former church—called The Crypt. The vampire I talked to—Ian, who's probably back in London now—told me that the group and their leader have been here for a long time and they keep a low profile. But recently some new bloodsuckers—the ones I'm pursuing—have come to town and they're killers. Ian said that the one he's most afraid of is called Bryce."

I visibly started in my chair, sucked in all the air in the room, and made a loud gasping sound.

Alan jumped in his chair. "What is it?"

"You just said the name of the psychopath who barged into my office last night and attacked me."

He pulled out a small notebook and pen from his pocket and began scribbling down everything I'd just said. "You were attacked last night? Tell me what happened."

I told the entire story of the evening before, right up to the point where Devereux entered the scene. Lying, I said that while I was passed out something must have scared Bryce and Raleigh off because when I woke up, they were gone. I didn't know why I wasn't willing to talk about Devereux, but I just wasn't. After all, he had rescued me.

Alan put the notebook and pen down on the table, stroked an invisible beard and frowned at me. "You're holding out. There's more that you aren't telling me. What is it?" He reached over, lifted my hair out of the way and turned my head, eyeballing the technicolor puncture marks on my neck. "I told you that counseling vampires was dangerous.

No wonder you look like death this morning."

Prince Charming has nothing on this guy.

"Gee, you sweet talker, you."

"Sorry. Tact isn't my strong suite. In fact, being so blunt and thoughtless is why I never seriously thought about being a psychotherapist. I'd be alienating clients left and right. Actually, you couldn't really look bad if you tried."

He grinned, reached over and picked up a renegade lock of my hair and tucked it behind my ear.

"Thanks, I think." I'd not only been surprised by his touch, but also by the pleasant sensation that lingered where his finger had brushed my skin.

I've definitely got to get out more. Maybe Denver's started putting hormones in the water.

Suddenly feeling awkward, I reached into the cookie bag and pulled out a chunk of chocolate chip heaven and chewed loudly. Too loudly.

The smirk on Alan's face told me he'd picked up on my discomfort and was enjoying it. He slouched down in the chair and lifted an ankle to rest on his knee.

I pushed farther away from the table, crossed my legs and put way too much effort into removing the cookie crumbs embedded in my teeth.

Once again, my confidence with men is underwhelming.

"So, you said you can show me? Prove to me that vampires exist?"

He grinned again, obviously enjoying my unease. "Yeah. I can. But right now I need to head back to police headquarters and see if there's anything new on the whereabouts of Emerald Addison. Are you free tonight?"

Smug bastard.

"That depends on why you're asking."

He got up and filled his coffee cup again, then paced around the kitchen. "I think it's time for you to find out what you've stepped in. I want to take you to that club, The Crypt, and give you a dose of an alternate reality. How about I pick you up at 10 p.m.?" He reached into the bag on the table and ate yet another cookie.

There's no justice in the world. The man doesn't have an ounce of extra fat on his body. And I've made a thorough inspection.

"Why would you want to go to a place you believe is a vampire coven? Aren't you afraid you'll be attacked again? Why would you want me to go there with you?"

He stood gazing down at me, shaking his head. "Whoa! For someone who doesn't believe in any of this, you ask a lot of questions. I'll give you a taste of what Ian told me. Becoming a vampire doesn't automatically change someone into an evil monster. That's all fiction. The personality you had before you died is carried over into your new existence. And, most important for our purposes, if you were a psychotic human being, you'll be a psychotic vampire. Now, that's a totally different level of psychopathology."

He picked up his notebook from the table and tucked it back into his pocket. "So, from what I've learned so far, the vampires in the coven at The Crypt are, for lack of a better word, more mellow than the ones I'm searching for. They've been able to stay below the radar for so long because the leader keeps them on a tight leash and he doesn't tolerate any behavior that draws attention to their existence."

Sitting there while he loomed over me had started to

make me nervous, so I stood, expecting him to step back out of my way, but he didn't. He remained there, staring at me with those lazy eyes, displaying the same overconfident smirk I'd seen at the hospital.

I raised my chin. "Excuse me."

He laughed.

Arrogant jerk.

I waited for him to give me room to move, and when he did, I strolled over to the counter, refilled my coffee mug and returned to sit at the table. I decided to ignore his bad manners.

I inspected the contents of my cup. "Have you met the vampires at that club?"

"Yeah, I've been over there several times. The head honcho is called Devereux and he's been very cooperative. I'll introduce you."

At the mention of his name, my body immediately revisited the kiss I'd shared with Devereux, and I felt the heat rise on my cheeks. I think it was safe to say that introductions had already been taken care of.

"But what about all the stuff about vampires drinking human blood? There isn't anything mellow about that," I said quickly, hoping to divert Alan's attention from what I was sure must have been my obvious reaction to his mention of Devereux. Either he didn't notice or he chose not to comment, because he nodded his head and answered the question.

He paced around the room again. "Ian told me that the blood thing is highly misunderstood. First, he said it isn't necessary to kill someone. Small amounts of blood from several donors works just fine. As I already said, some vampires—same as humans—have more evil tendencies than others. For those vampires, killing is the thrill. For them, not killing would be like sex without the orgasm. And, speaking of orgasms, Ian said that drinking blood is better than sex. Which they can have, by the way."

I concentrated on keeping my face neutral. "It sounds as if Ian was very talkative."

Alan rested his hip against the counter. "Yeah. We spent hours together and I took great notes. Then I got more information from the coven at the club. It's been a very educational experience. And it's helped clarify who and what I'm searching for."

"Wait a minute. You said the vampire leader doesn't draw attention to his group. Why would he volunteer to talk to you? What's to stop you from turning them over to the local police?"

"Well, think about it. You've been visited by the craziest vampire in Denver, you have clients who sit in your office and tell you about vampires, and I've just spent the last hour trying to convince you that vampires exist, yet you still don't believe. What are the chances anyone would actually think the owner of The Crypt is the leader of a vampire coven? Devereux can tell me the truth because he knows that no one would buy it. And, when you see the club you'll understand how easy it is for them to just blend into the fantasy."

"And what about the FBI? Have you told them the truth? Do they know what you're up to?"

"Let's just say that they are under the impression I'm tracking humans who are pretending to be vampires. They might amuse themselves by laughing at my Mulderisms, but the FBI is pretty conservative, and if they knew what I was really doing, I'd be out on my tail. Okay. I'm really outta here now. I'll see you tonight at 10. And, oh yeah. Thanks for the java."

And he was gone.

Chapter 7

It took me a minute to realize I was sitting there—my mouth hanging open, catatonic—staring at the door that had just slammed.

Moving only my eyeballs, I surveyed the cookie crumbs, coffee drips, and crumpled napkins surrounding Alan's empty coffee cup. Then I shook my head and broke into semi-hysterical laughter. The kind of laughter that makes you grab your midsection because it's almost painful in its intensity. I let the crazed frivolity roll through me for a few seconds then started talking to myself, out loud, which, in some quarters, might be construed as a bad sign.

"I choose Fictional Creatures for $500, Alex!"

Propping my feet up on the chair that'd been recently vacated by the firm hindquarters of the cutest FBI agent I'd ever seen, I raised my coffee cup in a solitary toast to the memory of his tight jeans exiting my kitchen and loudly vocalized the theme song from the TV game show, "Jeopardy."

I put on my best Alex Trebek voice. "These bloodsucking, undead denizens of the night have taken over the rational minds of the populace of Denver."

I pretended to press an invisible button on the table. "What are vampires?"

Imitating Alex again. "Yes! Our new winner is Dr. Kismet Knight, formerly a respected psychologist, now a permanent resident of Denver Psychiatric Hospital."

I sang the theme song again, applauded myself and heaved a huge sigh.

"I *definitely* didn't get enough sleep."

I stared out the window, transfixed by the streaks of color floating across the morning sky, and drank my coffee. It was exactly one week ago that Midnight walked into my office for the first time, and since then, my life had turned into a cliché-ridden, afternoon-matinee, horror movie. And I was apparently playing a lead role.

I'd fantasized about having more excitement in my life and I must have inadvertently rubbed some genie's bottle, because I definitely got my wish. Unfortunately, it fell under the category of "be careful what you ask for because you might get it." If I was as smart as I thought I was, I'd cut my losses and run. I could refer Midnight and Ronald to other therapists and just go back to my regularly scheduled programming. No harm, no foul. Only a madwoman would purposely visit some dance club allegedly run by vampires—vampire wannabes, no doubt—or listen to fantastical stories told by delectable FBI agents.

But then I tried to imagine never seeing Devereux again and my solar plexus clenched up. Definitely not a desirable option.

I decided to have one more cup of coffee—there's nothing like being wired and sleepy at the same time—and jot down some notes for my book. Agent Stevens' fertile imagination had given me lots of ideas for chapters and I'd have to remember to ask him for permission to use the material he'd shared with me. He wasn't a therapist, so there were no confidentiality issues. Maybe I'd even give him credit in the finished manuscript.

I brought my laptop computer over to the table, wrote for a while, then stretched the cramped muscles in my arms and checked out the time. Since it was still early, I figured I could either go back to bed for a couple of hours, or I could break my routine and do something different. Maybe go take a walk in that big neighborhood park I'd been meaning to explore. Jefferson Park was Denver's equivalent of Central Park in New York City, and it had lots of trees, benches, and trails and was only a couple of blocks from my townhouse.

Yes, exercise. That was the ticket. Whether I liked it or not, it had recently come to my attention that being physically inactive had a downside, and I'd promised myself I'd rectify that situation and gain some muscle in other places besides my brain. Never again would I be held hostage by any kind of wannabe. Svengali hypnotist or not.

I changed into a comfortable, dark blue sweatsuit, put on my unworn, still-in-the-box walking shoes and headed out the door. Denver could be counted on to have over 300 sunny days per year, and this morning was a prime specimen. Actually, the fact that it was mostly sunny in Colorado was one of the few things I would have changed about a state that was, otherwise, paradise. Coming from the Midwest, I loved a good rainstorm and relished the introspective embrace of a gray, overcast day.

The first thing I noticed was how many walkers, joggers, runners, bicycle riders, skateboarders, and pet owners were out on the trails this early in the morning. And, even more interesting, how many of them were holding Starbucks cups in their hands as they did those activities. I marveled at the level of physical coordination it would take to run and drink coffee at the same time.

"Kismet, is that you? I thought you lived around here someplace."

The voice was familiar. I froze, turned around slowly and stared into the dark brown eyes of Dr. Thomas Radcliffe, my astrologer-humping ex-boyfriend.

Shit.

This wasn't how I'd imagined our first meeting would be after all this time. In my vision, I was dressed to the nines— painted, polished, and gorgeous. He'd be overcome with remorse for his treatment of me and would beg me to take him back. But, instead, here I was looking like something the vampire dragged in, wearing an old, baggy sweat suit. I couldn't even remember if I'd brushed my hair before I left.

There was absolutely no justice in the universe because he hadn't changed a bit. He was still classically handsome, impeccably groomed, and he could've been a model who'd just stepped out of *Healthy Living Magazine*. And, to add insult to injury, he'd finally grown his thick black hair out, which I'd asked him to do repeatedly during the time we were together. There's just something about a man with great hair.

"Tom. How nice to see you," I lied, silently pleading with my face muscles to transform what I was sure was a grimace into an acceptable smile.

He came over and almost-hugged me. One of those not-quite-embraces—complete with an air kiss on either side of my face—so popular among the rich and famous. "You look just as I remember you." Which made me want to kick him in the shins.

He grinned. "You just popped into my head the other day, and I decided to make it a point to see you when I came to Denver."

Hmmm. I popped into his head. So much for my fantasy of the daily inner torture I hoped he'd endured as he replayed the loss of me over and over in his mind.

I retreated from his pseudo-hug and made my face as neutral as possible. I observed the colorful skin paint that passed for running pants and noticed he still wasn't reluctant to advertise all his products and services. I coaxed my eyes up to his face, straining my brain for something brilliant to say, but instead came out with the verbal equivalent of elevator music. "You're still running every day?"

"Yes, indeed. I've got to keep one step ahead of Father Time." He smiled and patted his tight stomach.

Dr. Cliché. I wonder if this man ever has an original thought.

He pulled my arm and guided me over to a nearby bench and sat. "Can we sit for a minute? Now that I've got you here, I'd love to catch up. What are you up to? Are you writing? Are you married?"

I joined him on the bench. "Well . . ." I managed to get that one word out before he launched into:

"Things are going so super for me. My private practice in San Francisco is booming, both because of the success of my last book and my radio program. You wouldn't believe how busy I am and how in demand I am as a speaker. Did you see me on Dr. Phil? I was one of the experts for a recent segment. Oprah's people are talking to my people. Can you imagine what an appearance on her show will do for my books? I live in a fabulous house in one of the finest sections of town and I just ordered a brand new Ferrari. I'll take you for a ride the next time I see you . . ."

I just stared at him as he went on with his manic rant. He didn't seem to notice that I hadn't spoken or that I was gaping at him like he was a nasty squished bug on my windshield. Had he always been this way? What had I been thinking? Had I really been so dazzled by his appearance that I'd ignored his self-absorption? I amused myself for a few seconds by mentally thumbing through the list of personality disorders he fit into.

"So, whatever happened to Summer, the astrologer?" I interjected loudly.

"Who? Oh, yes. She was a sweet thing. Simply adored me. Thought I walked on water. But we were from two different worlds and she wasn't a good fit for where I was going. We parted the best of friends."

Yeah, sure. I'll bet. I wonder what her version of the break-up is.

He glanced down at his diamond-studded watch. "Oh, damn. Look at the time. I've got to hurry back and get dressed for my presentation. Hey, here's an idea. Why don't you come to the conference with me and you can listen to my lecture. I'll bet you'd really learn a lot from it. What do you say?"

"Well, as tempting as that sounds," I said sarcastically, which, judging by his solemn head-nodding, he'd totally missed, "I'll have to pass. I have clients this morning."

"Bummer! It's a shame you can't attend, but I know how seriously you take your work."

He said that as if it was a bad thing. He'd always viewed my refusal to join him in the fast lane as a character flaw, as well as a personal disappointment.

"I was going to keep this as a surprise for you, but I guess I can tell you now. I expect I'll be seeing a lot more of you because I'm doing a series of workshops in Colorado and I'd love to discuss the possibility of my using your office part-time while I'm here. Could we get together for dinner tonight and talk about it?" He flashed me a California smile.

Welcome to the wonderful world of Tom Radcliffe's ego. Plenty of room for everyone, folks. Step right up. Enter at your own risk.

He stood, and began running in place. "Tell you what, I'll just drop by your house after the conference is over at 9 p.m. I got your new address from the APA Directory." Before I could answer he jogged away backward, yelling "I'll see you then."

I sat on the bench, shook my head and laughed out loud. Luckily, no clients were around to witness my temporary joyful insanity. I did have a reputation to uphold, after all.

Suddenly, everything about Tom Radcliffe seemed hilarious. How could I have been in love with such a narcissistic egomaniac? Such a superficial moron? I'd spent the last two years grieving and miserable, and now I couldn't, for the life of me, remember why. And, as long as we kept enough miles between us and a bedroom, I might never be tempted to recover the memory.

I smiled through a brisk walk around the park and whistled all the way back to my house. Maybe things were looking up.

The first thing I noticed when I got off the elevator in my office building a while later was a bulging manila envelope propped against my waiting room door. I picked it up, tucked it under my arm and unlocked the doors leading to my reception area and then to my office. I sat down at my desk and inspected the package. There was nothing unusual about it—no address on the front, postage or writing of any kind. I opened the clasp. Inside the envelope was some kind of light blue fabric with extensive stains on it. I had an immediate bad feeling and picked up a pencil to lift the cloth out of its container. I'd seen enough cop shows to know about not contaminating evidence, and my intuition told me that I was in possession of something awful.

Using the pencil to spread out the fabric on top of my desk, I could see it was one of those flimsy gowns they use in hospitals. The ones that never close in the back. The stains looked and smelled like dried blood.

Something about dried blood made me think of Emerald. Would she have worn this kind of gown?

No. There must be hundreds of explanations for this gown turning up in front of my door. It probably had nothing to do with Emerald at all. Just a case of someone leaving the package at the wrong place.

Even though I tried hard to delude myself, none of the rationalizations were working and I began to feel nauseous. The smell of the package reminded me of my dream, and I unconsciously reached up to touch the wound on my neck, which I'd covered with a band-aid. I had the unpleasant realization that if I didn't get to the bathroom in ten seconds, I'd throw up on the floor. I made a mad dash and reached the toilet just in time to lose my morning coffee.

Feeling hot and cold at the same time, my stomach completely empty, I went over to the sink and swished some water around in my mouth. It was a good thing I always carried a toothbrush, toothpaste, and mouthwash in my purse. I stared into the mirror and reaffirmed Alan's earlier assertion that I did, indeed, look like death today. Sometimes even the best makeup job wasn't enough. Having such fair skin was a blessing most of the time, because I always appeared younger than I was, but today I had definitely crossed the line between an ivory glow and an anemic pallor.

I shuffled back into my office and rummaged through my briefcase, searching for the business card Alan had given me, and I called the number. He answered on the first ring.

"Stevens."

"Alan, someone left me a bloody hospital gown."

"Kismet? Is that you? What about a hospital gown?"

I told him what I'd found. He said he'd alert the local police and they'd be right over.

I fished the dental hygiene products out of my purse and scurried to the bathroom, where I brushed and swished until I felt almost normal, then headed back to my office.

I sat at my desk, scrutinizing the blood-stained material, and I wondered again what I'd gotten myself into. I'd spent the last week bouncing back and forth between fear, confusion, and arousal, and I was exhausted. I didn't think I'd been of help to anyone, and I certainly hadn't done myself any good.

Staring off into space, I realized I hadn't checked my messages, so I punched in the retrieval code for my business voice mail and found several. The first was from Ronald, asking if we could reschedule his appointment because he'd been up all night searching for Emerald. It was a good thing he couldn't make it, because he'd be due at the same time the police would likely arrive and I hadn't even taken that into account. In fact, I'd totally forgotten I had a client coming. Another indication of my impending mental breakdown. I made a note to call him back later.

I paused the messages and scanned my appointment book to make sure I hadn't neglected any other important business, and smiled. Fran, my 76-year-old UFO abductee client was scheduled in this morning for her long-standing appointment, but it wasn't going to work today. One of Fran's challenges was a deep distrust of authority figures. I could only imagine what would happen if the police were still here when she arrived. Fran, who weighed no more than 90 pounds soaking wet, had been known to start screaming and flailing at the sight of a uniform, which usually guaranteed problems with whoever was wearing the offending garment at the time. Yes, I was definitely going to reschedule Fran.

And after Fran was Spock. Spock's real name was Henry Madison, but he got very upset if anyone called him that. He lived in a perpetual *Star Trek* episode, even going as far as having his ears surgically altered to be "Vulcan." He had his costumes tailor-made and shaved his eyebrows so he could draw on the "correct" ones. Interestingly enough, Spock hadn't come to therapy for any of the reasons one might assume. He'd come because he wanted to explore his poor choices with women. He just couldn't seem to find the woman of his dreams. He suspected Mother issues. I thought that was only the tip of the iceberg.

Continuing with the messages, up next was my daily reminder from Brother Luther about the current state of my immortal soul. He usually gave me a portion of the sermon-of-the-week, and kept his remarks very general and impersonal. Today's message had a different tone. He seemed agitated, and he talked a lot about being "washed in the blood," and made a comment about being a warrior for God. He continued on until the allotted message time ran out and he was cut off mid-tirade. That was the first time one of his messages caused me to feel uncomfortable, and, in light of the other events of the morning, I considered whether or not I needed to tell the police about Brother Luther, too.

Chapter 8

Within an hour, my office was inundated with police officers and forensics specialists. They bagged up the manila envelope and its contents, confiscated the pencil I used to move the cloth around, and were in the midst of seeking clues by crawling inch-by-inch along the hallway in front of my waiting room door. Alan stood next to my desk, silently observing the investigation and writing in his ever-present notebook.

A noticeably physically substantial female officer approached me. She was big the way that a weightlifter is big. Not fat, but solid and muscular. She must have been six feet tall. Dressed in a no-nonsense, dark blue pantsuit, she appeared to be in her late forties, but the years hadn't been kind. Her gray-streaked hair was cut very short, in a style that required little upkeep, and the lines in her face had formed themselves into a continuous scowl. I'd guess she'd been someone for whom high school had been hell, and she'd taken the Gold in the Olympic Holding A Grudge competition. Not someone I'd want to mess with, even if she hadn't been wearing a gun at her waist.

She marched purposefully over to me and snarled, "You Dr. Knight?"

"Yes." Gazing up at her, I suddenly felt six years old, called to the principal's office.

"Lieutenant Bullock. I need to get your statement." She pointed with her thumb back over her shoulder. "Let's go over there."

I nodded. We walked over to the couch, sat down, and I told her everything about finding the envelope, taking out the bloody, blue gown and calling Special Agent Stevens. She stopped writing and cocked her head, observing me, waiting, I supposed, for me to say something else. When I didn't, she prompted, her voice deceptively even, "I understand you have a missing client?"

"I'm afraid I'm not able to respond to that question."

She lowered her chin ever so slightly. "Why is that, Dr. Knight? You're the one who called us." Her voice became very quiet and controlled.

Feeling the chill of her frosty gaze, I swallowed loudly and cleared my throat. "Under the rules of confidentiality, I'm not able to discuss whether someone is or isn't a client. I called Special Agent Stevens because finding a package containing a bloody anything is out of my area of expertise. I thought it might be something he could deal with."

She held my gaze for a moment. "Why would someone leave a blood-stained hospital gown in front of your door, doctor?"

"I have no idea."

She gave an unfriendly smile and raised an eyebrow. "Do you know Emerald Addison?"

I sat silently, keeping my face pleasantly neutral.

She moved closer and locked eyes with me. "I know

Emerald Addison is your client. You're obstructing a police investigation by refusing to cooperate. I'll need copies of the records you have on her friends, who are also your clients," she demanded, her voice getting louder.

I tensed. "Lieutenant Bullock, I can only repeat what I've already said. I'm unable to respond. I'm bound by the rules of confidentiality."

She bolted up off the couch. "You're starting to piss me off, Dr. Knight."

She paced around in front of me, stopped and bent down so that our faces were inches apart. She whispered loudly, "If the blood on that gown matches the blood of the missing girl, you're going to have a lot more questions to answer. Maybe you didn't just find the gown. Maybe you had it all along. Maybe you're hiding something. Maybe I'll get a court order to force you to give me your records."

Every time she said the word "maybe," she accented and held out the first syllable, allowing each repetition to rise in pitch.

My heart pounded in my chest and I felt sweat breaking out on my forehead. I'd never had anyone get in my face and threaten me that way before, and I didn't know what to say, so I didn't say anything. That seemed to make her even angrier.

I knew she couldn't force me to divulge information, and I assumed she knew that, too.

"Wilson," Lieutenant Bullock barked at the tall, lanky policeman who hovered next to her, "make sure you get all the good doctor's contact information. I want to be able to find her day or night."

"I have it," he said, giving me cold eyes.

She squinted at me and growled, "Don't leave town."

And, like a fiery comet pulling meteorites in its tail, she left, taking all the officers with her.

Alan came over, sat next to me on the couch and patted my hand. "Now you know why her nickname is 'Bull'."

I reflexively flopped back against the cushions, letting my shoulders slump. My mouth was so dry it took me a couple of attempts before I could speak.

"What just happened here? All I did was find something and call it in. I was being a model citizen. Why am I suddenly a suspect?"

"You're not, really. They're all freaked out because they haven't been able to solve any of the recent murders or find the missing girl. This is the first lead they've had in days. Lieutenant Bullock is taking this case very personally because she knew the first murder victim. He was a friend of hers and she's a very loyal person. Don't let her get to you. I'll try to run interference."

I angled my head in his direction. "What about the gown? Do you think it was Emerald's? Why would someone bring it to my office?"

He shrugged. "Yesterday when you brought Emerald into the hospital, I was hanging around in intensive care, hoping to catch a glimpse of her after they cleaned her up. My persistence paid off because after they got the transfusion started, the nurse walked away for a minute, and I got a good look at Emerald. The gown in the envelope was exactly the same as the one she was wearing in the hospital. Now, whether or not the blood is hers, only the lab guys can tell us, but my money's on the likelihood that it is."

He studied his notebook, absently flipping through the pages, lost in thought, then gave me that serious eye contact he was so good at.

"You were the one who brought Emerald to the hospital, so maybe giving the bloody gown to you was a message. Can you think of anyone who'd want to get something across to you that way? Any unusually psychotic clients? Anyone wanting to hurt you? Have you gotten any threats?"

He chewed on the end of his pen, observing my face expectantly.

As soon as he mentioned psychotic clients, the memory of Bryce and Raleigh's visit invaded my brain, but I wasn't sure how much I could tell Alan—how much I could trust him. And, if I implicated Midnight in any of this, that was definitely a breach of confidentiality. I decided to fall back on an old therapy technique: When in doubt, say nothing. It wasn't actually lying if I simply held back information. Therapists are required to be discerning. But I did take note that my comfort level with bending the truth was expanding. I mentally added that to my list of things to worry about later.

I kept my expression relaxed and called on my Inner Sociopath. "No. I don't understand any of this. I can't imagine it has anything to do with me. Do you think Emerald is still alive?"

He studied the carpet and shook his head. "I wish I could be more encouraging, but if they've drained her blood again, it doesn't bode well. I'm hoping we can find out more tonight." He lifted his eyes to mine. "Are you still up for visiting The Crypt?"

Damn. I'd forgotten all about that. Maybe I could catch

Tom at his conference and cancel our visit. I wasn't inclined to let him use my office part-time, anyway, and I knew better than to be alone with him and a bottle of wine.

"Yes. I guess so. I'm not sure what good it will do, but since I'm involved now, I can't just walk away." And I had to admit I was curious about the place. Right. Who was I kidding? I was curious about Devereux.

Imagining the possibility of getting another glimpse of the platinum-haired fantasy object, I drifted off for a few seconds, indulging in a brief, R-rated mental interlude.

Sensing Alan's eyes on me, I shook myself out of my daydream and wondered what the FBI profiler had seen on my face to cause the eyebrow-elevated, semi-suspicious expression he wore on his.

I was about to inquire as to the meaning of that expression on his face when I got a strong intuitive hit that he thought I was hiding something. I simply knew what he was thinking and feeling. Just my usual. Daydreaming about Devereux must have distracted me from my mental stress-a-thon long enough for me to sense the subtle layers and become aware of Alan's energy. It did seem that my ability to psychically know things worked best when I wasn't consciously trying to use it. Yeah, that's helpful. Or maybe it was more accurate to say it worked best when I didn't get in the way.

It didn't seem possible that Alan could know anything about my erotic interest in Devereux, so his flash of distrust had to have something to do with Emerald. But it really didn't matter what he thought, because I wasn't hiding anything. Not really. In fact, I'd never felt more ineffectual and clueless.

And, besides. Even if he somehow did know about the

contents of my fantasy, it wasn't any of his damn business, anyway.

He opened his mouth to speak and I stood, surprising him. The best defense is an offense. I'd had just about enough intrigue for one morning.

I turned to him, straightened my posture and checked my watch. "I have a client coming soon, so I need to get ready. Thanks for contacting the police and handling everything. I really appreciate it. I'll see you tonight."

He remained seated for a few seconds, his face still registering confused surprise.

Shit. Now he really thinks I'm up to something. He's sending out wave after wave of questions. I should've just asked him why he was staring at me that way. Now I've turned it into some big, strange deal. Why does he make me so nervous?

He finally stood slowly, his eyebrows contracted into a V, and offered a tight smile.

"Yeah, tonight, sure. See you then."

He walked to the door, glanced over his shoulder at me once and left, closing the door behind him.

"Well," I said out loud. "I certainly handled that with finesse and style. Let's hear it for the Queen of Mixed Messages."

I forced myself to turn my attention back to work and settled in at my desk, intending to grab onto anything that seemed even remotely normal. Anything I felt competent to handle.

As I sat there, I remembered that I'd forgotten to tell the police about the phone calls from Brother Luther. It was probably just as well I hadn't, because it was most likely nothing. I'd been so caught up in the drama of the last few days that I was getting paranoid. Plus, telling Lieutenant Bullock something that might prove to be a false alarm was the last thing I intended to do.

Since Ronald had canceled his appointment and I'd rescheduled Fran, I had some time to myself before Spock was due for his session. I tried writing some case notes but kept getting distracted and staring out the window. I decided to stroll over to the 16th Street Mall, a pedestrian-friendly, outdoor shopping area in the heart of downtown Denver, and pick up some office supplies along with a bit of much-needed protein.

I roamed around the mall for a while, checking out the window displays and then made a beeline over to my favorite food cart. I didn't normally buy food off quirky carts in the middle of shopping malls, but one of my clients had raved about the quality of Maria's breakfast burritos, and because I was a fan of Mexican food, it was inevitable that I'd go sample the goods.

Since I'd emptied out the contents of my stomach before the police arrived, and I couldn't remember the last time I'd eaten before that, it was definitely time to refuel. I gave myself a quick, internal lecture about needing to take better care of myself, and my mouth was already watering in response to the heavenly aromas wafting from the gastronomical oasis. The handsome young man standing at the cart was Juan, Maria's son, and we were on a first-name basis.

"Doctor Kismet! What's it gonna be today? Spicy or mild?" he teased, as he scooped steaming scrambled eggs into a soft tortilla. He'd told me that he could tell what kind of mood I was in by the amount of hot peppers I asked for in my burrito. He called it Burrito Psychology.

"Better leave out the peppers today, Juan. I've had a rough morning."

He gave me a big, friendly smile, displaying perfect, white enamel. "Let me give you a couple of peppers on the side. I get the feeling that your day's about to change. Juan knows these things."

I smiled back at him, paid for the food and said I'd see him later, noticing with a chuckle that Juan's usual fan club— a crowd of giggling teenage girls—had swooped in on him the moment I walked away.

I sauntered down the mall and found a seat on a small wall enclosing an absurdly large sculpture of a cowboy-hat-clad man atop a bucking bronco. No doubt another sports symbol. Denver idolizes its football team. Maybe I should write a book about the psychology of spectator sports addiction. Or, maybe not. I already seemed to have enough enemies without stirring up the local Neanderthals.

I sat there, thoroughly enjoying the melt-in-my-mouth taste of Maria's masterpiece, and began to catch snatches of conversation coming from two women sitting at a folding table a few feet away from me. A little sign next to the table proclaimed, "Psychic Tarot Readings."

"No, that's not going to happen. He's not for you. Let go of him," said the woman facing me. She was spreading out Tarot cards on a colorful tablecloth, decorated with astrological symbols. Her fingers were adorned with rings, her long fingernails painted sparkling silver, and there was an intricate tattoo on the back of her right hand. She wore a bright red dress with a shiny black vest and her long, gray hair flowed down into a pile in her lap.

The woman sitting with her was less than happy with her reading, because she sprang up, almost knocked over her chair, and yelled, "That's bullshit. You don't know what you're talking about. He's my soul mate and you're wrong." She stomped off, muttering to herself about quacks and phonies.

I didn't want to embarrass the Tarot reader by letting her know I'd overheard the exchange, so I focused on my burrito, finishing up the last few tasty bites. The sound of laughter caught my attention and I raised my head to find her staring at me, making hand motions, inviting me to come to her table.

"Finish your breakfast and come on over. I've been waiting for you."

I scanned the area to see who she was talking to and when I couldn't find anyone else in the vicinity, I pointed to myself, "Me? No thank you. I don't believe in fortune telling."

She kept smiling at me and I had to admit I was impressed by her sales technique. Let people think that you had information just for them, and they'd probably sit down and fork over some greenbacks. It was basic psychology.

"No charge. Just come and listen for a few minutes. If you don't resonate with what I have to say, you can call me names and walk away."

Hmmm. This approach must work or else she wouldn't keep using it, but I couldn't see how she'd make a living by giving people the option of not paying. She had me, though. My curiosity was piqued. I wiped my hands on a napkin, folded up the paper that'd held the burrito, and carried it over to the trash can.

The Tarot reader was still smiling at me, shuffling her cards, waiting.

Curious, I walked over to her table. "Why would you want to read my cards for free? That can't be a very good way to make money."

"It's not my job to worry about where the money comes from. I just follow my intuition and everything seems to work out perfectly. Come on. Sit down. I am Cerridwyn."

Well, why not? Things had been so weird for the last week that this just fit right in. Why not let a Tarot reader on the mall tell me that I'd win the lottery, or that I was Cleopatra in a past life? How much more bizarre could it be than my morning so far?

She stopped shuffling the cards and handed them to me. "Just move the cards around, any way you wish. Put your essence into them."

I shuffled the cards and she continued to grin at me. Her eyes were a deep, dark purple—living amethyst—and they were surrounded by a network of fine lines, which were exaggerated when she smiled. Her eyes sparkled, and she always seemed on the verge of laughing out loud. At first, I assumed she was old because of her gray hair, but sitting close to her, I could see she was much younger. Maybe not even forty.

She reached out for the cards, and I stopped shuffling and gave them to her. She inhaled a deep breath, closed her eyes for a few seconds, reopened them and began laying out the cards in a specific pattern. She gazed into my eyes. "You have been chosen. From this time forward nothing will ever be the same for you."

Well, that was nice and vague. It was right up there with "You'll meet a tall, dark stranger."

She chuckled. "How did one so young become so skeptical?"

Oh, goodie. Another mind reader.

She studied the cards and declared, "I see you surrounded by men. Two of them will offer you love, one brings danger. But he is only a messenger of the larger darkness. Your refusal to see things as they really are will put you and those you care about at risk."

She was quiet for a few seconds, unfocused eyes staring off into the distance, then she smiled widely. "Ah, you are playing with the vampires."

I must have let my mouth fall open, because she started laughing.

"You're surprised that I know?"

"Yes. I do work with people who believe they're vampires. You're very good."

"But you don't believe?"

"No, of course not."

She seemed to think that was very funny, because she shook her head, put one hand on her chest, and laughed until tears flowed from her eyes. "I envy you your journey. If you are courageous, your life will become extraordinary. Even as stubborn as you are."

I let the stubborn comment pass. "What do you know about the vampires?"

"I'm very psychic. I have always been aware of non-humans—not only vampires—and of a growing darkness that is pure evil. There are a few places in the world where this evil is manifesting. Denver is such a place. You are to play a key role. But, even more important, you are to learn to love and be loved."

Cerridwyn certainly had a flair for the dramatic. Pure evil in Denver? Non-humans?

"Well, I have to say that I was expecting a canned prediction and you've been very creative. I want to pay you for your time."

She reached across the table and grabbed my hand, her expression suddenly serious. "There is danger tonight. It's too late for the young woman you seek. Don't be afraid of your own abilities. They will save you."

The breakfast burrito churned in my stomach. I was afraid to ask what she meant by the comment about the young woman, so I just sat there staring at her.

"I hope this reading was helpful to you. Come and see me again when you're ready to ask the right questions and to hear the answers." She reached into a pocket in her shirt. "Here's my card. Call me when you find your courage. Remember that nothing comes to you without your invitation, even if you don't realize you're sending it."

What invitation?

She handed me her business card, gathered her Tarot deck back into a pile, and wrapped it in a red, silk scarf.

I fished in my pocket for some money and pulled out a $10 bill. I put it on the table, stood and said, "You frightened me." I was surprised to hear those words come out of my mouth because it wasn't like me to share my feelings with strangers—or with anyone, for that matter.

She laughed. "Good. Being frightened will help you pay

attention."

She palmed the money, put it in her pocket and closed her eyes.

I took that as a dismissal and walked back to my office, replaying her words in my mind. The logical part of me tried to take charge, reminding me that there was no solid research to back up the validity of psychic readings. It had really only been cosmo-babble, anyway, and the strange feeling in my midsection was simple indigestion.

But the instinctual part of me ignored all that, and reminded me of the story of "The Three Little Pigs," and the one little pig who built his house with bricks. What was my unconscious trying to tell me? Was there really a big, bad wolf out there that could blow the house down?

Chapter 9

The rest of the day was pleasantly routine. I'd scheduled several clients. The task of concentrating on their concerns kept my mind off the ghoulish madness and bizarre chaos that had penetrated the edges of my life. The key to successful denial is to keep busy.

Actually, it turned out to be quite a satisfying afternoon.

Spock had a moment of illumination in the midst of waxing euphoric about the latest *Star Trek* convention he'd attended. It seemed he'd had a close encounter with a protester—I couldn't imagine what anyone would protest about a *Star Trek* convention—out in front of the building, and it had upset him. The woman was handing out flyers and bumped into Spock, accusing him of being a "sick-o with no life."

He paused in the middle of his passionate diatribe about the injustice of her accusations and said, a horrified expression on his face, "Is that true? Am I a sick-o with no life?"

I asked him what he thought, and we had our first authentic, meaningful dialog about his role-playing.

All in all, a significant session.

Then Wendy, a member of my Fear of Commitment group, came for her first individual appointment to tell me that she'd read a book I'd suggested and had courageously allowed herself to go on a fourth date with a particularly intriguing man she'd been seeing. Since she usually ended every relationship after the third date—thanks to the number of times her father visited her as a child after abandoning the family—this was indeed exciting news.

Witnessing client breakthroughs reminds me why I chose this work to begin with.

Feeling good, I finished up with my last client, went home, poured a glass of wine and crawled into an aromatic, hot bubble bath.

Enjoying the blissful sensations and playing with the bubbles, I recalled my talk with Cerridwyn on the mall and thought about how silly I'd been to take the Tarot reader seriously. It was totally rational that the strange events of the morning had caused me to be anxious. It really wasn't so unusual that she'd picked up my fears about Emerald because I knew my own intuitive abilities often opened me to information from others, whether I wanted it or not. I had no doubt that Cerridwyn had skills, but she was only a mirror. Impressive, but not supernatural.

I was just thinking about how great it would be to take a nap, when I heard a voice downstairs in my living room.

"Kismet? It's me, Tom. Your door was unlocked. I knocked but nobody answered."

My door's unlocked? What's the matter with me? Damn. I forgot to call Tom and cancel. And then the little psychologist in my head suggested, "Maybe you didn't want to cancel."

"I'll be down in a minute," I yelled.

I heard footsteps tromping up the stairs and then Tom poked his head into the bathroom, beaming a toothpaste commercial smile.

Same old obnoxious Tom.

Surprised and highly annoyed, I sat up in the water, pulled a couple of big clumps of bubbles toward me and raised my knees up to my chest. "Hey! I'm taking a bath here. I wasn't expecting you so early. Why don't you wait for me downstairs?"

Why am I being polite to this jerk?

He ambled over, lowered the toilet lid, sat down and made himself comfortable. "No. I enjoy having you as a captive audience. And besides, I've seen you naked hundreds of times."

He was right about that. From the first moment I laid eyes on him during our internship at the psychiatric hospital, I was putty in his hands. All he had to do was give me one of those dazzling smiles or glance at me with his bedroom eyes and I'd follow him anywhere.

Okay. So I'd led a sheltered life.

Tom had been the first man that I'd had a sexual relationship with. Oh, sure, I'd fumbled around in the back seats of cars with various high school and college dates, and I even managed to find a willing participant to initiate me into womanhood when I determined the time was right. But until Tom, I'd been an emotional virgin.

He was eight years older than I and he taught me things about the sexual arts I never knew existed. We spent four years together and amassed quite a collection of sexual aids, books, toys, and videos. Unfortunately, while it was all about pleasure and orgasms for Tom, it was all about love for me. He'd been so disappointed that I'd muddied the waters.

I gathered more bubbles around me. "That's ancient

history," I sneered. Unfortunately, I realized too late that it's hard to pull off an effective sneer while sitting naked in a foamy tub.

He perched there watching me, making no effort to hide the fact his eyes were lingering on certain parts of my body and he was enjoying the view. I remembered that wicked expression on his face and I felt a tightening low in my body—as if my libido had sent out an invitation that went into the mail before my brain could retrieve it.

"Is the water getting cold?" He leered at my breasts and smiled.

I followed his gaze down and noticed my nipples were large and hard.

Shit. Apparently my body didn't get the memo about this lusting after Tom thing.

He smiled. "I always appreciated how quickly your body got aroused. It was very exciting to watch you respond to me in such an obvious way."

He stood, moved a step closer to the bathtub and laid his hand on his zipper. "Look," he said, rubbing his hand up and down the front of his pants, showing me his erection. "See what you do to me?"

Geez. It had been two years since I'd had sex and my body was screaming *yes!* Despite his heartless rejection and empty promises, I still wanted him inside me. Even though he was the poster boy for superficiality, I still lusted after him. I was torn between being disgusted with myself and being overwhelmingly aroused. I started to suggest that we move into my bedroom when he uttered the immortal words, "Tell me how bad you want it."

Yuck.

I'd been expecting a sensual seduction scene and instead he gave me a worn out line from one of the porn movies he collected. His words hit me like a cold shower, putting out the flames of my romantic fantasy. All of my desire for him immediately evaporated in the crystal clear realization that he'd never been who I imagined him to be and I'd been fooling myself all those years.

I raised my voice and gave it a cutting edge.

"Very tacky, Dr. Radcliffe. Tell me. Does that approach usually work for you these days? Are more women responding to 'Mr. Macho' than responded to 'Mr. Sensitivity'? Hand me a towel and get out."

With a shocked expression on his face, he reached over, picked up a towel and handed it to me.

I stood and slowly wrapped the towel around myself, noticing he was still enjoying the show. "There's some wine downstairs. Go help yourself. Get out."

He opened and closed his mouth a couple of times but no words emerged. The color had drained from his face, and his expression veered back and forth between confusion and disbelief. He finally turned and silently retreated.

After he left, I stepped out of the tub and stood in front of the mirror. My cheeks were flushed and my eyes were shining. At least it was good to know that my body was still capable of sexual arousal. I'd started to wonder. But it was clear that anything personal between the two of us was finished. I was actually glad Tom had shown up, because who knew how long I might have carried the torch if he hadn't reminded me of who he really was.

Love truly was blind.

"If I promise to go back to being Mr. Sensitivity, can I come up and talk to you while you put your makeup on? I always enjoyed watching you do that, plus I'm getting lonesome down here," Tom crooned, standing at the foot of the stairs.

I shook my head and smiled. He was trying to schmooze me again, but it wasn't going to work. I had come to my senses.

"Sure. You can come up, but I'm almost done. Bring the wine bottle with you."

I might need a weapon.

He came upstairs and leaned against the door to the bathroom, lowered the bottle down onto the counter by the sink and stood there quietly, sipping his wine.

He shrugged his shoulders. "I feel as if I should apologize, but you can't really blame a guy for trying. We've got such a long history together. You've gotten even prettier since we split up."

"I *can* blame a guy for trying, so feel free to come up with one of your brilliant, meaningless apologies. I'm all ears."

I'd pulled my hair up into one of those large hair clips so it wouldn't get wet in the bath, and I released it, letting the curls cascade down my back.

He reached out and picked up one of the wavy clumps. "Was your hair always this long? It's very sexy."

He cocked his head and inspected the band-aid on my neck. "What's this?" He touched it with one finger.

I smacked his hand away.

"A nasty hickey, if you must know. Nothing I'd want my clients to see."

He raised his eyebrows, smiled.

"A hickey, eh? Someone claiming his territory?"

"You, Dr. Radcliffe, are a sexist pig."

He trailed a finger across the top of my breast, and gave me his "Aren't I a naughty boy" face I remembered so well.

I guess you really can't teach an old horndog new tricks.

I smiled and grabbed the offending finger and bent it backward, causing him to yelp with pain.

He rubbed his wounded digit and rambled about how irrational I was being, how women were all so emotional, and how he was just showing me that he found me appealing.

I didn't address anything he said, because I knew what he was up to, and I was already tired of his games. He just couldn't believe that a woman would turn him down—that his routine hadn't worked. I remember being jealous for most of the time we'd been together because Tom just couldn't resist flirting with every waitress, clerk, or secretary he encountered. Why hadn't I noticed his pitiful insecurity before? And why had I blamed myself?

"A friend is coming by pretty soon and we're going out to a club downtown. I meant to call you and cancel for tonight, but I forgot," I mumbled, my face close to the mirror so I could finish putting on my mascara without smudging it.

And, right on cue, there was a knock at the door.

Tom turned and raced down the stairs, yelling, "I'll get it." I'd put money on the fact that he assumed my friend would be female.

The sound carried easily in my small townhouse.

"Is Kismet here?" Alan asked, giving each syllable a slightly higher pitch, as if he momentarily thought he'd come to the wrong door.

I didn't hear anything for a few seconds and then Tom obviously recovered from his dashed expectations and reclaimed his innate pomposity. "Yes, of course, please come in. I'm an old friend of hers. Tom. Tom Radcliffe."

I called down the stairs. "I'll be right there, Alan. Just give me a few minutes. Get him something to drink, Tom."

I went into my bedroom and put on the outfit I'd laid out for the evening, then went back into the bathroom for some finishing touches to my makeup and hair. I even squirted on a hint of the perfume a friend had sent me from Paris on her last trip.

Feeling rather excited about the evening, I came down the stairs and joined them in the living room.

"Wow, you look great," Alan said. "Positively edible. And you smell wonderful."

"Yes, you really do," echoed Tom.

I said a silent "thank you" to the helpful sales clerk who'd talked me into buying some bright colors and current fashions. Maybe it was time for me to go visit her again.

I hadn't known what to wear to a dance club because I hadn't been to one in years, but I figured jeans would probably work. I had an expensive pair that I'd bought a few months back and hadn't worn yet, and the length was great for the high heels on my favorite black boots. I'd be even taller than usual tonight, but I felt like taking up space.

It was great to have an excuse to wear one of my new

shirts. It was the color of a summer sky, form-fitting, and low-cut. I'd had to buy a special bra for this top because none of my regular undergarments were skimpy enough. I'd briefly considered getting a Wonder Bra, but found that the extra padding and lift were overkill.

Going out gave me a chance to put on the beautiful azure, Victorian drop necklace and earring set that I'd bought for myself as a birthday present last year. They matched my eyes perfectly and made me feel feminine. An unfamiliar feeling.

I felt pretty good, and I had to admit I was enjoying the appreciative expressions on their faces. It had been a long time since I'd dressed up on purpose. It was nice to see that my efforts had paid off. Hell. It had been a long time since I'd had two handsome men paying attention to me. A long time? Try never.

Alan continued staring at me, and I frowned. "What?"

He laughed. "I'm just amazed by the transformation. I came to pick up Kismet Knight, Ph.D., conservative scientist, and instead I find Xena, Warrior Princess. Not that I'm complaining."

I laughed, too, feeling surprisingly light-hearted. Evidently, kicking Tom's metaphorical butt had perked me right up. "You don't know me yet. Who can say what other personalities might be hiding in here?"

"I'm looking forward to finding out." His eyes moved down my body.

I could swear I physically felt the movement of his eyes. *Oh, my. Either the wine is going to my head, or my pilot light just got turned up.*

"Ahem," Tom said, drawing my attention back to him. "I'm surprised, Kismet. It used to be worse than pulling teeth to get you to attend a dance club with me. You never enjoyed them. What's special about this one?

Well, well. Dr. Cliché is jealous.

"We're doing some research. Alan is also a psychologist, and he's introducing me to a subculture I'm interested in writing about."

"Hey, that's terrific. Can I go?" Tom asked.

I turned my head to Alan and he shrugged his shoulders. "It's okay with me."

What are you up to, Tom?

"Are you sure, Tom? Because it will probably be field study—just observation—and I remember how you felt about that in grad school. You thought it was boring."

But I could almost see the wheels turning in his mind as he imagined the sweet, young, scantily dressed subjects he'd be observing. No. Not boring at all.

"I'm sure it will be fun," Tom asserted, flashing another of his game show host smiles. He ran his fingers through his abundant hair and wiggled his eyebrows at me.

"Okay," I sighed. "Who wants to drive?"

Chapter 10

$\mathcal{W}$e wound up taking Alan's Jeep Cherokee because Tom and I had already sampled the fruit of the vine.

On the drive over Tom queried from the back seat, his tone disdainful, "What kind of subculture is it that we're observing tonight?"

Alan and I glanced at each other, smiled and voiced in unison, "Vampires."

Tom fumbled madly with the clasp of his seatbelt, making a frenzied effort to extricate himself from the restraining device. The fastener apparently put up great resistance, because he snorted, swore and made grunting sounds as he proceeded to pound the offending hardware into submission.

Tom always did have a short fuse.

I'm shallow enough to admit that I loved hearing every pitiful, Three Stooges second of it.

Go ahead and struggle with it, you moron. Come to think of it, you never did have much finesse with any hands-on activities, did you? Maybe someday you'll grow up and figure out the benefits of a tender touch.

Either my thought burrowed its way into his brain, or he simply exhausted his temper tantrum, because after a few seconds of quiet, I heard the "snick" of the clasp opening. He scooted forward and hurled himself against the front seat.

"Excuse me? Vampires?"

I had to give Alan points for keeping his eyes on the road and not laughing in Tom's face.

I half turned within the confines of my seatbelt, fixed my eyes on Tom and gave him my best blank face. "Yes. Vampires."

He rested his hand on my shoulder. "*Please* tell me you're not serious."

My tone of voice raised its chin, and I shook off his hand. "I've stumbled across a group of people who believe they're vampires, and I'm going to write about them. I think it's a valid topic for research."

I sounded way more defensive than I meant to. As if I dared him to contradict me. I didn't know why I felt the need to explain my work to Tom, but I did. Or maybe it was me I was trying to convince.

Tom shook his head slowly, exaggerating the theatrical back and forth motion, his lips tightly compressed.

"Kismet, Kismet. You had so much potential. You could have gone to California with me and shared the lime-light. You could have been interviewed by Leno. You could have taken a meeting with Dr. Phil. But here you are, study-ing pathetic fringe elements in Cow Town. I had no idea my breaking up with you would hit you so hard."

I straightened rigidly in my seat, kept my eyes riveted directly in front of me and took a deep breath. My hands automatically fisted in my lap and I bit my lower lip to hold back the avalanche of words gathering there. I wasn't going to allow the only female psychologist in the group to have a public meltdown. I wouldn't let him push me over the edge.

The arrogant jerk. The self-centered, obnoxious, smarmy asshole. No amount of making him jealous is worth listening to this pompous drivel. Once again, his brain is caught in his zipper.

My muscles tensed and moisture dampened my armpits. It was all I could do to keep myself buckled into my seat, because I was seriously fantasizing about diving into the back and pummeling a little color into Dr. California's face with my knuckles. Maybe give him youthfully puffy lips without him having to go visit his plastic surgeon. Of course, he might have to check in with his dentist afterward. It was so thoughtful of him to remind me he hadn't invited me to accompany him to the West Coast, and that he was now a big shot.

Alan studied me with raised eyebrows, his tongue pushing against the side of his face from inside his mouth. "Tom," he quickly interjected, obviously catching my hostile intentions. "Do you remember a series of murders in Los Angeles a while back? They got a lot of media coverage. Several bodies found, drained of blood? I'm searching for those killers, and I'll find them in the vampire subculture."

Alan sounded a lot more formal than I'd ever heard him. Psychologists are a competitive lot and we never miss an opportunity to puff ourselves up for each other. Or, maybe it was Tom's hyper-pomposity that brought out the pretentiousness in everyone. But, regardless, he did give me a moment to rein myself in. Lucky for Tom.

Oblivious, Tom droned on. "So, what are you? A forensic psychologist? What are you going to do with the killers after you find them?

Alan ignored the superior attitude Tom displayed in his over-pronunciation of the words "forensic psychologist," but

I heard him sigh.

"I work for the FBI. I'm an expert on serial killers, in addition to other things, and I'm the agent assigned to the case."

"How did Kismet get involved in all this?"

"She's the Vampire Psychologist," Alan said, grinning. "Here we are."

Our heads pivoted toward the window as we passed The Crypt, cruising for a place to park. Milling about in front of the main entrance were large groups of 20-somethings: Goths, vampire wannabes, heavy metal gods and goddesses, Britney Spears pretenders, androgynous individuals covered in body art and piercings, and some reincarnated hippies.

"It appears we're going to be the oldest people there," Tom noted, with a hint of annoyance in his voice.

"Especially you," I teased, smiling sweetly. Okay. Just because I'm a psychologist doesn't mean I can't be as nasty as anyone else. I knew Tom was sensitive about his age and that he'd avail himself of every plastic surgery procedure possible in order to stave off the ravages of time. Not that I was above a little nip and tuck myself in the future.

We finally found a place to park several blocks away, and walked back to The Crypt. It was huge, taking up almost the same space in square feet as it did in height.

The building had its own personality. The closer we got to it, the more ominously powerful it seemed. I could hear music throbbing on the airwaves.

The first thing I noticed about the building was its eyes—the stained glass windows that filled half of each wall. Extraordinary colors and shapes formed pictures and abstract patterns in each window. There were images of angels, demons, religious symbols, Celtic crosses, and spirits rising from graves. I could imagine how amazing they'd look with the sun pouring through them.

The windows were brightly lit and the colors splashed down onto the dark sidewalk like rainbows of light, bathing everyone standing there in etheric hues.

The building was gothic in design, with ornate towers and archways. The upper level had many nooks and crannies, and standing guard at various outposts were large gargoyles.

As we approached the crowd gathered in front of the main entrance, the smell of marijuana permeated the air, and I felt a heavy, pulsating rhythm moving in through the soles of my feet.

We climbed up the stairs leading to the entrance and passed through the massive double doors, which were made of heavy wood with beautiful carvings. A wall of sound hit me when the doors opened and the intensity of the vibration took my breath away. At the far end of the club a rock band commanded the aural landscape with screaming guitars, booming bass notes and primitive rhythms. Musicians cavorted wildly on the large, multi-level stage, and the acoustics were such that the sound exploded as it poured out of the mounted speakers.

A smoke machine pumped out a continuous layer of fog that hovered near the floor and had a life of its own, curling and twisting like a ghostly serpent.

A bouncer stood inside the door, blocking our entrance to the rest of the club. He was extremely tall, very thin, and deathly white. He didn't seem to give much credence to the idea of personal space, because he bent down very close.

"Welcome to The Crypt. ID please."

His breath was hot with an odd, sweet scent. He reached out a hand with long, dirty fingernails and I jumped back, without even thinking, stepping behind Alan while I retrieved my driver's license from the pocket of my jeans. It'd been a long time since anyone carded me.

Apparently not offended by my reaction to his hygiene, he smiled—showing discolored fangs—and waved us inside with a sweep of his arm. "Enjoy."

Tom tapped me on the shoulder and pointed at the bouncer, his expression telegraphing distaste. "Is he one of your clients? It appears he could use a little help."

I glared at him. "Very funny. I just might give him one of my business cards. He could be a perfect case study for my book."

Down girl. I don't have to justify myself to Tom or anyone else. This is starting to feel like a nasty little case of sibling rivalry—not that I have any idea how sibling anything would feel.

"Hey, you two. Check it out." Alan pointed to the interior of the club.

The entire place was decorated like a cross between a graveyard and Dracula's castle, and it was big enough to hold hundreds of people, most of whom had already arrived.

We maneuvered our way over to the main bar, which ran along an entire wall, and was shaped to resemble a long, wooden sarcophagus. Standing there, waiting to catch the attention of the bartender, Alan leaned toward me and shouted in my ear, "I forgot to tell you. Never look vampires in the eyes. They'll entrance you."

I was going to say something about that being ridiculous,

but that was too many words to scream over the music so I nodded and mouthed "okay."

Judging by the expression on his face, Tom was already in lecher heaven, scrutinizing the nubile, bouncing female body parts on the dance floor. I didn't think a grin could get any wider. He started to remind me of the "Joker" character in one of the *Batman* movies. He turned back to the bar to put in his order and caught sight of the bartender. "Holy shit."

She was spectacular. A leather fantasy right out of the centerfold of a men's magazine. Her hair was cut short and it stood up in stubby little spikes all over her head. It was hard to tell under the dim lights, but the color appeared to be pink—or maybe orange. Her eyes were almond-shaped blue orbs. She leaned over the bar and plopped her considerable assets in front of Tom. "What's your pleasure?"

After a few seconds, he finally raised his eyes up to hers and stared, his mouth slowly relaxing and hanging open.

Alan shook Tom's shoulder and snapped his fingers in front of his face. "Wake up!"

Tom came back to himself with a start, shook his head from side to side and peered at Alan. "What happened?"

Alan explained, "Never look a vampire in the eyes."

We all stared at the goddess behind the bar and she smiled at us, displaying a fine set of fangs.

Tom laughed, "Yeah, right." But he seemed rattled.

We ordered Bloody Marys—the house special—and went in search of a table.

The interior of the building had many small rooms, raised platforms, and cozy hideaways for customers seeking privacy for one activity or another. Miraculously, we happened to be in the right place at the right time and were able to snag an intimate circle booth in a raised area off the main room. The walls enclosing the booth muted the volume of the music and we could talk without yelling. From that vantage point, we could see almost the entire club while remaining unobtrusive ourselves.

Tom, who'd been very quiet since his close encounter with the centerfold at the bar, expressed the need to find the restroom. He started the long process of wading through a sea of humanity to reach the other side of the club. I watched him go, and about halfway across the room, he got hijacked by a tall brunette who pulled him onto the dance floor.

"Hello, Alan." A familiar voice enveloped me, velvet in my ears.

Alan rose from his seat. "Devereux, please join us. It's nice to see you again."

Devereux sat down next to me in the booth, lifted my hand and kissed it. He cocked his head then gave a slow blink of his turquoise eyes. "Hello. I am Devereux, the owner of this establishment."

The touch of his lips on my hand caused a strong reaction in several parts of my body. I couldn't sort through my emotions fast enough to say anything, so I was relieved when Alan spoke.

"This is Kismet Knight, she's a local psychologist. I've been consulting with her about the missing girl."

"It is a pleasure to meet you," Devereux said out loud, while whispering in my mind, "I am very happy to see you. Alan does not need to know that we have already met."

I just stared at him and nodded my head, because I was

overcome by a desire to crawl into his lap and cover his mouth with mine. And until I was sure I wasn't going to make a fool of myself, I sat very still.

What was it about Devereux? Why was it that whenever I was near him I turned into a hormonal teenager? Was it chemical? Did his pheromones communicate with mine in some mysterious way? Was he a master hypnotist? Or was I just dazzled by the obvious?

No doubt about it, he was a beautiful man. There was no other way to describe him. A work of art. Something about his face was masculine yet soft at the same time and it made me want to touch him, to run my fingers over his pale skin and through his long, silky hair. I shifted my head and tried to avoid his sparkling eyes, not because I feared he'd entrance me, but because I was afraid of what he might see in mine.

"Yes, I desire you, as well," Devereux murmured in my mind, the words caressing some invisible part of me.

Alan's cell phone rang and he lifted it out of his pocket and answered, "Stevens." There was a brief pause and then, "Shit, I'll be right there."

Turning to me he explained, "They've found a body. I need to go to police headquarters."

I started to get up but Alan put a hand on my shoulder. "I'm afraid I can't take you with me, Kismet. You'll have to wait here. I'll come back for you and Tom as quickly as I can."

I didn't care for the sound of that. I just wasn't the type to sit waiting for someone to chauffeur me around, and leaving me here with Devereux made me nervous in ways I couldn't even understand.

Devereux turned his attention to Alan. "I will look after

Dr. Knight and her friend until you return."

Alan put his hand on my cheek then stood. "I won't be gone long." He headed for the door.

"He is attracted to you," Devereux offered, nodding in the direction of Alan's retreating form. He smiled. "And you to him. But you are also attracted to me. And there are some confused emotions about your friend on the dance floor."

I frowned and studied his face. How did he do that? And why didn't it bother me as much as it should have?

"I thought you promised me that you'd stay out of my mind."

He nodded. "Yes, of course. I apologize. You are quite right. I do not wish to spoil the mystery between us. You are especially lovely tonight."

He angled toward me, waiting, his lips close enough to kiss. I breathed in the soft, spicy fragrance of him and closed the gap between our mouths before I even had a conscious thought about it.

We kissed long and deep, our tongues exploring, melting into each other. It was as if our physical bodies merged together and we shared the same heartbeat—the same life force. Every cell in my body desired him, and there was no one else in the room except the two of us. All of the noise disappeared and we floated in a private universe.

When we finally pulled apart, I gazed into his eyes, which glittered like jewels.

He whispered, "My gaze will not entrance you tonight."

I didn't care about making sense of that. I only wanted to drink him in with my eyes, to touch him, to kiss him again. In fact, in that moment, nothing else mattered. But then I asked myself, why didn't it matter? It wasn't like me to give into my physical desires in public. Why was I suddenly so uninhibited?

"Why am I so fascinated by you?" I asked, running my fingers along his cheek.

He took my hand in his. "We have that effect on some humans. I am very pleased you feel that way about me. I hope to fascinate you even more."

I got distracted watching his mouth for a moment.

"Kismet?"

"What?" I pulled away from him and blinked my eyes a couple of times to rouse myself. "See? That's what I mean. Why do you have that effect on me?"

"Do you remember when you asked me what Bryce had done to you and I said he had altered your brain waves?"

"I remember you said that, but it didn't make any sense to me. How can someone alter my brain waves just by staring at me?"

"It is about entrainment. I have done a lot of reading on this subject over the last twenty years. One benefit to living a long time is the acquisition of knowledge."

"Entrainment?"

"Allow me to explain. Think of an old clock, the kind with a swinging pendulum." He moved his hand back and forth, as if he was conducting an orchestra. Sharing his wisdom obviously pleased him and I smiled as I watched his enthusiastic presentation. Professor Devereux.

His graceful motions expanded into wider arcs.

"The rhythm of the swing is very strong, very powerful. Then think of putting several smaller, newer clocks on the same wall with the old clock, each pendulum swinging in a different pattern. Soon, all the new clocks will begin swinging in time with the old clock. The power of the old clock called to the newer ones and they joined with it. Am I explaining correctly?"

I skimmed my fingertips over the top of the hand he'd rested on the table. I couldn't seem to stop touching him.

"Yes, I know about that. It's like when women all start having their cycles at the same time. As if we get in sync with each other or something. But what does that have to do with you?"

He nodded and held up his index finger, prepared to continue with the lecture. "Let me put it in musical terms. Vampires . . ." He paused, frowning. "What is wrong?"

He saw me shift my eyes down when he said the word vampires. I brought my hands together in my lap. Saying that word reminded me I was taking advantage of someone who might be delusional, or at the very least, mentally confused. There I was, making out with a virtual stranger and encouraging him by listening to his stories. That felt bad as a woman and as a psychologist. I raised my eyes to meet his and he was smiling at me.

He shook his head. "You are the most stubborn woman I have ever met. It is becoming troublesome that you will not accept what I am. But I will continue to answer the question you asked and you will simply have to indulge me."

He lifted one of my hands, brought it up to his mouth and kissed my palm with those incredibly soft lips. Even that small contact caused my heart to race and my libido to tap me on the shoulder. His lovely turquoise eyes sparkled, and he somehow managed to appear sexy, angelic, and danger-ous all at the same time.

"As I was saying about musical terms, vampires give off such a powerful energy or tone that everyone entrains with us. The vibrational song that emanates from us is stronger than any other, and so it overrides whatever was there before. And that is without our even looking at anyone. If we gaze into a human's eyes without holding back, it is a form of mind control. We are able to change your brain waves."

"Are you talking about hypnosis?"

"It is much more similar to brainwashing than hypnosis because in hypnosis you are always free to choose."

I reached over and played with a lock of his hair. "So, you're saying the power of what you are is so strong that I'm pulled in whether I want to be pulled in or not?"

"Exactly," he said, with a quick nod.

"And when you said your gaze wouldn't entrance me to-night, you meant you'd hold back?"

"Yes."

I slid my index finger along his lower lip. "Then, does that mean my desire to kiss you is only there because you want me to kiss you? That you are irresistible to me because of that power and not because of anything I feel about you?"

He flashed a dazzling smile. "I am pleased to hear I am irresistible to you, but no. I am old enough to be in total control of my power and I hold back with you always so that you can make your own decisions. You kiss me because you desire to kiss me."

I trailed my fingernail lightly over his cheek. "Show me the difference."

He raised his eyebrows. "What do you mean?"

"Use your eyes. Turn on the full power. Let me have it. I want to know what you're talking about."

"Are you certain?" he asked, smiling mischievously.

I nodded my head and stared into his eyes.

I felt a wave of heat move through my body, my scalp tingled, and my eyelids got heavy. The next thing I knew, I was in his lap, my knees straddling his legs, with my arms wrapped around his neck, passionately kissing him.

In my mind he sighed, "This is how it could be between us."

"Ahem."

I heard a sound from somewhere in the distance, but nothing was more important than kissing Devereux's soft, warm lips. Nothing mattered except keeping my body pressed against his.

"Ahem. Kismet?"

In slow motion, I turned toward the sound. There, at the end of the table, were three sets of eyes, staring at me.

Chapter 11

Tom's shocked face leaned in toward me. "Kismet?"

Whatever had happened wasn't over with yet, and I was having a hard time concentrating on the fact that I needed to focus on the audience we'd suddenly acquired. I vaguely recognized Tom but couldn't place the two women standing on either side of him.

A woman's voice said, "She's entranced."

"Do you mean she's drugged? Did this guy put something in her drink?" Tom demanded, his voice dripping anger.

"No. She's not drugged. She's bespelled," said a different woman's voice.

"I seem to be missing something here. If someone doesn't clue me in right now, I'm going to cause a scene," Tom yelled.

"Kismet. What's going on? Where's Alan? Do you know this guy?"

I squinted up at Tom, nodded my head yes and buried my face in Devereux's deliciously scented hair.

"I do apologize. You must be Tom. We have not been properly introduced yet. I am Devereux, the owner of The Crypt. Please excuse our rudeness in not acknowledging you sooner. I take full responsibility. We were doing a little . . . experiment . . . and we got distracted."

The fog was clearing in my brain and I started to grasp that I was sitting in Devereux's lap and that Tom and two strange women were gaping at me. I remembered making the decision to leap into his lap, but for the life of me I couldn't recall why I'd do such a thing.

Devereux whispered in my mind, "That was wonderful. I await the opportunity for us to continue our experiment."

He effortlessly lifted me off his lap and set me in the booth next to him. The sounds of the room began to swim back into my consciousness and my eyes reclaimed the ability to focus. I wanted to ask him a thousand questions about what had happened, but it didn't appear I was going to have the chance.

"Please join us." Devereux waved his arm through the air over the booth.

Tom and the two women sat down. His eyes shifted rapidly back and forth between Devereux and me. "Kismet, what's the matter with you? I've never seen you do anything like that before."

"Give her a moment," urged the woman sitting next to him. "She's not herself yet."

She turned her attention to me. "I'm Zoë, Tom's new friend. I remember how it was the first time I was taken under. It's almost too amazing for words."

"Taken under? What do you mean taken under? What the *hell* is going on here?" Tom glared around the table.

I ignored him and focused my eyes on the woman speaking to me and recognized her as the tall brunette who'd waylaid Tom on his way to the men's room. She was very dynamic with her dark hair, pale skin and large, distinctive eyes. It was too dark for me to see the color, but they seemed unusual. I became momentarily fascinated by her eyelashes, which were the longest I'd ever seen.

Finally retrieving some of the ability to speak, I mumbled, "It's nice to meet you."

Devereux touched my arm and pointed to the other woman who'd joined us. "This is Luna. She is one of the managers of the club and my personal assistant."

I hadn't noticed through my brain fog earlier, but Luna was an exceptionally attractive woman. In fact, finding out that this femme fatal was Devereux's personal assistant bothered me way more than a little. I hardly knew Devereux, and a few passionate kisses shouldn't cause me to feel this jealous about another woman. Especially a woman who might not be interested in Devereux at all.

Yeah, right. Not interested in Devereux. Welcome to Denial Central.

Luna's silver eyes studied me like a specimen in a lab. She leaned across the table, shifting from side to side to get a better view, and I got the sense she'd have prodded me with a stick if she could.

"So, you're the one. You're the human who's caused all the fuss." She twirled a strand of her long, straight, jet black hair. "I expected more. You're very pretty, and I see what he means about your eyes, but I still don't understand the obsession."

She turned to Devereux. "What is it about her?"

The two of them stared silently at each other for a moment and then Luna nodded her head and sighed, "Yes, yes, I know. I'll be good. But I don't have to like it."

She turned back to me. "Have Devereux take you on a

tour of the rest of the club. I'm sure you'll find it illuminating." She stood, nodded at Devereux and walked away, moving like a sleek panther on the prowl.

Devereux said in my mind, "Luna does not understand my interest in humans. She believes it is dangerous for us to risk exposure by allowing ourselves to be known. There is no reason for you to be jealous of her. She and I have never had an intimate relationship."

I frowned at him and sent the thought, "I'm not jealous."

He smiled, nodded his head and thought, "As you wish."

"Hey, what's going on? Why is everyone just gawking at each other? I think I missed the beginning of this movie. Are you going to tell me what you were doing in this guy's lap?" Tom panted, his brows contracted.

I lifted my chin and locked eyes with him. "Well, even though I don't owe you an explanation, and you're sounding ridiculously like a jealous boyfriend, I'll tell you. Devereux and I have a special relationship. We are very attracted to each other. That's all you need to know. And I'll sit in the lap of anyone I wish, and I'll kiss whoever I choose!" I declared, giving him a stern look.

Although it was totally out of character for me to say all that out loud, it felt good to do it.

Tom scrunched down a little in his seat and nodded. "Okay. I hear you. I was just worried about you. You've been acting funny all night. Where's Alan?"

"He was called to the police station. There's been another murder."

His eyebrows rose. "A murder?"

"Yes, it's the case he's working on. He told you about it

in the car, remember?"

He frowned. "Oh, yeah. The vampire thing. So, how are we supposed to get home?"

You could always count on Tom to think about himself in the midst of whatever else was happening.

"He said he'd come back for us as soon as he could."

Zoë reached over and pinched Tom's chin between her fingers, guiding his face to hers. "Who knows, Tommy Boy. Maybe you won't want to go home. The night is young. Come on, let's dance." She pulled him out of the booth toward the dance floor.

"Don't leave without me!" Tom called back over his shoulder.

Devereux chuckled. "Your friend is an interesting person. Seeing you with me caused quite a storm of emotions inside him. He is concerned that he was wrong to let you go. He is reconsidering."

"Are you jealous?" I blurted, without thinking. What was I, a fourteen-year-old?

He snuggled in close and enveloped me in that wonderful spicy scent again. His eyes shimmered in the dim light and his voice flowed like music. "No. I am not jealous. I am certain of your feelings for me. What you and I have is beyond petty human emotions."

I briefly thought about insisting that I had no feelings for him, but how could I lie to someone who seemed to have the ability—whether I believed it or not—to know what I was thinking and feeling? Was that every woman's dream or worst nightmare?

Instead I asked, "If I stare at your eyes again, will I jump back into your lap?"

He laughed, a full-throated sound that washed over me like warm honey. "No. You may look at me and remain in your seat."

I locked eyes with him and thought, "Kiss me."

"Your wish is my command." And he pressed his soft, warm lips against mine, taking me once again into that deep, blissful, timeless universe where only the two of us existed. The sounds in the room receded into the background. Everyone else in the club disappeared. He gently teased his tongue into my mouth, exploring me, and I returned the favor. I heard myself making little moaning sounds. He spoke in my mind, "I want you."

My body ached with desire for him. Maybe it was the build-up of sexual need during the last two years, or maybe it was my reaction to his incredible kiss, but I couldn't think about anything except having mad, passionate sex with Devereux.

We reluctantly pulled apart.

"Come. Let me show you the rest of my club."

He stood and held his hand out to me, and I took it.

I slid out of the booth, raised up on my toes, and scanned the room. "I should tell Tom where I'm going. Not that he deserves it. It'd serve him right if I just left him here to fend for himself."

Devereux cocked his head. "The two of you had a disagreement?"

"Sometimes, even though I know better, I let his arrogance get to me. In a sick way, he's sort of like family."

He smiled. "Ah. Well, not to worry. Zoë will tell him you are with me."

"What do you mean, Zoë will tell him? How will Zoë know?"

"I have spoken to her, in her mind, and she will convey the message. Come."

We walked down the set of stairs that led from our cozy booth into the central part of the club. Devereux held my hand and guided us through the crowd, which seemed to flow aside magically, creating an impossible path through the jammed-in bodies.

We wound our way near the sarcophagus-shaped bar where the Leather Goddess entertained a group of slack-jawed males who were enthralled by her bartending talents. At the far end of the bar was an old-looking, wooden door. Seated on a stool in front of the door was a large, muscular man with long gray hair, dressed in standard biker gear.

When we approached, the biker guy jumped up off his stool, quickly pushed it aside and opened the door. Either this fellow had ingested too much caffeine, he was naturally nervous, or seeing Devereux triggered an anxiety attack, because he stared at Devereux with wide eyes. I could almost feel his adrenaline pumping. This guy was afraid.

Devereux said, "Thank you, John," as we walked through the entryway, and the door closed behind us. We were standing at the top of a long, wide staircase that descended down into the bowels of the club.

"Why was that man so afraid of you?"

He shrugged. "There are some humans who seek out that which terrifies them so they can be afraid, which is the only way they know to feel alive. Much like watching a movie that causes one to feel fear. John is addicted to vampires."

Listening to Devereux talk about vampires again was definitely taking the edge off the lust that had just been there moments ago. It was becoming clear that I either had to accept his vampire fantasies, or I wouldn't be able to see him. And seeing him had become non-negotiable.

I still hadn't made sense out of all the things Alan had told me about Devereux being the leader of a vampire coven, but I couldn't pretend I'd completely discounted that information. In fact, it had been replaying in my mind all day, eating away at my logical explanations. Alan was a psychologist, after all. Would he lie to me? Was he caught up in the delusion as well?

We walked down the stairs, which led to a long hallway with many doors on each side. I was reminded of Midnight's comment about the lower level being a dungeon, because the walls were stone, and the heavy doors appeared as if they'd been created to keep screaming prisoners locked away. A cool dampness pervaded, and I was almost surprised to see electric lights instead of torches lining the walls. But even though the place resembled a medieval castle, it really couldn't be that old because the church itself had only existed for just over 100 years. And yet, there was an ancient feel to it.

Some of the doors were open. As we passed I could see offices, meeting rooms, storage rooms, a lounge area with a movie-screen-size television, and the velvet curtain-covered entrance to the special gathering place Midnight had told me about during her first visit.

Devereux stopped in front of that room and pulled back the curtains. He nodded at me to check out the large group of people gathered inside. "I will introduce you to some of my companions later. Right now I selfishly wish to keep you to myself. You are a precious gift."

I wasn't used to men paying such attention to me so I didn't know what to make of all the emotions that swept over me as he said those words. Something about them triggered an old need and I suddenly felt vulnerable. I gazed up at his beautiful face, and he bent over and kissed my forehead tenderly, as if he knew what I was thinking.

He closed the curtains and took my hand, walking me further down the hallway to a set of ornate double doors. He used a funny, old-fashioned key to open the door and ushered me into a huge room filled with lovely antiques, tapestries, and artwork. The room was big enough to contain my entire townhouse with space to add a garage. Along the walls were beautiful candelabra holding lit candles which, combined with the prisms of light shining from an overhead chandelier, gave the room a soft illumination. The stone walls must have created a natural soundproofing, because I couldn't hear the music from upstairs anymore. The silence was rich.

I scanned the details of the room and noticed that all the modern office equipment was there—computer, fax machine, printer—built into antique desks, armoires, and tables, interspersed among colorful couches and chairs.

One half of the room was obviously used as a library; the walls were lined with bookshelves holding thousands of books, some of which appeared to be very old.

"Welcome to my private office." Devereux bowed. "Make yourself at home."

"Wow, this is amazing," I said, mostly to myself, as I wandered around the room, exploring. He had wonderful taste in furnishings and a remarkable sense of color. Appreciating the care he'd put into creating his workspace made me remember my own sparsely appointed office and I vowed to give it more attention. If it was true that someone's outer world was a reflection of his inner world, then Devereux was, indeed, a complex and multi-faceted person.

Turning back to him, it occurred to me that I hadn't seen him in bright light since he'd come to my office to interrupt Bryce's attack. As attractive as he appeared to me upstairs in the dim lighting of the club, now the combination of his shining blond hair and luminous blue-green eyes was almost overwhelming. He wore leather pants that were a dark version of the color of his eyes and a silk shirt of nearly the same shade. His boots had a full heel that made him even taller than he already was, which caused his lean, muscular body to seem even more impressive.

I moved over to him, stood with our bodies almost touching and gazed up at him. "What do you want from me?"

"Everything." He pulled me against him and his lips reclaimed mine.

My body came alive with sensations and desires. The longer the kiss went on, the more I became convinced I wouldn't survive the intensity of the feelings I was having. My knees were weak and all my pleasure centers throbbed with need. I felt him hard and thick against the front of my blue jeans. He made sounds that were part moan, part growl.

My heart beat so loud and fast it took me a minute to figure out that both of our hearts were beating together in a synchronized rhythm. I could almost hear the blood pumping through my veins.

He suddenly jerked away from me and retreated a step, observing me from beneath his dark eyelashes. He threw back his head and ran his tongue over his top lip. I got a quick glimpse of fangs.

I gasped in surprise, still lost in the web of desire we'd spun.

He closed his eyes and breathed out a heavy sigh. As he did that, the long canines retracted back up into his gums.

He opened his eyes again, his expression serious, and studied me. "It has been many years since I have lost control of myself that way. You do, indeed, have a great power over me. I hope I did not frighten you."

I knew that I'd just seen Devereux's teeth do the same thing Bryce's had done when he forced me to put my finger on his tooth in my office, and I didn't have any better explanation now than I had then, but I really didn't care. I kept feeling that I should care, but I just didn't.

"You didn't frighten me," I whispered.

"Come. There is something I wish to show you."

He took my hand and walked over to one of the bookcases, ran his fingers along the inside panel and did something that made a slight clicking sound. The large bookcase swung backward, creating the entrance to an adjoining room.

Devereux eased me through the opening in the wall of books into that other space, roughly half the size of the huge area we'd left, but still very large.

Saying this was the most extraordinary room I'd ever seen would be an understatement. The floor was white marble etched with Celtic, astrological, alchemical, and other magical symbols in patterns of various colors. False walls of rich wood had been constructed over the natural stone, and paintings, which appeared to have been done by the same artist, covered most of the available space.

The air held a gentle fragrance, a combination of incense and herbs.

On one side of the room was a large, antique bed, with bright-colored bedding.

I had expected the bed to be our destination, and I felt both nervous and excited about the prospect. But to my surprise, Devereux guided me to the other end of the room, where there were shelves and tables full of strange bottles, odd substances, and peculiar items. In addition, there were candles of every color, shape, and size. Further along the wall was an artist's easel, many canvases, and paint supplies.

Devereux walked over to the easel. "I want you to know me." He held out his hand.

I joined him at the easel and let my eyes take in the beautiful scene of a sunrise that was partially completed. He pointed to the rising sun in the picture. "Perhaps we all want what we cannot have?"

"All these paintings are yours? You're an artist?"

He nodded.

I moved around the room, closely inspecting the paintings hanging on each wall. There was a mix of breathtaking outdoor scenes alongside portraits of people dressed in clothing from other centuries. As amazing and etheric as the landscape scenes were, the portraits were even more spectacular. It was as if he'd captured the essence of each person's soul and added that mystical element to the final painting in some magical way.

"They're beautiful. You're very talented."

He bowed. "I have had a very long time to practice."

One painting in particular drew me and I walked over to stand before it. The woman in the picture had the same hair and eyes as Devereux. She was dressed in a flowing white gown, which reminded me of an angel. Around her neck was an exquisite pentagram on a silver chain.

"That was my mother," he said, coming to stand beside me.

I noted the "was" in his statement. "I'm sorry. Did you lose her recently?"

He turned to me and smiled, "No. She died very long ago, but I still miss her. She taught me everything I know. She was a powerful woman."

He walked back over to the shelves and tables of unusual things.

"What's all the stuff in the bottles? What do you do with all those candles?" I asked, moving back over to explore the strange objects.

He followed me. "Magic."

"Magic? You mean magic tricks, like a magician?"

He pivoted to stand in front of me and met my eyes with his.

"They are not tricks, but yes, magician is one of the names those such as myself have been called throughout the ages. We are also referred to as magus, shaman, or wizard. I have a particular fondness for the title wizard because it honors the lineage I come from—the same roots as the great wizard Merlin."

I chuckled. "Merlin? You mean the fairy tale about King Arthur and all that?"

His expression remained serious, which surprised me and made me anxious. I nervously studied his collection of

New Age paraphernalia on the nearby table.

"Ah, my dear Kismet. As a psychologist, you should know that all fairy tales contain a grain of truth. The actual stories of Merlin are not commonly known. But he was, indeed, a great Master.

"I do not expect you to believe everything—or perhaps even anything—that I will share with you, but I do ask that you keep an open mind. I want you to know why I am so drawn to you.

"Long before I became a nightwalker—"

I looked up from the crystal ball I was gazing into. "A nightwalker?" I interrupted.

"A vampire, the undead, an immortal."

I took a breath, preparing to ask more questions, but he held up a hand to stop me. "Please. Let me finish."

I nodded and picked up a colorful, crystal-encrusted wand.

"Since my human birth, I was schooled in the art and craft of magic. Generations of my family had apprenticed themselves to the witches and wizards who came before. The skills and abilities of each ancestor were passed along the bloodline. By the time the gifts came down to me, they were extremely potent."

He clasped his hands behind his back and paced to and fro, as if he was delivering a speech. I followed him with my eyes.

"In addition to my talents in the realm of the magical arts, I also inherited artistic abilities, which revealed themselves very early. It was not long before my ability to see the future blended with my love of painting to give me a very powerful way to express the prophecies and visions I could sense in my deepest mind. I became a seer."

He strode over to a large wooden cabinet and opened the wide double doors. Inside were scores of painted canvases, lined up like dominoes next to each other. He reached in and selected one particular canvas and drew it out of the cabinet, holding it carefully along the edge.

He carried the painting back to me, turned it around for me to see and held it up with both hands.

I gasped, staring. It was a portrait of me.

"Devereux! That's so beautiful. When did you have time to paint this? How could you have memorized my face so perfectly in the short time I've known you?"

I stood, speechless, taking in the details of the portrait. As I examined the exquisite artwork, something began to tug at my consciousness. Something was odd about this painting. I couldn't quite put my finger on what it was, until it rolled over me like a wave.

Suddenly, I felt tense.

"My necklace. You've never seen this necklace. In fact, this is the first time I've ever put it on, yet, it's in the picture. How can that be? And my blue blouse. How could you have painted me as I look tonight?"

He propped the canvas on an easel. "When I created this portrait, I did not know the woman in the picture or why I was compelled to adorn her with that particular piece of jewelry. As I always did when I am in the midst of a prophetic vision, I simply painted what I saw. But unlike the other visions that had been born on my canvases, this one would not release me after the image was complete. The woman in the portrait haunted me. She filled my dreams until I was sure I would go mad. She spoke to me in my mind and repeated one word over and over again."

He pointed to some writing at the bottom of the painting and I leaned in to read it.

Kismet

"I thought the word meant the woman in the painting was my fate. My destiny. I waited patiently for her to find me, and after a time, I put the painting away. And it has been locked away until now."

He closed the distance between us, his hands on my upper arms.

"It was not a word at all. It was a name. Your name."

I shook my head, searching the depths of his eyes for some clue to what he was talking about.

"I don't understand. Are you saying you didn't paint this recently?"

"Yes."

"When did you paint it?"

"Over 800 years ago."

Chapter 12

It was official. Like Elvis, my brain had definitely left the building.

At some point during the last few hours I'd apparently fallen through the Looking Glass. I didn't have a map of Wonderland, and nothing in my previous experience or education prepared me to deal with the strange, parallel universe I'd landed in.

Had someone slipped LSD into my Bloody Mary?

There I was, in the nether regions of Dracula's castle, staring at a gorgeous, self-proclaimed immortal who insisted he'd painted my portrait 800 years ago, and I couldn't find the instruction manual to put the pieces together. I couldn't even find the box the damn thing came in.

Devereux seemed to have that effect on me. One minute I was ready to rip my clothes off, leap into his arms and lose myself in a frenzy of body parts; and the next minute I rocketed between shocked horror, mind-numbing confusion, and righteous anger. My brain just wasn't equipped for that kind of neurochemical rollercoaster ride.

Then all hell broke loose.

I heard loud, angry voices out in the corridor and frantic pounding on the outer door to Devereux's office. Evidently, the villagers with lit torches had arrived.

"Master! Master! Come quickly. They're back and they've got Luna."

Devereux shoved the painting at me and ordered, "Stay here." He moved so quickly through the opening in the wall of books that my eyes registered only a blur.

He must have opened the outer door, because a cacophony of chaotic, fearful voices filled the air before the door clicked shut again and I was left in eerie silence.

Stay here? I seriously didn't think so.

I slanted another glance at the portrait and put it back into the cabinet. No matter when it had been painted, it was clearly high quality. Devereux was a talented artist. What was it with me? Why did I have to fall for brilliant men who were either egomaniacs, crazy, or both?

I walked out of Devereux's secret room and crossed his main office area, heading for the door to the hallway. The closer I drew, the louder the sounds became. I put my fingers on the handle, and gently pushed down, easing the door inward, until I could poke my head out and view the area directly in front of the entrance. I half expected to find a guard standing there, another of Devereux's motorcycle gang thralls, who would keep me in my luxurious holding cell. But this end of the hallway was empty.

Judging by the noise level, all the action was happening further up the corridor, in the area behind the velvet curtains. The sounds of crashing furniture, blood-curdling screams, Darth Vader-like rumblings, and screechings that had to be a demonic choir rehearsing the Satanic Mass for the Dead assailed my ears. Something unpleasantly red oozed out along the floor in front of that entryway.

The only way out of the basement was to pass the vampire-wannabe circus carrying on behind curtain #1.

I tiptoed up the hallway and stood with my back pressed to the wall, next to the entrance to the insane asylum. I peeked in long enough to figure out that all the people—if people was the right word—crammed into the room were locked in combat with willing and enthusiastic partners. The last thing I saw before I sprinted toward the stairs leading back up to the main floor was Devereux and Bryce, fangs bared, hair flying, levitating a couple of feet above the ground, clutching each others necks.

That was it for me.

The volume of noise swallowed my unintended scream, and I bolted away from the totally unbelievable up into the merely improbable.

I ran up the stairs like I was being chased by the Hounds of Hell, pushed through the door where John the biker, the vampire addict, had abandoned his post, and I smashed into Alan's chest. I screamed, instinctively tried to push away. He grabbed my upper arms, holding me against him. I was shaking so hard my earrings rattled.

"Kismet! I've been searching all over for you. What the hell's going on here? What's all that noise down there? What happened to you?"

"They're fighting."

"Who's fighting? I'd better get down there . . ." He started to pull away.

I grabbed his arms. "No. Trust me. You don't want to go down there. I don't know if this place really is filled with vampires or not, but I can say for sure that everybody is certifiably crazy. After what I saw, you wouldn't last five minutes. Please, I want to find Tom and go home."

"Okay. I'll call the locals while you find Tom."

"No! Devereux wouldn't want you to bring the police into this. Let's just go."

Alan tipped his head to the side and cocked a brow. "Devereux wouldn't, would he? And how would you know that?"

"I'll tell you all about it—all of it. But right now just get me out of here."

His eyes bored into mine, and he nodded. Either I was sufficiently crazed looking and he'd decided to humor me, or he'd read deeper between the lines and got that my terror was authentic. I could at least admit to myself I'd never dealt well with violent psychotics, and everything about what I'd seen in the basement triggered my worst nightmares.

He collected both my hands in his and stared into my eyes.

"Okay. Just breathe. We'll find Tom. You go check out the dance floor and I'll see if he's ogling the bartender again. Let's meet outside in five minutes."

I nodded in relief, pulled my hands free and started off toward the crowded dance floor. I took a few steps and turned back to yell at Alan to hurry, and saw him leap through the doorway to the basement. I should've known he'd have to be a one-man cavalry; an FBI agent, first and foremost. I filed away for future use the fact that he'd stared right into my eyes and lied to me.

Now more pissed than frightened, I stomped off in search of Tom. Alan could splash around in the madness if he wanted to, but I was going to find Tom, catch a cab and get the hell outta there. The further removed I got from everything that had happened downstairs, the more the idea of drugs in my drink began to seem reasonable.

I wandered around the club for several minutes, even going so far as to stand in front of the men's room, sneaking peeks inside whenever the door opened. That got me a lot of unwanted attention, suggestive comments, and lascivious invitations. But what it didn't get me was a glimpse of Tom.

And, come to think of it, I hadn't seen Zoë either.

One good thing about being tall to begin with and wearing high heels was the elevated altitude. From my lofty vantage point, I was able to scan over the heads of half the blissed-out partiers and save myself from unnecessary body jostling.

If Tom was in the club, he had to be under a table somewhere, because there was no sign of him standing or sitting anywhere. And Alan hadn't emerged from the supernatural testosterone-fest below, so I was on my own. That was fine. I was used to being on my own.

It suddenly occurred to me that Tom might have gone outside, so I strode purposefully toward the front door and noticed the cadaverous bouncer was missing in action. I pushed through the heavy door leading out into the fresh night air and stood for a moment, coughing, as my lungs made it clear that I wouldn't be getting off so easy after spending an evening breathing in the chemical spewing of a fog machine.

I hadn't worn a watch, but I figured it had to be close to last call. Tom wasn't outside either, but he'd have to come out of the club eventually, so I decided to wait. Then it struck me that he'd probably left without me. There I was, waiting for him to make sure he got home safely, and he'd probably gone on his merry way without giving me a thought. That would be typical Tom. And typical of how I'd let him walk all over me. How could a woman be so bright and so dense all at the same time?

There were groups of people standing in front of the club in various states of inebriation, drug intoxication, and passionate embrace, so I strolled further down the block and rested against the building, folding back into the shadows, still exploring the art of breathing and appreciating the solitude.

I mentally reviewed what I'd seen in the basement. Nothing fit with any of my therapeutic experience. In all my reading and research, I'd never run across anything that included fangs, levitation, and the kind of unearthly noises that were yowling out of that room.

What if there really are such things as vampires? What am I supposed to do with that? If there are vampires, then I might as well pull up stakes—so to speak—and go work in a fast food restaurant somewhere, because everything I thought was true, isn't.

I dropped my head back against the cool of the old brick and closed my eyes. The moment I did that, a wave of dizziness swept over me and I braced myself against the wall, feeling as if the ground had actually moved. I held myself there, locking my knees to keep myself upright in the midst of the spinning, and opened my eyes. Everything was subtly different. I blinked a few times to clear my vision but couldn't shake the sense that something was wrong. Something had changed. The darkness was deeper, more textured. The air seemed thick, heavy, and scented with a sweet, coppery aroma. The smell got stronger until I could taste it in the back of my throat and I gagged.

"Come to me."

I gasped. The voice was repulsive; it crawled on my skin with slimy fingers. I automatically jerked my head over, raising a shoulder to block the sound entering one ear.

What the hell was that? I'm really losing it. I willed myself not to move.

"Come. Now."

I couldn't tell if I heard the voice with my physical ears or inside my mind, but it was unlike any I'd ever experienced before. It was as if the words attacked my eardrums. The sound split into dissonant octaves again and again, until it filled the entire vibrational spectrum, reminding me of those experiments by the government using audio frequencies to create madness.

But I also had the sense of feeling the voice kinesthetically, of being able to locate places in my body where it was resonating, pulsing, invading. My bones and organs vibrated in time with a powerful rhythm outside of me, and the pressure increased as the sound waves echoed around and through me, becoming more painful as they escalated.

The voice tore at my ears, repeating the same message over and over. I covered them with my hands and screamed, "No!"

"I am here. Come to me and I will show you miracles. I will grant all your earthly desires."

I felt myself moving away from the wall, pulled as if by a powerful magnet. My solar plexus tingled and ached, becoming hyper-sensitive, and I had the bizarre notion that an invisible something was attached to my midsection, physically compelling me. My head felt fuzzy, my mind disconnected. I couldn't stop myself. I couldn't resist. I walked away from the club into the darkness of the street beyond, the sense of dread and terror growing stronger with every wobbly step. Then everything went dark.

I woke up in a coffin.

That might seem unpleasant, unsanitary or maybe creepy to most people, but for me it was my worst nightmare.

This might be a good time to explain my greatest fear.

When I was young I saw an old movie called "Premature Burial," where—due to a strange illness that caused complete paralysis mimicking death—people were buried before they were dead. They were put in boxes, placed in holes in the ground and were very aware of the dirt being piled on top of their supposedly deceased selves. They couldn't communicate their aliveness to any of the grieving mourners, so they slowly suffocated. When the illness was finally discovered and the Unfortunate Buried Alive were dug up, it became clear that at some point in the process the paralysis had worn off and the bloody fingernails of the Unwillingly Interred were evidence of their vain attempts to escape. A hideous death, to my mind. I couldn't sleep for weeks after watching that movie.

A psychic later told me that I'd died in a previous life due to being buried alive or maybe drowned or perhaps suffocated with a pillow—just choose one of the air-restricted methods—and that was why the movie had affected me so profoundly. I can't verify the accuracy of my previous causes of death, but I do know that anything dealing with being unable to breathe thrusts me into spasms of terror.

As I said, I woke up in a coffin, but I didn't know that right away.

The first thing I noticed was a putrid smell. A unique stench consisting of backed-up sewer, rotted meat, blood, mold, mildew, and dead bodies. The smell was so horribly potent that it caused me to become aware of the second thing: it was very dark. The reason the smell triggered me to notice the darkness was because as soon as I got a good whiff of it, my stomach heaved. I tried to sit up, or roll over, because I didn't want to throw up on myself, and I was certain that vomit was in my immediate future.

My effort to sit up caused me to bang my head against an unexpected barrier, which led me to discover there was a ceiling directly above my body. I began to push against it and quickly deduced it was an immovable object—or at least a very heavy one.

Then I panicked.

The feeling of my hands pushing against the resisting material immediately triggered a cellular memory of the aforementioned movie, and I started to scream, which shifted my attention away from throwing up. This proved to be very helpful. Fear is a powerful motivator. Like the mothers who lift multi-ton vehicles off their children, imagining myself locked in a box for my ride onto the Entry Ramp to Eternity allowed me to become Hulk-like in my strength, and to force open what turned out to be the substantial lid of an old coffin.

I sat up, still screaming, the sound reverberating off the

walls of the small, decrepit building I'd awakened in. A building that smelled extraordinarily bad.

Raising the lid on the coffin allowed me to see the sunlight filtering in through the broken front door. I couldn't tell how much time had passed, but it was obviously day. A chunk of my life was missing. I valiantly tried to reconstruct the chain of events that had brought me to this moment, and failed.

I stopped screaming—mostly because it hurt my throat—and let my eyes adjust to the dim light. Being able to see where I was made things worse. Instead of only suspecting I was up shit creek, I now had verification.

The building was an old, rundown mausoleum. Low spots in the cement floor were filled with stagnant, rancid water mixed with blood from several blatantly dead bodies. Even in the limited light, it was clear that no human in any state of aliveness could be the color of the remains scattered around that room. The place looked like a human slaughterhouse. Back in the corner were bones and pieces of rotting clothing, which gave evidence to the likelihood that whatever was going on here had been going on for a very long time.

Needless to say, I had to get out.

I assumed that whoever had killed all those people was probably coming back to get me. I didn't have time to think about why I was still alive—why the murderer had left me in the coffin instead of adding me to the collection on the floor. It occurred to me I was probably in shock, which explained the strange, fuzzy feeling in my head.

Since the lid of the coffin had only swung back on its hinge and was still standing straight up on one side, I couldn't brace myself by holding onto both edges to lift up. I grabbed onto the available surface and put my other hand down alongside my legs and felt my hand sink into clumps of dirt or sand. I pulled my knees up and heard a soft clattering sound as something knocked against the side of the coffin. I reached my hand in to find what had made the noise and closed my fingers around a long, stick-like thing. I brought it up into the light and found myself in possession of a human bone. I had been lying on top of whoever had been buried in that coffin.

Holy shit!

My stomach lurched again. I rose to my feet as if pulled by ropes. Looking down, I could clearly see the remains of the original resident. I brushed off as much of the decomposed material as I could from the rear of my pants with shaking hands and apologized silently to the person I was scattering into the air.

The coffin I was now standing in was situated on a pedestal about three feet off the floor. The area close around it was filled with the dead bodies and pools of bloody water. I would have to jump, which under the best of circumstances called on grace I hadn't cultivated, and to jump while wearing four-inch heels would guarantee a painful outcome. But, if my choice was to wait in the coffin for the psychopath to return or take my chances with a sprained ankle, I'd choose the sprain anytime.

Not being adept in physical situations, it took me a moment to realize that I could crouch, sit on the open edge of the coffin and scoot down, finding a small space for the ball of my foot to land on one of the few dry spaces on the floor and then ease myself away from the pedestal.

That's what I did, all the while listening for any sound

that would alert me to the return of the insane person who'd brought me there.

I walked on tiptoes through the carnage to the door, unable to avoid wading through puddles of slimy, bloody water, and finally reached the stairs leading up to the light. My stomach had been clinched so tightly I'd barely breathed since I got out of the coffin. I climbed up the stone steps and shoved the door, which swung open on rusty hinges, making that sound always present in horror movies. Then I stepped out into the sunshine and found myself in the middle of an old graveyard.

I heard sounds of traffic nearby and moved in that direction. I kept glancing behind me to see if it had been a trap; if someone—or something—was going to spring out at me from behind one of the huge gravestones and haul me back into the pit of hell, but I was alone.

I must have been quite a sight as I walked out of the ornate, cast iron gates of the graveyard and crossed the parking lot of McDonalds.

Chapter 13

$\mathcal{I}$ had no idea where I was.

Another beautiful day in paradise had gotten all dressed up and started without me. The sun beamed almost directly overhead, making it about noon. Shielding my eyes with my hand, I spun in a slow circle, searching for the mountains to give me a sense of where I was. Denver is a consistent distance from various distinctive peaks and I always got my bearings by checking out my location in relation to the mountains, as well as the ever-present downtown skyscrapers.

Turns out I was within walking distance of Devereux's club. I never knew there was an old graveyard tucked away back behind fast food row. Well, you know what they say about learning something new every day.

High pitched giggles drew my squinty eyes down from the horizon and I found myself gazing at a clump of little girls, all holding dripping ice cream cones. As they surrounded me, one sticky-fingered angel said, "You're funny!" This caused another wave of gleeful laughter.

"I'm funny?"

That was apparently hilarious.

Another sweet cherub said, "What are you doing in the middle of the parking lot? Are you dancing? What's all that stuff on you?"

I looked down at myself and discovered I was covered in everything I'd found back in the death pit in the graveyard. Including dried blood, which was all over my hands.

Gasping, I immediately leaped to the most drastic conclusion: that the blood was mine. I inspected myself, searching for wounds or cuts, anything that would explain the stains, but I didn't find anything. And since I had no recollection of what'd transpired during the missing hours—and at that moment I wasn't up for exploring the disgusting possibilities—I gave myself permission to stuff the entire matter deep inside my psychological Do Not Enter zone.

A pretty little brown-eyed tyke ventured a couple of tentative steps in my direction, pointed and yelled, "You smell!"

That was definitely some kind of cosmic cue. Simultaneously, anxious mothers scurried forth from everywhere, retrieved their children and whisked them back to the play area.

"What did I tell you? Never talk to strangers!" one mother scolded, as she pulled her child away, tossing frightened glances back over her shoulder.

I raised my arm up to my nose and sniffed. Yuck. I did smell. In fact, I smelled worse than horrible. Just like that ghastly place. No wonder the moms had treated me as if I was a carrier of the black plague. And I could only imagine the visual I presented.

I fished in my pocket to see if the cash I'd put there the night before had survived my mysterious experience, and I pulled out a handful of bills and coins. Even though I could've walked to Devereux's club, the memories of the previous night left a bad taste in my mouth. I had no desire to make a return visit. All I wanted to do was go home, take off the toe-smashing boots and crawl into a hot bath.

I'd just spied a telephone booth and headed in that direction to call for a cab, when a police cruiser pulled into the parking lot and blocked my path. Either I really did appear suspicious enough to draw the attention of a passing cop car, or someone in the restaurant had called the police to deal with the crazy lady.

Two very young officers got out of the car and walked cautiously over to me. I don't know what I expected, but it wasn't what I got.

"Are you Dr. Knight?"

"How do you know that? I mean, yes."

"Are you all right?"

"Yes. No. I'm not all right. I just woke up in coffin in a graveyard and I'm covered in stuff I don't even want to think about."

"Are you wounded?"

"No. I don't think so. Not physically, anyway."

"Is that your blood on your hands, Dr. Knight?"

I held my hands out and inspected again, "I don't know. How do you know my name?"

"An FBI agent working with the Denver PD put out a red flag on you. Said you'd gone missing last night. Your photo's been running on the local TV stations all morning. You must be an important person, because we're not usually allowed to act this fast on a missing person report. It looks like you've had a rough night. If you'll come with us, we can sort everything out and get you some help."

He took another step toward me and scrunched up his nose

as he approached. "Wow. Where did you say you've been?"

A quick visual communication passed between them. Eye contact so covert that if I hadn't been trained to notice such things, I'd have missed it. The look said, "Potential Disturbed Person." I knew that look well, having shared it with other professionals in various mental health settings. It's a shorthand code for a set of behaviors—behaviors that calmed the patient and encouraged cooperation. And, while I could understand why they might slide me into that category, I wasn't willing to assume the role.

I was in no mood to be cooperative or polite. My brain had finally kicked back into gear. Along with the fear and confusion I'd experienced since waking up in one of the levels of Hades, I was also pissed. Pissed at whoever dragged me to this place and pissed at being handled. The officers clearly thought I was hallucinating about waking up in a coffin in a graveyard, so I decided to cut to the chase.

I'd been abducted, brought to a maniac's lair, and who knew what else. Now was as good a time as any to take the cops on a tour of Horror Central. I pivoted and trotted back toward the entrance gate to the old graveyard.

"Hey! Stop! Where are you going?"

"I'm going to show you where I've been."

I called on my last reserves of glucose and sprinted through the gate into "Capitol Hill Cemetery, an Historical Landmark," with the cops close on my heels.

"Dr. Knight! You've obviously had some kind of trauma; you're not thinking clearly. Let us take you downtown. Stop or we'll have to restrain you."

"Restrain me, my ass. You'll have to catch me first."

If they were going to assume I was irrational, at least I could add some interesting fuel to the fire. I didn't like being treated as an incompetent—even if they meant well—and I never had played nicely with authority figures. It occurred to me that the officers might not know the old graveyard was back there, either, since it was well hidden. If that were the case, it was little wonder my story sounded even more fantastic than it would've anyway.

My run through the graveyard was really quite impressive. I managed to find my way back to the ramshackle mausoleum without falling, being obstructed by the city's finest, or turning an ankle. There was something to be said for adrenaline.

I heard one of the officers yell into his communicator, requesting backup, as they chased along behind me, dodging gravestones and statues.

"Dr. Knight! Stop! We're only trying to help you!"

I skidded to a halt a few feet from the door of the death chamber, and pointed. The police hadn't expected the race to end so suddenly. It was all they could manage not to crash into me as they put on their own brakes.

"There!" I jabbed my finger in the air. "Through that door is a stairway. There are dead bodies inside."

"Come on, Dr. Knight. No more games. Let's get you back to the police station. You can explain everything to the detectives. We've been instructed to bring you in immediately. The orders came straight from the chief."

The shorter of the two officers reached out and grabbed my upper arm and tugged gently, coaxing me to accompany him as he started walking back toward the cemetery entrance.

"Did you know there was a cemetery back here?" he said

to his partner, who shook his head.

For some reason, getting me back to the police station seemed more important than investigating my story, so I opted for drastic measures. I wrenched my arm out of his hand and leaped over to the door and pulled it open. The smell made my stomach turn. I doubled over and yelled at the cops, "Go on! Nothing normal can smell that bad. You at least have to check it out!"

Each officer put a hand up to his face, covering his mouth and pinching his nose, trying to stave off the smell. The taller one gagged. "That is one godawful smell. Maybe some animal died in there. Let's take a look."

I moved away from the door, putting as much space as possible between me and the stench. I bent forward, bracing my hands just above my knees, still trying not to vomit.

"I'll go down and see what we've got. You stay up here with Dr. Knight."

The smaller cop went through the door and down the stairs, and only a couple of seconds passed before he yelled, "Jesus, Mary, and Joseph!" and scrambled back up the stairs, his face gone pasty and his eyes wide.

"What's wrong with you, McCarthy? You're pale as a ghost!"

"Go down and see for yourself, Landers. A picture's worth a thousand words."

Landers went through the door and I heard a gagging sound and then, "Shit!"

He raced back up the stairs and out into the slightly fresher air, just as the requested backup arrived and put their hands over their noses, too.

A few minutes later, I leaned against a large statue of an angel, drinking from the cup of steaming McDonald's coffee one of the officers handed me, while the new arrivals investigated the carnage inside the tomb. Finding something that grotesque had to be the worst part of police work.

McCarthy called for the officers whose job would be to get up close and personal with whatever was down there. He turned to me and stared, appearing a little green around the edges.

"I apologize, Dr. Knight. You were right. There are dead bodies down there. I haven't been on the Force that long, but this definitely qualifies as the worst thing I've seen. Were you really in there all night?"

"I guess so. I can't remember. All I know for sure is that I woke up there this morning."

"This place is going to be swarming with experts any minute, so it would probably be best if you let us take you downtown so you can get away from here. You know the media's going to show up, too, and I don't think you want to face the world in that condition." He pointed to my grisly attire and shook his head. "Do *you* have a psychologist to talk to?"

I snorted. "Well, now that you mention it, I'm not sure any of them would believe me. I'm not even sure I believe me."

He signaled to a female cop who'd just arrived and asked her to take me downtown. He studied me again. "I'm glad you were persistent."

"That's a nice word for it." I smiled at him. He walked away, talking into his cell phone.

Exhausted, I followed the policewoman out of the cemetery and into her black and white. She opened all the windows, glanced at me in the rearview mirror and said, "No offense." We pulled away just as the caravan of TV news vehicles arrived and I was glad I didn't have to string two coherent sentences together because I would have failed. I hoped the process at the police station would be quick, but I suspected I was doomed to disappointment.

Thanks to the manic media circus camped out around police headquarters, I had to be smuggled in through the underground parking structure and secretly ushered in through an old fire exit. It seems my fifteen minutes of fame had caused quite a frenzy. My abduction had gotten linked with the murder investigation, and the vampire theme was simply too rich for the tabloids to pass up.

Sitting at the police station was like having one of those dreams about being in high school again. The one where no one talks to you and everyone walks wide circles around you, staring, pointing, and laughing.

No one was laughing, but anyone who got within ten feet of me cringed, recoiled, and rebounded away, giving me a wide berth. They were shocked to find their nostrils assailed by smells better suited to battlefields than to a psychologist whose face had evidently been on television all morning.

As one officer so succinctly put it, "There just aren't words for that smell."

It didn't take long for me to give my statement, because all I could remember was the last couple of hours. I didn't know what'd happened prior to my waking up and I had no clue about who'd brought me there.

But it turned out I didn't have to worry about getting out of there quickly. In fact, taking my statement in the close quarters of the badly ventilated station proved to be such a challenge that my hosts eagerly arranged for me to be taken over to the lab.

I'd expected to be headed off to the shower and outfitted with one of those delightful orange garments, but that didn't happen.

In fact, ever since I'd arrived at the police station things had been strange.

I'd been the focus of several whispered conversations, each containing the words "the chief."

I was escorted to the lab and was waiting for a blood sample to be taken, when the double doors burst open and a heavyset, white-haired, fifty-something male strode into the room. Everyone around me froze in mid-action and came to attention.

The new arrival signaled to the others, who scurried over immediately.

I would have just stared out the window, waiting for the bureaucratic huddle to end, if it hadn't been for the fact that various faces kept turning in my direction.

I might have been in shock, but I wasn't a complete vegetable. Clearly, those people were talking about me.

For a brief moment before the older man left, all the eyes in the group turned to me.

What the hell was going on? What weren't they telling me?

I hadn't had much experience with the police, but being treated like a skin-sloughing leper wasn't anywhere in my expectations.

The lab technician who'd earlier been preparing my arm for the blood sample came back and I said, "Who was that?"

He kept his eyes riveted on his task and said, "Chief Cassidy."

"Why was he talking about me?"

Ignoring my question, he responded, "There, all finished. The officer will take you back now."

He wrote my name on the samples, gathered up his materials and nodded to a uniform officer standing by the door.

The officer led me back to the detectives' bullpen. I figured I was going there to answer more questions—not that I had any answers—and I mentally prepared myself for a long stay. I was surprised when they quickly said I was free to go. It seemed they were taking me home and someone would come to my house later to pick up my contaminated clothing.

That piece of information drew several incredulous "What?" responses from various detectives, and I heard someone say I must have powerful friends who could roust the chief out of bed before the crack of dawn to start the search for me, postpone the interrogation and over-ride all the proper procedures.

Powerful friends? I was sure they had me confused with someone else, but that didn't matter. As long as this ordeal was over and I was being taken home, I'd claim to know the Queen of England. Hell, I'd claim to *be* the Queen of England.

In addition to everything else this situation was, it was humbling.

The pleasure of driving me home once again fell to the policewoman who'd brought me to the station, because, after all, the back seat of her unit was already tarnished. I half expected her to put down newspaper for me to sit on and, frankly, that wouldn't have been a bad idea.

"You're Dr. Knight, right? I'm Officer Colletta. I saw your advertisement in the paper. The one they were talking about on TV this morning. The one that says you're the Vampire Psychologist." She examined me in her rearview mirror.

"Yes. I'm Kismet Knight. I'm afraid to know what they were saying about me on TV, so I'm not even going to ask."

She didn't volunteer the information.

"That must be an interesting job—being the Vampire Psychologist. I mean, what do you do, exactly? Are there really people who think they're vampires?"

She lowered her voice and gave me serious eyes in the mirror. "Are there *really* vampires?"

"If you'd asked me that question a week ago, I'd have said there are people who are disturbed enough to believe they're vampires, and that it's all mental illness and acting out. But after the things I've seen in the last week, all I can say now is 'I don't know'."

She seemed almost magically able to keep the car on the road and watch me in the mirror at the same time. "We've had murders lately. Murders where the victims are drained of blood. Do you know about those?"

"I heard something about that."

"Maybe the murderer is one of your clients?"

Well. Thank you for raising a horrible possibility I hadn't considered. "I hope not."

We rode in silence the rest of the way to my house. As we pulled up in front, Officer Colletta said, "I'm surprised the cameras aren't here yet. You'd better prepare yourself for a media blitz. You probably won't have much privacy for a while."

I sighed. "I'm afraid you're right. Thanks for everything."

She met my eyes again and nodded. I got out of the cruiser and she pulled away.

I'd just stumbled up to my front door when I heard the screech of tires and the slam of a car door. I assumed the news vans had caught up with me, and was surprised to hear a familiar voice.

"Where the *fuck* have you been?" Alan demanded, bounding toward me. His face was red, deep frown lines etched the skin between his eyes, and the veins in his forehead bulged.

"I've been out all night searching for you. I told you to wait in front of the club. Where did you go? You look terrible. What's all over you? And what's that gross smell?"

He stepped away from me like he'd received an electrical shock.

As he yelled at me, the psychic numbness that had kept me from feeling the depth of the hideous experience receded, and I stood there trembling. The inner dam broke. Tears raced down my cheeks. I slumped onto the porch, tumbled over on my side, and sobbed loudly.

Alan cursed under his breath.

He kneeled down next to me. "Geez, don't cry. I'm sorry, Kismet. I didn't mean to be a jerk. I was just so worried. I heard on the police scanner that they'd found you, and then something about dead bodies. I guess I added up the numbers wrong and overreacted. I felt responsible for taking you to that club and for whatever happened to you.

"And now you stroll up to your front door, obviously in one piece, and I'm so relieved to see you and so pissed at myself for putting you in danger."

He sniffed the air.

"But we need to get you into the house and out of those clothes, because I never thought I'd say this to you, but you smell worse than anything I've ever smelled. Plus, the media vultures will be here any minute."

The professional part of me knew that I was sobbing because it was a natural physical reaction to the kind of trauma I'd experienced, but the little girl part was simply crying because it had been a terrible night and she wanted to be held on someone's lap and rocked to sleep. She wanted to feel safe again. To feel normal again.

"Let's take these boots off out here, okay?" He slid them off my feet and tossed them into the bushes. He pulled me up, put his arm around me, asked for my alarm code and opened the door.

I still couldn't stop crying long enough to speak in full sentences, so I was grateful he seemed intent on helping me. Once the reality had melted through the defenses I'd created to weather the nightmare, I was hanging by very thin threads and was happy to have a friend running underneath me with a net. Hopefully, the net wasn't accompanied by men in white coats.

Still holding onto me, he helped me up the stairs to the bathroom and propped me against the sink while he turned on the water for my shower.

"I'm going to leave the door open, if that's all right with you, because after you step into the shower, I'm going to take these clothes and bag them up for the forensics team. They'll want to analyze all the various . . . substances."

He shook his head. "I can't believe the chief made them let you wear the clothes home."

He really did look like he'd been up all night, and I was touched by the concern in his eyes.

I gave a limp shrug. "Sure. Leave the door open. That's fine," I sniffled, as I peeled off my clothes without waiting for him to leave the room.

"Uh, uh, I'm gonna go find that bag. I'll be right back." He flew down the stairs.

Sometimes things get very simple. Standing under that stream of hot water was the best thing I'd ever experienced. Not even chocolate or orgasms could top it on the list of wonderful things at that moment.

I washed my hair several times and used every good-smelling soap product I had on the plastic shelf that hung from my shower head. I scrubbed my nails and finally just laid down in the tub and let the water beat down on me. Ambrosia.

"Kismet? Are you okay?" Alan yanked back the shower curtain.

I just stared up at him, unable to move even one muscle in response.

"I'm sorry. I didn't mean to burst in on you like that. I couldn't see you in the shower and I thought you might have fallen down or something."

I didn't seem to have any opinions about him opening the shower curtain or seeing me lying naked in the tub. Nothing was more important than enjoying feeling like a warm, limp noodle. I couldn't get worked up about my blatant nudity or anything else. I was so happy to be home—so happy to be safe. And clean. It would have taken an earthquake to jar me out of my Zen tranquility.

Now that I smelled better, I realized I'd shared my aromatic carry-out with Alan, and he was less than springtime fresh. Whatever had been on my clothes was now on his.

I raised my arm. "Give me a hand, would you?"

He pulled me to my feet, his eyes moving slowly down my body.

I pinched my nose closed. "Anything strike you about your state of hygiene since you helped me upstairs?"

He glanced down at himself, half grinned and scrunched up his nose.

"I think you'd better add your clothes to the bag for the forensics team and step in here with me. That smell doesn't work any better on you than it did on me."

His eyebrows shot up and then he shrugged. "How can I refuse such an enticing invitation?"

He sloughed off the fouled clothing and gingerly stepped into the tub, making sure he kept his back to me.

He had an astoundingly nice ass. Firm, round, and begging to be palmed. I stood at the far end of the shower and watched the muscles in his back ripple as he soaped his arms.

After he'd washed everything he wanted to without turning around, he finally shifted his body and faced me, his compass enthusiastically showing true north. My eyes feasted on the impressive erection and he stared at me as he lathered himself there.

I felt an earthquake.

"Oh, my," I uttered without thinking. I fought the urge to reach out and touch someone.

We admired each other in silence, eyes caressing where

hands wished to be.

He turned off the water and ran his fingers through his wet hair, pushing it back from his face. His lovely purple-blue eyes sparkled mischievously, and his cheeks were flushed. Moisture beads glistened on the muscles of his chest.

He stepped forward, brushing my arm as he reached for the towels on the rack outside the shower. My arm tingled and became the epicenter for waves of pleasure sensations. He handed me a towel, slowly dried himself off and stepped out of the tub.

I stole another quick peek at his admirable erection and argued with myself about what I was thinking. I followed him, fastened the towel above my breasts and moved over to the sink. I wiped off the mirror with my hand, leaned in and stared at my reflection. None the worse for wear, if you didn't notice my spacey, glazed-over eyes. The normally sparkling sky blue didn't seem so vibrant right then.

Alan made good use of the extra toothbrush I found, and we stood side by side, silently gazing at each other in the mirror. I don't let just anyone watch me take care of dental business.

I brushed my teeth, flossed and used every kind of mouthwash that I had in my medicine cabinet before I finally felt semi-normal.

"What do you need now?" he asked.

Knowing exactly what I needed, I turned to him and met his kind eyes. "I want to curl up in my bed, under my covers, and I want you to hold me."

The corners of his lips quirked up in an amused grin, which I interpreted as an affirmative. I grabbed his hand, led us into my bedroom and pulled down the bed covers. I dropped my towel and slid between the sheets. Giving him my best "come hither" smile, I patted the mattress next to me, sending a clear message. It had been a long time since the Brazen Hussy part of my personality had a chance to come out and play.

He stood and gazed down at me, hesitating only a few seconds before he joined me.

I wrapped myself around him, feeling finally safe, and sighed. "Thank you for being here with me. You're a good friend."

"A friend? You're giving me way too much credit. I'm not having very friend-like thoughts at the moment."

I met his eyes. "What kind of thoughts are you having?" As if I didn't know, even without the compass to point the way.

"I'm-in-bed-with-a-beautiful-woman thoughts. And I know this isn't the right time to be romantic, because you need to rest and recuperate."

"It's very sweet of you to take care of me."

I didn't want to think about where I'd been all night, or what might have happened, or the media frenzy that was waiting for me. I absolutely didn't want to think about the probability that there really were vampires. All I wanted was to be held, touched, connected without any expectations or rules or complications.

I brushed his lips lightly with mine and slid my hand down the muscled plane of his belly, down over the warm, firm length of his erection. He moaned, grabbed a handful of my wet hair and pulled me tight against him as he closed his lips over mine with hungry need.

"I haven't even begun to take care of you," he breathed against my mouth.

Our bodies melted into each other as we took the kiss deeper, allowing all the emotions and tensions of the previous hours to find release through the firestorm of our mutual attraction.

We kissed until every nerve in my body was sizzling and burning.

He pulled away, his breathing ragged and his voice husky. "I don't want to take advantage of this situation. Tell me to stop and I will."

All I could think of was how good he felt next to me, how warm and sweet his mouth was on mine. And after the freak circus I'd experienced the night before, the pleasure of being with a normal male felt overwhelmingly right. Safe. Pure, primitive desire with no insanity attached to it. No fear.

"Don't stop." I ran my hands over his smooth chest.

He rolled me over onto my back and began licking and sucking my nipples, trailing his hand down my stomach. His body was fever hot and his touch like liquid fire.

He brought his face up to mine. "Your body is beautiful. I've imagined this since the first moment I saw you."

We kissed each other wildly, hands exploring, his erection rubbing against my leg rhythmically as he slid his finger into the hot wetness between my thighs. I arched my back and opened myself to him, as a wave of ecstasy built inside me. He straddled me and licked his way down my body until his tongue finished what his finger had started. I screamed and dug my fingernails into his shoulders as he laved me over the edge. Quivering, I grabbed his hair and pulled him up onto me, aching for him to fill me, longing to be joined in that primal way with someone. Wanting to give him what he'd given me.

Then there was loud pounding on my front door.

"Dr. Knight? Denver PD. Your door was unlocked. We heard a scream. Are you all right? Do you need help?"

Alan leaped up and ran into the bathroom.

I sat up in the bed and yelled, "No. Everything's fine. Stay where you are. I'll be right down."

Damn, damn, damn! That's twice I've left my door unlocked in as many days, and both times I got interrupted in the middle of something delicious.

Still reveling in the spell cast by Alan's magic mouth, the muscles between my legs contracted with desire as I breathed to recover myself. I heard the shower start in the bathroom and I was tempted to sneak in there so Alan wouldn't have to finish without me. Thinking about that provided an unexpected orgasmic aftershock and I forced myself to swing my legs over the side of the bed and stand up.

If only the cops had waited 15 more minutes. Nothing about my world made sense anymore.

I walked over to the closet, pulled on my pink terry-cloth bathrobe, tied the sash, and shuffled down the stairs.

Chapter 14

$\mathcal{D}$r. Knight? I'm Detective Robles and this is my partner, Detective Nyland. We have a few more questions for you, and the forensics team is sending someone by to pick up the clothes you were wearing last night. Do you have them bagged and ready?"

"Almost. I'll get them."

I pointed to the interior of my house. "Why don't you go into the living room and have a seat. Just give me few minutes."

I went up to my bedroom, peeled off my comfortable pink robe, put on fresh underwear and stood in front of the closet, trying to decide what would be appropriate dress for a police interview. I rifled through my professional clothes, considering whether a skirt or pants would be better. Then I stopped and shook my head. Who was I trying to impress? The cops had seen me covered in blood and gore and smelling like an outhouse. I pulled one of my new sweatsuits off the hanger and slipped it on.

I was going to run a brush through my hair, but it had already dried in long curls and sometimes it was better to leave it alone, otherwise all the curl would turn into frizz.

I listened for a few seconds and couldn't hear the shower running in the bathroom so I approached the door and knocked lightly. "Alan?"

"Yeah. Come on in."

He was sitting naked on the edge of the bathtub, in the pose of that famous statue, The Thinker.

Something about the incongruity of the situation made me laugh out loud.

He snorted. "Well. I'm glad someone thinks anything about this day is funny."

I went over and knelt down in front of him, taking his face in my hands. "I'm sorry we got interrupted before. It was wonderful. You were wonderful. I'm upset you had to finish without me."

He grinned. "You might not have been in the bathroom with me, but—trust me—you were there."

I shifted forward and kissed his warm lips. "Can I have a rain check?"

He pulled me in for another kiss. "You have a standing invitation. I hate to change such a titillating subject, but I assume the locals have come to collect your clothes. Before I got back into the shower, I went through the pockets, retrieved everything and tucked the filthy duds into that yellow bag there."

He pointed and shook his head. "Unfortunately, I should've been more careful when I was enthusiastically tearing off my clothes to join you in the tub, because my brand new Fruit Of The Looms wound up getting tossed on top of a really nasty hunk of something on your jeans, and they're trashed. I don't think sending my stuff to the lab would be helpful, since they're just a repeat of yours. When the officers leave I'll use your washing machine, if you don't mind. Otherwise, I won't have any clothes to put on."

A tantalizing visual formed in my brain. "Wow. That raises all sorts of interesting possibilities. A stranded naked man in my house, at my mercy. And who said dreams don't come true?" I laughed. "Certainly. My appliances are at your disposal. It's the least I can do." I waggled my eyebrows at him.

"Well, it might be the least you can do, but it isn't all you can do . . ."

I smiled at him, "We'll have to talk about that later. I'd better get back down there." I kissed him again, picked up the bag and closed the door.

The detectives stood when I entered the room and I handed over the yellow bag. It resembled one of those biohazard containers from a disaster movie; an eye-searing slap of color. All it needed was a skull and crossbones.

I offered to make coffee and invited them to follow me into the kitchen, so we could continue talking while I ground the beans. A few minutes later a woman from the forensics team joined us and we all drank coffee while the detectives asked me the same questions they'd asked earlier. I had little to add to my original statement, and in less than a half-hour I was showing them out.

I walked them to the door and paused with my hand on the knob. "Thank you for being so kind to me today and for coming over here to pick up the clothing."

"Just doing our job. Your Mr. Devereux can be very persuasive."

"My Mr. Devereux?"

The detectives stole a quick glance at each other. "Yes. It was at his request the Chief bent the rules for you. They seem to have an *unusual* relationship. Mr. Devereux is a very influential man. By the way, you've got quite a bit of company out there. You might want to . . ."

I opened the door and was immediately overwhelmed by voices screaming questions, bright lights shining in my eyes and cameras in my face. Even knowing I'd be the focus of attention, however briefly, hadn't prepared me for the reality of finding my front lawn filled with aggressive strangers who were competing to record my smallest utterance.

The detectives took charge of the situation, strode through the door and reminded all the reporters that they were trespassing on private property. I closed the door and pressed my weight against it.

I'd learned my lesson. This time I made sure all the locks on the door were securely engaged and the alarm was on. I didn't want any more juicy experiences thwarted by unexpected company.

After giving the detectives a couple of minutes to disperse the crowd, I peeked through the slightly raised slat of a mini-blind, and saw several uniform police officers holding the reporters back near the street. I hoped the media would lose interest in me before Monday because I had a full client schedule and I wasn't willing for things to get any more out of control.

And what was that about Devereux? A relationship with the police chief? Thinking of him reminded me of the violent scene I'd witnessed in the basement of The Crypt. It also reminded me of my overwhelming desire to crawl into his lap. Both those things seemed like they'd happened in another life. I didn't know whether to be disgusted with myself for letting my raging hormones get me into so much trouble, or be grateful that my long dry spell with men might be over.

But, what if he really is a vampire?

I decided all of it was too much to deal with and I'd think about it later. Yeah. Me and Scarlett O'Hara. I might get tossed out of the Psychologists Club for saying this, but a little denial never hurt anyone.

"Hey," I yelled up the stairs. "They're gone. You can come down now. There's coffee."

I went into the kitchen to forage for snacks to go with the coffee and then picked up the phone to check messages. A synthetic-voice from the phone company notified me that my message queue was full and I'd need to delete some before I could receive anymore. I didn't know how many the system held, but I'd apparently exceeded the limit.

I listened to the first few seconds of several messages, saving them if they were from clients or potential clients, deleting them if they were media calls, and then heard the sweetly sensual voice of Vaughan the chiropractor saying something about our dinner date tonight.

Shit!

I'd totally forgotten about Vaughan. It seemed like weeks since I'd made the date—back when there were no men on the horizon—and now I couldn't even imagine keeping it. I didn't feel remotely like the same person anymore. But as I listened further, he went on to say that he'd seen my story on the morning news and hoped I was okay, and of course, our date was off, but would I please call him and let him know I was alive and well. Very sweet. I wrote a note on the white-board on my kitchen wall, reminding myself to call him.

I heard the sound of bare feet padding into the kitchen and turned, expecting to find a luscious naked man, and instead burst out laughing. Alan had rooted around in my closet and found an old pair of torn, pink sweat pants that rode up to his mid-calf and fit him like a second skin, and a very small, tight T-shirt that said "Woman Power!" Even though he should've looked ludicrous, it was all I could do to keep myself from leaping on him and finishing what we'd started earlier.

He smiled at my reaction, and strutted around in a circle so I could see all sides of the spectacular presentation.

"I didn't want to put on anything that I might stretch out and ruin, and I figured you probably weren't too attached to these. Besides, I look great in pink."

"I think you probably look great in anything." *Not to mention in nothing.*

He gave a slow blink and sauntered over, his face very serious. "Thank you. I believe you mean that."

The close proximity of his body and the sudden shift in intensity surprised me, and I felt myself melting into a puddle on the floor. I leaned against the counter and cleared my throat. "Of course I do."

We stared at each other for a moment, then I forced my eyes away. As delicious as it would have been to return to my bedroom and spend the rest of the afternoon exploring each other's erogenous zones, the shock and confusion of the morning had worn off and fatigue was setting in. And it was time to face all the things I didn't want to think about.

My stomach growled. "Are you as hungry as I am?"

He smiled.

"For food, I mean?"

"Yes, as a matter of fact I am. Shall we have something delivered? What'll it be? Pizza? Chinese? Mexican? Lady's choice."

"How will the delivery person get through that horde of reporters out there?"

"I'll call in and request a police escort to the front door," he said.

We negotiated the food and I went into the living room to collapse on the couch while Alan performed the phone duties.

"I'm going to put these filthy clothes in the washing machine, then we need to talk. Something traumatic happened to you last night. Obviously, you didn't disappear of your own volition and I want to hear every detail. No matter how inconsequential." He hesitated for a few seconds. "And I have something to tell you."

The tone of his voice indicated I wasn't going to like his news, so, being my usual impatient self, I dragged myself off the couch and followed him into the laundry room.

"What do you have to tell me?"

"Hold on a minute."

I drummed my fingers on the counter while he loaded the washer.

He shook his head and smiled. "Such a control freak. Come on. Let's go back into the living room."

He grabbed my hand, pulled me to the couch and we sat.

I didn't say out loud that I thought we had control freak

characteristics in common.

I sighed impatiently.

"So? You're starting to make me nervous. Did something bad happen? I mean something in addition to what happened to me?"

He nodded. "Yes. Something bad happened. Do you remember the call I got last night at the club? The one where I was told there was another body?"

"Yes, I remember."

"The body they found was Emerald Addison's."

All the air leaked out of me like a punctured balloon and I sagged back into the couch cushions, speechless.

Alan patted my hand. "I'm sorry. This must be hard to hear. She was your client."

I didn't correct him. "What happened to her?"

"She was found in the alley behind an apartment building in Capitol Hill. The report said she had a friend living there named Eric Weiss. Her body was drained of blood, same as the others. It was a vampire attack, although the locals aren't seriously considering that angle."

I sat silently, staring at the wall.

Poor little Emerald. I wished she really had been my client so I'd have more memories of her than just our brief trip to the hospital. I wondered if Midnight and Ronald had been notified and how they were coping. And if they'd heard about my situation, they were probably worried about me, too.

I jumped up and strode to my desk, searching for my briefcase and my current client files.

Alan stood. "What's happening? What're you doing?"

"I've got to call a couple of my clients, friends of Emerald's. You saw them with me at the hospital. They must be feeling terrible."

I sat down at my desk, located the phone numbers for both of them, called, and got their answering machines. I left messages giving them my home phone number, and asked them to return the call, no matter what time they got my message. I had to do something to help, and I hoped someone would give me a clue as to what that might be.

Alan walked around behind my chair and rubbed my shoulders. "Do you want to talk about Emerald, or are you ready to tell me what happened to you last night?"

"Both, I think."

He swiveled my chair around until I was facing him, took my hands, guided me up from the chair and back over to the couch.

I studied him, searching for answers in his eyes.

"You said Emerald was killed by vampires. Do you really believe that? Are you telling me the truth? There really are vampires?"

He nodded. "Yes, I'm telling you the truth. Nothing in my background, education, or training prepared me to believe vampires really exist, but that's what I discovered. Beyond any reasonable doubt. And, for some reason I don't understand yet, more of the mindless, demented vampires are showing up in Denver."

None of that made any sense to me.

"Why is this happening all of a sudden? Has Denver had other murders in the past where the victims were drained of blood?"

"According to my research, there have been sporadic

deaths attributed to massive blood loss, but they were few and far between. It makes sense, because there've always been vampires, and some of them would have been the type who needed to kill. The death toll only became significant over the last few months."

He picked up our coffee mugs, refilled them in the kitchen and brought them back. The pink sweatpants were almost glued to his skin, leaving nothing to the imagination. The view, coming and going, made me smile, but then I remembered what we were talking about.

"Why Emerald?"

He shrugged. "That, I don't know. But I can promise you, I'll find out. So, tell me. What happened to you last night?"

He stretched out his long, pink-encased legs and crossed his ankles on the coffee table, and I curled up, my legs tucked underneath me, at the end of the couch.

"Well, after I saw you in the club and we split up to find Tom . . . Hey, that reminds me. You lied to me. You said you were going to help me search for him and then I saw you charge through the doorway to the basement. How am I supposed to trust you if you lie to me? And how do I know you're not lying about other stuff?"

He studied the carpet and shook his head. "Spank me. I've been bad." He shifted his eyes, gazing up at me from under his unfairly long eyelashes, and grinned. "I'm sorry I lied to you. But you need to know this about me: I'm dedicated to my work, and it wasn't even in the realm of possibility that I'd go off searching for Tom instead of finding out what was happening with the vampires downstairs. It's part of the job description of being the kind of obsessive-compulsive I am."

I frowned at him, but had to admit to myself that I did understand what he was saying. Having a curious mind has gotten me into more sticky situations than I could count.

"What was going on with the vampires downstairs? Why were they fighting? From what I saw, it was going to be a blood bath. Talk about *Night of the Living Dead*."

He scooted excitedly to the edge of the cushion, eager to share.

"By the time I got there, things had started to wind down and the interlopers were gone. From what I could gather, there are vampires who are challenging Devereux's rule of the coven. Bryce, the one we talked about before, is determined to take Devereux down. It seems very personal to him. The two of them definitely have unfinished business. He and his followers threatened the club manager, knowing it would piss Devereux off, and the fun began. The room was one unholy mess after the combat ended."

I grimaced. "Yeah. I saw some of the body fluids oozing out from the doorway."

He nodded. "Vampire bodies heal very quickly, so even the worst injuries repaired themselves within minutes. If it hadn't been for the blood everywhere, you wouldn't have known a vampire war was being waged."

"What did you do? Just run in and start swinging? Do you have a death wish?"

He laughed. "No. I'm adventurous. I'm courageous. I'm relentless. But I'm not stupid. Plus, I'd found out from my vampire source Ian—Deep Fang—you know, like the Watergate informer, that when a vamp loses blood, the first thing he does is seek a donor. I didn't want to be anyone's dinner, so I kept my distance until Devereux was alone in the room."

A little energy rush charged through my body. "You talked to Devereux?"

As Alan started to answer, the doorbell rang. I went over and peered through the peephole to make sure the visitor was welcome company. It was more than welcome. It was food. Police-escorted food. I cracked the door, handed out enough money to cover the bill plus a generous tip, reached out to grab the bag, offered my thanks, and closed and relocked the door. I carried the large sack of Chinese food to the kitchen table.

"Do you want to wait on the rest of the story until you've eaten, or can you continue?" Alan asked.

The smell of the food was driving me mad, and I moved around the kitchen in a blur, gathering plates, cups, and utensils. "I can eat and talk at the same time. Wow. You ordered lots."

"Oh, did you want something, too?" He laughed.

"Very funny."

I opened a new bottle of wine and poured some into each of our glasses.

We sat at the table and dived into the feast. Neither of us gained any points for table manners during the meal. The food was glorious and we ate with silent enthusiasm for a few minutes. There's nothing like stress and hunger to bring us back to our primitive roots.

For some reason I suddenly thought about the fact that vampires don't eat food. I wouldn't ever be sitting at the table sharing a meal with Devereux. At least not any meal I could force myself to contemplate. Unless, of course, we've all gone mad or there are hallucinogens in the water supply, and none of this really happened.

I paused in the food shoveling process and drank several sips of wine. "You spoke to Devereux? What did you talk about?"

Alan had already cleaned up his first helping and reached for reinforcements.

"It was strange, actually. He was in the middle of telling me about his long-standing rivalry with Bryce and all of a sudden he stopped talking and closed his eyes. Then he said, 'She is gone; he has taken her.' I started to ask who was gone, and who is 'he,' but before I could get the words out, Devereux vanished."

I claimed seconds on the egg rolls. "You mean he left the room?"

"No. He literally vanished. Vampires don't acknowledge the same limitations about time and space that we humans do. They can move through both with just a thought."

"I don't understand what you mean. Physical matter does have certain limitations. Flesh and blood bodies can't just disappear from one place and rearrange their molecules in another. We haven't caught up with *Star Trek* yet."

Alan polished off his second helping and went for the championship round, adding an impressive third layer to the sustenance already on its way down to his deceptively flat stomach.

"Devereux would say there are limitations if you believe there are. But, I've seen him vanish and reappear many times so I don't have any problem accepting that vampires can travel by thought, not only in this dimension but in all the others."

I pushed my plate away, finally satiated.

"Other dimensions? You know, every time we talk, your

stories get weirder and weirder. Are you going to tell me next that the vampires are really aliens, preparing to take over the earth? Or maybe they're controlling us with their minds, and we'll be herded into holding pens—walking blood receptacles—waiting for an impending undead feeding frenzy?"

He chuckled. "No. I'm not going to tell you any of that, but you have to admit they'd be interesting hypotheses to pursue. I'll make a note of them. Shall I continue telling you about Devereux, or would you rather make fun of my proclivities?"

"Oh, by all means, please continue."

"Anyway, after he vanished I went back upstairs, and then outside, looking for you. Of course, you weren't there, but I found Devereux leaning against the building about a half block down from the entrance to the club. He was just standing there, with his eyes closed, and when I approached he said, 'The one who has her is not only evil, but he is also insane. His mind is splintered and he is more animal than vampire'."

Alan had altered his voice, imitating Devereux's accent and unique speech patterns.

"At that point I still didn't even know who he was talking about. He said, 'I am linked with her mind so I should be able to sense her, but he has done something to mask her energy signature. He has overwhelmed her mind with his and is keeping us from communicating with each other. I have met few others who were powerful enough to do that. She is in great danger. She must be found'."

I smiled at his clever Devereux impersonation and shook my head. "You actually remember what he said, word for word? That's quite the memory you have there, Special

Agent Stevens."

"Yes, it does come in handy. I have the auditory equivalent of a photographic memory. Remember that in case you tell me something and then say you didn't."

I reached out and patted his arm. "Okay, I'll remember that. Then what happened?"

We headed back into the living room and reestablished ourselves on the couch.

He cleared his throat and shrugged. "A whole lot of nothing. Devereux vanished again and I went back into the club to search for you. I was still thinking that you were in there somewhere. And, just so you know, I kept an eye out for Tom, too, but I never saw him. I ran into Devereux's personal assistant, a snarly vamp named Luna, and I asked if she'd seen you. She said she couldn't believe so many people were interested in one, ordinary human and Devereux was beside himself that you had been taken. That was the first time I realized it was you."

He reached over and stroked my leg. "I didn't want to believe you were missing—I'm stubborn that way—so I kept looking in the club and giving people your description and asking if they'd seen you. Finally, I went back to the cop shop to see if there'd been any reports. I knew they wouldn't put out a missing person report that soon, but I was rattling cages as much as I could. Turns out I didn't need to. A couple of hours later the chief showed up in person and ordered that you become top priority. All available units went out on the street, searching for you. And they alerted the media. I've never seen anything like it before. I still don't know what happened to get the chief riled up."

"I was told Devereux called the chief."

"Devereux? What would Devereux have to do with the police chief . . .? Of course. I should've remembered. So much for my famous tape-recorder memory, eh? During one of our discussions Devereux told me he'd used his ability to control minds to create relationships with several powerful people in town. People who could smooth away any difficulties.

"It makes perfect sense now. He simply called the chief, suggested he rally the troops, and that's all it took. No one would question it. And the Chief would always think it was his own idea. Ingenious, really."

"Do you mean Devereux used mind control on the police chief?"

"Yep. The chief and a few other highly placed cops."

"Doesn't it bother you that Devereux manipulated the police? What if he uses mind control on you?"

He grinned. "I have a healthy respect for his abilities. He's the most powerful vampire I've ever run across. It might be worth it to let him take over my mind for a little while, just to see how that feels. And you have to admit, it got the job done. The cops found you."

"Actually, I found the cops. But I'll have to thank Devereux the next time I see him."

And why does thinking about seeing him feel good and bad and the same time?

"Okay, stop stalling. Tell me what happened last night."

I rearranged myself on the cushions. "I'm not stalling. There really isn't much to tell. I went outside to wait for Tom—or you—and I walked down the block and rested against the building. I suddenly had an overwhelming bad feeling—instant terror—and heard a grotesque voice calling me. I couldn't tell if the voice was coming from outside of me or inside my mind. It was like fingernails on the blackboard from hell times a thousand. The voice kept telling me to come to it. I remember thinking I just needed to stay where I was and everything would be fine. That I could just ignore it. That's the last thing I recall until I woke up this morning in the cemetery."

I told him everything about the mausoleum, the coffin I'd awakened in, the dead bodies and my encounter with the police. He sat silently while I spoke, shaking his head.

"I've had some horrible experiences since I joined the FBI, but none of them come close to being worse than what you just told me. Now I'm really sorry I was such an asshole when you came home."

"Apology accepted. We were all stressed out. I'm glad it's over. Well, except for the media fallout. I guess I can't avoid it any longer. Go ahead and tell me. How bad is it? What did they say about me on TV?"

"Pretty much what you'd expect. They played up all the occult aspects and continually referred to you as the Vampire Psychologist, with accompanying snickers. I think you're going to have to make a statement when you feel up to it. I don't think they're going to go away until you talk to them. I imagine this isn't the direction you envisioned your career moving?"

Suddenly there was a popping sound, a slight breeze and Devereux materialized in the middle of my living room.

hapter 15

"Kismet!"

What the hell? How'd he get here? And holy shit. Wouldja look at him?

Instead of his usual tight leather, Devereux was decked out in a luscious charcoal gray suit and a magnificent turquoise silk shirt. The color of the silk made his eyes appear even more spectacularly kaleidoscopic than usual. His hair shone like liquid moonlight. He could've stepped right out of the pages of a European high fashion men's magazine.

Since I had no idea what he actually did with his time, I couldn't even imagine where he'd been, spiffed up like that. I felt a brief twinge of jealousy at the thought of him dressing up for a woman. Maybe his assistant, Luna, or one of the other perfect female specimens he had working for him at The Crypt.

But then, who was I to be jealous when I'd spent part of the afternoon taking a shower and playing "show me yours and I'll show you mine" with a fixated, well-endowed FBI agent?

Devereux glided over to me, swung me up off the ground with his arms around my waist, and thoroughly kissed me. And then kissed me again.

I was stunned, but apparently willing, because I'd thrown

my arms around his neck at some point and kissed him back. Interesting to discover this entire new set of instinctual behaviors I seemed to have acquired regarding Devereux.

Pulling back slightly, he slid his lips close to my ear and whispered, "I have never felt so helpless as when I could not find you. There would have been no end to my vengeance had you been harmed."

My own, personal avenging angel. He looks like a god but talks like a character from a historical romance novel. I can sure pick 'em.

"Are you well? Did the dark one harm you?"

"Uh . . ."

There it is again. That brain-melt thing that happens to me whenever I'm within ten feet of Devereux. But, talk about bad timing.

Alan leaped up from the couch, his face a mixture of confusion and outrage. "Hey! Devereux! What's going on here? What are you doing?"

Despite that fact that it was difficult to appear threatening while wearing short, pink sweatpants and a decidedly feminist T-shirt, Alan managed to gather up sufficient testosterone to get his point across.

But Devereux wasn't interested in butting heads with anyone. He lifted me up into his arms, glanced over at Alan and whispered gently in that amazing voice, "You are tired, my friend. Lie down on the couch and sleep now."

Damned if Alan didn't do just that.

He arranged himself into a fetal position, made a few soft, snorting sounds and drifted off, smiling.

Wow. That's impressive. And disturbing. Shouldn't I be putting up some kind of fuss? And should I worry about getting used to being carried around like this?

Devereux turned his attention back to me. "You must come with me now."

There was a swoosh of air, a sound reminiscent of the crackle of electricity, and we were suddenly standing in the middle of Devereux's private room, underneath The Crypt.

He released me and I stood, head spinning, stomach churning, trying to make sense of something that was impossible to make sense of. Whatever had just happened definitely messed with my equilibrium. I wasn't sure if my legs were up to their usual task of keeping me upright.

"Please. Come and sit. You do not look well." Devereux fetched a small chair, pushed it gently against the back of my knees, and I sat. I scanned the room, recognizing all the paintings on the walls, the art supplies and the strange stash of bottles on the table.

As I perched there, trying to reclaim my balance, I got more and more annoyed. The journey through Devereux's invisible transporter—or whatever it was he'd used to get me from where I had been to where I was—had definitely rained on the good feelings that kissing him had inspired in me, and I was royally torqued. Not to mention extremely tired of finding myself in locations chosen for me by some male or another without my consent. Something in my brain snapped.

No. That's it! No more manipulating me and jerking me around.

I vaulted up from the chair—the fury of a woman pissed—shaking with rage, and got right in Devereux's face. All the anger that had been stuffed during the previous hours burst out like a five-alarm fire as I yelled at him.

"I don't want to sit. I don't want to be here. You had no right to bring me here. I didn't tell you to bring me here. I'm tired. I want to be in my own house, in my own bed, away from all your bullshit!" I punched his stomach with my fist, and then, outrageously shocked at myself, retreated a couple of steps. Definitely a case of temporary insanity.

He gasped and bent forward slightly. I'd finally done something to surprise him. He stared at me, his mouth hanging open, his eyes wide, eyebrows creeping up toward his hairline. Then he barked out a laugh, and slapped his thigh.

He straightened and grinned. "Well. I wondered when you would let your feelings out. I am glad you have chosen to share them with me."

I gave him a hard frown. I didn't appreciate that he seemed to be enjoying my outburst. In fact, he was acting downright superior about my outburst. As if he'd arranged it.

With that, the last remaining fragment of the dam burst. "Share them with you?" I screamed. "I'll show you how I'll share them with you. You pompous bastard!"

I had no idea how, but I managed to fling myself on him— flying through the air, as it were—my hands out in front of me, grasping toward his neck. It didn't occur to me that if he really was a vampire, attacking him might have larger ramifications than I'd anticipated. There was still some part of me that refused to accept Devereux could be something as horrible as a blood drinker. But I had to admit he did seem to have an extraordinary amount of physical strength. Not to mention that traveling-through-thought thing.

In an effortless movement, he caught my wrists in one of his hands, curled his arm around my waist and wrestled me down to the floor, laughing.

Of course, listening to him laugh only made me angrier,

and being restrained pretty much undid any remnants of control I still pretended to have. I struggled to get away from him and screamed at his apparent amusement. He hadn't even worked up a sweat keeping me his prisoner on the floor.

"Are you laughing at me, you Fabio-wannabe?"

He laughed harder, and then stuck out his lower lip in a pout.

"Fabio? Is he still around? My dear Kismet. You know very well that the two of us do not resemble each other. My hair is much lighter, my eyes more soulful. I have been told I am much more handsome and desirable than that particular gentleman."

Okay. It was a cheap shot. Devereux is more beautiful than most men, Fabio included. But what arrogance!

I vainly struggled to get loose. "Well. *You're* not conceited. Tell me more about how handsome and desirable you are."

He shifted so he straddled me, still holding my wrists down against the floor. The bright turquoise of his eyes was noticeably heightened by the color of his shirt. In fact, they radiated a surreal shine, as if his irises were gemstones come alive. Long, pale hair fell across my face and he threw it back with a toss of his head. His signature fragrance wafted through the air and into my nostrils, caressing the pleasure centers of my brain.

It appeared that no matter what else was happening, my attraction to Devereux remained parked at the curb, motor running.

He gave me serious eye contact. "Shall I tell you how beautiful and desirable you are?"

That seemed to squeeze some of the juice out of my anger

and I forced in a couple of deep breaths to keep my chin from quivering.

Well, I'm just pitiful. One compliment and I regress back to being a needy five-year-old. I must be exhausted.

Embarrassed by both my erratic behavior and my sloppy wardrobe, I stared down at my crumpled sweatsuit. "Oh, yeah, tell me how beautiful I look and how arousing this outfit is, Mr. Fashion Model."

He scrunched his eyebrows together and studied me for a moment.

"You are indeed beautiful, and if you wish to dress accordingly, I can accommodate you." He chuckled. "Is it safe to let you up now?"

I snorted and tried to shake him off of me, which made him start laughing again.

How annoying that he has such a great laugh.

"I will take that as a yes." With another burst of his unexplainable speed, he suddenly loomed over me, reaching down to take my hands to pull me up.

The temper tantrum had exhausted most of my remaining energy, and I frowned, giving him my hands. "What do you mean, you can accommodate me?"

After he assured himself I was up and steady on my feet, he glided over to the bed I'd seen during my first visit to this secret room. Spread out there, were several beautiful evening gowns in various colors and fabrics.

He pointed to the dresses. "I bought you a few gifts. I hope you enjoy them. I would be pleased if you would wear one tonight."

I scraped the bottom of the energy barrel and revved my

anger back up again. "Oh, I see. You have another plan for me to follow? Something else you'll manipulate me into doing, whether I want to or not?"

He flashed a wide smile. "Absolutely not. If you prefer to wear your charming sweat ensemble, that is perfectly fine with me."

I glanced down at the baggy sweatsuit again and then over at the silky creations on the bed, and was torn between wanting to touch them and not wanting Devereux to know the colorful dresses had captured my interest.

He waited silently while my inner demons fought with each other, and I saw the corner of his mouth twitch slightly as he tried to suppress a smile. I hated that my emotions and thoughts were apparently so transparent to him.

I mumbled under my breath and inched over to the bed. The gowns were lovely. Almost works of art. Even someone with my limited fashion sense could see they were amazing. My eyes were immediately drawn to a shimmering blue garment. I ran my fingers along the soft fabric with a sigh. The dress already felt as if it belonged to me.

"I love the dresses. They're beautiful. But I don't understand why you bought them for me. Where would I wear such things? And, it isn't only the dresses." I examined my bare feet. "If you'd told me you were going to zap me out of my living room, I would've put on shoes."

He smiled and strolled over to an ornate wooden armoire, opened the tall doors and pointed to boxes of shoes and drawers of exquisite lingerie. All conveniently in my size.

He bowed from the waist, a sweep of his arm indicating the collection, as if he was one of those game show models.

"I believe we have everything you require."

What is this? Vampire Cinderella? Should I be flattered or creeped out?

"Why did you get all those things for me? And why do you want me to wear them?"

He sat on the corner of the bed near me. "You are a beautiful woman. You should adorn yourself with beautiful things. And, it is appropriate for you to dress for the ceremony."

I instinctively stepped back. "Ceremony? What ceremony?"

Sacrificing a virgin? Not in this lifetime. Bride of Dracula? Dinner for the coven? Whatever it is, count me out.

"A ritual of protection. You have been taken by the darkest spirit I have ever encountered. I can feel his presence even now."

"Ritual of protection? Wait a minute. How do you know who kidnapped me? Did you have something to do with it? What do you know about my ending up in a graveyard?"

He held up a graceful hand, palm out. "I had nothing to do with your abduction, but as soon as I awakened this evening, I reconnected with your mind, read your memories and discovered what had happened. You are in great danger and I must protect you."

I don't know if he's Merlin's ghost, a vampire, a nut case, or all three, but I'm done.

"You know, this is sounding more and more like something from a B horror movie, and I don't think I want to play. I want you to call me a cab so I can go home."

I moved rapidly toward the door and he was suddenly there, standing in front of me, blocking my path.

He placed a finger under my chin and lifted my face up

so that we locked eyes, his expression very serious.

"I should have been more forthcoming with you from the beginning. I should have anticipated your need to understand and analyze everything. I did not wish to frighten you away by acting too quickly, but I see now that I have blundered. Please allow me the opportunity to make it up to you."

He bent down and pressed his lips against mine in a sweet kiss, and I took the first exit to Euphoria. Again.

I reached up and held his face in both my hands and pressed my body against his, deepening the kiss.

First I punch him, then I kiss him. I've given new meaning to the words "mood swing."

We stood melded together for not nearly long enough. I let my hands slide down his face, then stepped back. It took me a couple of tries to find my voice.

"What is it you should've told me?"

He reached for my hand. "This might take some time. It is better to be comfortable."

Hmmm. The vampire version of "Let's get in the back seat?"

He led me over to the bed, gathered up all the dresses and draped them across the back of a throne-like chair. He crawled onto the bed—which was a very arousing thing to watch—sat against the headboard and patted the space next to him, inviting me to join him. I did.

I had a brief thought about what it meant that I was in bed with another man after spending the afternoon in a very intimate encounter with Alan. Was I now being unfaithful to Alan even though we'd made no promises to each other? We hadn't pretended our sexual attraction had any future implications. Or had I been unfaithful to Devereux? For some reason that choice felt more troubling.

Wait a minute! Am I channeling a soap opera or something? I barely know either one of them and I haven't made any commitments to anyone. I'm a free agent and can do as I please. A curse on all those old Sandra Dee movies my mother used to make me sit through! Any minute now I'm going to get up and go home.

But I was immediately distracted by the fact that the bed felt so soft and welcoming, and I was half tempted to close my eyes and drift away. I forced myself to open my eyes very wide and concentrate on the painting of Devereux's mother that was visible from my vantage point.

She was so beautiful. Almost as beautiful as her son. I think her eyes were slightly more greenish blue and his are bluish green. Or maybe not. They strongly resemble each other, but I couldn't quite put my finger on what made Devereux so masculine. Perhaps his jaw was slightly stronger than hers, or his cheekbones more defined. Something. But whatever it was, there was no way I could ignore his pure maleness. Dangerous male. Yummy male.

I giggled, of all things.

"Kismet?"

"What?" I realized my mouth was hanging open and my eyelids were at half-mast.

"You are clearly more exhausted than I thought. Perhaps you should lie down and rest for a while."

"No, really. I'm fine. Just let me catch my second wind." I blinked my eyes several times and sat up straighter, turning to him. "Or coffee, maybe. Yeah, that'll do it."

He crawled down to my feet, grasped my ankles and tugged on them gently until he'd pulled me into a prone position, with my head on the pillow.

"Hey, I don't want to lie down. I don't want to . . ."

Sleep must have ambushed me, because that's the last thing I remember.

Until the dream.

Chapter 16

I'm walking through an old, run-down, abandoned house. The darkness is relieved only by the full moon shining through the large, broken windows. There's an unpleasant, musty smell masking something metallic—sweet—something familiar I can't identify.

I hear a child crying somewhere in the house, and I run toward the sound, yelling, "Where are you?" The corridor stretches out ahead of me, extending itself as I stumble along, feeling like I'm wading through tar.

Now the child's voice pleads, "Help me, help me," and my feet become heavier with every step. "Help me, help me." A heart-wrenching cry.

I scream, "Please, tell me where you are. I want to help you."

My mouth is dry, my heart pounding and I force myself to keep moving. I open every door along the unending hallway and finally come to a furnished bedroom where a sobbing boy sits on a huge, four-poster bed next to a small table where a candle burns. The child reaches out his little arms, as if to hug me, and I lean in to embrace him. His arms encircle my neck and he rests his cheek against mine. I rock him gently as he quiets, and then he resumes his chant, "Help me, help me, help me . . ."

I ask, "How can I help you?" and he suddenly rears back, exposing long, pointy fangs, and sinks the horrible teeth into my neck. I fight against him, trying to push him off of me, to break his vice-like hold on my neck, but he has strength beyond imagining.

Finally, I fall back onto the bed, barely breathing, and another voice—a terrible, disgusting voice I've heard before—takes up the child's plea. "Help me, help me, help me . . ." I close my eyes, expecting death, and the familiar voice says, "Ah, we meet again." My dream eyes fly open and I'm no longer lying on the bed in the old house. I'm buried alive in a rotting coffin . . .

"No! Let me out!" I screamed, struggling to sit up. My heart raced and my skin felt hot, as if I'd been near a fire.

Twin points of pain throbbed on my neck and my lungs ached as I gasped for air.

The hideous tones of the voice echoed in my ears and slithered across my skin. The same repulsive voice I'd heard outside The Crypt before my brain shut down.

I pushed and fought against the hands holding me as if my life depended on it.

"Shhh. Kismet, it was only a dream. You are here, safe with me."

I gasped and forced my eyes open.

Devereux sat next to me on his bed, holding me down, a concerned expression on his face. I realized I'd been flailing my arms and kicking my legs. My cheeks were wet and my body trembled.

"It was only a dream. No one will harm you." Devereux pulled me up into a hug, and rocked me as I'd rocked the child in my nightmare.

"Only a dream. I don't know what that means anymore." I didn't feel normal with my eyes open or closed, and somewhere along the way I'd lost hold of the thread of sanity I'd been clinging to.

I closed my eyes again for a moment and sank into the

soothing motion, enjoying being close to Devereux. I burrowed my face into his silky hair, loving the spicy smell of it. I didn't know what it was about him that felt so right to me. So familiar. But in the midst of the madness my life had become, I was almost willing to stop thinking and just trust.

He picked up a bottle of water, cracked the seal, removed the top and handed it to me. I downed half of the water in one long pull and only realized how dry my mouth had been after it wasn't dry anymore. I set the bottle on the table next to the bed and suddenly felt awkward. There I was, in a magnificent bed being held by a blond god, and all I could think about was that my sweatsuit was all rumpled and my mouth tasted sour. Which didn't bode well for the state of my breath.

Devereux smiled and stroked my hair.

"Your breath is fine, but after you rest a while longer if you wish to refresh yourself in order to feel confident, I can provide everything you need. But now I think you ought to lie back. You still seem pale."

"That's something, coming from you," I teased self-consciously, in an attempt to change the subject.

He grinned. "Yes, I suppose you could say I have no need of suntan lotion."

He put his hand behind my head, grasped it gently, and guided it down toward the pillow. It did feel wonderful to surrender into the soft mattress again. He stretched out next to me, our bodies touching, his head propped on his hand, facing me.

"Kismet, are you having more dreams lately? More than usual?"

I thought about the child's fangs in my neck and my skin went clammy.

"It isn't that I'm having more dreams. I always dream. It's that the dreams, the nightmares, are horrible. Graphic and bloody and violent. Completely unlike my usual dreams. Why did you ask me that?"

"The same thing is happening to me and many others of my kind. An increase in dark visions and nightmares."

I lifted my head, stared at him and raised my eyebrows. "Are you saying that vampires dream?"

He opened his eyes wide and raised a brow. "That is the first time you have referred to me as a vampire. Do you realize that you have just accepted what I am?" He cocked his head. "What has happened to change your belief?"

"Well, I'm not all the way over on your side of the coffin yet, but it was mostly because of talking to Alan. And what I saw at your club last night."

At the mention of Alan, a heavy feeling settled in my stomach. Chinese food with a side of Guilt poured over Shame, followed by a dessert of Feeling Like a Slut. I hoped Alan was still sleeping soundly on my couch. I didn't know if Devereux was aware of my sexual interlude with Alan earlier, but I knew Alan wasn't aware of my relationship with Devereux.

What a tangled web we weave . . .

"Yes. I am aware of your time with Alan, but you are a grown woman and able to make your own decisions. As much as I wish I could have been there for you this morning, that was not possible. I am glad someone was. Alan is a fine man."

Then he chuckled. "A slut? You surprise me. I would not have expected such a thing from a modern woman. That would imply something that I sense no evidence of. Why would you think that about yourself?"

"Well, Mister Mindreader, I don't really. It's just old programming. Most women have some of it. The idea that we're bad if we express our sexuality freely. Cultural baggage. I know all the therapeutic reasons why guilt isn't useful, but I still feel it anyway."

I sighed. "Yesterday Tom walked in on me in the bathtub and if he hadn't behaved extremely badly, I might have had sex with him. Then last night I just about tore your clothes off at the club, and today I was with Alan. After two years of celibacy, that's a lot to deal with."

His voice wrapped me in aural fur as he stroked my cheek with the side of his finger. "It is not necessary for you to be so hard on yourself. You have had a lot of changes to integrate and understand. Turning to Alan for comfort was a natural thing to do. You had been through a terrible ordeal."

Anger flashed in his eyes, I felt the air crackle and my skin tingled.

"An ordeal that will never happen again, I promise you. You are *mine* to protect now."

Wow. He's capable of some impressive mood swings himself. This probably isn't a good time to talk about the "mine to protect" thing.

He took a slow breath and his eyes returned to their calm, magical turquoise.

The corners of his mouth curved into a gentle smile. "But we were talking about dreams. You asked if vampires dream. Yes. We have access to levels of consciousness that are unavailable to most mortals, and when we turn inward during the daylight hours, our minds—or souls, if you will—journey to other realms. Dimensions that cannot be explained with words. Worlds that exist beyond the waking and sleeping dreams that humans know. Are you willing to share your nightmare with me?"

"I thought you could read my mind. Why do you need me to tell you the dream?"

"For some reason, I can only sense it as a series of emotional impressions—fast-moving pictures. If you tell me what you experienced, perhaps I can help you understand what it is trying to communicate to you. That is what psychology believes, yes?"

"Yes. That's true. But I still don't understand why you want to know."

"Honestly, I am not sure. I simply feel compelled. Unless it is too unpleasant to recount again so soon?"

"No. I believe that dreams are metaphorical messages, so I might as well figure out what this one really means."

I gave him all the details of the nightmare, along with all the feelings it triggered in me. He listened quietly, his brows contracted, his lips compressed.

"We must make time very soon to discuss the symbols in your dream. It is fascinating that so many are having similar visions. It is also important for us to have a conversation about vampires and what acceptance of us will mean for you. I wish we had time to begin the dialog now because I would have preferred to explain tonight's ceremony to you in greater detail, but we must hurry."

My solar plexus tightened. "Wait a minute. I don't care for the sound of that. What will this ceremony consist of? What would you have explained?"

A knock sounded at the door and a petite, five foot nothing, twenty-something woman stepped into the room. She appeared more pixie than vampire. That is, until she spoke and exposed fangs that were distinctive and highly visible. She had bright red hair that curled around her shoulders, large, brown eyes and she wore a sheer black dress under which was, apparently, nothing but skin.

"Master, it is nearly time for the ceremony. The others are arriving."

Master?

Devereux nodded at her and she backed out of the room.

He climbed off the bed, stood next to it and held out his hand to me. "I swear to you that no matter how strange the ceremony may appear to you, no matter how unfamiliar, no harm will come to you. A ritual of protection is one of the oldest, most potent types of magic. In its simplest form, it is a focusing of intention—surrounding the one needing protection with a powerful aura of well-being that repels all energy unlike itself. It will be as if you are floating in an invisible bubble of safety. Not very different from current Pagan rituals."

Pagans with fangs?

I sat frozen on the bed, my mind spinning out ever-more-gory, blood-soaked scenarios about the mysterious ceremony. No matter how logical his explanation, I barely knew Devereux and had no reason to trust him. Whether he really was a vampire—which was still mentally incomprehensible to me—or "only" a disturbed man, I was at his mercy. Inhuman or human, what I'd observed about Devereux and his colleagues didn't fit into any reality I knew about. I had no frame of reference and the lifeboat I'd been riding in up until then had sprung a leak and I had no idea if there were sharks in the water.

My stomach contracted so tightly I could barely breathe.

Devereux bent down and met my eyes. "No harm. I swear."

I gazed into his blue-green depths and believed him.

So, the Head Shark just said he won't eat me. Should I laugh or scream?

The door opened again and several women—none of whom I'd ever seen before—entered the room and lined up a few feet away from the bed.

Devereux indicated them with a sweep of his arm. "My companions have come to assist you with dressing. They will prepare you for the ceremony."

He kissed me lightly on the lips and turned to walk away.

My throat tightened and the sound came out like a squeak. "Wait! What do you mean, they'll prepare me for the ceremony?"

Why does this remind me of the cartoon where the cannibals have a huge pot boiling on the fire, waiting for the hapless hunter to arrive?

I didn't see any ropes, chains or anything else that could be used to restrain me. No cooking utensils or things with an edge that could cause bleeding. But my imagination was working overtime, creating scary and unspeakable possibilities.

"Ah, my apologies. I forget that you have not given yourself permission yet to read my thoughts. You still choose to resist. They are here to help you select one of the beautiful dresses and to make sure you have everything you need."

He pointed to a tall, slender woman with long brown hair and golden eyes. Her rangy body was encased in what used to be called a "unitard," a one-piece body suit worn for exercising. Except during the disco era, when these skin-tight, shiny numbers showed up on the dance floor along with six-inch platform shoes and big hair. Her suit made her look like she'd been dipped in a glittering rainbow, since every color imaginable was present. And the form-fitting garment left no doubt about her voluptuous shape.

"This is Nola. She will see to your hair and makeup."

I ran a hand through my tangled hair. *The disco queen will see to my hair and makeup?* "My hair and makeup? I don't think so."

I rolled off the bed and walked a wide circle around the women standing between me and the door.

Devereux repeated his disturbing habit of suddenly appearing in front of me, frowned and laid a hand on my arm. "Why do you object to being adorned? You usually wear makeup."

He said the last with impatience in his voice. I guess my resistance had unpleasantly surprised him. Maybe he wasn't used to anyone saying "no" to him. I wasn't the only one who had a lot to learn.

I summoned my best, no-bullshit facial expression. "You need to fill me in on what's happening here. I'm not going anywhere or letting anyone do anything until I'm clued in."

He heaved a heavy sigh and shook his head.

"As I have said before, you are the most stubborn woman I have ever known. Are you not ever willing to be spontaneous? Must you be in control at all times? Are you unable to even sense the truth of my words?"

Well, that stopped me. He'd managed to trespass into my

psyche and find the hottest buttons to push. I'd often been accused of lacking spontaneity, and my controlling nature was legendary. How else is a woman supposed to rise to the top of her field if she doesn't take control of her reality? But he had pulled the scab off a painful wound. I did wish that I was able to relax and trust more—that I could follow my intuitive guidance. That I wasn't so . . . anal.

But it was the expression on his face that really turned the tide. In one breathtaking gaze he'd managed to communicate that he thought this ceremony was for my benefit. That he'd arranged it to keep me safe. That he was worried about me.

Shit. Now he's gone and done it. He's got me feeling guilty about letting him down. How did that happen?

My shoulders sagged. I met his concerned eyes and nodded. "All right. I trust you."

Maybe. Where can I find some shark repellent?

He flashed a brilliant smile. "Thank you." He bowed from the waist and glided toward the door. "I will return for you shortly. It will be an extraordinary evening."

He left and the women surrounded me. Nola floated over to the chair where the dresses were draped.

"Which dress do you prefer?" She smiled, showing even, white teeth.

I expected her to have fangs and was surprised she appeared so normal. Except for the golden eyes.

She smiled again and her canines descended.

Can everybody read my mind?

She laughed and nodded. "Probably."

I'm in a parallel universe where everyone is telepathic except me.

"No. You can do it, too. The Master told us. He said you are a special human."

"Why do you call him Master? Is he holding you here against your will? Are you brainwashed?"

She cocked her head to the side, confusion flowing across her features.

"He takes care of us. He is more powerful than any who came before. We aren't prisoners here. We are privileged to attend him. To be in his presence." Her face shone with rapture.

Eeewww. Devereux has a harem of bloodsucking handmaidens. Worshipping devotees. Disempowered females. If he thinks I'm going to join the cult, he's sadly mistaken. This is the twenty-first century, mister, and I'm a liberated woman. I wonder what other services they perform for him? What if this ceremony deal is some kind of bizarre sexual ritual?

"Can you tell me about the ceremony we're going to? What should I expect?"

She smiled, which confused me until I figured out that she'd obviously read my mind and knew about my judgments and speculations.

She met my eyes briefly then shifted away. "That information is not mine to share. Have you decided on a gown?" She pointed to the dresses on the chair.

I'd felt a mild tingle wash through my body as she'd turned her eyes to me. I didn't know if all vampires could entrance with their eyes, but I had to admit I'd felt something.

I walked over to the chair.

Remembering the beautiful, shimmering blue dress, I lifted the others out of the way until I found it. It was floor-length with a plunging neckline, made of a soft, lustrous material that might have been woven moonlight.

"This one will be fine. You know, I'm perfectly able to dress myself, so you and your friends can go and do whatever you need to do now."

"We are here to attend to you. It is the Master's wish. We shall remain."

Okay. Maybe we could have an informal consciousness-raising group here. These women must have slept through the '60s.

Nola draped the blue dress over her arm and floated over to the armoire containing the shoes and lingerie. The other women, all dressed in colorful, flowing gowns, posed like goddess statues in a semi-circle where they'd remained since they entered.

My newly acquired assistant opened the drawers, pulled out the shoe boxes and rifled through them. She seemed to be searching for something in particular and got excited when she found whatever it was.

Her voice raised in pitch. "Yes. These are lovely."

She held up a pair of open-toe, blue high heels, the same shade as the dress, and a strapless, satin corset with garters for silk stockings. Which, what a coincidence, were also available.

I waited next to her, watching. "Just out of curiosity, how do you know what's in there? Did you buy this stuff?"

She nodded. "The Master asked several of us to observe you and to discern your clothing sizes. Then he told us what he had in mind and gave us free rein to purchase all manner of clothing from the Internet. It was very entertaining."

"What do you mean, 'observe me'?"

"Physically and astrally, of course. We watched you in your home and joined you in your dreams. The usual ways."

The usual ways?

My eyebrows shot up. "You spied on me?"

She nodded enthusiastically. "Oh, yes. You are very interesting. Come now. There is a room for dressing and hygiene."

Why does everyone around Devereux speak so strangely?

She stepped over to the nearest wall, touched a symbol carved in the wood and a panel slid aside, exposing an opening into yet another room. The "room for dressing and hygiene," or more commonly, the bathroom. But it was a very large, ornate bathroom.

She took my hand and pulled me, as if I was her little red wagon. The rest of the team remained behind.

Gee. Devereux's private bathroom. Should I genuflect or something?

The room was big enough to be a public restroom, but much too luxurious for the masses. There was a faint hint of his scent in the air, perhaps more easily recognized because no incense was burning to mask the fragrance. Mirrors lined each wall and opulent, silver-streaked marble counters were abundant. Multiple sinks with sparkling, modern hardware were interspersed along the counters and the floor was pristine white marble.

A huge silver bathtub sat on a raised platform, enclosed by glass etched with figures of nude men and women dancing. Next to it, in another glass-surrounded area, was a double shower.

Fluffy white towels sat in piles on the various counters and hung in artistic racks on the walls next to the bath and shower areas.

Painted along the top of the walls, like a happy little border, were more men and women, frolicking in all their naked majesty.

This is unsettling. Devereux really seems to enjoy the nude human form. That makes me both anxious and excited at the same time. Back to my question about the nature of the ritual.

White leather chairs and a loveseat sat off to the side in an alcove, and a clothing rack stood next to a small mirrored makeup table with a fancy matching chair. On the table was a small box, wrapped in shiny paper with a rose pinned to the top instead of a bow. A small card had my name on it.

Nola watched me as I opened the gift. She rocked back and forth from heel to toe, smiling a cat-who-ate-the-canary smile.

Inside was a black velvet jewelry box containing a beautiful silver pentagram on a chain, identical to the one Devereux's mother wore in her portrait.

I was speechless. My mouth opened into an "ah" that remained silent. The weight and craft of the piece suggested it was high-quality and probably very valuable.

I turned to Nola and shook my head.

She cocked hers and raised one sculpted eyebrow. "Are you unhappy with your gift? The Master was very pleased to choose it for you."

"No. I'm not unhappy. I'm confused. Why would he give me something so valuable? He barely knows me."

She tilted her head to the other side and studied me. "Perhaps that is not true. You must dress now. The night awaits."

Just then, as if there'd been a silent signal, the other women filed into the bathroom. I decided to let all the rest of my questions wait until I could talk to Devereux.

After some initial stubbornness on my part, when I insisted on adjusting my own breasts in the cups of the corset, I finally gave up and let them take over. It turned out they were pretty good with the makeup and hair stuff, and when they finally stepped away to survey their work, it was declared good.

They'd managed to enhance my features through their cosmetic witchery and kept my hair down long and curly. Subtle silver sparkles had been dusted on my curls and the lovely pentagram necklace was added as a last touch. It dangled in the cleavage created by the low-cut dress and tight corset.

Although cleavage was usually the least of my concerns. In fact, eliminating it had always been a thornier problem. Thinking about my genetic heritage from my mother made me wonder what she'd say if she saw me at the moment. If she and my father had thought I was strange before, now they'd probably move to another state and leave no forwarding address.

Suddenly, all the women raised their heads as if they were listening to something I couldn't hear, then Devereux's enticing voice floated through the opening of the door.

"Kismet? Shall we go?"

My entourage escorted me back into the other room, as I wobbled a bit on my shoes' thin heels. Not quite stilettos, but in the neighborhood.

He literally gasped when he saw me. And I had the same reaction when I laid eyes on him.

He waltzed elegantly over to me, held out both hands and took mine. "You humble me with your beauty. I am overwhelmed."

"Uh . . ."

It's becoming annoying that my brain goes on vacation whenever I'm around Devereux. I had no idea lust could be so intoxicating.

He smiled and twirled me around in a dance-like movement, which caused my dress to spiral out around me, lifting off the ground.

He looked spectacular.

Dressed in cream-colored soft leather, his pants were obviously cut specifically for his lean, muscular frame. They fit his body like a perfect glove, the waistband riding just above his hips. A line of soft platinum hair snaked down his lower stomach and disappeared into his pants. With the exception of those enticing little strands, his chest was smooth and hair-free. The state of his chest was apparent because he wasn't wearing a shirt. The muscles in his abdomen were toned and obvious, and his nipples peeked out occasionally from beneath the open floor-length duster, which moved like something much softer than leather. Or, maybe that's how expensive leather moves.

Shining in the center of his chest was the same antique medallion he'd worn the first time he'd come to my office.

The color of his hair matched his clothing and it spilled down over his shoulders, long, soft, and delectable. The blue-green of his eyes sparkled with a fire from within and they shone like the alchemical blending of emeralds and sapphires.

As he swayed with me in our inadvertent dance, I became entranced by the sight of him in all that leather without a shirt. The pink of his nipples peeped out from the edges of the coat, vivid against his pale skin and captured my attention—and my imagination. A trick of the light made the medallion seem to pulse against his skin. I had to fight the desire to touch him, to run my hands over his chest.

We stopped moving and I finally found my voice.

"You look amazing. I just want to run my fingers through

your hair and lick your chest."

My outburst startled me and I felt my face grow hot with embarrassment. *Geez, did I really say that out loud? Have I been sucked into the cult?*

He let go of me and laughed until his eyes glistened. He wiped the moisture away, then took my face in his hands.

"Thank you for that. I have never been so flattered. I hope you will still feel that way when we are alone later."

When we're alone later? At least he assumes I'll get through this ceremony in one piece.

He cocked his head and smiled.

"As I have said, I swear that you will be safe."

"Has anyone ever told you that reading minds without permission is rude?"

He nodded. "My apologies."

He bent his arm at the elbow and lifted it out for me to take.

"The journey to the ceremonial site might cause you to be dizzy and momentarily uncomfortable. It will pass quickly."

What? Every time I start to get comfortable, he says another weird thing.

I had a brief panic attack and considered bolting out the door, but decided I wouldn't get far in the high-heeled shoes. I had to clear my throat a couple of times before I could speak.

"Where are we going? How will we get there?"

We walked into his main office and headed toward what appeared to be a solid wall.

"Our destination is another dimension and we shall move through thought."

Before I could complain or raise my hand up to keep my head from colliding with the physical boundary in front of me, I heard a swoosh of air again, as I had when Devereux brought me from my house. I felt my hair being blown back gently from my face and my equilibrium shifted. I'd say we'd been moving, but it wasn't like any kind of motion I'd felt before. It reminded me of an experience I had in an elevator once, when the car plummeted down several floors in free-fall before the automatic controls took over and stopped the downward motion. My stomach churned and if Devereux hadn't been holding me, my knees would have buckled.

I'm not sure when, but I'd apparently closed my eyes, because when I sensed we were stationary I opened them.

And words failed me.

I was standing on a cloud in a huge, candle-lit room with what seemed like hundreds of other people.

Devereux brushed his finger gently across my cheek and I turned to him.

He took my hand and walked me forward a few steps.

"It is my pleasure to introduce you to Lady Amara."

A beautiful woman with long, pale blond hair approached. She wore a breathtaking white gown and a warm smile. She resembled Devereux so strongly that she could have been his sister.

She moved in very close to me, lifted the pentagram necklace resting on my chest and met my eyes.

"Welcome, Kismet. You have come at last. I am Devereux's mother."

Chapter 17

$\mathcal{D}$evereux had been correct in predicting that I might feel queasy after our inter-dimensional road trip. My head was fuzzy and there was a loud buzzing in my ears. Part of me figured that I'd fallen and hit my head and that was why I was having both auditory and visual hallucinations.

Talking to Devereux's dead mother? Walking on a cloud?

After I accepted my temporary madness I relaxed and enjoyed the experience. After all, it was obviously just a dream. A marvelous, esoteric, lucid dream. It made perfect sense to me that I'd called up the beautiful blond woman's image from the portrait in Devereux's room and that the cottony feeling in my head might be symbolically translated into a cloud.

I gave what I thought was a supportive smile and trilled, "Okay. Sure. Absolutely. Devereux's mother. It's nice to meet you, Lady Amara."

She nodded. "Amara, please."

The two of them exchanged a look and Devereux stepped in front of me, put his finger under my chin and lifted my face so he could search my eyes.

He frowned. "Kismet? Are you well? Your mind is racing like a film on fast-forward."

He removed his finger from my chin but continued to stare at me.

I smiled. "Oh, sure. This is a great dream. Much more fun than all the bloody, scary ones I've been having."

He turned his head toward the blond woman and they both laughed playfully. Devereux moved over to her and drew her into a hug. "It is wonderful to see you, Mother. It has been so very long."

They held each other tightly, both seemingly reluctant to let go.

Amara finally stepped away from his embrace, wiped a tear from under her eye and stood in front of us. Shifting her gaze to each of us in turn, she said in a trembling voice, "My beautiful son. I am so happy you have found your mate and that your heart will be at peace. I cannot remain long, so we must begin."

His mate?

Surprised by this confusing new development, I scanned the immediate area, searching for the mate Amara had referred to.

Before I could ask any of the multitude of disturbing questions which had commandeered my partially functioning brain, Devereux positioned himself in between both of us. He offered us each an arm, and we were suddenly in the middle of a cavernous room. The dreamy quality of the experience began to recede. The sounds, colors, and sensations lost their vague edges and became hyper-focused. My sensing system shifted into high and my inner defenses rallied the troops and pulled up the bridge over the moat.

I was suddenly afraid. All around me were people I didn't

know, and we were still walking on a damn cloud. Candles floated in the air of their own volition, just as in the Harry Potter movies, and the flames were overly large and multi-colored. Every few seconds each candle sent up a spark of mini fireworks, but no one else paid any attention.

Maybe there was something funny in that water he gave me. Some kind of weird drug from one of those strange bottles he has in his bedroom.

The air was thick and heavy, as if it were very hot, but it wasn't. There was a wall of murmuring sound, which I soon discovered to be the whispered conversations around me.

Devereux guided us into a large, cloud-free, open circle. As if on cue, all the other guests encircled us, forming themselves into several concentric rings, each behind the other. On the floor of the open area were symbols similar to the ones in Devereux's private room. Sitting in the center of the circle was an ornate, jewel-encrusted chair with a high back.

Amara grasped my hand and led me over to the fancy chair, indicating I should sit. I gazed into her eyes, searching for any sign that I was in danger, but all I saw was kindness, warmth, and compassion.

Since I didn't know what else to do—or what else I *could* do—I sat in the chair. The moment my hind end touched the seat, the people in the circles began singing. Or maybe chanting would be a better word to describe the sound. Some repetitious melody in a language I didn't recognize. The vocalizing started out softly, harmonies flowing over and under the tonic, but as it went on, it got louder. Then louder still, until I could feel the vibration of the sound in my bones.

The song was mesmerizing. Eerie and lovely. My eyelids drooped and my head fell forward. I was still fully conscious, but had the distinct impression that my body had gone to a different time zone. I concentrated on lifting my head and was finally able to raise it just enough to have the motion cause it to flop back against the chair.

Out of the corner of my eye, I saw Amara step next to me. I felt her take my hand and tried to produce sounds, but nothing came out.

I don't know what Devereux had been doing all this time, but he suddenly appeared next to me in the center of the circle and all the singing stopped. I mean they literally stopped chanting at exactly the same second. Devereux raised both his hands in the air.

"Welcome, my friends. I am grateful for your willingness to join us in this ceremony of protection today to hold the sacred space. It is truly a momentous occasion and a special time for me because my Mother is here. Welcome my mate Kismet to the circle."

What? I'm his mate? Why isn't my brain working?

He made a graceful, flowing gesture with his hand and arm, pointing to me, and everyone said words in unison in that exotic-sounding language.

Ever since the singing ended, my mind began to clear and my body operated at my command again. Amara released my hand, but continued to stand next to me.

Devereux extended his hands out in front of him and a large, golden chalice appeared out of nowhere. He held the chalice over his head, moved around the inside edges of the circle and kept up an ongoing monolog in that mysterious, sonorous language.

He was quite a sight to behold. Gliding like a dancer, his

duster billowing out behind him, his naked chest gleaming in the candlelight.

My mind was clear enough to find him compelling, and my body was aware enough to be aroused. In fact, for some reason I was intensely aroused. My suddenly hard nipples thrust against the silky fabric of my dress, threatening to burst free from the restraining corset, and the area between my legs grew slick with liquid heat.

Then he came and stood in front of me, set the chalice on the floor at my feet, threw off his duster and, for lack of better words, did an erotic dance for me.

His movements were totally unlike his usual elegant, contained presentation. His hips undulated, his stomach muscles rolled and his arms sliced through the air in deliberate, graceful motions. He threw his head back, his platinum hair flying, and his face was slack, as if he'd gotten lost in ecstasy.

A potent energy fired off Devereux as he danced. I felt the tension building inside myself and thought that if he didn't touch me soon, I'd literally explode. As I caught some of the expressions on the faces of the other participants, I saw I wasn't the only one having that reaction.

Devereux's skin shone with sweat, like liquid diamonds. He moved his hands seductively over his body, locking his eyes with mine. Bending toward me, he opened his mouth and slowly and deliberately licked his upper lip with his tongue. His canines were fully extended and he kissed me, caught my lower lip with his fangs, then backed away.

I gasped, thinking he'd bitten me, but I tasted no blood. All my erogenous zones were frantic with desire—aching with need. My heart pounded double-time. I'd gotten so excited and aroused by his dance that I doubt if I'd have complained even if he'd taken a pint.

I noticed I'd scooted to the edge of the chair, ready, I supposed, to leap onto Devereux at the earliest chance. Oddly enough, thinking about making a public display of myself with Devereux didn't seem to upset me.

All that mattered was doing whatever I had to do to get him to touch me again.

He picked up the chalice, glided over to the circle of people, and pandemonium broke out.

As Devereux approached the crowd, a madness built—excitement spread around the circles. All variety of wails, moans, groans, and howls rent the air. Some of the bodies of the participants convulsed, limbs twitching and jerking in random spasms, as their heads flopped back and forth on boneless necks. Others jumped up and down with manic intensity, as if they'd been taken prisoner by a sadistic puppeteer.

Holding the chalice in his left hand, Devereux magically manifested some kind of knife or dagger which appeared in his right.

He stared into the eyes of the woman in front of him in the circle and she offered her arm. Using the knife to make a small cut on her wrist, he caught the dripping blood in the chalice. A roar went up from the crowd.

Arms shot out from everywhere as the noise level rose.

Devereux navigated the ring, repeating the process with as many wrists as it took to fill the chalice with blood.

I'd been so shocked and enthralled by Devereux's sudden shift from lust object to phlebotomist that I hadn't noticed the other really bizarre thing that was unfolding.

People were sucking on each other's wounds.

Well, technically, I guess you couldn't call them people.

Vampires were sucking on each other's wounds.

And not merely sucking. Feeding frenzy would be more accurate.

I felt my jaw drop as I watched the bloodsuckers attaching themselves to wrists and necks, some falling to the floor together in passionate mid-suck. A few of the revelers seemed to have gotten so swept away by the feasting, that clothes were discarded and other parts of the body were invited to play.

Vampire orgy. Perfect.

I instinctively sat back in the chair, hoping the lunacy wouldn't spread to me. Amara took my hand again and I turned to her. Her eyes were large and shining, more green than Devereux's, and she said, "He would never hurt you. You must trust him."

At that moment, he stalked toward us, his hair fanning out behind him, holding the chalice in his hands. His eyes were feral, expressing a wildness he'd never shared with me before, and his face was startlingly beautiful. A fallen angel.

Taking the chalice in his left hand, he held it away from his body and embraced his mother in a one-armed hug. He met her eyes and she nodded, tilting her head to the side. Devereux leaned into her, exposed his fangs and sank them into her neck. She gasped and laid a hand on the back of his head.

I didn't know what to do with myself—where to look. Devereux had just assaulted his mother, and she was apparently enjoying it. There was something very sensuous about him sucking on her neck and I couldn't imagine that was a psychologically healthy mother-son activity.

But then, she's dead, so do the rules apply?

After only a few seconds he raised his head, embraced her again, said something in that strange language and turned to me, licking blood from his lips.

Devereux raised the chalice into the air and the chanting started again. Vampires rose from the floor and disentangled themselves from each other, adding their voices as they re-formed the circles.

As the intensity of the sound increased, I felt the curious, entranced feeling again.

Devereux knelt before me, offered the chalice and said, "One sip, my love."

There was a major firestorm of resistance in my brain. One part of me was already struggling to get up from the chair, begging the muscles in my legs to report for duty one more time. But the muscles were hanging out with the other part of me that was thinking about tearing off Devereux's clothes and jumping on him. One sip of blood wasn't much of a price to pay for being able to get my hands on this blond Adonis. Good thing this wasn't really happening.

My hands reached out for the chalice and he gave it to me. It was warm. I raised it to my lips, stared into his astonishing eyes over the rim, and drank. For some reason I'd imagined blood would taste like tomato juice. It didn't. But by the time I discovered that the taste was thick and unpleasant, I'd choked and swallowed the entire gulp. I coughed and sputtered and finally stuck my tongue out, maybe thinking that would dissipate the taste.

Definitely a dream. I'd never drink blood if I was awake. Nothing to worry about. Just a dream.

He mouthed the words "Thank you," retrieved the chalice from me and drank the remainder of the blood. Saying more of those unfamiliar words, he held the cup out in front of him and it vanished.

The chanting grew louder and another portion of my consciousness drifted away.

Devereux stood, pulled me out of the chair, wrapped his arms around me and kissed me passionately. I made an effort to hold onto him, but my bones had mysteriously dissolved and all four of my limbs were now only useful as paperweights.

Bending me over backward he whispered, "No harm." He kissed his way down from my mouth, along my neck, finally resting his mouth on the fullness of my breast. The part of me that wanted to roll around with Devereux sighed contentedly. He planted little kisses on my skin then there was a flash of pain, followed by the most blissful feeling I'd ever experienced.

After a few seconds, he lifted me into his arms, brought his lips to mine and held me. I briefly wondered how someone who drank blood could have such sweet-smelling breath, but I decided to add that to the list of things to think about later.

Besides, this is my dream and I'm not likely to give my lust object stinky breath, right?

He returned me to the chair, kissed my cheek and walked out toward the vampire chorus. The chanting immediately ceased.

This was too weird. I'd been in lots of choirs and I knew how hard it was to get people to all stop singing at exactly the same moment. There was always at least one person not paying attention or something. But this was downright eerie. As if sound itself had disappeared.

And, just as before, as soon as they stopped chanting, I began to come back to myself. Not that I knew where I'd been prior to that, but I didn't know how else to explain it.

Immediately, I noticed that my breast throbbed with pain. One quick glance solved the mystery. Standing out against my very-white skin were two neat puncture marks, surrounded by a sea of traumatized red tissue, which would soon be a colorful blue-green-purple.

Amara, who still stood next to the chair, took my hand again. She inspected my chest. "I will heal that for you before I leave. There will be no lasting mark. Devereux will explain."

My eyes darted to her neck to see if her bite marks appeared as bad as mine, and there was nothing to see. Her skin was smooth, white, and flawless.

She smiled and nodded. "Exactly so."

I don't know if this is a flaw or a virtue, but I have an innate need to be polite. To be a nice person. I couldn't blame Amara for what her son had done, but I had to turn away from her because it was temporarily impossible for me to pretend that I wasn't seething with rage. Something about the physical pain had jolted me into awareness.

Damn it to hell! This isn't a dream. It's a wide-awake nightmare. I can't believe the bastard bit me. He actually bit me. I'm probably going to turn into a vampire now.

Amara stepped in front of me, her eyes hard and serious. "No. It is not that easy to become a vampire. It requires intention." Her gaze went to the bite on my breast. "This was merely a symbolic gesture. I wish there had been more time to help you understand, but no harm has been done. You will be as you were."

I scanned the area for Devereux. He'd retrieved his duster and was slowly moving around the inside of the circle, pausing at each of the quarter points. Some of the words he spoke sounded like English, and I picked up the phrase "guardian of the four directions," along with a few others. I got the idea that each place he paused in the circle represented east, south, west, or north.

He pulled a gem-studded wand from the pocket of his coat and held it up in the air over each direction. A burst of brilliant white light emanated from the tip at each location and it hovered, forming a vertical line, floating in space.

I was tempted to rub my eyes, because I couldn't believe what I was seeing, but I remembered how much mascara Nola had insisted on plastering on my eyelashes, and I hesitated at the last moment. I didn't want to do an imitation of a raccoon or Alice Cooper.

By the time Devereux completed the circle, there were four beams of luminescence.

At a signal from Devereux, all the vampires in the inner circle took a step forward, which put them in line with the hovering lights. As soon as the radiance touched the vampire closest to it, the glow began to spread around the circle, flowing out to each circle in turn. Soon the white incandescence transformed into multiple colors, shifting and changing every few seconds. The mini fireworks put off by the candles became more pronounced and the medallion around Devereux's neck sparked like a floodlight.

I lowered my eyes to shield from the bright glare but was able to squint enough to see that all the vampires in the circles had clasped hands. And as they did that, the light began to pulsate and writhe, creating bursts of color and completely enveloping everyone in the circle until there was only pure energy.

Devereux turned in my direction and held out his hand.

I turned anxious eyes to Amara. She smiled and nodded.

My feet had a mind of their own and I found myself standing and inching over to where he waited. I stretched out my hand and the moment our fingers met, there was a sharp sound that reminded me of a whip cracking and the light exploded and engulfed us.

Then there was nothing.

Chapter 18

$\mathcal{I}$woke up naked in my bed. Naked except for the pentagram necklace.

At least I assumed it was my bed, because I couldn't open my eyes. I raised my hands up to investigate and found the source of the problem. All that mascara I'd worn the night before had somehow congealed into gummy clumps, hermetically sealing my upper lashes to my lower.

I spent a couple of minutes prying them apart, opening and closing my lids to test the equipment, and then discovered I'd apparently rubbed my eyes at some point because there was a big, black stain on the side of my right index finger. I knew the mirror would present me with even more delightful news.

But, thankfully, I was in my own bed.

Staring up at the ceiling, I listened to the sounds floating in through the window, appreciating the evidence that, for some people, normal reality still existed. Lawns were mowed, dogs were walked, greetings were called out from yard to yard, and cars were driven. Music still blared from the radios of passing vehicles and children played. The everyday world that I used to belong to—that I took for granted—evidently continued on as if nothing earth-shattering had happened.

Memory fragments from the night before bobbed like apples in the tub of my brain, waiting for me to capture one and take a bite.

Bite.

I bolted up, filled each hand with a breast and warily lowered my eyes, afraid to see what might be there. Instead of the torn, bruised, and traumatized skin I'd anticipated, there was nothing but the white, lightly-blue-veined expanse I'd always had.

Breathing a sigh of relief, I watched the patterns of sunlight play across the wall in front of me and felt numb.

There were only two possible explanations for what was happening to me. Either I was in the midst of a psychic meltdown—maybe even a psychotic break—and the entire sequence of events had only unfolded inside my fevered, twisted little mind or, I had truly entered a monstrous world, where vampires drank blood, levitated in the air, read your mind, and seduced your body.

Quite frankly, I didn't know how to deal with either option.

My mouth was as dry as the lunar landscape and it tasted like I'd scoured the floor of an ER with my tongue.

A wisp of memory floated into my brain and opened a Pandora's Box of horrible possibilities.

There's no way in hell I drank blood. Not one chance in this or any other universe. Not even if someone held me down and forced my mouth open. Yuck, yuck, yuck.

I held the palm of my hand in front of my mouth, breathed into it, and almost gagged.

No. I just must have eaten something funky. Something gross. I hope I didn't share this breath with anyone I actually like.

The digital clock on my nightstand showed 1:00 p.m. That information didn't really tell me much, because I wasn't even sure what day it was. Panicking, I picked up the TV remote control and clicked on CNN, assuming the data panel on the bottom of the screen would have the correct date. Sunday. Relief swamped me. I hadn't lost any more time than I already knew about and, more important, I hadn't missed any client appointments.

I swiveled my head around, stretching the tight muscles of my neck and shoulders, then swung my legs over the side of the bed. I turned off the TV, forced myself vertical and walked over to the closet to fetch my comfortable pink robe. I slipped it on, tied the sash and a sparkling blue fabric caught my eye. The lovely dress I'd worn the night before hung neatly in the closet, and on the floor underneath it were the matching shoes. Paying closer attention, I found the corset and stockings draped across the rocking chair in the corner.

I hoped it had been Devereux who'd brought me home, undressed me and tucked me into bed. But the startling possibility that it might not have been him, or that things I didn't want to know about might have happened, froze me like a statue.

Laying a hand against the wall to brace myself, I closed my eyes and sent my awareness through my body. I'd always been able to use my intuition to check out the state of my physical health and recently that ability seemed especially heightened.

Whether I wanted to know about it or not, I needed to find out if there'd been any sexual activity—either consensual or forced. I steeled myself for possible bad news and asked the silent question. None of my usual indicators fired a warning, so I asked again, just to make sure.

As before, calm silence.

I'd learned to trust the subtle "yes" or "no" reactions of my body and felt relatively confident that I hadn't been physically harmed while I was sleeping. Or unconscious. Or whatever I'd been.

A mini tsunami of relief washed over my fear-contaminated mental shoreline and I straightened, tightened the sash on my robe, and headed downstairs for desperately needed coffee.

Halfway down the stairs I remembered that the last time I'd seen Alan, he'd been sacked out on my couch. It had been eighteen hours since I'd left him sleeping there. I couldn't imagine he'd still be snoozing. Then I remembered how his unnatural sleep came to be, and decided that rational rules wouldn't necessarily apply. I figured he'd be rightfully confused and probably angry, and he'd want to know where I went.

Sure enough, the couch was empty. I walked around the room, checking for a note, but there was no sign of one. I scanned the white board in the kitchen. Nothing.

Remembering that his clothes had been in the washing machine, I lifted the lid and there they were. Still wet. He hadn't even transferred them to the dryer.

Why would he have gone out in those ridiculous pink sweat pants? Unless he got another call from the police and had to hurry out. But, even so.

I went over to the front window, lifted one of the slats in the mini-blinds—just in case the media circus still had its tent erected—and tried to find Alan's car. It was there. Right where he left it yesterday. And, thankfully, my lawn was media-free.

What the hell was going on?

I did another walk-through of my house, calling his name loudly, but got no response.

Still trying to figure out the mystery, I absentmindedly went through the motions of making coffee and then remembered the phone. I hadn't checked the messages yet, and if Alan'd had to leave quickly, he might have called. Plus, I'd contacted Midnight and Ronald and had left—or been snatched—before they could call me back.

While the coffee brewed and sent its heavenly aroma directly into my nostrils, I punched in the retrieval code to listen to my messages.

There were several from media outlets, a few from concerned clients, wondering about my safety, and one from a friend in Paris, who laughingly said she'd seen a report on CNN about a flaky psychologist in Denver who worked with vampires. So much for my career.

Midnight had left a message saying she and Ronald were not dealing with Emerald's death very well, and they were worried about me. She wanted to know if I could possibly see them for a joint appointment on Sunday.

I was just about to hang up so I could call her when I heard the first couple of words of the next message and the hairs on the back of my neck rose.

Brother Luther's familiar southern-accented voice screamed out of the earpiece.

"I know what you did. I know where you've been. Consorting with foul creatures of the night! You'll be punished! You'll burn in the fires of Hell! Unholy Jezebel! Whore of

Babylon! Suffer not a witch to live! No one can save you from the wrath of the Almighty! I am the messenger. You have been marked. You will burn."

My eyes and my mouth were wide open and after the message ended I felt slimed. As if someone had thrown a bucket of manure on me through the phone. The negative energy of the call hit my solar plexus like a fist. I saved his hateful tirade because I was definitely reporting him to the police. The call had to be some form of harassment, at the very least.

Finally, there was a message from Alan. He spoke in a very soft, subdued voice, as if he'd just awakened.

"Kismet? You're probably going to think I'm insane—if you don't already—but I'm home and I don't know how I got here. The last thing I remember is being at your house and seeing Devereux appear in your living room. It's Sunday morning, the sun just came up, and I'm still wearing your pink sweats. I went outside to look for my car and it isn't here. I think I left it at your house along with my clothes, but I don't remember. You're probably thinking I had some kind of blackout, or breakdown—and maybe I did—but I'd appreciate if you'd call me when you get this and help me figure out what the *hell* is going on."

I disconnected, put the phone down and poured a cup of coffee. I plopped down into one of the kitchen chairs. Sometimes there's just too much information for a brain to process.

Postponing the inevitable, I allowed myself the luxury of sitting still while I finished my first cup, then poured another one and picked up the phone.

Punching in Midnight's phone number, I got her answering machine. I apologized for not being able to return her call sooner, and told her I'd had to deal with personal business, but that I was fine and she and Ronald shouldn't worry about me. I said I was willing to meet them at my office later in the day if they still wanted an appointment, and left my cell phone number.

I dialed Alan's cell phone next and he must have been using it, because I went directly to voice mail. I told him I didn't think he was insane, and that his car was still here, along with his clothing. I said I had to meet with some clients, but he should let me know what he wanted to do about picking up his possessions. I'm sure my voice sounded as tired as my spirit felt.

What I wanted more than anything was to do absolutely nothing. To sit quietly without thinking. Without trying to interpret, understand or accept. Without being afraid.

Since none of that was likely, I rinsed out my coffee mug and went back upstairs to take a shower, carrying my cell phone with me.

Seeing my face in the bathroom mirror caused me to laugh out loud. I'd really done a job of spreading the mascara around my eyes and upper cheeks, and I looked like a child had scribbled on me with a black magic marker.

Gorilla breath and raccoon eyes. See what happens when you stay at the Ball past midnight?

I momentarily wondered if I'd made myself this attractive a sight before or after my pale knight dropped me off. Or, should I say, my pale bloodsucker? I'd better get used to calling a spade a spade.

As attracted as I was to Devereux, I wanted to keep

my distance from him for a while. To pretend to be normal again. But how did one remain distant from something that could come and go through thought? Something that moved through time and space like shifting from room to room? Something that didn't give a shit about anyone else's boundaries or needs?

I turned on the spray, dropped my robe on the floor, pulled the necklace over my head and laid it on the counter and stepped into the shower.

After blissing out for a few moments, letting the hot water cascade down my body, I poured shampoo on my hair and piled the soapy mass on top of my head. I picked up the plastic bottle of body gel and was spreading it across my breasts when my hand slid over something on my chest. The necklace. I'd forgotten to take it off.

Wait. No. I didn't forget. I did take it off. I laid it on the counter.

I pulled aside the shower curtain and squinted through the fog that the hot water had created in the small room and scanned the counter. No necklace.

I put my hand back on the pentagram and Devereux's voice whispered in my mind, "This necklace is your protection. You must never remove it."

What the hell?

I looked around, expecting him to pop in, but nothing happened. I thought vampires couldn't go out in the sunlight, so where'd the voice come from? But then, after what I'd seen, I could testify that there was no rule book for what Master Devereux could or couldn't do.

I lifted the necklace over my head again and in the nanoseconds it took me to do that, the pentagram returned to rest between my breasts.

The same words floated through my mind.

"This necklace is your protection. You must never remove it."

Apparently, Devereux had somehow implanted a message in the necklace and it replayed any time the pendant lost contact with my skin.

Well, to hell with it. I'd leave the damn necklace on. It was just another way that Devereux had reached out to intrude on my life, and I wasn't going to give it one more moment of attention than I had to.

I finished washing and rinsing, wrapped up in a towel and stepped out of the shower.

My cell phone rang. It was Midnight calling to schedule a time to meet.

We set the appointment for one hour later, which gave me time to get dressed and eat something. My empty stomach echoed like an abandoned cave.

A short time later, I'd just picked up my briefcase and purse to head out the door when my cell phone rang again. This time it was Alan. He sounded a lot more solid, and had retrieved his usual cocky attitude.

He launched right in.

"So, did I imagine it, or did Devereux plant a passionate wet one on you when I was there yesterday?"

"Uh, I seem to recall something of that nature."

"You want to tell me what's going on?"

"No."

"What?"

"I don't mean no, I don't want to tell you. I mean not right now. I need to get over to my office for an appointment. Plus, I'm seriously burned out on talking or thinking about all the weird stuff that's been going on. I'm running on empty. Could we talk about it later?"

He paused. "Sure. I just thought maybe you and I had possibilities, but after what I saw, I don't know anymore. What do you think? Do we have possibilities?"

Ah, shit. These are the exact messy kinds of things that I don't want to talk about. The stuff I don't have one clue about.

I couldn't keep all the impatience and frustration out of my voice.

I paced around the room. "Can I waffle and say that I'm confused? That I don't even know my name right now, much less what's happening with my love life? Seriously, can we put a bookmark in this discussion?"

Either he decided to humor me or he really caught the vibe. Or, maybe he really didn't care all that much.

"Absolutely. Things are still crazy for me, too. There've been some leads in the Emerald Addison murder case and I don't know when I'll have a spare minute. I'm going to have one of the black and whites drop me off at your place so I can pick up my car. I'll get the clothes some other time. I'm ready whenever you are. Ball's in your court."

I nodded, then remembered he couldn't see me. "Thanks. Talk to you soon."

Feeling like I'd just dodged a very large bullet, I willed myself to relax.

I stole one more peek out my window to see if any media types were lurking, didn't find any, and headed into my attached garage. I carefully pulled my car out onto the street and drove to my office, checking out the rearview mirror to see if anyone was interested in my whereabouts. It appeared I'd gone back to being unimportant. At least for a little while.

Even something as familiar and comfortable as driving seemed to require extra attention. I caught a glimpse of my eyes in the mirror, half expecting to see a shell-shocked reflection, and was surprised to appear so normal. As if nothing had changed. As if I hadn't lost my mind. As if I still lived in a world where there were no such things as vampires.

I was more comfortable believing I was nuts.

Midnight and Ronald showed up right on time and we spent the next two hours processing the grief and anger they felt about losing Emerald. Neither of them appeared to have slept in a couple of days and their vulnerability tugged on my heart strings.

They asked a lot of questions about what had happened to me—the abduction and waking up in a cemetery—and I gave brief answers. I let them believe a mental patient had lost control of himself and held me against my will. That was easier than getting into what really happened, and I didn't want to give either of them cause to be more concerned about their immediate environment than they already were.

Midnight said she'd returned to her parents' house temporarily because she couldn't face Emerald's empty bedroom in their shared apartment. As he had before, Ronald showed great strength and compassion. He sat next to Midnight, kept his arm around her, and had been her constant companion during the last couple of days.

In fact, at one point, they kissed each other on the lips and the sense I got was that it was more romantic than friendly. There was obviously more to Ronald than met the eye. Perhaps Midnight had radically misinterpreted Ronald's reaction to her relationship with Bryce. Maybe it hadn't been Bryce he was interested in, after all.

Watching them together gave me a hopeful feeling.

I walked them out to the waiting room, feeling tired but thinking I'd done something useful. I came back in the office, sat down at my desk and rested my head on my arms. I must have dozed off, because a sound caused my head to jerk up and it was no longer light outside.

The sound had been the throat clearing of the individual standing in my doorway.

I hadn't turned any lights on in my office except the small desk lamp, so the room was mostly dark. As had become my careless habit, I hadn't closed or locked my office door, thinking I would be leaving momentarily. Who knew how long I'd been sleeping.

I definitely had some karmic thing with doors.

The man standing in the entrance was very tall, but stooped over with rounded shoulders. The overhead light in the waiting room provided enough illumination for me to note that my visitor had shoulder-length dark hair with a rapidly receding hairline. He wore a black suit, white shirt, and skinny black tie. He held his hands together at chest level and twisted them, as if he was continually rolling a ball of clay or batter for a biscuit.

He edged forward, still standing in the doorway, as if reluctant to enter.

"Are you the vampire doctor?"

Chapter 19

I rose from my desk, turned on another table lamp and walked slowly toward him, still straining to make out his shadowy features. My solar plexus began to tingle gently. I rested my palm there while I determined if that familiar signal was simply information or a warning.

I kept a couple of feet of space between us. "I'm Kismet Knight. I'm a psychologist."

"Yes. You're the one. Can you help me?"

"I don't know."

Since I wasn't getting any particularly negative reaction from my sensing system and his uncomfortable, nervous gestures gave me the odd notion that he was more afraid of me than I was of him, I felt myself relax.

I pointed to the interior of the office. "Would you like to come in?"

He nodded and lumbered—as if moving his body around involved concentrated effort—over to the couch and sat.

I hesitated for a moment, watching him.

So, should I leave the door open because I don't know anything about this fellow, or should I close it to give him privacy? Should I lock it so no one else can surprise me today? Which would also mean I'll have to quickly unlock it if I need to get out fast. I can't believe I'm talking to myself about doors. In all my years of private practice, I've never given the door one thought. Never felt threatened. I guess I can kiss those days goodbye.

I gently closed the door, leaving it unlocked, and eased over to the dimmer switch on the wall. Rule number one: Never make quick moves with a frightened client.

"Would you mind if I turn on a bit more light?"

He lifted his chin from where it had been resting nearly on his chest, finally giving me a glimpse of his full face. "I don't mind."

I turned up the watts and claimed the chair nearest to him.

He had a thin, cadaverous face, dotted with deep pockmarks from a rough case of acne and lined with scars that brought to mind the sewn-together monster in "Frankenstein." His nose was hawk-like and took up lots of facial real estate. His eyes were a dull, washed-out gray, and were small and close together, which made his dark unibrow stand out starkly against his light skin.

He lowered his head again, twisting his hands in his lap.

I leaned forward slightly. "How can I help you?"

"I heard that it's safe to talk to you. That you won't tell anyone about us."

I sat back. "Who's 'us'?"

He raised his head and cocked it. The unibrow contracted in the center. He pulled back his upper lip so I could see his long canines. "Why, vampires, of course."

Okay, Kismet. Either there are vampires or there aren't, and after last night, there's really no doubt. You didn't think you'd be treating actual vampires, but you did ask them to come on down.

I tensed. "Uh, yes, of course. You can talk to me. How can I help?"

That explains the solar plexus tingle.

The hand-twisting escalated, and he lowered his head again. "I have an unusual problem. You know that vampires drink blood, right?"

I cleared my throat, wondering if this was a trick question. "Yes, I'm aware of that."

This is so amazingly ludicrous. How can I sit here and talk about drinking blood with a vampire? Where am I supposed to put this in my brain? Is my intuition out to lunch? Am I in danger?

He swiveled his head around, scanning the room, as if he wasn't sure we were alone.

"Well, I find the sight of blood disgusting." His shoulders sagged and his chest became even more concave than it had been. He almost whispered, "I avoid looking at it as much as I can. It's revolting."

Holy shit. Somebody help me. A vampire who doesn't like blood. Is this a joke? Am I being secretly filmed for some reality show?

But suddenly I remembered Devereux's mind reading tendencies and how he'd told me that all vampires are telepathic. Even if this was an individual of a different "species" sitting across from me, I didn't want to have my rude thoughts announced through the vampire radio network. I needed to ask some questions and set some ground rules.

I held up my hand in a "stop" gesture, and he brought his eyes to mine briefly before lowering them again.

"I'm sorry. I don't know your name."

He nodded, and spoke in a clear voice. "Yes. I suppose you would need that. I'm Apollo."

I raised my eyebrows before I could catch myself. "Apollo? Like the Greek god?"

He nodded. "Yes. The very same. I know I don't match my name very well—being decidedly un-god-like—but it was actually my last name when I was alive. Anthony Apollo. My human ancestors were originally from Greece. In the vampire world, catchy names are preferable to mundane, human-sounding ones, so I go by Apollo. Besides, it gives everyone quite a chuckle."

He smiled and relaxed his hands in his lap.

I returned his smile, pleased to witness a lighter side of him, and hopeful that letting him into my office hadn't been yet another bad decision.

"So, Apollo, you probably know that working with vampires is a relatively new thing for me. I'm still finding my way around. I'd appreciate if you could answer some questions. Would that be all right?"

He nodded. "If I can."

"I'd like you to tell me what powers you have. I mean, can you read my thoughts? If I look into your eyes, will I be entranced? That sort of thing."

He shrugged. "I'm pathetically weak for a vampire. I haven't been one long—less than fifty years—and the vamp who turned me was rather insipid himself. You know a vampire is only as powerful as the one who created him. Then add in my little 'problem' and I can honestly say that I don't bring much to the vampire gene pool. But to answer your question, I can read some thoughts. Specifically, strong emotions. If you're worried about what you've been thinking so far, I can tell you it's all gone over my head. Same with the eyes. Although I can probably give you a headache if I really concentrate."

I nodded, trying not to smile because I didn't know him well enough yet to decide if he'd be pleased I'd gotten his humor, or offended that I found him amusing. But I was impressed by his mind and his way with words. So many articulate vampires. Who knew?

"Well then, let's deal with the largest issue. You said that you heard I'm safe. That you can talk to me. I want to know if I'm safe with you. How likely is it you'll become interested in my neck?"

Gee, Kismet. That was graceful.

He laughed awkwardly for several seconds, deep smile lines creating bizarre shapes out of some of the pock marks on his face, which appeared to be unaccustomed to that much frivolity.

"Forgive me for laughing, but if you'd heard the warning Devereux gave the coven about anyone harming you in any way, you wouldn't even ask the question. Trust me. No one wants to have Devereux as an enemy. I think you will find that most of us have tremendous self-control. That is one thing I can say about myself, so you can rest assured you are safe with me."

Said the spider to the fly.

He pulled a tissue from the box on the nearby table and dabbed at his eyes, wiping away the gleeful moisture, and shook his head. "Ah, that felt very good. It's been quite a while since I laughed out loud."

I gave him a few seconds to collect himself.

"I'm glad the laughing felt good. Perhaps we can encourage you to do more of it. And thank you for explaining about what Devereux said. I'm pleased to know I'm safe with you, otherwise we wouldn't be able to work together."

Get a grip, Kismet. This isn't just another client you're setting boundaries with. This is a being who sucks the blood of people exactly like you. Is there no end to your political correctness?

"I noticed that your . . . er . . . fangs are descended. I understand that some vampires can will them in and out of their gums. Can you do that?"

"No. Unfortunately, I don't have that kind of power or control. My fangs remain in this position all the time." He raised his hand to cover his mouth. "I hope that doesn't concern you?"

I shook my head. "No, it doesn't." He lowered his hand again.

I cleared my throat. "Forgive the rudeness of this question, but I don't understand where vampires get the financial resources to come to a therapist. I'm pleased to speak with you this evening, but I usually require appointments in advance and some kind of payment arrangements. Will that be a difficulty?"

Aha! An escape hatch!

He smiled broadly and raised his eyes to mine. "No. The members of Devereux's coven are well taken care of. Money is the least of our concerns. I'll pay cash. The fee is irrelevant."

Well, now. Aren't those words that cause a therapist's heart to flutter?

"Thank you. Let's talk about your issue. How does your disgust at the sight of blood complicate your . . . experience?"

"I'm afraid I'm going to have to be quite graphic. Are

you sure you're willing to listen to this?"

I swallowed the lump that had formed in my throat. *No!* "I'll do the best I can."

I feel like a newbie, a brand new therapist sitting with my first client, trying not to screw up. Trying to convince the boogieman under the bed that there's no boogieman under the bed.

"Since you're the vampire psychologist, you probably know there are people who enjoy hanging around vampires because they want to have their blood sucked. They crave it."

I straightened in my seat. "Yes, I've heard that."

He let his shoulders visibly relax and inhaled a deep breath.

He's breathing. Do vampires breathe? Does Devereux? Why didn't I notice that small detail?

"Therefore, finding necks to suck on isn't my problem. People offer themselves to me all the time. All I have to do is tuck in. And as long as I can't actually *see* the blood, I'm fine. Like any other vampire, I love the taste of it, and the way it makes me feel is worth whatever it takes to get it. But it's impossible to suck blood without there being any . . . remains. Residue. Drops. Or, horror of horrors, actual uncontrolled bleeding.

"You see, sometimes in the midst of a feeding I can get carried away. It really is like having a body orgasm, if you'll forgive my bluntness, and I've been known to enlarge the wound with my fangs when my body starts reacting to the . . . uh . . . stimulation. It can be an overwhelming experience. Anyway, if I see even one drop of blood I immediately throw up everything I just swallowed. And then there is *more* blood, which makes me retch until the muscles of my stomach scream with pain."

His eyes had gone very wide and glassy as he told his story and he clasped his hands together so tightly that the white skin had become blue. He sat very stiff and straight.

The obvious terror the story stirred in him caused me to scoot to the edge of my seat in anticipation of having to perform some vampire CPR. I'd seen clients with that expression on their faces as they described fears of being covered in snakes, eaten by a lion, or burned alive. A phobia is a phobia.

Although I had to admit I wasn't really eager to put the vampire CPR thing to the test.

I took a breath and sat back. I noticed that my own hands clutched the arms of the chair so rigidly the veins stuck out. I consciously let go and wiggled my fingers to restore the circulation.

"That sounds very scary for you. I can totally understand why you'd avoid situations where you have to see blood. Do you remember the first time you had that reaction?"

"Uh, yes. Unfortunately, I do remember. I have to warn you that this might be difficult for you to hear."

He paused and studied me before he continued. I guess he was waiting for me to give an indication I was willing to proceed. I nodded.

"It was a few years after I became a vampire. Prior to the event I'm going to tell you about, I could swim in blood and it had no effect on me. It was the first time I drank from a child. A dying child. The little boy was near death from cancer and I heard him crying through the window. He said, 'please don't leave me.' I don't know who he was talking to because no one was there. The child was all alone in that room, but I could see people moving around in the other parts of the house. He was all alone."

He stared at me silently for several seconds. Despite the controlled mask he'd made of his face, his eyes betrayed him by expressing the fear and self-loathing he usually kept locked away.

The words "all alone" had been said with such raw misery that my heart ached.

In that moment I understood how difficult it had been for him to tell his story to a therapist or anyone.

I had a clear intuitive sense that he was afraid I'd . . . what? Run out of the room? Condemn him for being what he was? Grab a stake, hammer, and leap on him?

I gave him a gentle smile and nodded. "I understand. He was all alone. Then what happened?"

"I waited until everyone else had gone to bed and I went to the boy and held him in the dark. I don't know why I felt compelled to go to him. I usually had no interest in children. He was bleeding from his nose and mouth, and I licked the blood from his skin and rocked him. He began to remind me of myself when I was small. I could feel his pain building and, as he was ready to leave his body, I drank him dry. At the last moment he put his arms around my neck and pleaded, 'Don't leave me, Daddy.' After his soul left his body, I stumbled out into the alley and threw up for the first time."

Shit. Where do I begin?

I let him see the sympathy and compassion in my eyes and spoke softly. "That's a very heart-breaking story. Do you remember a time when you were small when you asked your Daddy not to leave?"

He stared at me with horrified, pain-filled eyes and nodded. He told me the story of his father abandoning the family when Apollo was only five and how he'd begged him not to leave. After he finished sharing the memory, he frowned and stared down at his limp hands in his lap.

A tear rolled down his cheek.

"Do you think my experience with that little boy has something to do with my blood phobia? Because of my own father?"

"I do, yes."

He plucked another tissue from the box and wiped away the tears streaming down his face.

"You must be right, because I already feel different. Would you mind if we ended our meeting for now? You've given me a lot to think about."

"I wouldn't mind at all. You do have a lot to think about."

We both stood and he reached into the pocket of his jacket, pulled out an envelope and set it on the table.

He sniffled a few times. "I don't know what your fees are, but there should be enough in here to hold me for a while. Just let me know when you need more. I promise to make an appointment next time."

He extended his hand and I took it. The coolness of his flesh surprised me and I caught my breath. He noticed my reaction and released my hand.

"I'm sorry. Since I don't drink enough blood, my skin is always cold. I hope I can do something about that. Thank you for today."

I smiled. "You're welcome. I look forward to our next session. You might want to consider hypnosis. Perhaps we can gently uncover more of the memory that's causing the problem."

I walked him to the door and opened it.

He blew his nose on a fresh tissue, nodded and left.

I briefly considered sitting at my desk and writing up case notes for Apollo, but I was tired and wanted to go home. I'd write up the notes at home later with a glass of wine.

It wasn't likely I'd forget any of the details.

I thought about Apollo's story and the poor child who'd died in his arms. As sad as it was, I'd actually heard much worse from my human clients.

Who would've thought that a vampire would have the same issue as anyone else? The universal experience of a crappy childhood.

Maybe vampires weren't really so different after all.

Yeah, right.

Chapter 20

It was a miracle. A quiet, drama-free evening.

After I wrote up my case notes for Apollo, I enjoyed a long, glorious, undisturbed shower, still wearing the necklace that wouldn't go away. I stood under the spray until the hot water cooled, which was saying something because I have a very large hot water tank. My skin had gotten satisfyingly pruned. I slathered myself with the exquisite and obscenely expensive skin moisturizer my friend regularly sent me from her European exploits

I snuggled into my Sigmund Freud pajamas—seriously, they're white silk with Sigmund's face splattered like black, Rorschach inkblots all over the fabric. They were a hot novelty item at the last American Psychological Association convention in Las Vegas. And, if that wasn't cozy enough, I dug out my furry Miss Piggy slippers, complete with snout and curly tail, and covered up with my ever-present pink robe.

I pulled my hair, which occasionally can feel very heavy, up into a ponytail on the top of my head, and let it cascade down in spiral curls around my shoulders.

I was in the midst of total and complete relaxation. Or total and complete denial, whichever you prefer.

I'd just poured a glass of liquid bliss in the form of white wine when the doorbell rang.

I turned on the porch light and squinted through the peep hole. Either there wasn't anyone there, or my visitor was hiding out of view. Or some other option I didn't even want to think about.

After the events of the last week, none of the possibilities were good news.

I chose the "when in doubt, do nothing" approach and was rewarded by a repeat performance of the doorbell tones.

Leaving the chain engaged, I cracked open the door barely enough to scan a small area, which basically wasn't in the least helpful. I still couldn't see anyone there.

I was just about to close the door, when it occurred to me I should ask an obvious question.

"Who's there?"

"It is I, Kismet. Devereux. Please let me in."

Devereux? If it was Devereux, why was he ringing the doorbell? Why didn't he just pop in unannounced, uninvited, as always? Why didn't he simply swoop in like an intrusive bat and snatch me off to another creepy-crawly adventure?

"Why are you here?"

I was batting a thousand with Questions for Dummies.

"I have come to make love to you."

"What?" I croaked. Couldn't say I'd heard that one before.

Since I was still staring at the floor in front of my door, I recognized the black leather boots that stepped into my line of vision.

I raised my eyes but could only see more black and a flash of what could've been blond hair.

Apparently, he could also see the floor on the other side

of the door because he said, his voice oozing amusement, "What are you wearing on your feet?"

I glanced down at the dual Miss Piggys and felt the need to defend them. Her?

"None of your business. What do you really want?" Although, I had to admit I'd rather enjoyed the previous answer.

"I spoke the truth. I have come to make love to you. Please open the door."

How arrogant! And you just assume that's okay with me? That I'm just going to open the door and make another deal with the devil? That I'm even remotely interested in having sex with you after our last trip to the Twilight Zone?

"How do I know it's really you? You usually materialize out of thin air."

"As you wish."

I heard that familiar little *pop* sound, felt a rush of air and suddenly knew he was behind me. I turned, hands on my hips.

"Hey! That wasn't an invitation!"

A dazzling smile spread across his face. "You forget I have that handy little mind reading ability."

He bowed from the waist, wearing a variation of his usual leather-god outfit. "I rang the doorbell because I thought you would prefer me to enter your home the normal, human way. I understand you are weary of the drama that has taken over your life. I do not wish to contribute any further to your discomfort."

He brought his hands around from behind him. They held a huge bouquet of pink roses and a ludicrously large box of chocolates.

"Gifts for you, my love."

He bent forward and brushed my lips lightly with his. The familiar, delicious scent of him took my nostrils hostage and my lips instinctively puckered in anticipation of more of the same.

He burst out laughing.

"You have pigs on your feet!"

He thrust the roses and box of chocolates into my hands, scooped me up into his arms and walked us over to the couch. As soon as he was seated with me on his lap, he reached over and lifted my feet, inspecting the colorful porcine coverings.

"I have never seen such a thing. Do modern humans wear all animals on their feet or only pigs?" The longer he stared at the fluffy piggy shoes, the harder he laughed. He thumped the snout with his thumb and first finger and pulled on the tail.

As annoying as it was to be laughed at, something about his mirth was infectious and I found myself chuckling, which eventually gave way to snorts and belly laughs.

Once again, whatever resolve I'd built up against Devereux had leaked away in direct proportion to the number of minutes I spent gazing at his perfect face. It was a waste of time for me to argue that I was immune to his charm, or his eyes, or whatever it was that caused my normal inhibitions to catch the first plane outta town.

At some point I must have put the flowers and chocolates on the coffee table, because my arms were free to ensnare his neck. Which then led to my being flat on my back in my Freud pjs and my piggy shoes with an absurdly gorgeous vampire on top of me, attached at the lips.

So much for a quiet, relaxing evening.

We made out like teenagers on the couch.

As always with Devereux, I couldn't stop touching him. Couldn't run my fingers through his long, silky, aromatic hair enough. Couldn't feast on his lips even remotely enough. Couldn't imagine anything more important than having him inside me.

Even counting my close call with Alan, I hadn't technically had intercourse for two years and the muscles in my vagina contracted in gleeful, moist anticipation.

He lifted his hot mouth from mine long enough to whisper, "Will you invite me to your bed, my love?"

Geez, the guy's voice should be a registered weapon. It could take you down in three seconds.

"What happened to all the mind reading? I've been sending out the welcome committee for the last thirty minutes."

He raised himself up just enough so I could see his smile. "I know, but it is important to me to hear the words from your own sweet lips."

He somehow managed to lift himself off the couch in a flowing motion while scooping me up at the same time.

"Shall we?"

He carried me up the stairs, the twin Piggies bobbing up and down, but my mind was no longer on footwear. In fact, my entire brain was focused on the fastest way to get us both naked.

We entered my bedroom and Devereux paused at the foot of my bed.

"You have not changed the sheets since you shared your bed with Alan. I can smell him. I wish to be the only presence here with you."

He put me down and stood in front of me.

I started to explain that I hadn't "officially" had sex with Alan and there really wasn't any part of him left behind, but Devereux gently pressed a finger to my lips, ending the flow of words.

"None of that matters. Nothing that happened before me matters. I simply wish to make love to you right now in your own bed on fresh sheets. Yes?"

He removed his black leather duster and threw it in the rocking chair in the corner.

Enjoying the view of the physique that'd been under the coat, I moved over to him, lightly kissed his lips and smiled. "Definitely, yes."

I opened a brand new set of silk sheets I'd had for a long time, but never used, while Devereux stripped off the old bedding.

Quite an efficient team, we smoothed on the new sheets, watching each other with hungry eyes.

"Do you have candles?" he asked.

Uh, did I? I thought for a moment and remembered which box in the closet I'd stashed them in. I wouldn't tell him that I'd only bought them in case the electricity went out and I needed emergency light. I was trying to learn to keep my unromantic explanations to myself. At least under certain conditions.

While I was in the closet I stepped out of the Miss Piggy shoes and put them back in their special place, next to my Glenda Good Witch sandals.

Okay. So I let my inner child out sometimes.

He took the candles and the holders I'd also retrieved,

placed them on the night stands on either side of the bed and stood back, appreciating his handiwork. He smiled, pointed a finger at each of the candles, and the wicks burst into flame.

He laughed and said out loud what I was thinking. "More parlor tricks."

I turned off the light switch on the wall and basked in the lovely glow of the candles. The soft illumination was the perfect setting for Devereux. His eyes sparkled, his hair was a shining radiance, and his skin assumed the hues of the firelight.

He glided over to the window and closed the mini-blinds, then circled back around to the door and silently sealed it. Ambling over to me, he gently released my hair from the ponytail and eased the long curls down over my breasts.

"Your hair is beautiful." He nestled his face in my hair and breathed in the fragrance, then ran his fingers through it and smiled. "You are beautiful. I had given up hope of ever finding you. And now you are here. Now you are mine."

"I'm yours? What does that mean?"

"It means we belong to each other. We always have."

I started to question his assumptions, and he silenced me with a kiss.

He reluctantly pulled away, and leaned against the wall to balance himself while he removed his boots. He pulled his shirt off over his head in one slow, elegant motion.

Vampire Chippendales.

Even though I'd seen him without his shirt before, the effect in the candlelight was almost overwhelming. The muscles of his shoulders, arms, and abdomen were perfectly chiseled. A magnificent work of art in flesh and bone. I started to think about what the odds were of a human being so exquisitely built, then remembered he wasn't human. Not even close.

But that didn't matter. In a very short, intense time period, I'd gone from thinking Devereux was mentally ill—an unfortunate having psychotic delusions about being a vampire—to waiting breathlessly for that very same vampire to fill me with what was already making its presence known inside his tight leather pants.

I splayed my hands on his chest, relishing the firm warmth of him, and moved close enough to take one of his nipples into my mouth. He moaned and relaxed his head back, embracing me with his strong arms.

I started to unbutton the waistband of his pants and he covered my hand with his.

"Wait. We must remove your shirt first."

Vampire rules?

I didn't ask why. He lifted my hair back behind my shoulders and unbuttoned my pajama top. Letting the slippery silk fall away, he used his fingers to guide the fabric from my shoulders and down my arms. He bent and slid his face over my breasts, taking one nipple at a time into his mouth with a gentle sucking motion. He cupped both breasts in his hands and laid tiny kisses all over them, before using his tongue to harden my nipples to painful, throbbing points.

He straightened, lifted the pentagram necklace, and brought it to his lips. He kissed the center of the circular design, then replaced it, all the time gazing into my eyes.

I already ached for him and couldn't imagine being able to hold out much longer. My knees were barely functional.

He stepped away and studied me, the expression on his

face a clear indication of the maelstrom of feelings and desires he couldn't hide.

He caressed my breasts again and said, "You are very lush and ripe for such a slender woman. In all my eight hundred years, yours are the most magnificent breasts I have ever seen. I shall never tire of touching them, of sucking them."

He demonstrated, as I fisted my hands in his hair.

After a few delicious seconds he kissed his way back to my lips.

Sliding his hands into the elastic waistband of my pajama bottoms, he eased the material down my hips, leaving my white cotton bikini panties in place. He stroked and massaged me, running his hands up my back and down to the mounds of my ass, pulling my lower body tight against his hard, thick erection.

I found my way back to the button on the waistband of his pants and successfully opened it. The zipper slid down easily and I quickly discovered that Devereux was an *au natural* kinda guy.

That realization was outrageously arousing for me, and I enthusiastically shimmied his pants down his hips, releasing the unexpectedly large organ jutting out from a thatch of blond curls.

I had a momentary thought about the myth that a man's feet or hands are correlated with the size of his penis. In Devereux's case, his normal-sized artistic hands and average appearing feet gave no indication of what had been sequestered away behind the zipper.

I sank to my knees, still pulling down the leather pants, and gently nudged him to sit on the edge of the bed. I raised my mouth to his, ran my tongue along his lips, then kissed him, while one hand stroked the warm, hard length of his throbbing penis. He moved rhythmically against my hand while he moaned softly. I slid my finger up to the drops of liquid oozing from the opening, then stroked his length again.

We used our tongues to taste and explore each other. I felt his fangs extend as I carefully avoided their needle-sharp tips. Running my tongue up and down the length of his fangs seemed to have the same effect as my hand on his erection.

I pulled away from his lips, kissing my way down his chest and his stomach until I reached his hard length and took it in my mouth. His skin was velvety soft over the taut muscle.

He gasped and held my head between his hands, moving gently to show me what he liked. I used my lips and tongue to taste every part of him, to whip him into a greater frenzy of desire. I was a quick study and he soon cried out and lifted my head from his groin.

"If you continue to do that I cannot hold back, and I wish for us to share our first orgasm together while I am inside you."

The crotch of my panties was already soaked with creamy desire and he lifted me up onto the bed as I kicked off the last clothing barrier between us.

Both completely nude now, we knelt on the bed, facing each other, feasting our eyes.

His body was astoundingly magnificent. Long, lean, and muscular with smooth skin and perfect features. The light blond hair that trailed down his abdomen to his crotch was soft and slightly darker than his long platinum mane. And rising out of that thatch of silk was an erection that belonged on a statue of a Greek god. Or a Celtic god. I never was sure what part of Europe Devereux came from.

We reached for each other at the same time and I palmed the mounds of his ass, exploring the firm muscles there as I pulled him tightly against me.

We embraced and kissed passionately, taking the joining of our lips deeper and deeper until it felt as if we were one being—merged.

He spoke that strange, musical language in my mind, a soft melody of words and spaces. Even though I didn't understand what he was saying, the sounds felt right. As if my body remembered them in some mysterious way.

He gently turned me and guided me down onto the bed, bringing his mouth to my nipples again while his finger slid into the wet heat between my legs.

He whispered in my mind, "I love that you are so wet for me. You make me feel alive."

Using one fingertip in a feather-light movement, he caressed my clitoris, making little circular motions which caused me to arch my body, spreading my legs wider, before he moved that clever finger up inside me.

He added a second finger, while still stroking me with his thumb.

A wave of something powerful built inside me and I made primal noises, instinctively moving my hips in time with the rhythm of his fingers.

I moaned and fisted my hands in his hair, lifting his head. "Devereux, please. I want you inside me."

He raised his mouth from my nipple, brought his lips near mine and whispered, "Inside your body and your heart."

Eagerly, I reached down and guided his thickness into my opening, wrapping my legs around his waist at the same time to take him deeper.

If I hadn't been so wet his size might have been uncomfortable, but under the circumstances, it was as if we were made for each other. One lock with a perfect key.

I don't know which one of us groaned louder, but he swallowed the sounds with his mouth on mine.

Still kissing, he thrust himself inside me. Long, slow, deep strokes. His controlled movements drove me mad with desire. I didn't know if all 800-year-old vampires had such skill in lovemaking, but this one certainly did. I'm not sure if I screamed or only wanted to.

Then he raised himself up, grabbed my hands and lifted them over my head, holding my wrists. His mesmerizing voice became lower-pitched and husky, sending waves of chills over my skin.

"Do you remember the moment in the club when you asked me to use my eyes to join with you? When we became one consciousness?"

I didn't want to talk. I wanted his mouth on mine, his hands in my hair, his hips thrusting against me. But his description of the passion that fired in me that night brought me back to the delicious memory and I had a body rush, causing me to gasp. The muscles of my vagina tightened around him involuntarily and he reacted with a deeper thrust and an intake of breath.

He smiled, obviously aware of my memory and the mental chatter. Or maybe it was just because what we were doing felt very, very good.

"I will take that as a yes."

I closed my eyes and mumbled something that could have been interpreted as an affirmative.

"Open your eyes, my love. Let me show you that everything before this moment was simply a small taste of what is possible."

I opened my eyes, connected with his and reality as I knew it faded away.

My world became the blue-green of his eyes.

A spinning, shining, universe of bodyless, yet extraordinarily physical, sensations. As if the pleasure volume on every nerve ending had been turned up while simultaneously having no awareness of being physical at all.

Floating in a stream of consciousness.

I hadn't done any experimentation with hallucinogenic drugs, so I didn't have actual experience to base anything on, but from what I'd read, I was in the middle of an altered state. The vampire version of an LSD trip.

Time had no meaning, so I didn't know how long we'd been there. His penis still moved inside me as we kissed wildly. It could have been hours. Or seconds.

Devereux and I communicated purely telepathically now, and as the orgasm built inside us, it was impossible to tell if the wave of pleasure had a specific starting place. Or, if we'd simply become the wave.

We'd fallen into each other's eyes and nothing else mattered.

Just as the peak of the orgasm began, Devereux pierced my neck with his fangs.

I gasped, but there was no pain. Only intense, reverberating pleasure.

Pleasure that was off the scale.

I screamed as wave after wave of bliss washed over me. Every muscle in my body—I think it was my body—contracted in ecstasy.

Somewhere in the midst of my own release, I felt Devereux spasm inside me, his mouth still at my neck, his silky hair flowing across my breasts.

He brought his lips back to mine and kissed me with profound tenderness, our souls merged as completely as our bodies. I tasted the sweet, coppery tang of my own blood on his tongue and found myself savoring the experience. I sucked on his tongue and ran mine over his teeth, wanting to take in more of the salty essence.

It occurred to me briefly that enjoying the taste of blood probably wasn't a good thing, but I was still lost in the rapture of the moment.

A soft groan from Devereux brought me back to sufficient awareness to notice that I'd been sucking on his fang, which seemed to be as stimulating to him as my sucking on other things.

I felt his erection expand inside me, apparently ready to have another go, and I lifted my hips to take him deeper.

In another of his amazing, seamless movements, he raised himself to his knees, and held me by my ass, our bodies still attached at the crotch. We locked eyes as he pressed me back against the headboard, one of his hands still underneath me, and the other braced against the wall.

He pounded into me and I heard a voice repeating, "Yes, yes, yes," and discovered it was mine.

I tightened my legs and arms around him, and he held me effortlessly, as if I weighed nothing. He'd told me that vampires possessed unnatural strength, but I hadn't had much personal evidence until then. I think he could have held me there, giving me one orgasm after another, until I cried for mercy.

Which I finally did.

I clung to him like a wet tissue as he emptied himself into me yet again, only then letting the resilient organ slide out of my vagina. Still straddling his lap, I snuggled into his warm arms and let myself be gently rocked.

He whispered lovely words, in English, French and what might have been Gaelic, and stroked my hair.

At some point I'd fallen asleep, because he swept his finger gently across my cheek and said softly, "I must go, my love. The dawn approaches."

My eyes flew open and I noticed I was tucked into my bed, and Devereux was fully dressed.

He sat next to me and brushed a lock of hair away from my face.

"For eight hundred years I waited for this night. I am very much in love with you. I do not expect you to return my feelings right away. I understand that this is all new to you. I only ask that you give me a chance to win your heart."

He leaned over, brushed my lips with his and vanished.

I fell back asleep with the lyrics of Heart's classic "Magic Man" flowing through my mind.

Chapter 21

The screeching of the alarm clock dragged me, kicking and screaming, back to the land of the living.

I groaned, rolled over and turned off the annoying siren.

I'd had the most amazing dream. Or to be more accurate, I was in the middle of it when the damn alarm went off. I knew I had to get up, but it was so tempting just to lie there and revel in the memories from the previous night and the remnants of the nocturnal fantasy.

In the dream I'd been with Devereux again, but this time we were outside, in the sunlight, on top of a beautiful mountain, surrounded by other peaks. I could actually feel the breeze blowing through my hair and across my body. Which was naked, by the way.

As was Devereux's. Yum.

The muscles of my vagina contracted as I remembered Devereux, stretched out like an alabaster nature god in the vivid green grass, with me on top of him, riding that impressive erection, as we both screamed with pleasure.

It seemed so real. The sun shining on Devereux's pale skin, the feel of the grass on my knees and lower legs as I straddled him, a wafting of evergreen in the air.

After sharing another cosmic orgasm I collapsed on his

firm chest and felt his arms close around me as his lips passionately reclaimed mine.

Then, in another of his smooth moves, he flipped me over so I was on my back in the grass and he kissed his way down my body. Faster than I could see, he bent my knees, opened my legs, and began to lick my clitoris. His tongue was soft, relentless, and had honed in on the perfect spot. Impossibly, within seconds I felt another powerful wave of ecstasy building. After he pushed me over the edge, he angled his mouth ever so slightly and gently sank his fangs into the soft lip next to my clit. There was a fleeting sting as his needle-sharp canines pierced the tender skin and he began to suck, but that was quickly drowned out by the mother of all orgasms.

Waves of intense pleasure built, one upon the next, as I screamed words in a language I didn't know. Just when I thought I would go mad if the sensations didn't stop, he ran his tongue over the tiny punctures, kissed me there and sat up, a wicked smile on his amazing face.

That's when I was rudely interrupted and forced to resurface into consensus reality.

But, damn if it wasn't the best dream ever. Even thinking about it gave me a hot body rush.

I stuffed my newly reawakened libido with a sigh.

Back to the real world.

All it took was the simple act of sitting up to remind me that my physical body, as well as my dream body, had undergone quite a workout only a few hours before.

That realization birthed a silly grin.

I guess it could have been the fact that, after two years, I'd been royally pleasured by the best lover I'd ever had.

Magnificently shagged. Awesomely boinked. Spectacularly screwed. We'd surely broken the world record for the number of orgasms a couple could have and still be alive to talk about it.

Well, one of us was alive to talk about it, anyway.

I sat back against the very same headboard that had been witness to the athletic portion of the performance and sighed happily, still unable to stop smiling.

It occurred to me that I'd never asked Devereux where he went during the daylight hours. Did he sleep in a coffin? Maybe sleep was the wrong word. But he'd told me he dreams. So how could he dream if he didn't sleep? How could he dream if he just died when the sun came up?

Now that I was actually beginning to accept the ludicrous idea that not only did vampires exist, but I was having a mad, passionate, sexual relationship with the Head Poobah, I realized I was very curious.

If I was going to counsel real vampires, I needed to ask lots more questions and get much better answers.

I needed to make sure I didn't simply shift from a total refusal to believe anything paranormal, to a complete acceptance of any and all vampire weirdness. That was just too extreme for me and not in the least scientific.

I threw the covers back, heaved my legs over the side of the bed, stood and attempted to stretch. All the major muscle groups in my body ganged up on me at once and started whining. If it hadn't been for the fact that I had a full client load for the next twelve hours, I'd have considered diving back into the bed and pulling the covers over my head. With any luck, I'd fall back asleep and have the mountain dream again.

But instead, I promised the complaining muscles a long, hot shower so I propelled myself in that direction.

I hoped I'd be able to wipe the goofy smile off my face when I got to my office. But, on the other hand, it might do my clients good to have their notions about me confounded, to help them realize that change really could happen. Even to me.

Walking to the bathroom reminded me, again, what happened to muscles if you didn't use them. The area between my legs was tender and sore, which was to be expected after considering the size of the object that'd been jammed in there.

I started the shower, adjusted the water temperature and stepped in. The soothing water flowed down my body, miraculously easing all the tight muscles while relaxing me into a boneless state. I washed my hair, then soaped the rest of me. The lathering came to an abrupt halt when I reached the area between my legs. Not only was it tender, but the soap caused a sudden, burning pain.

"Ow, dammit! When did this happen?"

Not sure who I was asking, I put the soap down and felt around the sore spot with my fingers. Beyond verifying that it was, indeed, uncomfortable, the examination didn't give me much additional information.

Finding wounds on my body that weren't supposed to be there had started to be a regular occurrence. It didn't take a psychic to figure out that the feeling of déjà vu I experienced was because I'd been through this same routine just a few days earlier, thanks to Bryce.

I finished my shower, toweled off and grabbed a hand

mirror from the top of the vanity.

Angling it so I could examine my nether regions, I touched a finger gingerly along the tender skin, but still couldn't make out anything in particular.

Maybe we'd just rubbed the poor little thing raw with our calisthenics.

When I pulled back the lip on one side, clearly visible were two not-so-tiny holes, floating in a sea of angry, red skin.

"What the hell?"

I reached over, opened the medicine cabinet above the sink, and retrieved the tube of antiseptic salve that I'd used for my last bite wound.

Dotting it carefully on the sore spots, I struggled to remember any time during the night when Devereux'd bitten anything but my neck.

I instinctively lifted my hand up to my throat, checking for evidence of what I clearly remembered, and felt only smooth skin. I raised the mirror, shifting around to display all sides, then shook my head.

Nothing. No sign of the sensuous neck nibble. Not even a red spot.

Either I'd blacked out and missed a very erotic chapter in our book of carnal knowledge, or something altogether different had happened.

Then, as if someone turned on a movie, I remembered the last scene of the mountain dream. The labial feast.

"It was not a dream" floated through my mind in a familiar voice.

I jumped up and ran into my bedroom. "Devereux?"

"We were in another dimension and I was careless. My

heartfelt apologies, my love. I will heal your wound tonight."

"Dever—" I almost got his name out before I realized the voice was coming from inside my head. Or, at least I was pretty sure that no one else could hear it.

At least, not anyone I could see.

I'll never get used to this.

I paused for a moment, waiting for any remaining astral proclamations, but the voice was silent.

Well, that's great. Now even my dreams leave scars.

I didn't know whether I was being open-minded or stupid, but one thing was certain.

Nothing surprised me anymore.

Well, almost nothing.

As soon as I stepped off the elevator at my office later that morning, I knew something was wrong. Not only did my intuitive radar system shoot off a warning, but my regular senses shifted into overdrive. I'd learned from experience not to ignore those kinds of signals.

I walked slowly down the short hallway between the elevators and my waiting room, steeling myself for what I'd find. That usually closed door was now open and there was a horrendous stench coming from my inner office.

I set my purse and briefcase against the wall opposite the entryway, gingerly pushed the waiting room door open with one finger, and discovered the main door was not only open, it was off its hinges, lying on the floor in front of my desk.

All the chairs and tables in the waiting area had been

overturned, some were broken and everything was coated in a dark reddish-brown substance. On the wall someone had scrawled, in childish print in that same horrible color, "i will not suffer a witch to live," and "you will be washed in the blood."

As bad as that was, I knew it had only been the prelude to the main concerto.

Holding my breath, I stepped to the doorway of my office and surveyed the scene.

Compared to the condition of this larger room, the mess in the waiting area had been child's play. Perhaps that wasn't an inaccurate diagnosis of the perpetrator's developmental level.

I shuddered out the breath I'd been holding.

Someone had taken a knife—clearly a honking huge knife—to all the couches and chairs, slashing wide gashes through every cushion. Then, just to make sure the destruction was complete, the furniture was tumbled and drizzled with more of that reddish-brown stain.

All the files in my locked file cabinet had been shredded and strewn around the room. Some appeared to have been partially burned, which explained one small portion of the odor. The metal file cabinet itself was oddly twisted, as if hands had pulled it apart.

The drawers in my desk had been opened and they, along with the top of the desk and my computer, were saturated with what could only be pools of blood.

The stunted artist hadn't spared the walls in this room either. On all four sides were scribbled various obscenities, threats, and a few things I vaguely noted as coming from religious sources.

Actually, I recognized everything that was written on the

wall because I'd heard it all before.

Brother Luther had screamed every word of it at me in one of the enraged messages I'd saved in my voice mail system.

As astounding as the damage was in both rooms, I still couldn't figure out what the ghastly smell was.

Had Brother Luther broken into my office and left a dead animal? Excrement? If it had been him, he must be a very large, strong man. Or maybe he brought somebody with him. In any case, the destruction was violent, thorough, and personal. I wasn't sure how much good it would have done, but I should've told the police, or at least Alan, about the telephone threats right after they started. Maybe Brother Luther—if he really was responsible—had done something similar before. He might even have a police record. Hindsight is always crystal clear.

I scanned the room again for the source of the smell and noticed that the door, which had been torn off its hinges, was lying strangely on the floor. Not flat, but at an angle, as if something was underneath.

My solar plexus tightened and my heart pounded. My brain treated me to a high-speed presentation of all the worst-case scenarios I could imagine.

I moved slowly and carefully through the debris, not wanting to disturb any more of the evidence than necessary, and knelt down near the dislodged door. A wave of nausea hit me. I lifted up one corner, which was all it took for me to discover the source of the smell.

A slender, young male was underneath. He was deathly white, clearly no longer alive, and drenched in blood.

I guessed he'd been there for several hours.

Startled, I pushed the door off of him and jumped when it bumped into a still upright end table, sending the lamp that had miraculously survived the onslaught crashing to the floor.

I was still staring at the unidentified young man when I heard someone gasp.

"Dr. Knight! What happened? Are you okay? Oh, my gawd! That's Eric!"

I turned so quickly I lost my balance and went down hard on my butt in a puddle of thick blood.

Midnight and Ronald had scheduled another joint appointment and they were right on time.

We all stared at each other for a few endless seconds, and then Ronald stepped forward, offering his hand.

"Let me help you up, Dr. Knight."

Midnight had locked both hands over her mouth and stood rigid, eyes wide.

I accepted Ronald's help to stand, and moved away from the young man Midnight had identified as Eric. The apprentice who'd crafted the little knives for blood swapping.

After helping me up, Ronald went back to Midnight. He put his arm around her and stroked her hair, but she didn't respond.

I noticed a fine trembling in her body. One of the first signs of shock.

"Ronald, would you help Midnight out to the hallway, please? I need to go out there and make some phone calls."

I kept my voice as calm and normal as possible.

He understood what I hadn't said, nodded and pushed Midnight gently in the direction of the door, holding her by the shoulders to keep her from stumbling or tripping over the chaos on the floor.

Once out of direct sight of her friend's body, Midnight lowered her hands away from her mouth and cried silently, her head on Ronald's shoulder.

I left them huddled together long enough to retrieve my purse and fetch my cell phone. The expression on their traumatized, young faces was heart-wrenching, and I wished they'd been late for their appointment. That I'd been able to meet them out in the hall instead of involving them in more psychotic madness.

But, ruminating about what should have been didn't do any of us any good. I joined them and rested my hand on Midnight's arm.

"I'm sorry, Midnight. But the police are going to want to talk to you and Ronald since you knew Eric. Why don't you sit down and relax until they arrive?"

They both nodded and lowered themselves to the floor.

I leaned back against the wall and closed my eyes, taking a moment to sort out my emotions.

Oddly though, instead of feeling frightened or upset, I felt calm. I'd been making the assumption that all of the terrible things that had happened—Emerald Addison's death, my kidnapping and everything else—had something to do with the vampire-wannabe community. I'd finally started to believe there were supernatural forces at work. And it was clear that somehow the vampire stuff was involved. But it was almost a relief to come to the realization I had a garden-variety psychopath on my hands. No doubt this serial killer had abusive childhood experiences, linked with religiously instigated guilt and shame. I'd hazard to guess he wasn't fond of women either. Classic. Textbook. A mentally defective, wounded child acting out in the most hideous ways.

Now, *that* was something I knew how to deal with.

And how convenient that he seemed to have taken a personal interest in me.

I walked down by the elevator and dialed 911 on my cell phone. I explained there'd been a death in my office and returned to the other end of the hallway where Midnight and Ronald sat, standing nearby to wait for the police to arrive.

The calm before the storm.

I glanced down and noticed my clothes were trashed. Again.

Having my cream-colored pantsuit covered in blood was a miserable reminder of the night I spent in the mausoleum. But since I didn't have any spare clothes to change into, I had little choice but to ignore the psychic flashbacks and distract myself by thinking about ways the police could use me as bait to catch the killer.

By the time they arrived, I'd concocted some creative and audacious scenarios, in which Super Psychologist would save the day.

I heard the *dings* of the elevators just before the doors opened, and I instinctively moved a few steps in that direction.

A dozen uniform officers swarmed out, followed by a forensics unit. From the tail end, preceded by heavy footsteps, came a familiar voice.

"Well, well. Dr. Knight. We meet again."

Lieutenant Bullock strolled over to me in the hallway,

clasped her hands behind her and walked around me in a circle. The edges of her mouth were quirked in a grim sort of smile. She raised her eyebrows when she noticed the large, messy bloodstain on the back of my pants.

"Up to your ass in blood once more, eh? Or, should I say twice more, since I last saw you? I heard about the cemetery deal, and your influential friend making sure you didn't have to go through normal channels. Oh, yes. Why so surprised? I make a point of keeping track of 'interesting' people. And you, Dr. Knight, strike me as very . . . 'interesting'. Funny, how often death follows you around."

She ran her fingers through her short, graying hair and shifted her attention to Midnight, then Ronald, then me.

She pointed at the couple huddled on the floor.

"I'll send some officers to begin their interviews and to get preliminary details from you. Then, after I do my job inside, I'll be back."

Her smile brightened. "I'm going to handle your statement. Personally."

She took a couple of steps toward my waiting room door, then partially turned, her face devoid of emotion.

"Don't go anywhere."

She pivoted and strode into my office, barking out orders to the officers already inside.

Surprise in his voice, Ronald said, "Wow, that policewoman doesn't like you, Dr. Knight. What did you do to piss her off?"

I almost responded by saying "What do you think I did to piss her off?" but caught myself before giving the automatic therapy reply.

Instead, I shrugged. "I honestly don't know. Something about me bothered her from the first moment she laid eyes on me. Maybe I remind her of someone else."

"Or maybe she knew you in a past life?"

I turned to the voice and was grateful and relieved to see Alan approaching.

He covered the short distance quickly and put his arm around my shoulders.

"I couldn't believe my ears when I heard the address of the homicide on my radio. What happened? Did one of your clients go berserk?"

"No. Someone broke in, destroyed my office."

He tightened his grip on my shoulders. "Well, your trusty FBI agent is always here for you. Who died?"

The shoulder resting against him relaxed. "A friend of Midnight's. A boy. One of the other vampire apprentices."

"This is a vampire thing?" He unceremoniously dropped his arm, leaped away, sprinted off into my office and left me with my mouth hanging open.

Well. So much for being here for me.

I sighed and backed up against the wall to wait for whatever Lieutenant Bullock had in store.

True to her word, she sent officers out to interview Midnight and Ronald and a detective to talk to me.

The detective politely asked questions that I only had one answer for: I don't know. With each similar response from me, his eyebrows inched closer to his hairline.

I couldn't blame him for being skeptical. This was the third police interrogation I'd participated in during the past week, and even I had trouble believing that I had no worthwhile information to share.

How had I managed to involve myself in so many situations where I appeared to be a chess piece being moved around on some cosmic board by unseen hands?

Somebody obviously had delivered the blood-covered material in the manila envelope. All I did was open it and make the report to the police. To the best of my knowledge, I hadn't purposefully lost my memory, strolled away from The Crypt and crawled into a disgusting mausoleum to take a nap in an occupied coffin. And, unless I've been abducted by aliens, causing me to have missed time, all I did this morning was come to my office.

But, I realized my protestations of unaware innocence might be wearing pretty thin for the authorities right about then.

Finally, Lieutenant Bullock emerged from my office, motioned to the ever-patient detective who'd continued to rephrase his questions in ways he thought might elicit additional information from me, and they shared an animated, whispered conversation.

The detective nodded and ambled over to the officers still questioning Midnight and Ronald. Lieutenant Bullock approached me, frowning.

"I'd like a private word, Dr. Knight. Is there a lounge area or break room on this floor?"

I'd prepared myself for many possible opening lines from her, but that one took me completely by surprise, which I'm sure was written all over my face.

I pointed past the elevators. "There's a small lounge area inside the women's restroom. Will that do?"

She nodded and launched herself down the hallway, indicating I should follow.

When we reached the restroom door she paused, pivoted and called to a uniform officer standing in the hall.

"Greenfield!" She motioned to him then pointed to the floor at her feet. "Here. No one comes in."

We waited while the officer stationed himself outside the bathroom.

Lieutenant Bullock pushed open the door, held it while I entered and surveyed the small lounge area.

My curiosity morphed into nervousness when she'd assigned the officer to stand guard at the door. At least that was what it appeared he was doing. She hadn't mentioned it specifically, but if no one could come in, it wasn't likely I could get out without obstruction either.

"Sit," she ordered, pointing to a red leather couch.

I sat. The dried blood on the seat of my pants crunched like cardboard.

She paced in front of me for a few seconds, her hands clasped in back, then stopped. She assumed a military style stance, feet so many inches apart, shoulders back.

I was totally out of my depth. And my comfort zone. I had absolutely no idea what we were doing in the women's bathroom, or why she'd taken me aside. I wasn't sure where to look, so I focused on her sturdy, black shoes.

I met her eyes when she finally spoke, her voice quiet.

"This is awkward for me, because it flies in the face of everything I believe in. Not only am I about to give police information to a civilian, but I also intend to raise an issue that will sound crazy and might reflect poorly on me as a law enforcement professional. Although, as a psychologist, I suspect you're used to having people tell you questionable stories."

She was silent again for a few seconds, then loudly cleared her throat.

"Stevens has been spinning some wild yarns about vampires. Or, wannabes, as he calls them. He says there's quite a community of them here in the central Denver area.

"He's got some bizarre theories, but he keeps the details to himself because he thinks I won't believe him. But what he doesn't know is that I've been following the same trail of deaths that he has, and I've come to similar outrageous conclusions."

I shrugged. "If he's keeping his theories to himself, how do you know what conclusions he's reached?"

She lifted her chin. "Let's just say I stumbled upon his notebook one day when he was using the computer downtown, and eyeballed enough pages to get the drift. Plus, I'd overheard enough of his strange telephone conversations to whet my appetite for more information."

I raised my eyebrows. "So, you're fundamentally saying that you read his private papers?"

She made a swatting-away-a-fly hand motion.

"Don't go there. The bottom line is that he believes there are actually such creatures as vampires. And the evidence supports it.

"Stevens thinks my interest in this case is due to the fact that my friend was one of the first Denver victims, and he's right. Webster's murder does play into it. But that's not where it started for me."

She brought her arms up and crossed them in front of her chest.

"I was a street cop in New York ten years ago when these murders began to pop. Long story short, I found my partner's body drained of blood. The perpetrator was never apprehended.

"The victim in your office was killed by the same method as all ninety-six others. He was drained of blood."

I blurted out, "Ninety-six others? I haven't heard anything about ninety-six murders. The news said there were five bodies. And there was no mention of the cause of death."

She nodded. "Ninety-six all together, twenty-six in Denver. Twenty-seven now. We haven't released that information to the public. I'm sure you can appreciate how the average citizen might react to finding out there's a serial killer who somehow removes the victims' blood while they're still alive.

"But there's another piece of this sick puzzle, and that's what I want to talk to you about."

I pointed to myself. "Me? I've already told the detective everything I know."

She pulled a small chair from the corner, arranged it in front of me and sat. She leaned back and rested one ankle on the opposite knee.

"Let's just call this a professional consultation between a law enforcement expert and a psychological expert. A psychological expert who calls herself 'The Vampire Psychologist'."

I realized I'd scooted up to the edge of the couch cushion and forced myself to slide back. All the muscles in my neck and shoulders were tight and I rotated them in an attempt to relieve the pressure.

"Okay. We're having a professional consultation. Go on."

She studied me, her face blank. I wondered if she played poker, because no one would be able to read her if she didn't want to be read.

"Remember I said that all the bodies had been drained of blood? In almost all the cases there wasn't a drop of the victim's blood to be found at the scene. Out of the ninety-six cases, only two bodies were covered with blood. The first was the body of Emerald Addison, and the second, the young man lying on your office floor."

She cocked her head, put both feet on the carpet and leaned forward.

"Any thoughts about the one thing both those murders have in common?"

I didn't care for the direction of the conversation.

"You're saying that I'm the common denominator?"

She nodded. "Very good, doctor. But that's not the interesting part. The blood found all over Emerald Addison wasn't hers. I'm not sure if I could even call it human."

"Are you saying she was covered in animal blood?"

She stood, replaced the chair in the corner and paced again.

"That's what we initially thought. But whatever the blood-like substance is, it doesn't have the necessary ingredients to be classified as mammal at all.

"I'd be willing to wager that the blood all over the victim in your office isn't his. I think we'll discover it's a match to what we found in the Addison case."

I rose and paced in the square she hadn't claimed, making 'I don't know' gestures with my hands.

"I don't understand. Where would the blood come from

if not from the victim?"

"Well, doctor, that's where you come in. As a psychologist, give me your professional opinion about why a killer might leave his own blood, or some synthetic liquid that looks like blood, at the scene of his crimes?"

I paused and thought.

"It would be symbolic. Metaphorical. If it only happened in two of the ninety-six cases, then something about those two cases was more personal for the killer. There was a reason for the killer to either spill his own blood or give that impression. Maybe something religious . . ."

I froze in mid-sentence and stared at Lieutenant Bullock.

I tried to wrap my mind around the notion of Brother Luther as the murderer of ninety-six people. The same Brother Luther I wrote off as a harmless windbag.

But if Brother Luther was the murderer, what about the bodies being drained of blood? That fit more with a vampire than a religious fanatic.

Maybe Brother Luther had a partner who was a vampire.

But, his telephone rants all centered around his hatred of vampires. None of it made any sense.

Frowning, Lieutenant Bullock stepped in front of me.

"What? Why did you stop? Did you think of something?"

I nodded and sighed.

"Yes. I think you and Special Agent Stevens and I need to get together right now for a serious talk. I want to tell you about some phone messages I've been getting, and you and Alan have to come clean with each other."

She narrowed her eyes and studied me for a few seconds, then bounded toward the exit. "This way."

Chapter 22

The next few hours were madness.

While I was in the bathroom with Lieutenant Bullock, the police had sealed off my entire office building.

I didn't have to imagine the reactions of the other occupants to the news that their Monday morning schedules had been completely disrupted, because they informed me in no uncertain terms.

The normally sedate building manager had bolted up the stairway before the police blocked it off and he was livid.

He blustered over to me, shaking his head emphatically, wagging his index finger in the air.

"This won't do, Dr. Knight. Everyone is very upset. This is the second time in a week the police have been called to your office. This is a reputable building and I have other tenants to consider. I'm sorry, but I'm going to have to terminate your lease and ask you to vacate.

"I haven't been allowed inside your office yet, but from what I've been able to determine, the space is no longer in the same condition it was when you rented it. I hope for your sake that your insurance is up to date and sufficient."

I opened my mouth to protest, but the words died in my throat. He was right on all counts. I just stared at his red face and watched the veins pulsing on his forehead as he launched into the second act of his diatribe, and felt very sorry for myself.

Two weeks ago I was a successful, respected psychologist with a calm, predictable life. Things might have been boring, but they were sane. No vampires, religious zealots, quest-obsessed FBI agents, mausoleums, dead bodies, or ruined offices. Why couldn't I have taken up yoga or belly dancing? Something that didn't come with an outrageous dry cleaning bill.

"Are you the building manager?" Lieutenant Bullock barked from a few feet away, as she marched toward us.

He pursed his lips and nodded.

She handed him a business card. "If you have complaints about the way this investigation has been handled, please register them at this phone number. Dr. Knight was simply being a law-abiding citizen, reporting a crime. I think you might want to consult your attorney about the legality of evicting her."

She turned her attention to me, placed her hand on my upper arm and eased me away from the trembling manager.

"Please come this way, Dr. Knight. Some of the clients you had scheduled for this morning are waiting downstairs. One of the officers will walk down with you."

I didn't know which amazed me more: her lecture to the building manager, his barely repressed rage or the fact that she was being nice to me.

After giving an explanation to my anxious clients, telling them I'd call to reschedule as soon as I had a new location, and facilitating several mini therapy sessions to ease their concerns, I contacted the rest of the clients I'd scheduled for the afternoon to fill them in on the situation.

In the middle of making those calls, I thought about the two new vampire clients on my schedule for that night. I had no way of contacting them. They'd only left messages on my voice mail informing me of their intention to come.

Maybe I should drop by The Crypt and leave a message for Devereux. Who knew if the place was even open during the daytime?

But that would have to wait until later. First, I needed to go back upstairs to check on Midnight and Ronald.

They'd been thoroughly and persistently questioned and had the dazed appearance of abandoned puppies waiting to be rescued.

Since their interrogation was complete for the moment, Lieutenant Bullock arranged for them to be taken home. I accompanied them downstairs and suggested we meet at my home the next day.

They both nodded, and Midnight gave me a quick hug.

As they drove away in the back seat of the black and white, Lieutenant Bullock and Alan entered the lobby. He'd retrieved my burgundy purse and matching briefcase from the hallway and had draped the long strap of the purse over his shoulder. He rested his hand on the top of the bag, as if carrying a purse was a normal, everyday thing. Observing the nonchalance with which he carried the fashion accessory made me smile for the first time in hours.

An eternity later I sat in my living room, stretched out in my incredibly comfortable oversize chair, my lower body attired in the finest orange, police-issue pants, the latest in paper footwear dangling from my toes. I thought about the events of the last few hours.

My trip to the police station had been the second in as many days and I could say with complete certainty that I'd rather be sucked on by vampires than return there again. Well, one vampire, anyway.

The chief didn't intervene this time.

As soon as we reached her office, Lieutenant Bullock snagged a passing officer, pointed to my pants and ordered, "Get Dr. Knight some clean pants and shoes, show her where to change, bag what she's wearing, then bring her back here."

I caught Alan's trademark smirk as the officer guided me down the hallway.

When I returned to her office in my neon pants, Lieutenant Bullock and Alan were in the middle of a shouting match, precipitated, I gathered, by her disclosure about his notebook.

They stood nose to nose, enjoying the verbal equivalent of a pissing contest.

After they zipped up and called a truce, I recounted everything I could remember about Brother Luther's telephone calls, then forwarded copies of the toxic harangues to Lieutenant Bullock's voice mailbox.

The lab report came back verifying that the blood in my office didn't belong to Eric. As before, it couldn't be identified.

We argued for and against various theories and hypotheses, going nowhere fast, until it was obvious that we'd exhausted the productive possibilities for the day, and we were all tired and hungry.

Lieutenant Bullock waved us out, said she'd be in touch and Alan walked me to my car.

"Well, you've had a crappy couple of weeks, wouldn't you say?"

I shrugged, not sure if he was kidding or attempting to be supportive. "I'd guess the dead people have had a crappier time than me."

He nodded and grunted some version of "huh" or "hmmm."

I fished my keys out of my purse and toyed with them, checking out the asphalt near my right foot.

"So, can I come home with you?"

"What?" I was sure my face clearly indicated I hadn't seen that coming. "Why do you want to come home with me?"

He smiled, and stepped closer. "I think we have stuff to talk about. Things to clarify. Questions to be answered. You know, the usual. Maybe you'd like to have your back scrubbed in the shower. Or maybe your front."

I barked out a laugh, then smiled and answered.

"I can't really blame you for running hot then cold, because you probably think that's what I did. And I can't say I don't find you attractive, in an obsessive-compulsive sort of way, because I do. But I spent four years with a man who kept me very low on his priority list, and something about you reminds me of him. Been there, done that."

His sapphire eyes darkened, he wrapped his arms around me and planted very soft, warm lips on mine.

I kept my arms at my sides, but felt my lips opening for his tongue as my mouth welcomed the pressure of his.

My body responded to the unexpected move by putting out the chemical welcome mat. I moaned softly.

After a few seconds, he released me and stepped back, leaning against the car next to mine.

"I've known lots of women in my life. I seem to be the kind of guy women make up stories about. They attribute my loner tendencies to some kind of yearning that only they can heal. They think if they have sex with me I'll suddenly be different. Not as work-obsessed. Not as crazy. But they all find out quickly that what you see is what you get.

"So, I've managed to have lots of experience with women, but zero experience with relationships. I just don't know how to do them. I'm not even from Mars." He laughed, referring to the trendy book. "There's no name for the planet I'm from."

He studied me as if he was waiting for something, and I found myself doing the "therapist nod," the gentle, slow, up and down head motion, not unlike one of those dolls in the back window of a car, that most counselors unconsciously perform while listening to someone's story.

I shrugged. "I'm not sure why you're telling me this."

He sighed. "You confuse me. Sometimes I think I've blown it, and that you're already emotionally committed to Devereux, so I back off. Then other times I get the idea that our attraction is mutual, like the way you just responded to my kiss, so I take a chance. Now, I'm just asking, flat out. Do I have a chance with you?"

I decided to be as honest as I could.

"I don't know. You're right about my being emotionally connected to Devereux. I'm not sure if that's because I really care about him, or if he's zapping me with vampire juju and I'm a puppet on his string.

"The truth is that I met Devereux before I ran into you at the hospital. I don't know why I didn't tell you. Maybe it was because I thought the whole vampire thing was bullshit and Devereux and you and all my wannabe clients were deluded and confused. It wasn't until Devereux put you to sleep and snatched me out of my living room that I actually forced myself to accept what my eyes were telling me.

"I was already a little bit in love with him before I met you. But, it's also true that I'm very attracted to you. So, I guess I can't tell you anything helpful. I simply don't know."

He pulled me into his arms again and whispered into my hair above my ear. "I'll play my hunch, then." He kissed my cheek, smiled and said, "Cover your back, Dr. Knight."

By the time I backed my car out of the space and turned to wave goodbye, he was already gone.

I tuned into the local evening news on TV for the company, poured a glass of wine and sat at my desk. It was time to make a new plan.

Even if the building manager didn't evict me, it would be quite a while before the police would let me back inside my office, and even longer for the space to be repaired. I'd have to check online for cleaning companies that specialized in bloodstains. Was there such a thing?

In the meantime, I needed to find a place to meet with my clients. Having a home office wasn't appealing at the best of times, and I certainly wasn't going to give a blanket invitation to every vampire in Denver.

Even if Devereux said the needing-to-be-invited-in thing was a myth, I wasn't taking any chances. From what I'd learned so far, just because Devereux could come and go as he pleased didn't mean that other vampires could. He seemed to be the Grand Poobah in more ways than one.

Hearing my name mentioned on the news jarred me out of my thoughts. I picked up the remote control and turned up the volume. The station was airing a story about the body found in my office. They replayed a video clip from my last trip to the police station, while the voice-over speculated about my "alleged vampire clientele." At the end of the story, the reporter gave us his best stern expression and said, "This reporter wonders how it is that Dr. Knight always seems to be involved in these murders? Maybe the police should be checking her alibi." His lips spread in a lopsided horse smile. "Wes Carter, live in Denver. Back to you in the studio, Bob."

"Thanks, Wes. It sounds like there's more to Dr. Knight than meets the eye. We'll be following the story 24/7 until we get to the truth."

Doing my best imitation of Jack Nicholson, I bellowed, "You can't handle the truth!"

I jumped up and made sure all the doors and windows were locked and the blinds and curtains were tightly closed. Until that moment, I'd forgotten about the media. They hadn't been in front of my house when I came home, but another carnival could arrive at any moment.

My doorbell rang and I said, "Shit!" out loud, wishing

my trusty intuition would've put in its two cents a bit earlier.

I peered through the peephole and saw black hair and felt a tingling sensation in my midsection.

"Who is it?"

"Oh, get over yourself. Open the door."

The voice was familiar.

I cracked the door enough to see X-rated Luna standing on my front porch, unaccompanied by reporters, cameras, or microphones.

"Luna?" I swung the door open. "This is a surprise."

She was dressed in a low cut black top, tight black jeans, and black, pointy, high-heeled boots. Vampire dominatrix. The dramatic makeup artistry on her pale skin was even more striking than the first time I saw her. Her silver eyes were embellished with Cleopatra-like wings. Very exotic.

"Yeah, well don't count on it ever happening again. I think the sooner he tires of you, the better. But I told him I'd come to your house and that I'd ring the damn doorbell, so here I am. He can't give me any more grief about you."

Luna's distaste for humans, and me in particular, was well known.

I nodded. "And to what do I owe this honor?"

"You've got that right. I have a message from the Master. He has serious business he must attend to tonight and he won't be able to see you. But he said he'll visit your dreams and explain. He said I had to tell you that you're in danger and not to let anyone remove your protective necklace."

"What does he mean, I'm in danger?"

"Hey, I just deliver the messages. I don't explain them. But I will tell you that something's up. Vampires are swarming into Denver in droves. Some of them make even us tough vamps nervous. Something dark and heavy is in the air, so to speak."

"Where's Devereux?" I asked.

She glared at me. "Not that it's any of your miserable human business, but he's off on some kind of inter-dimensional rescue mission. He's always saving somebody." She pursed her lips and brought her face closer to mine. "He simply can't resist a hard-luck case."

Her lips relaxed into a wicked smile, displaying fully descended fangs. "But who knows? You might get snatched away by the Dark One again and I won't have to hear about you anymore. Wouldn't that be great?"

She laughed and vanished.

I was never sure what to make of her attitude toward me. Clearly she didn't have much use for me, but I knew she'd follow Devereux's orders. I was sure she wouldn't hurt me. Probably.

Leave it to Devereux to choose a pissed off beauty queen for his personal assistant. No bug-eating, rotted-tooth Renfield for him.

I was still standing in the entryway with my hand on the open door. I poked my head outside and was relieved to find nothing. No one screaming questions, no bright lights, no car tracks on my grass.

I locked the door and went back to my desk.

The next task on my list was to contact all my clients, cancel or reschedule any appointments set for the next couple of days and assure them I'd be functioning again as quickly as possible.

I spoke with all but a handful and left general messages for the ones I hadn't reached, asking them to contact me.

Rubbing the back of my neck to ease the tight muscles, I shuffled over to my comfortable chair, found the remote control and clicked through the channels, searching for mindless entertainment.

I landed on a well-known national discussion program. The show's host was an abrasive, politically dogmatic, argumentative bully who only had guests to give him someone to shout over. I usually didn't have much time for television, and this show was particularly worth avoiding, but something about the topic caught my attention.

A diverse panel was talking about the end of the world. Normally, discussions about that topic have a decidedly religious flavor and don't appeal to me, but this group seemed to be comprised of all kinds of people: scientists, psychics, spiritual leaders, law enforcement officials, and politicians. Quite an unexpected amalgam of opinions.

An old, white-haired woman on the panel moved to the podium and spoke. "The world is being contaminated by a growing darkness. A cumulative negative energy so strong that it's eliciting the worst from all the earth's inhabitants. The idea that thoughts and emotions hold certain vibrations is no longer speculation. According to the Law of Attraction, like attracts like, and we are witnessing clear evidence of that all over the world today."

Where had I heard that before? It seemed so familiar. Then I remembered. Cerridwyn the Tarot reader had said almost exactly the same thing.

I hadn't realized the end of the world had become such

a hot topic.

I listened to the panel's discussion, waiting for the voices of ridicule and condescension that usually follow such proclamations, but none came. Everyone on the panel had a unique aspect of this "growing darkness" to share.

My ears perked up when they mentioned Denver as one of the cities on the leading edge of the escalating negativity.

According to a dark-skinned man wearing a turban, unexplained deaths and all forms of violence had increased in these cities at a higher rate than the national average.

They devoted the next few minutes to comparing ideas about why those certain cities and areas of the country had become the focus of evil, and decided it had to do with a psychic build-up of toxic human emotions: hate, fear, blame, guilt, rage, shame—conditions that prepared the ground for increased violence, manipulation, intolerance, control, and destruction.

The white-haired woman explained, "Peoples' focus on fear, hatred, and violence has caused a greater vibrational accumulation of those emotions in places across the country where powerful concentrations of hopeful, optimistic, and enlightening energy also exists. In other words, everything and its opposite is increasing in these locations.

"We are called to make a choice between love, compassion, and tolerance and hate, fear, and war. A true archetypal Armageddon."

The discussion sounded so New Age, I was shocked by the host's uncharacteristic lack of reaction. Strange. I'd never heard him be polite with anyone before. I guessed his behavior was as clear an indication of the impending end of the world as anything. Or maybe hell had frozen over.

I thought about the reading Cerridwyn gave me and all the weird things that had happened since then. I was no longer the same person who had concrete answers about what was and wasn't real. Maybe I should go and visit her again.

Wow. Did I just seriously consider going to a psychic on purpose?

The program went to commercial and a group of children in costumes screamed "Trick or Treat!" as an advertisement for Halloween candy filled the screen.

Halloween? Was it Halloween already? I didn't even know what day of the month it was, although I'd vaguely been aware it was October. Today was the 30th, so tomorrow was Halloween.

I loved Halloween as a child. It didn't take a psychologist to figure out what metaphor I was acting out by dressing up as a princess every year. Damn those Disney fairy tales!

In graduate school, I studied Samhain, the old pagan holiday that predated our current, consumer-driven observance. Samhain celebrated the time of year when the veil between the worlds was most transparent—when magic was afoot.

Unfortunately, our culture had become suspicious of true magic and had shrouded the holiday in fear, superstition, and nonsense. I'd attended a Wiccan coven's ritual once and walked around hearing peoples' thoughts again for a week afterward. Powerful stuff.

I read something in the newspaper recently about a big party or gathering on Halloween. A yearly event. Not that I intended to go. My life was bizarre enough without adding more occult madness.

A sudden pain shot across my forehead and my solar

plexus seized.

The light bulbs in both the overhead fixture and the table lamp simultaneously exploded, leaving the room illuminated by the eerie glow of the large TV screen.

"Harlot! Whore!"

The screeching voice from behind me startled me so badly I leaped out of the chair and landed on top of the coffee table, knocking over my glass of wine.

Creeping toward me, circling in front of the table I crouched on, was an emaciated-looking male.

The sunken cheeks of his white, cadaverous face appeared blue in the shadowy light, and his floor-length, black coat hung loosely on his tall, wiry frame.

His head was a luminous egg. Hairless with crisscrossing veins.

His coal black eyes were rimmed with swollen red tissue, something foul and thick oozing from the corners.

He looked like an experiment gone wrong. A body in search of its grave.

He pointed a finger at me, the elongated fingernail ragged and stained. He clutched a huge, battered black book in his other arm.

He snarled, displaying yellow and brown teeth. And fangs. I recognized the southern drawl from the phone calls.

Is this Brother Luther? He's a vampire?

The degree to which I'd missed the boat blew me away.

He screeched, "Evil Jezebel! You will burn in eternal damnation! Consorting with Satan's minions!"

His breath was horrible, reeking like a sewer. It provided nauseating contrast to the rancid odor wafting from his clothing.

I scanned the area, weighing my options and the distance to the nearest phone, then leapt off the table, landing as far away from him as possible.

There wasn't any way I was going to make eye contact with him, so I focused on his nose, which was a mass of bumps, missing skin and odd angles.

"Are you Brother Luther? What do you want?" I asked, using my least threatening therapy voice, my heart running a marathon.

As if he hadn't heard my question, he continued slinging vile epithets. He stared at me with his glassy dark eyes, tiny droplets of spit flying as he ranted.

Shit! What the hell's going on? How could this be Brother Luther? I thought he hated vampires.

Simultaneously, I reached for the cordless phone and he reached for me.

I grabbed the phone, managed to punch in 91, then lost my grip on it when he jerked me by the fabric of my blouse.

My eyes watered as he held me close to his face. It was almost impossible to breathe while being bathed in the noxious stink radiating from his mouth.

I pushed against him and had the clear impression that my wrists would break before I'd budge him an inch.

He was staring at me but his eyes were unfocused.

My bowels threatened to liquefy and I fought to turn my head to get away from the worst of it.

"She must be punished," he bellowed in my face, gathering more of my shirt in his grasp.

His head suddenly jerked down, his vacant eyes locked on something he now held in his palm.

He screamed as the necklace Devereux had given me lit up the room, burning his hand. He dropped his book, released me, and I fell to the floor. I speed-crawled a few feet away from him and slowly stood.

Evidently the necklace had done more than scorch him, because he put both hands on his bald dome and whimpered in a weak, shaky voice, "Don't hurt me, don't hurt me, please don't hurt me, help me, help me . . ."

Something about his words reminded me of the dream I'd had about the child in the house.

Lowering his arms, he clutched his stomach and rocked up and down, sobbing loudly.

I became momentarily confused and almost made a move to comfort him.

Suddenly he jerked upright, rose to his full height, which seemed taller than before, and held his arms out on either side of him. He closed his eyes and slowly let his head drop back, his mouth falling open.

It wasn't possible, but it looked like the coat that had hung loosely on him moments before, now stretched taut across his chest, shoulders, and upper arms.

As he'd spread his arms out, the coat flapped open, exposing his scarred, festering nude frame. His chest was a mass of oozing sores, surrounded by coarse, filthy body hair, which trailed down to a thick patch sprouting a huge, reddish erection.

His head snapped up, like a spring had been released, and the black coals in his eyes ignited into flames.

He eased his hand down his abscessed stomach, grasped his penis and began stroking the length, groaning.

He smiled the worst smile I've ever seen, and stepped

toward me, unoccupied hand outstretched.

"Come to me. Touch me."

He thrust his foul erection toward me and laughed, his voice burrowing holes in my ears, making my knees weak.

I backed as far away from him as I could.

What just happened? What is this thing? Why does his voice seem familiar? Where's his southern accent? Why does he look different? He obviously did something to cause me to believe he's physically bigger than he'd been just a few moments ago. Some mind control thing.

He began moving the hand on his penis faster and was momentarily distracted by what I guessed was an approaching orgasm. I didn't want to be standing in front of him when he got to that point.

I dropped to the ground, crawled toward the front door as fast as my legs would carry me and cringed when I heard him scream his release. The cry sounded more like pain than pleasure. Immediately I felt myself being lifted up by the waistband of the orange pants.

That hideous laugh washed over me again and I was just wondering if my death would be quick and painless or drawn out and torturous, when the front door burst open and a whole flock of vampires swept into the room.

Several of them leaped on my captor, causing me to be flung against a wall, where I sat, semi-dazed, watching my vampire cavalry be thrown around like sponge toys.

What the hell is going on? Is he some kind of vampire demon?

Brother Luther, if it really was Brother Luther, seemed to be able to control vampires, as well as humans, with his mind, but there were too many for him. Or else he simply lost interest. Because he threw down the hulking vampire whose neck he was sucking on, turned his red eyes to me and shrieked, "Soon."

He either disappeared or moved so quickly there wasn't even a blur, but one minute he was there, the next he wasn't.

The vampires lay around the room, scattered like bowling pins after a strike.

The silence was broken by a deep male voice saying, "Get the fuck off me," as a short, rotund man sprang up.

I didn't recognize any of the blood-covered warriors, except one. The last one I expected to see.

Still in shock, I crawled over to a woman sprawled out on the floor between the living room and the kitchen. Her long black hair was matted with blood from several head wounds and two large holes gaped at the top of her left breast where fangs had torn the skin. The wounds were already beginning to heal.

"Luna? Is that you?"

"No, it's the Avon lady. Are you always this dim?"

"What are you doing here?"

"Saving your unimportant ass, that's what."

I nodded and smoothed a clump of her long hair away from her frowning face. "Believe me, I appreciate that, but how did you know that . . . whatever he was . . . was here?"

She slapped my hand away. "Devereux expected trouble tonight and ordered me to keep watch on your house. He said I should bring reinforcements, just in case. I thought he was over-reacting because of his strange attachment to you, so I just hung out myself, looking through your window. I saw the skuzzy guy come in, summoned the others, and the rest is history."

She sat up.

I tried to help her and she slapped my hand away again.

"Who is that guy? Or, better yet, *what* is that guy?"

She shrugged. "I don't know, he was your gentleman caller, not mine. But Devereux's going to rip him a new one. I hope I get to watch."

"But, how is it he was able to control you and all the other vampires like that? I thought the mind control stuff only worked on humans?"

She nodded while tapping her index finger on her chin, deep in thought.

"It usually does only work on humans. It takes one helluva powerful vampire to control other vampire minds. The only one I've ever seen do it is Devereux. He's definitely going to go ballistic.

"Whoever the guy with the boner was, he's gonna find out what happens to vampires who mess with the Master's property."

Master's property?

I was way too exhausted and traumatized to open up that coffin of worms. But Devereux and I were definitely going to have to come to an understanding.

During the short time we'd been talking, the wounds on all of the vampire bodies had healed and, if you didn't count the blood all over every part of my living room, you wouldn't have known a life or death situation had just occurred. That I'd almost been dinner for a crazed vampire zealot.

How is it Brother Luther could have festering sores on his body? Why doesn't his body immediately heal them? Why didn't it occur to me he could be a vampire? Not too bright, Kismet!

But there *was* blood all over my living room.

A trashed office and a living room that smelled like a used sanitary pad.

Luna rose in a fluid motion, without the aid of bones, and brushed off her black ensemble.

I scrambled to my feet, not nearly as graceful, and noticed all the vampire eyes staring at me.

I was in room filled with vampires. Blood drinkers. Children of the night.

Well, hell.

What was I supposed to do with a room full of vampires?

I couldn't offer them coffee and bagels. Should I offer them the use of my shower? My washing machine? Should I open up a vein?

The problem was solved when one of them—the huge one the crazy vampire had sucked on—stalked over, bowed from the waist and said, "We serve the Master. We will hide ourselves outside and keep watch over you until the sunrise."

He raised his hand, made a "come on" gesture, and a dozen undead walked out my broken front door.

Luna surveyed the wreckage of my living room and said, "Do you want to stay here? Would you rather spend the rest of the night at The Crypt?"

On automatic pilot, I'd already started picking up papers and books that had fallen off my desk. I was too emotionally wiped out to deal with Luna's prickly attitude.

If anyone was in dire need of psychotherapy it was Luna. Anger and hostility rolled off her like toxic waves. It was a good thing there were rules against doing therapy with someone you know, but even if there weren't, I wouldn't be caught dead having her as my client. Oh, wait. Bad choice of words.

I probably would be dead.

I sighed, my voice shaky. "I'll stay here. There's no blood upstairs and I need a shower."

"Then I'll stick around, too. Devereux would stake me if I left you alone tonight."

Swell.

She walked to the kitchen door and looked around.

"Where's your washer and dryer?"

I pointed.

I reached down to retrieve another pile of papers, and when I turned to see if Luna had figured out how to operate the washing machine, she walked back into the living room, naked, her hands on her hips.

"Do you mind if I take a shower first if you're going to clean up down here?"

"Uh, sure. That's fine. Make yourself at home."

And it just keeps getting weirder.

I heard the little popping sound that indicated some vampire or another had just made an unscheduled arrival or departure, and then the sound of the shower running.

What was up with all the naked vampires? Was nudity a requirement to join the club?

The mentally ill sometimes act out childhood shame issues by getting naked and being sexually aggressive. Masturbation as an anxiety relieving and self soothing technique was common. That didn't surprise me.

And I wasn't a prude. I'd spent as much time as any other woman in health club locker rooms, making small talk with other naked women. But a naked vampire, built like a silicone-enhanced supermodel, calmly cruising around my kitchen was a little out of my comfort zone.

It was natural to be curious about a body that perfect, but actually gawking at it had to be out of the question. But what was I supposed to look at while I spoke to her?

I wondered how many times Devereux had seen her naked?

Geez. Together they'd look like a god and goddess.

Insecure? Me?

Chapter 23

I guess it made sense that a vampire wouldn't worry about human rules.

I mean, once you were undead, who were you trying to impress? And who would get in your face about anything, anyway, if the result would be having your throat torn out?

Luna glided down the stairs, moving with feline grace. Her calm exterior only partially camouflaged the power and violence lurking just under the surface. She was still naked.

She strolled over to the washing machine, noted the cycle wasn't complete and sat down at the kitchen table.

How weird was it to have a sky-clad vampire wandering around your house?

I'd replaced the light bulbs and done everything I could in the living room. Now it would be up to the cleaning crew.

I heard the washing machine spin cycle click off and walked over to shift her clothes into the dryer.

Like the moment in a horror movie when the forest goes strangely silent, and we know the monster is watching us through the trees, a chill ran through my body, sliding an ice cube down my back. I turned to look at Luna.

She was watching me, eyes narrowed, the tips of her fangs peeking out through parted lips.

"I need blood."

Terror took me hostage. In three seconds, I'd gone from being in denial about the predator padding around my kitchen, to having every ancestral alarm bell in my psyche clanging madly.

My stomach contracted, I felt hot and cold at the same time, my knees rubber.

Smart-mouthed, cynical Luna was gone and in her place was a vampire. A creature that drank human blood. A hungry predator.

I only had one card to play. My mouth had gone totally dry and I was only partially successful at keeping the fear out of my voice. I knew she could sense it, anyway.

"If you're thinking about having my neck as your entré, you'd better consider what Devereux will say. He is, as you said, attached to me."

My anxiety escalated. Her intention saturated the air. I knew exactly what she meant to do.

She stood and stalked very slowly across the room, closing in on me. She locked her eyes on mine, which caused me to get the fuzzy, floating feeling that meant she was pulling me into her gaze. Taking control of my mind.

I visualized the protective wall that usually kept me from drowning in other peoples' energy and felt it collapse. Nothing in my repertoire could hold up against the kind of power Luna wielded.

This wasn't vague energy. It was laser-sharp mind control.

I threw my hands up, palms out, in a reflexive action, which did nothing but give her something to grab onto.

Pinning me against the washing machine with her lower

body, she ran her hands up and down my arms, holding me still. Her silver eyes were large and foggy, as if the lights were on but no one was home. Her pointy fangs elongated as she caressed them with her tongue.

She leaned in and slowly licked the side of my neck.

I braced myself for the shock of pain I was sure would come and was surprised to hear a scream.

She'd slid her hand across my chest and encountered the necklace. It had the same reaction to Luna that it had to the bald lunatic. There was a flash of light and a sensation strong enough to cause Luna to drop the necklace and leap away from me.

As she stood snarling, the fog in her eyes cleared and her fangs retracted into her gums.

I wrapped my arms around myself and trembled. The part of my brain that had wanted nothing more than to do whatever Luna commanded threw cold water on itself and woke up.

I stared wide-eyed at the creature in front of me.

She'd known about the necklace, but the bloodlust apparently didn't waste time on frivolous details.

I didn't think there was any way I could ever truly understand the craving for blood. To have blood obsession to the point of being enthralled by the need. But I'd just gotten a psychic encyclopedia full of information that horrified and sickened me.

Mental postcards of all the bodies she'd drained, all the destruction she'd caused slammed into my brain.

She might not have wanted to kill me, but she would've. Even if it meant Devereux would destroy her.

My body shook, a delayed reaction to my second near-death experience of the night.

Luna backed away and reclaimed the chair at the kitchen table, still watching me, her fists clenched. She clearly struggled to regain control.

Her eyes were dull with dark smudges underneath, her skin pasty white.

She cleared her throat then spoke, her voice husky. "You're lucky Devereux gave you that necklace. If you hadn't been wearing it, I'd have bled you. I would've tried to only take enough to sustain me until I could find another source, but I probably wouldn't have been able to restrain myself. Hunger after being wounded is the worst.

"There's nothing in the human experience that comes close to being as powerful as the need for blood. Not even a heroin addict's craving for a fix."

She sighed and licked her lips.

"I have to go and feed. Until I do, I'm a danger to you. Not that I care, but Devereux does.

"Necklace or no. Even now I can't think of anything but the taste of your blood and the pulse pounding in your neck. I'll go and find one of my regular sources. One of my vampire addicts. It won't take long. Then I'll come back."

It was probably stupid to question a hungry vampire, but I couldn't help myself.

"Do you mean you're going to go kill someone?"

She shook her head. "No. I'll find one of the humans who regularly donate blood and sex. Getting both my needs met at the same time seems to take the edge off."

She cocked her head and stared at me with cold eyes, her

voice deep and serious.

"Don't make the mistake of thinking that vampires are just eccentric humans. That we simply have a nasty little habit or two. We're not human. We take blood from willing and unwilling victims. Killing is what we do. We enjoy it. All of us. You might be surprised to know what pleasure it brings me to fantasize about draining you dry."

She rose, sauntered over and gazed at me through her thick eyelashes, a cold grin on her face.

"In fact, you could say you and I have a date the moment Devereux dumps you."

I started to ask another question, but she flicked her fingers dismissively and said, "That's enough. If I don't leave now, you'll be sorry."

She blinked out and I slid to the floor, my back against the washing machine. Exhaustion swamped me.

I woke up in sunlight, lying on top of the covers on my bed, Devereux's voice an echo in my mind.

"My love. Luna told me what happened last night. I am sorry I was not there to protect you. Something very strange is happening. I was tricked into journeying into a difficult reality and was intercepted once I arrived there. The power necessary for someone to deceive me is beyond any I've seen before. We must be vigilant. I will come to you as soon as I rise. Oh, yes. Here is the address of your new office: 984 Lincoln Ave., #505. The building manager is expecting you. Until tonight."

A phantom vampire lover, a religious fanatic killer, and a beauty queen predator.

Just another day in Oz.

My first glimpse of the emergency room décor in my living room was depressing. For one brief moment I hoped it was a bad dream and I'd find my living space just as normally-cluttered and blood free as usual.

But no.

I spent a few minutes on the phone, interviewing cleaning services, being very up-front about the bloodstains, and settled on the one that specialized in taking "the jobs that nobody else wants."

The woman started to tell me about the last crime scene they'd been hired to restore, and how no one would ever have known that an entire family had been brutally murdered there, and I cut her off, saying I was sure they could handle my situation. Too much information.

They agreed to come later that day.

I also tracked down a handyman who'd done some home repair work for me in the past, and said I needed a new front door.

Luckily, he was also available.

I showered, dressed and decided to focus on finding another office. I wanted to make a change regardless of what my current building manager chose to do.

Unfortunately, I discovered immediately that my infamy had spread, and, suddenly, none of the vacancies in the paper were still available after the rental agent heard my name.

I couldn't really blame them because what property manager in her or his right mind would want to rent to someone who'd had her office recently trashed by a murderer?

Then I remembered Devereux's mental memo.

What had he said about an office?

I closed my eyes and allowed the address he'd imprinted in my memory to resurface. Grabbing my purse and keys, I headed out my broken door, wondering briefly if my guardian vampires had really spent the night out in my yard and if it had been Luna who'd carried me upstairs.

Cold chills ran through my body as I imagined myself sleeping and vulnerable as Luna crouched over me, maybe thinking about which vein she'd puncture first.

I drove to the address Devereux had given me, which turned out to be only a block away from The Crypt.

I pulled to the curb. The building was spectacular.

Delightfully old, it had been lovingly restored, remodeled and was the crown jewel of the neighborhood.

A parking garage, built to blend in with the architecture of the antique building next door, sported a sign that said, "Parking For The Crypt and Lady Amara Only."

The building is named after Lady Amara? Devereux's mother?

Come to think of it, Midnight had mentioned that Devereux lived in a loft near the club. It looked like he owned the whole building.

Damn. I'd been so caught up in trying not to believe Devereux was a vampire, that I hadn't given any thought to the fact he was also a rich vampire.

Deciding not to move my car to the parking garage, I plunked quarters into the meter in front of the lobby entrance and walked through the wood-framed, stained-glass double doors.

Breathtaking.

Gold etched marble floors stretched out for hundreds of square feet, and just past the bank of elevators stood a large reception desk. Plush leather couches and chairs were scattered throughout the room, Devereux's artwork filled the walls, and relaxing music flowed from invisible speakers.

Still gawking at the beautiful lobby, I walked to the reception desk and asked for the building manager.

The young woman seated behind the desk smiled brightly and asked my name. Upon hearing it, she rose and held out her hand.

I shook it.

"I'm Victoria Essex, building manager, receptionist, troubleshooter, and all-round wunderkind. I've been expecting you."

She sailed her arm through the air in the direction of the elevators. "Right this way."

The elevator was a mirrored affair. Lovely to look at, but it could be annoying to have nothing to rest your eyes on but yourself during your ride in the box.

Unless, of course, there were other people in there with you, and then you had total license to indulge your people-watching desires to your heart's content.

I'd just given myself permission to study my young companion in the mirror, when the ding sounded, the door opened, and we stepped into a lushly carpeted hallway. The ice blue of the floor matched the colors in the elegant, European style wallpaper. I could easily have imagined myself in a luxury, old world hotel.

Pausing in front of a hand-carved portal, Victoria slid a keycard into a slot near the handle, the red light changed to green, and the door clicked open.

There had to be some kind of mistake.

This place was big enough and extraordinary enough to be Martha Stewart's Denver corporate office.

We wandered through a space that would make a great waiting room, then entered a large, multi-room suite.

Victoria smiled. "Isn't it incredible? Mr. Devereux designed the renovation of the building himself and chose the interiors for every suite."

"So, Mr. Devereux owns this building?"

She nodded. "Yes. This one and many others, including the gothic wonderland down the street. Have you ever been to The Crypt?"

"Yes. It's really something. Does he live in this building?"

She cocked her head and raised her eyebrows.

"I'm sorry. Mr. Devereux gave me the impression that you two were close friends. I just assumed you were aware of his personal details. But, then again, he did tell me to answer all your questions. Yes. He keeps the penthouse as his residence."

The charming smile returned to her face.

She opened a set of double doors that led to a lovely, full bath.

"On the other side of the suite is a smaller bath, which would be perfect for your clients to use. Would you care to see it?"

He must have filled her in about my line of work. I nodded and she guided me across the expanse.

"What kinds of other businesses have their offices here in the building?" I asked.

"All the businesses here belong to Mr. Devereux and his associates. They run several international corporations. Yours will be the only outside business in the building. Well, what do you think? Would you like to move in?"

I chuckled. "You bet. In a heartbeat. But affording the rent is another issue."

She nodded and smiled. "Mr. Devereux told me you'd say that. He said to tell you he'll discuss the details of the rental agreement with you personally, and I should assure you that you can easily afford the space.

"I'm going to leave you here for a few minutes by yourself so you can get a feel for the place." She took a couple of steps toward the door, spread her arms wide and spun in a circle, pointing to the empty space as she twirled. "Start imagining where your furniture will go. Enjoy the view of the mountains from your windows.

"Oh, and by the way, he also asked me to tell you that you can have the suite unfurnished or furnished. He has a huge warehouse full of couches, chairs, desks, tables, lamps, anything you might desire. Wonderful pieces. He said to let him know what you require and it will be delivered immediately."

She stopped spinning, walked through the suite and closed the door behind her.

I laughed out loud at her joyful free-spiritedness and threw my arms out as she'd done, then let them return to my sides. If I'd ever managed to learn how to turn cartwheels in elementary school, I'd be tempted to turn one now.

I strolled through the spacious rooms.

Of course, it was out of the question. There was no way in hell that I could afford this place. The bathroom fixtures alone cost more than I paid for my townhouse.

Wouldn't it be great if I could afford it? I hadn't even started figuring out how I was going to acquire new furniture to replace the broken stuff in my office. My insurance would probably reimburse me, but that could take months.

But, if I moved into Devereux's building and let him give me a rent break, I'd be obligated to him. I was sure that's what he wanted. Where was the line between taking advantage of a good deal, and losing my autonomy? What happened if I decided I didn't want a vampire boyfriend? What if Luna was right and he dumps me? I'd have to move again.

Thinking about all that made my head hurt.

I glanced down at my feet, which had sunk deep into the rich pile of the carpet, and wondered if a rug this thick had to be vacuumed or mowed?

The view out the windows drew me like a magnet.

From this row of windows I had a panoramic view of Colorado's Front Range, the mountains that skirted the metro area all the way from south of Colorado Springs up to the Wyoming border.

Wind clouds hovered along the tops of the peaks, signaling that the Denver area might be in for some of our famous one-hundred-miles-per-hour, window rattling, roof lifting air blasts. But, if this building had been here as long as I suspected it had, it wasn't likely to get blown away anytime soon.

Giving in to temporary insanity, I'd just dropped down

onto the floor and was flailing my arms and legs and giggling, making a snow angel in the carpet, when Victoria reentered and clapped her hands.

"I knew you'd love it!"

Outrageously embarrassed, I was halfway up, when I glanced over to find her on the floor with me, following my example.

We laughed at ourselves and each other, spent a couple of minutes being five-years-old again and finally got off the floor.

We smiled at each other. After all, our inner children had bonded.

She handed me the keycard and a business card with her information on it.

"Mr. Devereux said for me to give you the keycard so you could spend as much time in the suite as you wish before you decide one way or the other."

She started toward the exit then turned, a wide smile on her friendly face.

"I think he really likes you. I look forward to having you here. If you need anything just call me, any day, any time.

"Blessed be." She waved and left.

Blessed be? That was a Wiccan greeting and parting. Of course Devereux had a witch as his office manager.

Did she know everything about Devereux? He must have told her something to justify the fact that he was never here during the daylight hours. He did tend to surround himself with people who were devoted to him. Maybe he secretly slept in a coffin in the basement?

I wandered around the suite for a few more minutes, stared out the window, then forced myself to head back out to the hallway.

I'd apparently decided to take him up on his offer. Providing, of course, the true cost wasn't higher than I was willing to pay.

Halloween.

The big news story in town was the yearly bash, which turned out to be called The Vampires' Ball.

How could I have lived here so long and never heard of it?

The event was the topic *du jour* on the radio.

According to the legend, twenty years ago, in the foothills west of Denver, an eccentric billionaire built a monstrously huge hotel that was designed to resemble the rich guy's favorite Scottish castle.

He'd even had a portion of the Celtic original dismantled and shipped here for his masterpiece, in the hopes that a ghost or two might tag along for the ride.

There are lots of stories about those ghosts, which might have contributed to the failure of the hotel as a successful enterprise.

Or maybe the hotel went belly up because the billionaire lost interest in it and didn't continue all the maintenance and upkeep required for a castle in the foothills of the Rocky Mountains.

Whatever the reason, the castle languished.

Until ten years ago, when it was purchased by yet another eccentric billionaire and transformed from a hotel to an event site.

Specifically, the site for The Vampires' Ball.

Gee. I wonder if I know any eccentric billionaires who might be attracted to a ghost-filled castle as the location for a celebration dedicated to vampires? Hmmm. Let me think.

It wasn't enough that Devereux was a vampire who could move through thought, a wizard who travels to other dimensions, and a gorgeous hunk of god-like masculinity. Now I had to deal with the fact that he's rich and owns half the world.

I didn't know whether to laugh or scream.

But, whether or not Devereux was involved, the gala sounded like it would draw every vampire, vampire wannabe, and fan of the paranormal on this side of the Mississippi.

It occurred to me that the ball would be a great place for the police to use me to capture Brother Luther.

Or whoever the hell he is.

But why would I want to do that? I wasn't the brave type. If I couldn't use my therapy skills to solve a situation, I was pretty much out of my league. Now that I'd actually seen him up close and personal, and witnessed his madness firsthand, why would I want to put myself in danger again?

Because until he was caught and put away, I was a prisoner. He could show up any time and destroy as many offices as I could move into. In fact, that reminded me I needed to talk to Devereux about whether or not he really wanted me in there if his beautiful building could be wrecked by Vampire Satan at any time.

But still, weighing all the pros and cons, I thought it was worth a phone call to Lieutenant Bullock.

Chapter 24

Within minutes of pulling into my garage, both the handyman and cleaning crew showed up, and my townhouse was a flurry of activity.

While the professionals put my living quarters back together, I sat at the kitchen table, deleting and saving voice mail messages.

I'd made the big time.

In amongst the calls from current clients, prospective clients, babbling psychotics, New Age seekers, Anne Rice fans, hopeful romantic partners—mostly prisoners or the recently released—and local media, there were messages from all the major networks.

I'd been invited to appear on every late-night, early-morning, afternoon and prime time interview program on the TV schedule. The segment would probably be called, "Let's ridicule, harangue and generally humiliate the allegedly professional woman calling herself The Vampire Psychologist."

I definitely thought that all advertising wasn't good advertising.

The one exciting message was from a well-known publisher, asking if I'd consider writing a book. That was definitely a keeper.

Tom would be so proud of my fifteen minutes of fame and fortune.

Thinking about Tom's shallow tendencies reminded me I hadn't heard from him since Zoë pulled him onto the dance floor at the Crypt several nights ago.

I would've said disappearing that way wasn't his style, but I really didn't know him well enough anymore—if I ever did—to guess what he would or wouldn't do. Especially if there was a woman involved. In fact, now that I thought about it, taking off with a gorgeous female was exactly something Tom would do.

I saved all the messages from the national media, just in case I ever did finish the book about vampire wannabes—or was it about vampires now?—and needed some New York and Los Angeles contact numbers.

Being productive felt good. I called all my current clients, told them I'd have a new location soon, and arranged for telephone counseling sessions in the meantime.

The prospective clients were willing to wait until I set up my new office. I was surprised by how many of them hadn't been put off by the gruesome publicity surrounding me. In fact, thanks to the national obsession with celebrities, some of the callers sought me out because they'd seen my face on the local news.

Maybe I'd come out of this mess with some parts of my life still intact.

By late afternoon, the new door was installed, the living room sparkled, and silence reigned supreme.

I'd left a message for Lieutenant Bullock, outlining my offer to be bait tonight at The Vampires' Ball, and hadn't heard back from her.

Taking advantage of the quiet, I drifted into a catnap on the couch and was startled when the doorbell chimed me into wakefulness.

I bolted up, heart pounding, and immediately checked the window for signs of sunlight. I was relieved to find the sun hadn't gone down yet. I was safe. Maybe.

It wasn't healthy to make assumptions about the limitations of the undead, but I hoped the not-being-able-to-go-out-in-the-sun thing was true.

I crept over to the door and yelled, "Who is it?"

"Your trusty FBI agent."

I huffed out the breath I'd been holding and stared through the peephole.

Alan's smiling face filled the view.

I'd had the handyman install additional locks on the door—not that locks would keep vampires out, but I had to do something—and going through the unlocking process took a bit longer than before.

He noticed.

"Hey, is this a different door? Did you have more locks installed?"

After carefully relocking the doors, I led him into my disinfectant-scented living room and offered him a seat on the couch.

He sniffed the air and raised his eyebrows.

I sat in my fluffy chair and explained the events of the previous evening as he shook his head and wrote in his dog-eared notebook.

When I finished, he frowned and smacked a hand down

on his leg. "I knew I should've come home with you. None of that would've happened if I'd been there. Why wasn't I called? You know I've been on this case for months."

I did the therapist nod and spoke in my most reasonable voice.

"Well, first, you wanted to come home with me so we could have wild and crazy sex, so I might've been even more vulnerable when the maniac showed up if I'd been on my back, screaming Johnny Depp's name."

He barked out a laugh.

"And second, I don't have to tell you what violent psychopaths do to people who stand in the way of their fixated object. If you'd been here, even if we were just talking in the living room, he'd have seen you as a threat and taken you out. For some reason I've become important to him."

I tucked my legs underneath me and sighed. "I didn't call you because it simply didn't occur to me. From the moment Brother Luther showed up, 'til Luna's vampires arrived and the room got too crowded for him, to the second I fell asleep on the floor, I was on automatic pilot.

"Actually, by not letting you come home with me, I probably saved your life. Therefore, clearly, you owe me."

I cocked my head and gave him my sweetest, most innocent smile.

He snorted, laughed and slouched into the couch cushions.

"Let's entertain the possibility that your suppositions are correct and he would've torn my throat out if I'd been with you. That makes what you proposed to Bullock even more dangerous and lame-brained. How many people would he take out at a huge gathering in order to get to you?"

I nodded. "Well, that's why the police would be there. Don't you think it makes sense to call him out? If I don't, I'll be looking over my shoulder every day until he either loses interest in me or gets caught. And what's the likelihood that a psychopath will lose interest?"

He folded his arms across his chest. "Okay. I hear you. But I can tell you that Bullock isn't going to go for it. She can't put a civilian in danger. It'd mean her badge. But I think having the cops show up at the ball is a great idea."

"Tell that to Lieutenant Bullock. Are you going?"

He grinned. "Would I miss an opportunity to schmooze with every vampire in the western USA? And, after all these months of following the trail of bloodless bodies, I might be in on the take-down. That's definitely worth the price of admission."

That gave me the opportunity to ask him the questions I'd wanted to ask since I met him.

"Why are you so obsessed with this case and vampires in general? What do you really want?"

He lowered his head and got very quiet. It wasn't only that he didn't speak. It was as if he stilled his body to the point that I was tempted to get up and put my hand on his chest to see if he was breathing.

After a few seconds he studied me, moving only his eyes, and nodded.

He sat up straight, brushed off some imaginary substance from the front of his shirt and spoke, voice low.

"I've never told this to anyone. Not anyone. Ever. I'm not sure why I'm telling you. Maybe it's because I really do want to have that wild and crazy sex you were talking about, or maybe it's because I just want to tell it to someone. Finally. And you've got that mystical therapist vibe happening."

He smiled, but it didn't reach his eyes.

"I wouldn't have been able to tell you this even a week ago, but after everything you've seen and heard, my story won't seem so farfetched or delusional. Maybe."

He stood and paced around the room for a few seconds then propped himself against a far wall, his arms folded over his chest again.

He stared at me.

"Ready? Wait for it." He paused. "My mother is a vampire."

I opened my mouth, but no sound came out. My brain spun for a few seconds, trying to concoct the perfect response, and failed.

Was this his way of telling me he wasn't going to answer my question? Was he trying to be funny again to deflect from whatever the truth was?

He returned to the couch and sat, reading my face.

"You're trying to figure out if I'm kidding, or messing with you or if I've gone barking mad, right?"

I raised an eyebrow and smiled. "I always did great on multiple-choice tests."

He hand-combed his thick, chestnut hair, which left a couple of the shorter bits on top sticking straight up. "Okay. Let me rephrase. My mother *might* be a vampire."

I sat back in my chair. "I'm all ears, Special Agent Stevens."

He sighed and ran his hands over his face, like he'd splashed water on it and was wiping it with a towel.

"It happened when I was twelve. My father had taken

off for parts unknown a few years before, leaving my Mom and me by ourselves. Mom was great. She worked two jobs to keep the roof over our heads. She never complained. One of those jobs was tending bar at an upscale watering hole in Manhattan."

He got up and paced again, as if the very telling of the story required movement.

"My mom was beautiful. I mean seriously great looking. Her beauty made her attractive to men, but she always picked the wrong ones. She was too soft-hearted for her own good.

"She used to take me to work with her sometimes and I washed and stacked glasses behind the bar. It was illegal to have an underage kid there, but everyone was cool. No one would've turned my mom in. They loved her."

He ran his fingers through his hair again, strode to the window and peeked outside.

He was giving off so much nervous energy that I could've asked him to hold the plug end of my portable razor and shaved my legs while he talked to me.

"About a month before she disappeared, she started hanging out with this slick guy. Expensive clothes, big car, diamond stud earring. He seemed okay to me at first. I thought he might be sick because he was so pale, but he was nice to me when I saw him."

Alan walked into the kitchen and I heard the cabinet open and the faucet run. He carried his glass of water back to the couch and sat.

Patience, Kismet, patience.

He rubbed his palm of his free hand repeatedly against his pant leg. "I was happy for her. She really liked him.

He treated her well. But she started to stay out all night, then ignored the alarm clock when it went off in the morning. Wound up losing her day job."

He set the glass on the table without drinking.

"And she started looking different. Now I'd call it anemic, but then I was just worried about her and I didn't know what was wrong. One evening when I came home from my after-school job, I found her still in bed, barely breathing, with two hellacious holes in her neck. I ran out to get help and when I came back with the nurse next door, she was gone."

He slumped back into the cushions, his chin almost resting on his chest.

I drifted over, joined him on the couch and laid my hand on his forearm.

"You made the vampire connection because of the holes in her neck?"

He shook his head. "Not for a while. I thought she'd been kidnapped or ran away or that she died and someone took her body away and didn't tell me. The police investigated, but it went nowhere. I went to live with my mother's sister in Jersey and didn't make the undead association until I saw my mother."

That came out of left field. I paused long enough to stifle my initial, knee-jerk reaction and forced myself to remain companionably calm, detached. "You saw your mother?"

"Yeah. During college. A bunch of us guys went out drinking in Manhattan at this new, trendy bar. I got up to go to the john, and I saw the guy. The slick guy my mom had been dating before she disappeared. He looked exactly the same. I was ten years older than the last time he'd seen me, but there was a spark of recognition . . . and surprise. Just then the person sitting next to him at the bar turned in my direction, and it was my mom. Very pale and not one day older."

He leaped up and paced again. I was getting tired just from watching him.

"I yelled, 'Mom!' and before I could say another word, the slick guy pulled her by the arm and they were out of the bar faster than it was possible to be out of the bar. I bolted after them, but they'd both disappeared when I got outside. I ran in both directions, hoping for a glimpse of the long, red dress she'd been wearing. Nothing.

"My friends came piling out, thinking I was drunk, and I got crammed into a taxi."

He plopped down next to me again, sighed and shook his head. "Of course, nobody believed me. They wouldn't even check out the possibility that she'd been abducted and held against her will. I didn't begin to explore the vampire angle until I read a couple of small articles in the New York paper about dead bodies with holes in their necks. Then it clicked."

I took his hand. "So, you're searching for your mother?"

He gave a sheepish smile.

"Pitiful, eh?"

I shook my head. "No. Not pitiful. Understandable. What will you do if you find her?"

His eyes welled up. One perfect drop of liquid pain rolled down his cheek. "I just want her to tell me why she left me. She loved me. I know she did."

I gathered him into my arms and gently rocked him.

He let me hold him for a few minutes, then pushed away.

He snatched a tissue from the nearby box. "Some FBI

agent I am, eh? Blubbering on your shoulder like a kid. I'm sorry. I didn't mean to turn you into my therapist."

I stroked his cheek and smiled, letting him see the compassion in my eyes.

"You didn't come to me as a therapist. You came as a friend. And, as someone said to me recently, I'm here for you."

He blew his nose and smiled.

"I guess the wild and crazy sex is out? I'd be willing to settle for pity sex."

I laughed and took his hand again. "How about a chaste, platonic kiss?"

I angled my head and pressed my lips to his.

He pulled back and whispered, "How about this instead?"

He used his body to shift me backward until I was prone on the couch. His lips were soft and warm as they captured mine. He gently rubbed his groin against me and teased his tongue into my mouth.

My arms tightened around him, and his erection came to the door and waved hello.

He broke the kiss and slowly sat up. He wore the expression of a man who was certain of his sexual charm.

"Yes. When it finally happens, it will be very good."

He smiled and stood.

I sat up, relieved I didn't have to enter the murky territory of Alan versus Devereux, but aroused, all the same.

Men were so good at disguising vulnerability with sex.

He straightened his clothes and nonchalantly ran his fingers through his hair, as if he hadn't just reintroduced me to Mr. Happy.

But the physical contact had done what he wanted it to

do: it distracted us from the hurtful topic.

"I'm going to go home and put on my costume for the ball. Do you want me to come back and pick you up?"

Driving up to the mountains alone was always fun in the daytime, but at night—with more vampires afoot than usual—company sounded like a good idea. Besides, I didn't have any idea where the ghostly castle was or how to get there.

"I'd appreciate the ride. What are you wearing?"

He grinned. "Guess."

"Garden variety vampire, or something unique and interesting?"

"I'll surprise you. Is an hour enough time?"

"Sure. I'll just throw on a low cut black number, put on some white paint, false eyelashes and red lips, and I'm good to go."

He headed for the door, glancing back over his shoulder. "Okay, then. It's a date. Be back in an hour."

Before doing anything else, I trailed him to the door and locked it.

I raced up the stairs, started the water in the shower, then went into my bedroom to find out what kind of long, black dresses might be hiding in my closet.

It was entirely possible I'd accumulated dresses that I only wore for one professional event or another then forgot about.

As I'd suspected, pushed against the far wall of the closet was a plastic bag, stamped with the name of an expensive chain store, which contained the perfect black dress.

Finding the price tags still attached meant I'd never worn it, or I'd gone out in public with the papers flapping underneath my arms.

Unfortunately, both options were possible.

Well, I couldn't help it if my inner world was more interesting to me than most of the mundane details of the outer world.

Would I trade my expertise in the emotional, psychic, and psychological realms to be more socially savvy? No. But I wouldn't mind being more balanced.

Maybe I just needed a wife. Yeah, that was it. Someone to do all the stereotypical things we attribute to wives.

Or, maybe a harem. Yum, a male harem.

I imagined Devereux, Alan, Tom, Vaughan the chiropractor and the cute doctor I'd met in the ER all dressed up in slave costumes. I spun the wheel of various scenarios and envisioned them feeding me grapes, rubbing my feet, and carrying me in one of those Egyptian-type chairs.

Then I got totally distracted by a quick visual of the six of us having a private party in a luxurious, curtained bed.

Maybe a cold shower would do me more good than a hot one.

I laughed out loud, removed the dress from the plastic bag, and spread it out on my bed.

Then I clipped off the price tags.

An hour later my makeup was done and the curls of my hair were picked out into a long, shining thickness. I was perfumed, high-heeled and poured into a slinky, floor-length, cleavage-exposing black dress.

The ever-present, recently-life-saving necklace was nestled in the valley.

Not too shabby.

After checking out the pale hue of my natural skin tone against the black of the dress, I'd decided against putting on even whiter makeup. Sometimes it came in handy to have a ghostly complexion.

Right on time the doorbell sounded and I scoped out the peephole.

I turned on the porch light and felt a ripple of dread fan through my body. It was dark.

Standing on my porch was Dracula strolling the streets of London, a la Gary Oldman: top hat, long curls, blue glasses, and a silver-knobbed walking stick.

There was no mistaking that charming smile.

I opened the door. "Alan! You look amazing!"

He strutted into the entryway, preened, and bowed.

Adopting a thick Transylvanian accent, he said, "Mina, I mean, Kismet, I vant to drink your blood. But I could be persuaded to do something else instead."

He stepped around behind me, lifted my hair away from my neck and ran his teeth over my skin.

He sported the same kind of tiny, well-crafted fake fangs Midnight had worn.

The touch sent goose bumps down my skin and I turned to face him.

"We'll never get out of here if you keep on doing that."

He slid his fingertips down my arms, still speaking in the thick accent. "It would be my pleasure to rip off this incredibly sexy dress and ravage you right here on the floor. Do you prefer to be on the bottom or the top?"

"Oh, Count, you take my breath away, but I fear we'll be

late for the vampire staking if we dawdle."

He lifted my hand and kissed the palm.

"Then, I shall come to visit you in the night."

We both laughed.

"Aren't they adorable, Raleigh?"

Alan and I both jerked our heads toward the voice.

Once again, my living room hosted unexpected visitors.

Bryce stood in the center of the room, his long, dark hair resplendent against a blood red, floor-length, velvet coat. White ruffles peeked out of the lapels and sleeves. Black leather pants hugged his well-proportioned lower body.

It had to be some kind of cosmic injustice that such an evil being could be so devilishly handsome.

He could've been a candidate for Vampire Pin-Up of the Year if it hadn't been for the struggling human he held in an effortless headlock under his arm.

I recognized Ronald's auburn hair immediately.

Bryce held Ronald in a choke-hold so tight that only grunts and moans emanated from the young man's lips.

My stomach contracted, and I gasped.

Could this day get any worse?

As he'd done before, Raleigh laughed maniacally while performing munchkin-like kicks and steps in circles around the room.

Instead of the sleeveless muscle shirt he'd worn last time, in honor of the ball he was decked out in a miniature version of traditional movie vampire garb: slicked back burgundy hair, white shirt, and long, sweeping cape with a raised collar. He'd painted black circles around his icy blue-white eyes.

Creepy.

Alan dropped his walking stick, pulled a gun from somewhere under his jacket and pointed it at Bryce.

"That's enough. Release him. Now."

"Well, well. Things just keep on getting better. I do love a good drama."

Bryce ignored the gun and, moving faster than we could see, planted himself directly in front of Alan, surprising him. He gazed into Alan's eyes, which fluttered then closed completely, his chin nodding against his chest. Alan's arm fell to his side. The gun slipped from his hand onto the floor with a thump.

Bryce kicked the gun aside. "What a disappointment. Not a worthy adversary, after all. Just another squawking blood sack."

Bryce turned and moved toward me, dragging Ronald along like a crash-test dummy.

He cocked his head and gave his favorite evil smile.

"I see you're all ready for the festivities. Excellent. We have a special room reserved just for you."

He pointed to Ronald. "I'm afraid your little friend here had quite a hissy fit when I sucked most of the blood out of his girlfriend Midnight's body. He insisted on coming along to tell you all about it. Unfortunately, he seems to be a little tongue-tied at the moment."

Bryce laughed robustly, tightening his grip on Ronald's neck with every chortle.

Ronald gasped for air. He wasn't going to make it if Bryce didn't release him soon.

I didn't know what to do, so I did something stupid. I took a step toward Bryce, got in his face and screamed. "Let him go, you bloodsucking coward. Showing off for idiots and children. We'll see how big and bad you are after Devereux gets through with you."

Bryce flinched. He didn't like that. His handsome features contorted into a ghastly mask, his eyes narrowed and grew darker. He growled, showing razor-point fangs.

I figured mentioning Devereux's name would push his buttons, but I didn't think it through beyond hoping he'd turn his rage on me and drop Ronald.

So much for that.

Bryce simply appeared at my side, circled my waist with his free arm and yanked me against his body. He raised his chin in unconscious Alan's direction and barked at Raleigh, "Bring Dracula."

Chapter 25

Traveling by thought might be miraculous, but it certainly messed with my equilibrium. When Bryce suddenly released me, I stumbled backward, straining to catch my balance.

We'd materialized, or metamorphosed, or whatever we'd done, in the center of a lavish balcony.

I shuffled a few steps toward the railing and my mouth fell open.

We were definitely at high elevation.

I reached that conclusion because mountain peaks were visible through high-placed windows, and from my vantage point, the angels-with-fangs painted on the vast ceiling seemed close enough to touch.

I'd never imagined such a place. It reminded me of a photo of a European opera house I'd seen in a magazine, except much bigger.

Was this the famous ghostly castle?

The walls were lined with ornate balconies, one underneath the other, each filled with people in costumes.

The terrace we'd popped onto seemed to be the only one with limited occupancy.

Stretching out below me was an extraordinary ballroom.

Everything was gold. Sparkling gold. From the designs

in the antique wallpaper, to the water fountains strategically placed throughout the room, to the nude sculptures.

Dazzling chandeliers burst down from the painted ceiling, dangling like mammoth crystal earrings.

It wasn't an exaggeration to say there were thousands of people milling about in the main area.

The costumes were incredible. Assuming they were costumes.

An amplified voice floated through the airwaves, "Welcome to the Vampires' Ball."

I raised my arms over my head, signaling, calling to the partiers across the stadium-size space.

A commotion behind me caused me to turn my head in time to watch Bryce pull a screaming Ronald by his hair toward a door in the far wall. Raleigh followed, dragging the still-unconscious Alan, whose wig, glasses, and hat were missing in action.

I guess Bryce didn't care if I yelled or drew attention to myself by waving my arms madly. He left me standing against the railing, turning back only once to laugh at me before disappearing through the doorway.

The noise level told me why he didn't care. Even if I set myself on fire and screamed, no one would've taken it seriously. I couldn't be heard over the ear-splitting music, or the hysterical frivolity, and if I'd been inclined to turn myself into a human torch, they'd probably think it was part of the night's entertainment.

Jumping from the balcony wasn't an option.

Even if I made it to the next balcony down, the distance was great enough that I'd not only kill myself, but the unlucky soul I landed on.

After making a futile effort to communicate to anyone that I needed help, I gave up and followed them through the door.

I felt numb. I didn't know if I was getting used to being terrified or if my adrenal system had simply gone into overload and shut down.

Under any other circumstances, the beauty of the room on the other side of the doorway would've taken my breath away. As it was, words failed me.

All the walls of the expansive room were mirrored. Several large chandeliers, like light-flowers in bloom, hung from the hand-painted ceiling and reflected the never-ending glow of the clusters of illumination.

Instead of angels with fangs, the painting overhead depicted fanged Greek gods and goddesses playing musical instruments.

I wondered if the original owner of the castle had been the one to order the vampire-inspired artwork or if it had been a more recent addition.

There hadn't been anything like these fanged characters in Devereux's art gallery under The Crypt, but it wasn't out of the range of possibility that he'd painted these, too.

The exquisite music room contained several grand pianos, each a different style and color, forming a widely spaced square around the perimeter of the room.

Harpsichords, antique harps, and other instruments filled the spaces between the pianos. Music stands holding what appeared to be hand-written notation sheets waited patiently for musicians who might never arrive.

In the center of the room, Midnight lay, deathly white. Bryce must've released Ronald when they'd entered, because he sat on the floor with Midnight, his legs underneath her head. He gently stroked her hair, murmuring softly.

I rushed over to the couple, knelt and felt for a pulse in Midnight's neck, which was dotted with fang-sized holes. The beat was there. Faint, but present.

Ronald and I shared a look that communicated relief, frustration, and fear.

Bryce swaggered into the center of the room, his crimson coat and dark hair reflected in every facet of the mirrors.

Once again I was struck by evil's ability to be beautiful.

"Is she going to die?" I asked, standing.

Bryce walked a circle around Midnight, studying her as if she were a mildly interesting display, smiling.

"Perhaps. Perhaps not. It all depends on whether or not I choose to finish what I started."

He raised his eyes to mine. "Maybe I'll give her the immortality she always wanted."

I remembered what happened the last time Bryce pulled me into his eyes, so I didn't meet his gaze, but instead focused on a spot between his eyebrows. Even being in that close proximity to his dark green orbs caused me to have a fuzzy, tingling feeling in what Devereux had called my "third eye."

For some odd reason, Cerridwyn's words floated through my mind: "Don't be afraid of your abilities. They will save you."

I still didn't understand what she meant, but the words seemed important. And comforting.

I knew I had no chance of doing anything physical to get away from Bryce. And even if I managed to escape, I couldn't leave Ronald, Midnight, and Alan behind.

My only hope was to use my mind. Maybe if I could get him talking, I could discover something helpful.

"Why have you brought us here? What do you want?"

"You, my dear Dr. Knight, are bait."

Bait? Was he trying to catch Brother Luther, too?

"Bait? For what?"

He hesitated. "Well, I guess since the curtain is about to rise on the first act, it's prudent to tell you. Lucifer seems to want you for some reason, so I brought you here for him, then he'll get me what I want."

"What do you want?"

He smiled, licked his lips and ran one hand slowly down the zipper of his leather pants, cupping himself.

"I want Devereux."

What? Does he mean he wants Devereux sexually? Or was that gesture a show of power like in some street gangs?

Something about the way he said Devereux's name sent chills up my body. My pulse quickened, stomach contracted.

Where is Devereux, anyway?

"You aren't strong enough to do anything to Devereux."

He gave a Cheshire cat smile.

"Perhaps not. But Lucifer and I together. Well, let's just say we're an unbeatable team."

That's the second time he'd mentioned that name. Was he talking about the Devil?

"Who's Lucifer?"

He laughed and moved his hand. "You'll find out soon enough."

Suddenly the air was filled with the familiar popping

sounds, and at least two dozen vampires materialized into the room. They carried bottles, carved boxes, enormous gemstones, ancient-looking books, statues, and swords.

A couple of the new arrivals resembled the old, bearded characters in *Lord of the Rings*.

I didn't think they were there to hold a renaissance faire.

Bryce nodded, pleased.

He grabbed my arm and pulled me toward him.

"We'll go and enjoy the party while the ritual is prepared."

"What ritual?"

"The ritual of High Magic which will render Devereux helpless long enough for me to take control of him. Lucifer already began the binding process in Devereux's dreams. Even now his power weakens."

Devereux had mentioned he'd been experiencing strange dreams. And he said something about being tricked into entering a "difficult reality," whatever that was.

Until that moment, I hadn't seriously tried to contact Devereux telepathically. I didn't believe I could. But I put everything I had into sending a burst of thought to him, and for a second I could've sworn I *heard* him say my name.

I didn't know if that was good news or not. It certainly would be great for me if he turned up, but if he did, he'd be the guest of honor at the Ritual from Hell. And I didn't care for the sound of this Lucifer guy.

"What about Midnight and Ronald and Alan?"

Bryce spoke pleasantly, waving a hand in the air. "They're perfectly fine." He lowered his chin and whispered. "For now."

"Can you save Midnight?"

Harsh laughter burst from his mouth. "Silly human.

"Raleigh, drag the girl and her savior over to the corner with the FBI agent. We need the space in the center of the room to cast the circle."

Raleigh gave a dramatic bow and skipped over to Midnight. He pulled her by the arm, her head slamming onto the floor as it fell off Ronald's lap.

"Please! Don't hurt her!" Ronald's eyes glistened with tears. It feels horrible to be helpless.

Raleigh barked at Ronald, "Get over here under your own steam or I'll be happy to drag you, too. Of course, your arm might accidentally be pulled out of its socket, but by that time you'll have passed out and won't notice."

He made a braying sound, which was probably laughter.

Bryce smiled like a proud parent watching a precocious child. He seemed to be having a very good time.

He turned to one of the bearded vampires who'd brought over a jar of something for him to inspect.

Movement in the mirror caught my eye.

A man, dressed not in vampire regalia but in an old-fashioned waistcoat and breeches, stalked across the room and stood at the edge of the activity, watching.

In his hands he carried a violin and bow.

He began gesturing angrily with the bow, his face contorted, his mouth forming soundless words.

None of the vampires in the middle of the room responded. Apparently, they couldn't hear him. Neither could I.

I shifted my head so I could see the man directly instead of reflected in the mirror. He wasn't there. Turning back to the mirror I found him right where he'd been before.

I tried the experiment again with the same result.

What the hell? Am I the only one who sees this guy?

It was obvious from his body language that the violinist was becoming progressively more upset the longer he was ignored.

He moved toward Raleigh, who was hefting a large black stone into place in the circle, and poked him with the bow . . . which passed right through his body.

Not getting the result he desired obviously enraged the man further and he stamped his foot, throwing his bow on the floor.

When he bent over to pick it up, his eyes met mine in the mirror. Surprise flashed across his face and he disappeared.

No. I didn't just see that. Bryce must've messed with my brain again. No more supernatural weirdness. I refuse to believe one more unbelievable thing.

At that moment, Bryce dismissed the bearded vamp and turned to me. He closed his arm around my waist. I felt a feather's breath of air against my face, then we were down on the main floor, in the middle of the party.

I almost asked him how he managed to come and go without smashing into or landing on top of anyone, but caught the words before they left my mouth. I didn't want him to mistake my nervous chatter for actual interest in anything about him.

I craned my neck, searching the area for Brother Luther and was relieved to come up empty. Since I hadn't heard back from Lieutenant Bullock, and Alan was incapacitated upstairs, I hoped the lunatic wouldn't show up. According to what Bryce had said, there was already a full dose of misery on tap for the evening.

Misery and a ghost in the mirror.

A velvet voice floated through my mind. "My love."

I started to say "Dev—"

"Speak to me silently. In your mind."

I didn't waste any time questioning whether or not I could communicate telepathically. I sent him a bundle of thoughts, emotions, and pictures, sharing everything I knew about Brother Luther, Bryce's intentions, the ritual to trap him, and someone named Lucifer.

"I will not allow harm to come to you. Do not let anyone know you have spoken to me. I will be close by. No matter what."

I felt an odd emptiness and knew he was gone.

Bryce's mouth was moving, so I assumed he'd been talking to me. I focused on his words, hoping he'd provide more useful information.

". . . why he would be interested in someone like you."

"What?" I blurted, annoyed that I'd missed the first part of his sentence.

I held my hands over my ears, pretending I hadn't heard him because of the loud music.

He scowled and raised his voice.

"I was saying, Devereux knew when he brought me over that I'd be powerful. He also knew how I felt about him. He's as bisexual as the rest of us. I never did believe his song and dance about waiting for some soul mate or whatever. It's bad enough he's making a fool of himself over a woman. But a *human* woman is beyond belief."

The evil grin slid across his face again.

"He'll have a long time to regret and reassess his choices. I might still take him back. If he begs.

"Let's dance."

Before I could protest or think of a way to avoid the close contact, Bryce pulled me onto one of the table-free areas where couples were slow dancing.

He put his hands on my rear end and ground his lower body against mine.

I struggled to free my arms from his rigid embrace. He didn't even notice.

He was busy studying my cleavage in the low cut dress.

"I might just have to sample the goods Devereux is so hot for before the night is over. You've got big tits. I like that."

He reached a hand around, grabbed my breast, squeezed and laughed.

"More than a handful."

He slid his hand from my breast to the hair resting beside it and lifted a curl. "And your hair is long. It's almost as pretty as mine. Almost."

If he was waiting for me to compliment his hair, he'd be a rotted corpse in vampire hell before that happened.

Thankfully, he didn't have a reaction to my lack of response.

He palmed my butt cheeks again, moving us assertively through the crowd. He clearly fancied himself the vampire Fred Astaire. As we circled the dance floor, I searched for familiar faces.

I thought it might be easy to pick out the vampires in the sea of wannabes, but it turned out to be more complicated than expected.

The high quality of the costumes, makeup, wigs, and fake fangs, along with the fact that just about everyone in the room wore dramatic vampire costumes, made identifying the bloodsuckers more challenging.

Everybody looked like an authentic bloodsucker.

But the longer we danced among them, the more I began to notice the familiar tingle when I was in the vicinity of a vampire. And not only that. I was able to intuitively sense the level of the vampire's powers.

Some of them barely sent out enough buzz to charge a flashlight battery, while others came across like a mini cattle prod to the solar plexus.

My stomach muscles had repeatedly contracted since Bryce kidnapped us out of my living room—fear tends to do that—so it was a good guess he belonged in the second category.

Apollo had told me that a vampire was only as powerful as the one who made him, so if Devereux was Bryce's maker, his abilities were probably beyond the norm. Or whatever passed for normal in vampire reality.

Vampire. Reality.

Two weeks ago I'd never have put those words in the same sentence.

The slow song ended and the band launched into one of those World Beat compositions that combined African and Latin rhythms. The primitive drumbeats called to the celebrants and the dance floor filled.

I had to admit, most vampires might be sick puppies, but they could dance.

Bryce flipped me around so my rear end nestled against his groin. His arms encircled my waist, pulling me tighter against his apparently ever-present erection, as he propelled us through the cavorting masses.

He boogied, shifting his hips from side to side, forcing me

to mimic his movements.

Ever since we'd popped onto the main floor, I'd been so occupied with Bryce, spotting Brother Luther if he arrived, and trying to communicate with Devereux that I'd missed some interesting developments.

I'd always thought most men were overly fond of their penises. They were always ready, willing, and able to talk about them, show them to you, touch you with them, or try to sneak them into any warm, wet, available place.

It would appear that vampires have elevated penis fixation to an art form.

All around me on the dance floor was sexual activity. Penises being stroked by either the owner or a willing partner of either sex.

I'd stumbled into a vampire porn video.

Was that what being immortal meant? Blood sucking and masturbation? And why was it only the male vampires?

Did something weird happen to testosterone in the transformation?

Was that the best we could do with eternal life? Perpetual sexual adolescence?

Lost in thought, I startled when a woman screamed a few feet away from me. I was only able to hear it because the tone of her cry was higher pitched than the music.

I jerked my head in the direction of the scream saw a woman pinned to the floor by a vampire whose fangs were embedded in her neck.

I'd guess she wasn't a willing donor.

None of the bystanders offered to help her. In fact, the attack seemed to excite the strokers.

I struggled to get out of Bryce's grasp and he clasped me tighter, rubbing himself against me, making soft moaning sounds.

It was completely stupid of me to think I could do anything to make the vampire release his victim, but I absolutely couldn't just stand there and watch.

I stomped down hard on Bryce's foot with the heel of my shoe and he relaxed his arms enough for me to slide down through them. I don't think he let go because I hurt him, but because I surprised him. He was obviously distracted.

I leaped onto the back of the sucking vampire, who turned out to be a very large, muscular, smelly bloodsucker who flicked me off without even lifting his mouth from the woman's neck.

Laughter echoed around me as I fell to the floor on my back. A hand reached out of a full-length, hooded robe to help me up and I caught a glimpse of a familiar face inside the hood.

Even the clown-like vampire makeup couldn't disguise Lieutenant Bullock's distinctive features.

I started to acknowledge her, and she stopped me with the slightest shake of her head.

Bryce's arm snaked around my waist again and he jerked me up off my feet, holding my back against his chest.

"Ordinarily, I'd punish you for your absurd actions, but I still need you for a little while longer. You're lucky Lucifer wants you.

"Playtime's over. Let's go back upstairs."

The woman on the floor had stopped screaming and was clearly dead.

The crowd actually applauded.

Vampires suck. In more ways than one.

I managed to catch Lieutenant Bullock's eyes and shifted mine in the direction of the high balcony, showing her where we were going.

She gave an almost invisible nod, lowered the hood over her face and merged into the crowd.

Just before Bryce popped us out, I caught a glimpse of several robed figures winding their way toward a doorway.

The music room had been transformed into the Church of Satan—or the setting for a Black Sabbath concert. Something that required lots of black draperies, upside-down crosses and pictures of ugly guys with horns.

A large circle with an inverted pentagram had been drawn in the center of the room and the massive gemstones placed in probably meaningful positions.

Some of the mirrors had been decorated with elaborate symbols, and the light from the chandeliers was replaced by the soft, eerie glow of black candles.

When we materialized in the room, Raleigh scurried over to Bryce. He frowned as he noted that Bryce held me off the ground, tight to his chest, and that one of his hands had moved from my waist to my breast. Raleigh shot me a dirty look and snarled, showing his pointy fangs.

Jealousy?

Bryce noticed and enjoyed Raleigh's reaction. He laughed out loud, removed his arms from around me, and I fell in a heap on the floor.

Raleigh clutched Bryce's hand like a child.

It took a minute for my eyes to adjust to the dim light, but I was finally able to make out the shapes in the corner. Ronald cradled Midnight in his arms and Alan sprawled next to them, still as a corpse.

I hadn't allowed myself to consider the possibility that Alan was actually dead, but since it had occurred to me, I had to know. I started crawling in Alan's direction.

I'd just reached Alan, picked up his wrist and detected a light pulse, when the familiar limb closed around me again.

Bryce held me under his arm like a rolled up newspaper.

"Playing Florence Nightingale, Dr. Knight? Trying to save the handsome FBI agent? My, my. How many men are you servicing these days?

"But you mustn't rattle the blood sacks. I need at least one of them for the ritual. Maybe two."

"What are you talking about? What do you need for the ritual?"

"Blood."

"Do you mean you need to drink blood?"

"You really are a tedious human. Of course I need to drink blood. But this blood's for the ritual. It's the final step. We're going to smear it all over the circle. Quite a waste of food, if you ask me, but the wizard geniuses say it's necessary.

"It will be worth it to have Devereux under my power."

He laughed, carried me near the circle and set me on my feet.

He positioned himself in front of me, shoved one of his hands down the front of my dress and roughly grabbed a breast.

LYNDA HILBURN

"You didn't answer my question, Florence. How many men are you servicing?"

His grip on the tender flesh hurt, but I didn't want him to know that. I breathed in slowly through my nose, using a relaxation technique to lessen my awareness of the pain.

"None of your business."

He squeezed harder and I yelped. My knees gave out. It hurt like a mammogram times a thousand, and he wasn't even trying. My entire breast was going to be black and blue. If he didn't rip it off.

Apparently, the protective necklace only worked if it was touched directly. What kind of magic talisman was that?

Smiling, he released his hold, pulled his hand out of my dress and let me fall to the floor.

Standing over me, he unbuttoned his pants and was sliding down the zipper of his fly when the silence was shattered by an extremely loud pop and Brother Luther appeared.

Chapter 26

$\mathscr{B}$ryce physically jumped back a few inches, visibly startled. "Lucifer!"

Lucifer? This isn't Brother Luther? Then who's Brother Luther?

The tall, bald vampire growled, his discolored fangs bared. He stepped over me and stalked toward Bryce, whose eyes had gone wide.

It didn't take a psychologist to figure out that Bryce was afraid of the foul-smelling creature backing him into a corner.

Bryce's voice quivered. "Lucifer, I wasn't really going to do her. I was saving her for you, just as we agreed."

Lucifer picked Bryce up by his throat, piercing his neck with long, filthy fingernails. Bryce struggled uselessly as rivulets of blood trailed down his neck and Lucifer licked them with his long tongue.

Bryce screamed, "Dammit, Raleigh! The song! Play the song!"

Raleigh sprinted over to a boom box propped on a chair. He pressed a button and Brahms's *Lullaby* floated softly from the speakers.

Lucifer continued to suck on the wounds on Bryce's neck, while using his other hand to fondle his own favorite body part.

"Crank it up!" Bryce yelled.

Raleigh turned the music up eardrum shatteringly loud and Lucifer pulled back, dropped his hand from Bryce's neck and let him fall to the floor. He relinquished his grasp on his swollen organ and shuffled over to the boom box. He sat in front of it, swaying to the music, humming tonelessly.

Bryce leaped to his feet, massaging his neck.

Raleigh rushed to him. "I did good, didn't I, Master?"

Bryce kicked the small man in the stomach, causing him to double over.

"You almost fucking got me killed, you moron. You should've started the damn CD the moment Bizarro Man showed up. You know that's the only way I can control him. Otherwise, he goes fucking ballistic."

Raleigh, who wasn't even as tall as Bryce's waist, hugged him. "I'm sorry, Master. Don't punish me!"

Bryce hesitated for a few seconds, appearing to consider the possibilities in the location of Raleigh's face, then peeled the mini vampire off his body.

I'd gotten to my feet during the chaos and retreated behind a spectacular, mahogany grand piano.

I studied the bald vampire who'd inexplicably ceased his rampage and sat hypnotized in front of the CD player.

Shit on a stick. Lucifer's affected by the music. Not only affected, but manipulated—controlled. I've never seen a reaction that strong before. He transformed from being a dangerous predator into an almost-childlike state. I never would've suspected. This is one for the psych journals. If they believed in vampires, that is.

My silent diagnostic session was abruptly interrupted.

Shoving Raleigh out of his way, Bryce scanned the room

and quickly found me. He stalked over, grabbed my upper arm forcefully enough to leave bruises and pulled me to the circle.

The pain of his fingers burrowing knife-like into my arm was so intense I gasped, struggling to catch my breath.

He barked, "That's enough bullshit. On with the show."

Several vampires had been busy placing objects inside the circle and drawing geometric shapes around the outside. Others worked in another part of the room, blending the contents of small bottles into a silver cauldron, which bubbled over a fire.

All of them came to attention at Bryce's command.

I hadn't noticed before that each wore a black robe. Vampire monks? Vampire devil worshippers?

Lucifer swayed gently, oblivious.

Except for one of the bearded vampires who scooped thick liquid from the cauldron into a black cup, everyone else assumed their places in the circle and began chanting.

The sound of the chant was different from what I'd experienced with Devereux. That had been melodic. This was more like a deep rumbling sound.

It reminded me of a performance I'd attended by a group of Buddhist Throat Singers. They have the ability, through years of training and practice, to sing two, three or four distinct low tones at the same time. They use it for meditation and trance induction.

Eerie and powerful.

These guys were doing the same thing. It sent chills through me just like it had at the concert.

The other bearded vampire walked the circle, holding a sword straight up over his head. The blade sparkled in the candlelight. He mumbled words under his breath and paused at regular intervals to lower the sword's tip to the floor and up again.

He came to a stop at the point nearest to where I waited with Bryce, whose claw-fingers were still cutting off the circulation in my arm. Using the sword, the vampire made a downward swipe and reached his hand through an invisible slash in an imaginary entryway, pretending to hold something open.

Bryce dragged me through.

The growling chant rose in intensity.

If I hadn't participated in the Wiccan coven's ritual years ago, I'd have been surprised by the energetic change I experienced inside the circle.

The air felt thicker, as if it exerted more pressure on my skin. My body seemed to move in slow motion, cotton candy filled my head.

Bryce released me with a push and I splatted onto the floor. Again.

Not only was my arm throbbing, my hip screamed. I must have fallen on it earlier.

I kicked off the only shoe that had made it into the circle and stood.

Bryce yelled to Raleigh, "When I tell you, turn off the music."

He studied me, amused. "I'm going to summon your blond vampire lover now. Fix your hair. You're a mess!"

I rubbed my arm and gave him a blank stare.

He can't really force Devereux to appear, can he? He's acting very smug and arrogant. Even more than usual. What if all these vampires together have more power than Devereux?

He laughed and strutted over to the invisible opening, where the bearded alchemist who'd been stirring the foul-smelling brew at the table handed him the black cup.

Bryce muttered something that sounded like strings of vowels and drank whatever was in the cup.

He grimaced, shook his head and bellowed, "Devereux. Come to me."

There was a moment of unnatural stillness. My skin itched as currents of air gathered in the ring. The velocity increased, blowing my hair back from my face and the light flickered, becoming suddenly brighter.

A sound—not a pop this time but a full-fledged sonic boom—resonated only seconds before Devereux's shirtless body burst into the circle.

The momentum was powerful enough that he landed on his hands and knees.

Bryce dropped the cup he'd been holding, clapped his hands and laughed. He bowed to the circle of chanting vampires.

"Bravo, gentlemen! You've exceeded all my expectations and will be abundantly rewarded."

Whatever had happened to cause Devereux to arrive had clearly taken a toll on him, because he struggled to get to his feet and appeared dazed.

Bryce cocked his head and watched his guest, who'd finally managed to rise.

Devereux turned his head in my direction and I instinctively moved toward him.

His eyes held an emotion that almost looked like fear.

He whispered in my mind, "This is impossible."

Bryce intercepted me, stepped between us. He gave me his back and ran his hands over the muscles of Devereux's chest.

He frowned. "Don't look at her. Look at me. I told you what would happen if you didn't cooperate."

Devereux rubbed his eyes. "What is this spell? You are not powerful enough to summon me."

Bryce clapped his hands again, laughing.

He swung his arm in a wide arc, indicating the robed participants. "When you have the right bargaining chips, anything is possible."

He hollered at Raleigh, "Now!"

Raleigh hit the "stop" button on the CD player and the lullaby abruptly ended.

I hadn't realized how loud it had been—what a counterpoint the lullaby was to the chanting—until it was gone.

I had a vague idea of what Bryce had in mind, but I couldn't figure out anything I could do to help Devereux. Or myself.

"Raleigh, bring me one of the blood sacks. Now! Move it!"

Raleigh, who enthusiastically enjoyed his role as Bryce's flunky, smiled—or more accurately leered—as he scurried over to the corner where Midnight, Ronald, and Alan waited.

He grabbed Alan by the neck and pulled him to the edge of the circle, dropping his head with a loud thump.

I was glad Alan was unconscious, because that had to hurt.

The bearded vampire with the sword reached his hand through the invisible entrance and pantomimed holding a curtain open.

Bryce seized Alan and dragged him inside.

He picked up a ceremonial athame that had been placed

strategically in the ritual space.

The confident, wicked smile on his face faltered as he darted a glance in Lucifer's direction and found him standing. Moving toward us.

I wished there was a volume control knob to turn down the chanters, because the repetitive sound was giving me a headache.

Devereux's voice whispered in my mind, "Stand back."

Bryce had gotten so distracted by Lucifer's approach and finding the knife to bleed Alan, that he'd underestimated Devereux's recovery.

Bryce knelt down next to Alan, raised the athame and repeated some words in Latin. Before the blade reached Alan's skin, Bryce was forcefully lifted into the air by Devereux's arm around his neck.

The blade flew from Bryce's hand and clattered to the floor.

The two of them tore at each other, snarling and swearing. They levitated, then wrestled down to the floor, pounding on each other like human fighters on angel dust.

I stood frozen, feeling like a helpless idiot.

As Devereux and Bryce flailed, they crashed into the chanters, who had nowhere to go, because the circle was protected by its own, weird force field.

Apparently, the only way in or out was through the imaginary opening.

The fighters struggled back to their feet, separating long enough to hiss and growl at each other.

Devereux spoke, deep and slow. "You are the mistake I have paid dearly for. It is finished."

With a ferocious roar, he launched himself at Bryce and

ripped his throat out.

Bryce crashed to the floor like a downed tree.

Blood spurted everywhere, drenching the circle. A sizzling sound, like butter in a hot pan, could be felt as well as heard. Faint static electricity caused the hairs on my arms to raise. Tiny sparks ignited around Devereux.

I pulled Alan as far away from the oozing blood as I could.

Although copious amounts of blood still flowed from the wound, the skin of Bryce's throat had already begun to knit itself back together.

I shifted my eyes away from Bryce in time to see Lucifer plow into the circle and grab Devereux.

On a good day I was sure Devereux could hold his own with the ghoulish vampire, but he was weak and things looked bad.

Lucifer lifted Devereux into the air, holding him by his hair, trying to sink his fangs into Devereux's neck.

Bryce's throat was healing so quickly he'd be back on his feet within seconds, and I didn't think Devereux had a chance of fending off both his enemies.

I cast my eyes around frantically, searching for anything I could use to help Devereux.

My eyes caught movement in the mirror. The waistcoated violinist, still holding his instrument and bow, was waving his arms excitedly to get my attention.

He moved his mouth, offering more silent words, and pointed his bow at something on the floor.

My eyes tracked where he pointed and didn't see anything except the sword.

I glanced back at the image in the mirror; he nodded

and mouthed, clear enough for me to understand, "Yes! Pick it up!"

The sword!

I really am dense.

What happened to the ZZ Top vampire who was guarding the opening?

I scooped up the blade, which was much heavier than I expected. I intended to stick it in Bryce's chest, because everyone knew you could kill a vampire by puncturing his heart. I hoped that wasn't another movie myth.

Bryce's neck was almost completely healed and he'd just lifted his head off the ground when I brought the sword down, aiming for his chest.

I whacked his head off instead.

This time the blood oozed instead of spurted.

I heard Raleigh scream Bryce's name.

The collective gasp of the now-silent chanters made me raise my head to investigate. All their surprised eyes were on me. A few of the vampires moved a step forward, as if they intended to take the sword away.

I didn't care about that. My brain had clicked on "automatic." All I knew was that I'd missed my target.

Before they could do anything, I raised the sword again and plunged the tip directly into Bryce's heart, holding the grip with two hands.

Sword in the Stone in reverse.

In my prevailing shocked and traumatized state, that decision made perfect sense.

I'd never again scoff at a story of a mother lifting a car to save her child. That was one heavy sword, but I'd wielded it like it was made of aluminum foil.

The electrical sensation increased and the sparks of light surrounding Devereux ignited crackling fire sounds.

Bryce had said the blood was the final part of the ritual. He just never thought it would be his blood. But what would it mean for Devereux that the circle had been saturated with the thick, red stuff?

He'd managed to pry Lucifer's hands off his hair, but wasn't making much progress in getting free.

"Kismet?"

I turned to find Alan sitting up, staring at me, his mouth open. He still wore the fake fangs.

He shifted his eyes to Bryce's body—both parts—then to the sword, then back to my face.

I can only imagine how I must've looked.

Well, I probably looked like what I was: a blood-soaked, traumatized, barefoot, ghost-seeing, vampire slayer.

In my demented state, I wondered if I should add "vampire slayer" to my business card. But I figured it wouldn't do much for my vampire therapy business.

I wasn't even particularly surprised that Alan had rejoined the land of the living. Since Bryce had been the one to put the whammy on him, and he was now undergoing an accelerated decomposition process, it made sense that Alan would be released from his evil eye.

It's funny how lucid you can become in the midst of a psychotic break.

Bryce's handsome face had regressed to his true age and the massively wrinkled skin began to crumble like ancient papyrus. Chunks of his now gray, brittle hair blew across the floor in the air currents caused by Devereux's continuing struggle with Lucifer.

I turned toward my ghostly helper in the mirror and mouthed the words "Thank you." He bowed from the waist, raised his violin to playing position and moved the bow vigorously over the strings. I wished I could've heard the tune.

Apparently, seeing ghosts is another one of my skills. Who knew?

A groan from Devereux brought him back to center stage in my attention.

Something was happening to him. He stumbled, not able to remain erect. His eyes met mine and I saw fear again before he collapsed on the floor.

Lucifer loomed over him, slowly bending down.

Devereux whispered in my mind, "I love you."

Something about the hopelessness and finality of the feeling he sent along with the words terrified me. A bone-chilling cold that rose from the horror of killing Bryce and the possibility of losing Devereux washed over me. I dropped to the floor and crawled to the vampire I loved. I stroked his cheek, calling his name over and over. He didn't answer.

Alan grabbed the athame from where it had fallen on the floor, leaped up onto Lucifer's back and stabbed him repeatedly. Lucifer seemed more annoyed than injured and flailed about, trying to dislodge the irritant between his shoulder blades.

Lucifer finally reached over his shoulder, grabbed Alan by his thick hair and threw him into the former chanters. One of the vampires held onto Alan for a few seconds, a confused expression on his face. Maybe he wasn't sure where his loyalties belonged since I killed Bryce. He must have decided that it wasn't wise to be on the losing team, so he let Alan go.

Grasping at straws, I screamed up at Lucifer, repeating all the words he'd said to me in one of his other personalities. "She must be punished. You are the warrior of God. The redeemer of lost souls. She's a harlot! Jezebel! Whore!"

Lucifer froze. He reached down and grabbed a big chunk of my hair, pulling me up as he straightened. He locked his red eyes on mine and I felt my brain slide out my ears.

I closed my eyes to break the eye contact and kept repeating the words, trying to remember everything else he'd said, until I felt him relax his grip on my hair.

Even before I opened my eyes I could tell he'd transformed. But I knew for sure when he launched into his southern-accented rant.

"Whore! Jezebel! You'll be washed in the blood!"

He seemed to shrink before my eyes. The stained, horrible smelling black coat now larger than his shriveled frame. His eyes black coals again.

He backed away from me, clutching his coat around him, rocking slightly.

I became aware of Alan standing next to me, his eyes wide, fascinated by the spectacle unfolding in front of him.

I hoped the transformation from one of the split-off personalities to another might release Devereux from whatever power-hold Brother Luther—or Lucifer, whoever he really was—had on him, but Devereux lay still as death.

The ritual Bryce set in motion had taken on a life of its own and fulfilled the original intention: to control Devereux.

Then several things happened at once.

A loud noise drew my attention to one of the mirror

panels on the other side of the room, which turned out to be a hidden door.

Lieutenant Bullock's costumed police officers stormed the room, yelling, "Police! Freeze!"

The human rescuers were followed by Luna and too many vampires to count.

The arrival of Devereux's coven caused the vampires who'd been in the ritual to dash through the imaginary opening in the circle and pop out of the room.

Luna barreled toward the ritual space and smashed into the invisible force field.

"Fucking magic bullshit!" she screamed. "They had the whole building protected so we couldn't enter through thought. We had to follow the stupid humans who'd found a way in. Now we'll have to erase their memories."

Her expression became suddenly serious as she got a closer look at Devereux lying helplessly on the floor.

Her face contorted. Enraged, she screamed at Brother Luther, thinking he was Lucifer, not realizing that for all intents and purposes, he was a different person. Er, different vampire.

Trying again unsuccessfully to enter the circle, Luna vented her anger and frustration on the stooped, pitiful vampire standing over Devereux.

The longer she yelled, the more upset he became until he covered his face with his hands and sobbed loudly.

I knew what would happen if he reached a breaking point in his anxiety, so I tried to convince Luna to stop haranguing him.

"Please, Luna. You've got to stop. He's calm for now.

Trust me, if you keep screaming at him, something bad will happen. He's sick."

"Fuck that. This asshole did something to Devereux and I'm going to find out what he did. Take your human psycho-babble somewhere else."

She'd been prowling around the perimeter of the circle, testing for an opening. Not finding one made her even angrier.

I stared down at Devereux's beautiful face and remembered the music.

Keeping the dangerous, psychotic vampire subdued so we could remove Devereux from the circle was the highest priority. Maybe when he was freed from the influence of the spell, he'd revive.

Playing the lullaby, which would make Brother Luther shift into his child personality, seemed to be the best temporary solution. Perhaps he'd be immune to Luna's threats in his regressed state.

All I could think about was saving Devereux, so I didn't consider the repercussions when I sailed through the opening in the circle, heading toward the CD player.

Alan called out, "Where are you going?"

"No time to explain." He'd missed the musical portion of the evening.

When I got there, the little CD drawer was open and empty.

Where was the CD?

Where was Raleigh?

Luna yelled, "About fucking time," and leaped through the opening I'd shown her. She strode toward Brother Luther, snarling, fangs bared, a true vampire Amazon on the warpath.

Too late, I realized my mistake and ran after her. I tried to step in front of her and she pushed me aside effortlessly, shoving me into Alan so hard we both hit the floor.

The sight of her caused Brother Luther to shriek in terror. He clutched his stomach and performed the same up and down rocking motion he'd done at my house. In between sobs he begged, "Don't hurt me, don't hurt me, help me, help me."

Luna kicked him, screaming, "What have you done to Devereux, you festering piece of shit?"

He whimpered, "Mama!" Then dropped to his knees, covering his head with his hands and arms.

A physical spasm rocked his body. He threw his head back and gave an ear-piercing primal scream.

As before, the transformation was rapid and astonishing.

Alan and I stood and watched Lucifer.

Shocked, Luna backed away. "What the fuck?"

He rose slowly to his feet, his no longer emaciated body filling the previously loose coat.

Alan sucked in a breath. "Jesus Christ."

Somehow Brother Luther's body had become taller, bulkier—more muscular. His actual bones had shifted. His eyes were on fire.

He advanced menacingly toward Luna, his mouth open, exposing his still-elongating fangs.

She assumed a fighting stance, crouched low, waiting.

Several of the vampires Luna had brought with her crowded into the circle. They growled deep, flashed fang and surrounded Lucifer.

He took a step toward Luna, hand reaching for her throat.

Just then, Lieutenant Bullock crashed into the circle, gun

pointed. "I said freeze!"

All eyes turned to her for a split second, and in that tiny window of opportunity Lucifer scooped up Devereux and they both vanished.

We all froze for several seconds, stunned.

Staring down at the empty space on the floor, my brain finally registered that Devereux was gone and I lost it.

I screamed like the Banshee from Hell. The walls reverberated.

All the pain, fear, confusion, and grief I'd tried to hold inside burst forth in one long, gut-wrenching, soul-shattering cry.

Then the tears began. I dropped to the floor, laying my forehead on the spot where Devereux had been.

Everyone was silent while I sobbed.

Alan knelt down beside me and stroked my hair. "I'm sorry, Kismet. We all tried to save Devereux. He's very powerful. If anyone can get away from that lunatic, it's him. You've got to keep hoping."

I raised my head and met his eyes to see if he believed what he'd said, or if he'd chosen that moment to dredge up his unused therapy skills.

His warm eyes beamed sincerity. And compassion. I sat up, exhausted, tears streaming down my face.

I was grieving for his competition and he was being remarkably understanding.

Luna snorted in disgust. She narrowed her eyes, pressed her lips together tight and covered the few steps to where Lieutenant Bullock still stood pointing her gun.

She knocked the weapon away, growled and brought her

face nose-to-nose with Lieutenant Bullock's.

"Bitch! You distracted us. I almost had the fucker. I'm trying to decide if I should kill you now, or wait until we find Devereux so he can do it himself."

Lieutenant Bullock retreated a couple of steps. "You're interfering with police business. Step away."

Luna barked out a laugh and turned to the other vampires. "Police business? Gather 'round, everyone. This cow thinks she has something to say about what's happening here. She thinks she knows one fucking thing about anything."

Lieutenant Bullock still didn't seem to understand who, or what, she was talking to. She might've understood vampires in theory, but she had no personal experience with them. She probably thought all the bloodsuckers in the room were dressed in their ball costumes. It's likely she didn't know she was conversing with the real deal.

"There's a body on the floor and blood everywhere. You bet your ass I have a lot to say about it."

Luna plastered on her most evil smile. "And what kind of body do you think is on the floor, human?"

Alan rightfully sensed that things were going south at the speed of light, and he jumped up and squeezed himself in between Luna and Lieutenant Bullock.

But instead of helping, he leaped into the fray.

The three of them argued at the top of their voices.

The other cops and vampires lined up on opposite sides, facing each other like the Sharks and the Jets in *West Side Story*. Though I doubted if they'd break into a dance routine.

I tried to intervene a couple of times but didn't have the energy to involve myself in anything as meaningless as blame or police or whether vampires exist.

Devereux was gone. Maybe dead.

That was all the pain my heart could hold.

I staggered out of the circle and walked aimlessly in no particular direction.

The sound of someone crying penetrated the fog in my head.

"Shit!" How could I have forgotten about Midnight and Ronald?

I raced over to where Ronald still cradled Midnight in his lap and knelt. He was crying, his shoulders shaking. "She's so cold. She's dying, Dr. Knight. I'm losing her."

I stroked his cheek with the backs of my fingers. "Hold on, Ronald. It's not over yet."

I leapt up and hollered, "Call an ambulance!"

That stopped the argument.

Everyone ran over to see what I was yelling about.

There'd been enough death and loss for one night. Midnight wouldn't be on the list if I had anything to say about it.

Having a positive goal seemed to galvanize everyone. Soon Midnight and Ronald were being carried on stretchers out of the music room to a Flight For Life helicopter, waiting on the castle's roof.

I noticed that everyone in the room took turns watching me, as if they expected me to pick up the sword and behead someone else. Since I hadn't known I was capable of that kind of violence to begin with, I couldn't give anyone any guarantees about my future actions.

With Devereux gone, nothing really mattered anyway.

After the medical tech got Midnight prepped and stabilized, he told me her vital signs were incredibly good for someone who'd almost been drained.

I don't know why he spared the time to talk to me again and be so encouraging. Maybe he saw something in my eyes.

Anyway, he said her outlook was great.

Except for some missing hair and scalp, Ronald was completely fine. A nasty souvenir of his first ever Vampires' Ball.

I was morbidly drawn to the edge of the circle, which no longer held together, where I obsessively stared at the red velvet duster filled with ash.

The sword still rested nearby, clear evidence of something I knew logically but resisted emotionally.

I sat down, trying to feel bad. Trying to feel ashamed. Trying to feel anything. But I was numb.

Alan had finally gotten across to Lieutenant Bullock that it was a vampire body rotting on the floor in the Dark Magic circle. So, no forensics team would be arriving to collect evidence.

He reminded her that if she told anyone she'd spent the last couple of hours with vampires, she'd be taken away in one of those delightful coats with long arms that lock in the back.

Luna still prowled the area, mumbling under her breath about the stupid humans and what she wanted to do to Lieutenant Bullock. We each deal with pain in our own way.

I wasn't sure how I was going to deal with mine.

I rested my forehead on my bent knees. Another river of tears poured down my face.

It wasn't fair. I'd just accepted that Devereux was a vampire and that I had strong feelings for him, then he was gone.

Weren't vampires supposed to live forever?

I knew that after the shock receded, I'd have to deal with all the stages of grief. Was I supposed to move into an office in Devereux's building, seeing constant reminders of him every day? I'd have to be a glutton for punishment to do that.

Maybe I'd take a sabbatical from my practice. Hide away. Take some time. Go to Paris to visit friends.

I don't know how long I'd been sitting there in front of Bryce's remains, but for some reason I had an urge to raise my head. The ghost in the mirror was once again working hard to get my attention.

Nobody else has the ability to see this ghost but me?

He was beside himself with joy.

He smiled very wide, danced in circles and thrust his bow vigorously in a pointing motion toward the far end of the room.

Since he'd been a reliable resource, I rose and shifted my eyes in the general direction the bow indicated.

There was something on the floor, half underneath one of the grand pianos.

My heart pounded and I gasped.

My body knew before the rest of me did.

I ran full out across the room, skidding to a stop a foot away from flowing platinum hair.

Devereux looked like he'd been hit by a truck. Or exposed to the vampire equivalent of kryptonite.

I screamed again, this time with pure joy, which quickly followed by the sound of running footsteps and excited voices.

He was sprawled on his back, his hair partially covering

his face.

I dropped to my knees, held his face in my hands and kissed his parched lips. His skin felt icy cold to the touch.

I was suddenly terrified that Lucifer had sent Devereux's dead body back as a sadistic parting shot.

I checked for a heartbeat on his pulse points and didn't detect anything. But, if he was already dead, did it matter that he didn't have a heartbeat? I didn't understand enough about vampire mortality to even know what signs to watch for.

Luna, who'd dropped down next to Devereux across from me, closed her eyes, cocked her head and pressed one hand against his forehead and the other to his chest.

I watched her, not sure what she was doing, but hoping she knew some kind of vampire trick that would bring Devereux back to consciousness. I couldn't help myself. I started crying again.

She slanted a glance at me. "I can feel him. He's in there."

"What does that mean?" I choked out between sobs.

"Stupid human," she said gruffly, and then cleared her throat and spoke softly. "Take his hand and find out for yourself."

I picked up his hand and held it in both of mine, waiting. I didn't know what I was supposed to be listening for, but touching him felt wonderful. Even if his skin was as cold as marble. I closed my eyes and clearly *heard* him say my name. His finger twitched almost imperceptibly.

I burst out laughing, still crying, and a joyful roar rose up from the bystanders.

My vampire was alive. Or whatever.

Epilogue

$\mathcal{L}$una transported Devereux back to his underground room at The Crypt. He didn't really regain full consciousness for six weeks. I spent as much time sitting with him as I could. Luna humored me. She assured me that he was aware of my presence, even though he couldn't communicate beyond an occasional telepathic whisper of my name or a tremble of a finger.

I read the entire Harry Potter book series to him. Not only because I thought he'd enjoy it, but the books were the written equivalent of a teddy bear for me.

It turned out that the magic Bryce and Lucifer used was ancient, powerful, and had been stolen from the same line of wizards Devereux claimed as his ancestors. Maybe that was why it worked so well.

All of Devereux's inter-dimensional caregivers told me he'd recover completely. Whatever "recover" means for a dead guy.

My private practice is busier than ever. Moving into the new office in Devereux's building was the best thing I ever did. All my old clients returned, plus a full evening caseload of vampires. My waiting list, for both humans and the undead, is long.

Tom really did run off with the gorgeous woman . . . er, vampire. He left me a cryptic voice mail message saying Zoë had accompanied him back to California, but that they'd be returning soon. He said he needed to speak with Devereux about living forever.

Lieutenant Bullock held a press conference about the "vampire murders," which got the media off my tail. She said the City of Denver was still actively following leads, but that there had been new deaths in other cities, taking the focus away from me. I'm a blissful nobody again.

The Lieutenant started visiting me for "professional consultations" about all things vampire. She said she'd made mistakes because of her lack of knowledge and wanted to rectify that situation. She asked me to call her by her first name, which turned out to be Amy. I never would've guessed. It's been nice having another human around who knows the truth.

Midnight spent less than a week in the hospital and was released to her parents. She's still seeing Ronald, but is content to live at home for now. Our sessions are more about her and less about vampires.

Brother Luther/Lucifer hasn't contacted me. Yet. Discovering a vampire with Dissociative Identity Disorder, formerly Multiple Personality Disorder, has piqued my interest in the diagnosis, and I've been doing research. It's clear we haven't heard the last of the demented bloodsucker, so I want to be armed with as much information as possible when he circles back this way. According to the reports of blood-drained bodies, he's moved on to another one of those pockets of escalating good and evil: Sedona, Arizona.

So has Alan.

He stopped by my townhouse to say goodbye one afternoon about a week after the insanity at the haunted castle. After a couple of awkward, silent moments, we practically leaped into each other's arms. I don't think either of us expected that. His lips were as soft, warm, and inviting as always, and I don't know what to do with the feelings I have for him.

I can't be in love—or lust, or whatever it is—with two men, can I?

I don't know. Stranger things have happened. But, I do know that vampires exist. Vampires and ghosts and who knows what else.

What does that mean for me? Hell if I know.

But I'm actually excited to find out.

Don't miss Lynda Hilburn's next exciting novel:

DARK HARVEST

LYNDA HILBURN

ISBN#9781933836614
US $15.95 / CDN $19.95
Trade Paperback / Paranormal
OCTOBER 2008
www.lyndahilburn.com

A special presentation of

THE DREAM THIEF

HELEN A. ROSBURG

PROLOGUE

Venice lay beneath the velvet pall of a moonless night. Though the city's mood throughout both day and evening was carnival-like, no sound of revel disturbed the midnight hour. What boats remained on the canals glided silently through the dark water. Even the lap of tiny wavelets against the wooden hulls and stone steps seemed muted.

Within the Villa Santonini, only the plaintive cries of the *doge's* daughter could be heard. Valeria cried out in her sleep, but did not wake. She lay soaked with sweat, her thin, silken shift sodden. Her tongue flicked in and out of parched lips, and her hands kneaded her breasts. Her back arched, lifting her body from the bed, and she tossed her head from side to side.

1

He was back again, in her dreams. There, at the foot of her bed. He wore a ruffled white shirt, its ties undone so she could see a tantalizing bit of his well-defined chest. Thick, wavy, sun-streaked brown hair kissed the tops of broad, muscular shoulders. Knee-high black boots of the softest leather embraced his calves. Skin tight leggings caressed his heavily muscled thighs. Her eyes moved to the V of his groin.

He followed her gaze. His hand moved lazily downward; he touched himself.

Valeria watched him harden. The sight inflamed her, sending rivers of molten blood through her veins. He reached out to touch her where he had touched himself and she arched to meet him, pulling up her night shift. Then, suddenly, he was gone.

Groaning with the pain of loss, Valeria pulled herself upright. Where had he gone? She looked desperately about her bedroom, but he had vanished. Just like every night before. But this night was different. This night she had to have him. Had to. She could not wait any longer.

The tapers in the silver candelabrum had long since guttered, and no light came through the tall, gold-draped windows. But she would have known her way through her father's palace had she been blind-folded. Valeria tip-toed to her door and opened it.

"You," she gasped. "You're here. You're really here."

By way of reply, he raised a finger to his lips. He reached for her hand.

Valeria shuddered with desire when she felt his fingers twine about her own. His cool flesh surprised her. She had thought his touch would burn her.

Together they moved silently down the long, window-lined gallery. Valeria felt as if she moved in a dream. And as if it were, indeed, a dream, she did not pause, did not question. What happened went beyond her control.

The night air was cold against her skin when they left the palace. She smelled the canal, and let him lead her down the steps to her father's dock. A strange boat swayed gently atop the water.

She noticed it was not secured, yet waited like a patient horse for its rider. It was painted black, one with the water on which it rested. Gilt paint decorated its sides in whorls and flourishes. Its small cabin was completely enclosed and windowless. The man at her side gestured and she stepped down into the vessel. It barely rocked. It moved not at all when he followed her.

Silken pillows lined the floor. She could not see them in the darkness, but she felt them. When he placed his hand on the small of her back, passion surged through her entire body and her knees turned to liquid. She sank down into the pillows.

He did not have to court her body. She came to him. Ready. Her thighs glistened with moisture when she opened them to him.

Suddenly he was naked before her. He knelt between her knees, his flesh gleaming palely in the dark, as if he were illumined by a magical light within. And he was ready, as ready for her as she was for him. He was hard and very large, within her delicate hand. Small animal sounds came from the back of Valeria's throat.

Beautiful. He was so beautiful. And he had seemed to become more so each night. Gaunt and pale when she had first seen him, he had come each night to tempt and torment her, growing more and more beautiful each time, irresistible. She had thought him a dream, only a dream. But here he was. Entering her.

Valeria screamed. He filled her, ignited her. When he moved against her she screamed again. The pleasure grew too intense, too overwhelming. Her entire body became composed of strings, all being pulled down at once, down and down to the secret place between her legs. Tighter and tighter they wound as they rocked together until the cords suddenly snapped, and she was released in a spasm of pleasure, an explosion of sensation. Heat poured from his body into hers.

And then, suddenly, the warmth began leaving her. Even as she floated, she felt herself growing cold, colder. She tried to move, but her body had no strength, no power. And she had no sight. Everything was black, black. . . .

He pulled down her shift, covering her naked legs. Her arms

he arranged over her still breast. Carefully, almost lovingly, he pulled her long, brown tresses artfully about her shoulders.

He left her, a single passenger. The black boat drifted along through the night and into the dawn.

CHAPTER

The streets of the Ghetto Nuovo teemed with life. Pina picked her way around market carts stalled in the throng of humanity, piles of offal left by numerous equine drudges, and lean, opportunistic dogs and cats staying alive on fat waterfront rats. Uncountable bodies pushed past her: Jews with the circle of yellow sewn onto their outer garments; well dressed merchants visiting the money lenders; dandified young men taking in the sights. Pina glanced back to make sure her servant, Andrea, still followed, and quickened her pace.

It was still cool so early in the spring. Early in the morning as well. It had been barely two hours since the beadle, the Shomerim la-Boker, Watcher for the Morning, had been round from house to house knocking on doors to wake the ghetto denizens. The street was shady, too, as the Jewish population had nowhere to build but up, and haphazardly constructed buildings towered over the busy streets. Pina clutched her shawl more tightly to her breast.

The poorly built housing was the reason she hurried. Another building had collapsed recently, killing scores and injuring more. Her skills, and coin, were sorely needed.

Pina turned a last corner and found herself in front of the unimposing façade of The Scola Grande Tedesca. Externally, the Venetian synagogue did not present features of particular merit or interest. It was not prudent to attract the attention of the Rulers of the Republic, who had explicitly forbidden the construction of synagogues. She looked up at its five windows and hesitantly pulled open the massive door.

The synagogue's benign exterior belied the sumptuous, gilded interior. She glanced up at the women's gallery, then heard the sharp click of footsteps on the beautifully inlaid floor.

"Rabbi Levan?" Pina called tentatively.

"Oh, good. You're here, child. I am grateful. As many others will be." The traditionally garbed Ashkenazi teacher took Pina's hands in his own and squeezed them gently. He tilted his head in acknowledgement of her servant. "We should leave at once."

"Of course." Pina's eyes drifted to the large basket Andrea cradled. "I brought as much as I could. I know it's not enough. It's never enough. But . . ."

"Hush, child." The Rabbi held a finger briefly to his lips. "Come. They're waiting."

Pina followed the black clad figure back onto the street. His slightly hunched back became the center of her focus as they wound their way along the crowded, narrow thoroughfare. Several minutes later the Rabbi opened the door to a tall, shabby tenement and gestured her inside.

The stench assaulted her immediately: unwashed bodies; the coppery odor of blood; human waste and vomit; the pungency of fear and despair. Pina heard the moans of the injured and dying, the murmuring of prayers. She followed the Rabbi out of the corridor and into a room packed with too many bodies to count.

Almost all the furniture had been removed. People lay in rows on the floor, only inches separating them. Several women, all with the yellow circles sewn on their breasts, moved among the maimed, offering what comfort they could. Two men working in bloodstained outer coats were doctors she recognized from previous missions to the ghetto. One of them looked up when she entered.

"Thank the Lord," he groaned, and pushed to his feet. His yellow patch was nearly obliterated by his patients' effluvia.

"God's angel has visited us once again in our time of need," the Rabbi said. His coal black eyes pinned her, and she looked away. She felt absurdly guilty, as if the plight of the people was her fault.

"You are not the cause of this," Rabbi Levan said softly, startling Pina with the accuracy of his statement. "Neither will you be the cure. But you are a blessing, and a light in the darkness."

The doctor who had risen stood before Andrea, who offered him the basket.

"There is material for bandages," Pina said shyly. "Herbs and salves as well. It's so little, but it was all I could manage. We're running low as well, and . . ."

"We know your dilemma," the doctor interrupted in a kindly manner. "We thank you for your generosity. And your courage." With that he turned away to resume his work.

"Can I . . . can we help?" Pina looked up at Rabbi Levan. "You know my skills. I've helped before."

But the Rabbi shook his head. "You must not risk yourself by tarrying."

Pina couldn't disagree. It was becoming harder and harder to think up excuses to leave the villa, particularly for any length of time. And with the recent murders her mother was getting more and more protective.

"All right," she conceded reluctantly. "But I'll be back as soon as I can gather more supplies. Oh, and take these." Pina dug into the velvet sac tied to her belt and withdrew a few gold coins. She pressed them into the Rabbi's palm. His black eyes glittered, and she turned away before his tears of gratitude could spill.

ISBN#9781932815207
US $6.99 / CDN $9.99
Mass Market Paperback / Paranormal
Available Now
www.helenrosburg.com

For more information
about other great titles from
Medallion Press, visit

www.medallionpress.com